I'M SURE YOU W
MICHAEL EXPLA
TIME I'VE FORG
ON . . .'

Joy's mind was moving very, very slowly, reluctant to accept this new reality. Put on what? Pregnant . . . ?

If she had a baby and was unmarried, she could never be Head of Department at St Ignatius'. She probably wouldn't even have a job at St Ignatius'. So she would have to get married; she would have to marry Michael. As if someone had turned on a light switch in a darkened room, Joy knew absolutely and finally that she did not want to marry Michael. Not only that, she never wanted to have sex with him again.

But what about the baby, if there was a baby?

Now she really did have something to worry about.

ABOUT THE AUTHOR

Sherry Ashworth was born in north London and educated at the City of London Girls' School, St Hugh's College, Oxford, and the University of York. She lives in Manchester and is married with two daughters. She teaches English part-time at Bury Grammar School for Girls in Greater Manchester.

Her other novels, *A Matter of Fat*, *Personal Growth* and *The Perfect Mother*, are also published in Signet.

SHERRY ASHWORTH

No Fear

A SIGNET BOOK

'The world too is set firm and
cannot be shaken.'

Psalm 96

PENGUIN BOOKS

Published by the Penguin Group
Penguin Books Ltd, 27 Wrights Lane, London w8 5tz, England
Penguin Books USA Inc., 375 Hudson Street, New York, New York 10014, USA
Penguin Books Australia Ltd, Ringwood, Victoria, Australia
Penguin Books Canada Ltd, 10 Alcorn Avenue, Toronto, Ontario, Canada m4v 3b2
Penguin Books (NZ) Ltd, 182–190 Wairau Road, Auckland 10, New Zealand

Penguin Books Ltd, Registered Offices: Harmondsworth, Middlesex, England

Published in Signet 1996
1 3 5 7 9 10 8 6 4 2

Set in 10/13pt Monotype Plantin Light
Typeset by Datix International Limited, Bungay, Suffolk
Printed in England by Clays Ltd, St Ives plc.

Special thanks to Holy Cross College, my BGS
A-level groups and to Brian, again.

This novel is for
Colette, Linda and Claudia.

CHAPTER ONE

She stood at the very edge of the diving board, feeling its concrete firmness beneath her toes. Below her was the translucent ice-blue surface of the water, as still as in a painting. As she gazed down, unseeing, into the inscrutable blue depths, she felt no fear. Every muscle and nerve was taut with anticipation. One moment, and she would plunge into the nothingness. Just a fraction of a second more to enjoy the sensation of being there, poised on top of the world –

The phone rang. Joy started from the armchair, letting the newspaper fall from her lap, turned off the diving on the television (How can people actually want to *do* that?) and ran into the hall. Good news? Bad news? A cocktail of dread and anticipation coursed through her veins, as it did whenever the phone rang or the doorbell buzzed. As she glanced at her dishevelled curly hair in the mirror it occurred to her that she didn't look tidy enough to answer the phone. She would have to adopt her best telephone manner to compensate.

As it turned out, it was only the college secretary.

'Fran!' Joy declared. 'How are you? Did you have a good summer?'

'Not bad,' Fran said cautiously. Joy understood the tone. It was best not to tempt fate. If you said you'd had a good holiday, then something bad might happen next. 'I was looking for you in college,' Fran continued. 'I thought you might be in today.'

Joy immediately felt guilty, although the beginning

of term at St Ignatius' did not start for a few days.

'I was working,' she explained. 'I was working at home. I *was* planning to come in tomorrow – or later on – or –'

'Oh good,' Fran said. 'Because Sister wants to have a word with you. She told me to find out where you were.'

'Sister!' Joy repeated, as an enemy of the Corleones might mouth 'the Godfather'.

'Nothing serious,' Fran warbled. 'I think.'

'She thinks,' thought Joy, weaving in and out of the traffic on the road leading out of Manchester. 'Nothing serious, she *thinks*.' If it was something serious, then Sister might very well not tell Fran. Or perhaps Fran did know why Sister Maureen wanted to see Joy, and the words 'I think' were a gentle indicator that the matter might be serious after all. *Nothing serious, I think.* Perhaps it was code. Perhaps, had she bothered to read the avalanche of documents the college was producing in the run-up to its forthcoming inspection, she would know what the phrase meant.

If it wasn't serious, why did Fran ring her at home? With one part of her mind Joy obsessively ranged the facts of the situation before her, examined possible causes for Sister's summons; with the other part of her mind she wondered why she was doing this. It was pointless worrying. She would find out sooner or later.

It was going to be later. When she arrived at St Ignatius', feeling as if the summer holiday had been a mirage and that only yesterday she'd walked out of the entrance with a box of books and papers to peruse during July and August, Sister Maureen's door was firmly shut. Joy stood on the other side of the heavy oak door and waited.

She glanced at herself to check that she was respectable. The navy linen shirt she had thrown on was a mistake, as it had creased badly when she was in the car. Her jeans were reasonably clean, for jeans. She ran her fingers through her hair, more for comfort than in an attempt to tidy it.

Ought she to knock? Joy reflected that if she did knock, and Sister was occupied – with a parent, or even with a governor – she would be told to go away. Which would be most embarrassing. So instead she stood very close to the door and listened, her heart pounding. She could detect the silvery tones of Sister Maureen's voice, but heard no one talk back. Did Sister talk to herself too? Or did she have a hot line to the Almighty? Perhaps Sister was just on the phone.

Joy decided it would calm her to think through, just once more, the reasons why Sister might want to see her so urgently. That way she would be prepared. Was Sister unhappy with the A-level results? Although senior management claimed St Ignatius' Sixth Form College educated and cared for the whole student, A-level results were prodded and examined as eagerly as were beasts' entrails by ancient priests.

Was it that? Did Sister think her students should have done better? Joy wondered next if she'd forgotten to fill in some vital form. Or worse – had a parent complained about her?

Joy reviewed what grounds a good, God-fearing, Catholic parent might have for objecting to her. The obvious one was that she was Jewish. For that reason she had never expected to get the job at St Ignatius' when she'd applied four years ago. Except Sister had said something in the interview about it being a positive advantage to have faith. Joy had been on the verge of

3

admitting she was more of a wandering Jew than the kosher-eating, holy-thinking, Yiddish-speaking variety, but said nothing. And Sister had believed her to be an expert on Jewish affairs ever since.

It was still possible that a parent had objected to her Judaism, or to what there was left of it. Joy's mother had taught her to sniff anti-Semitism everywhere. Yet all the students knew she was Jewish, and no one really cared. So it probably wasn't that. Could it be that she'd decided to teach the upper sixth Defoe's *Moll Flanders*? All that sex and shoplifting. Hardly part of a good Catholic education.

Then another possibility struck Joy. Sister had found out about Michael. Joy thought she had been careful. She thought she had excised every mention of Michael from her polite conversations with the principal. Joy had forbidden him ever to set foot in St Ignatius'. Perhaps Sister Maureen had discovered his existence.

As you know, Joy, St Ignatius' differs from other tertiary colleges in that we still endeavour to set moral standards. I didn't see your being Jewish as a barrier to your teaching here, as you know. In fact, I often feel that Catholics and Jews have a great deal in common. Neither way of life condones a cohabiting arrangement. Joy, you are living in sin. I'm afraid it's either Michael or St Ignatius'!

No one was in the corridor. Joy screwed up her mouth so that she could bite the side of her cheek, another of her comfort habits. As she chewed, she wondered if it was one of those apparently innocent activities that the medical establishment will one day tell you is bad for you; for all she knew, excessive chewing could be a cause of mouth cancer. It was possible. All that constant friction. Joy wondered how she could tell if she did get mouth

4

cancer. She felt with her tongue for lumps. The inside of her cheek was bumpy and slightly tender, and there was a slight ache in her tongue. Did she have tongue cancer? Or perhaps she'd strained a muscle in her tongue. Joy poked it out and extended it fully to check she'd done no permanent damage.

At that moment Sister Maureen opened the door.

'Joy!' she exclaimed. 'It's good of you to come so soon.'

Stepping into Sister Maureen's study was for Joy like entering another world. It was partly Sister's fragrant odour of sanctity, and partly the thrill of being alone with the one person who *was* St Ignatius'. Power is intoxicating, thought Joy. Through the large windows the tennis courts were visible, empty now, as term was yet to begin. An imposing wooden crucifix hung on the wall over the desk. The books on the shelves were arranged in perfect order. There was a faint aroma of lavender, which seemed to cling to Sister Maureen's person.

Joy contemplated the principal's lined but lively face with admiration and not a little envy. She wished she was Sister Maureen. Not because she was principal and everybody did what she said, but because she always seemed so certain of what was right and what was wrong. Joy wished she was a nun too. Perhaps it was worth giving up sex just to be *certain* about everything.

'Coffee?' Sister offered, and turned her back to Joy to pour some from the Kenco jug on the hotplate. She was a slight woman, and her habit accentuated her trim figure. Joy's anxiety diffused as she reminded herself how much she valued Sister's good opinion, and she determined not to say anything in this interview to jeopardize that. Joy sat to the side of her desk, trying not to look at the paper spread out on it, and failing. Sister Maureen sat down, and smiled.

'Will you be wanting days off for the Jewish New Year?' she asked.

'Yes please, Sister. Just the Friday this year.'

'Now, I've often wondered why it is that you celebrate the New Year for two days. Why is that?'

Was this the reason Sister had summoned Joy to her office? To clear up an abstruse point of theology?

'I think, Sister, it's because the rabbis aren't certain what day it falls on.'

Damn, thought Joy. That makes rabbis sound like a set of good-natured incompetents. *Well, Rabbi Epstein, you think Rosh Hashanah should be on Wednesday this year, and Rabbi Cohen thinks Tuesday, and I say Friday. What say we go for Wednesday and Thursday? You're happy? Good. I want that everybody should be happy.*

'How interesting. Judaism is a fascinating religion. Now, if your New Year falls in September and is a festival of renewal, how does it differ from Pesach, which links with our own Easter, which is a festival of rebirth?'

Joy launched into a convoluted explanation of Pesach as a celebration of freedom from slavery and hoped the principal wouldn't sense her ignorance. If only, thought Joy, she'd get on with it and tell me why it is she has to see me. Why doesn't she realize that all this polite chit-chat makes it worse?

'I expect you're wondering why I asked to see you, Joy.'

Joy wondered if the students' joke that Sister Maureen could mind-read was true.

'Joy, I want to say at the start that this is highly

6

confidential, and I'm not altogether sure I should be speaking to you like this, but I think it's in your interest.'

At that moment Joy knew for certain that it was something bad. *It was in her interest.* That meant Sister Maureen was going to tell her off. Joy Freeman, thirty-one years old, BA (Hons.) English, householder and taxpayer, melted away to reveal a child, clumsy and fumbling and immersed in a sweaty self-consciousness.

'I think it's in the college's interest too.' Sister Maureen carried on serenely, apparently unaware of the knot of fear in Joy's intestines. 'It's about Betty Murphy.'

Betty was Joy's head of department. She'd been head of English for over twenty years, from the time St Ignatius' was a girls' grammar school and Shakespeare was taught from little red books that had been thoroughly bowdlerized. Joy guessed immediately why Sister had mentioned Betty. She was ill. That was it. Almost certainly something life-threatening. Life-threatening and sudden, because she'd only had tea with her a few days ago. Or perhaps, Joy thought, she was dead already.

'Betty has come to see me to ask for early retirement.'

Praise the Lord, thought Joy – she's alive!

'She mentioned early retirement several times last year, so I wasn't entirely surprised when she made a formal request. I told her I would take her case up with the governing body and that I was fairly certain they would agree. The college owes Betty a good deal.'

'Yes,' Joy enthused. 'She's a brilliant head of department.' Her praise was genuine. Betty's dry sense of humour and unusual dress sense had delighted Joy, and she respected her intellect and judgement enormously. Joy tried to imagine St Ignatius' without Betty, and it seemed a hostile place. Betty was like a mother to her.

'We'll all miss her. Of course, her departure leaves me with the problem of finding a replacement.'

Joy nodded eagerly. She always nodded a lot at Sister Maureen as it seemed a safe sort of thing to do.

Sister Maureen had stopped speaking. Below the window two of the groundsmen had begun to cut the grass, and their motor mower was vibrating throatily. Sister's phone rang with an insistent trill. She picked up the receiver and said rather sharply to whoever it was that she was busy. Joy felt honoured.

'I shouldn't think in this case I would have to go to the bother of inviting external applications, as there are such good candidates in the English department, and – I wondered, would you be applying?'

Me? Head of English. Joy felt as awestruck as the diver she had watched earlier. Why was Sister asking her if she was planning to apply? In order to warn her not to? Joy decided to think out her answer very carefully.

'I haven't really thought,' she said. 'I mean, you know. Well, it's a bit of a surprise. Unless . . . If you . . .'

'I know this is rather sudden,' Sister continued. 'But I've called you here to tell you that I think you'd make a very strong applicant. The reason I'm mentioning it so early is because there is just something that I feel might stand in your way, and an early conversation with you might help you to address it.'

It *was* Michael, Joy thought. She had to chuck Michael. No. It was because she was Jewish. She would have to start receiving instruction. She would have to convert. It would break her mother's heart, she knew. A daughter in Holy Orders.

'Sometimes our greatest strengths are our greatest weaknesses. What we love about you is your commitment to the college. We know how much you care about the students, about the results, about carrying out your job to perfection.'

Joy nodded.

'To say that sometimes someone can care too much seems a little odd. Being head of the English department is a stressful job, Joy. There are changes in the A-level syllabuses under way, and the government inspection some time next year. That's a lot to care about. Sometimes, to protect ourselves, we need to care a little less. To worry a little less. To be blunt, Joy, my concern about you is – how shall I put this? – that sometimes you worry too much.'

Worry too much? Do I worry too much?

'I know you do it because you care about us here, about the students. But I have to take into account the toll on you. My point is this: If I could see, in the coming months, that you were worrying just a little less, that you were taking things a little more calmly, I really think you would be a very strong candidate indeed. A very strong candidate.'

'Thank you,' Joy said. Worry less. What did Sister mean, worry less? How do you worry less? Joy was worried, but decided to bluff.

'I see what you mean,' Joy said. 'I do worry rather a lot. I'm flattered that you think I should apply for Betty's job. It'll be my New Year's resolution – to worry less. Worrying is a very unproductive emotion. Like guilt.'

Oh Christ! I shouldn't have said that. All Catholics suffer from guilt just like all good Jews suffer from anxiety. But Sister Maureen seemed unaffected by the *faux pas*. Obviously she wasn't feeling in the slightest bit guilty for having lacerated Joy's self-esteem.

'I knew you'd take my comment in the right spirit, Joy. I do admire the way you can take criticism.'

Joy looked at Sister Maureen and loathed her.

'Now I want you to know that I and all of the senior-management team have the very highest opinion of your academic standing, your popularity with the students and the respect your colleagues have for you. Just remember that you must look after yourself as well.'

The principal's praise spread like dye in water, colouring the criticism to a lurid shade of pink. Everyone thought highly of her, respected her, except – she worried too much. Joy felt a little confused. Was Sister Maureen warning her that because she worried she wouldn't get the job, or was she praising her, or . . . Best, Joy thought, to salvage this excruciatingly embarrassing interview with a joke.

'Right, Sister,' she said. 'I'll make a start immediately. I'll go home, take the rest of the day off, lie down and worry about how to stop worrying.'

'A good idea,' Sister said. 'And perhaps you might get Michael to cook you something nice tonight.'

Joy emitted a chuckle of laughter to mask her astonishment. Sister knew about Michael after all. She'd probably known for years and years. Sister Maureen was wasted at St Ignatius'. She should have joined the CIA years ago.

Sister Maureen's phone rang again. Joy rose, muttered her goodbye, left the study and closed the door with what she desperately hoped was an air of insouciance.

What puzzled Joy most, as the soles of her trainers thumped through the empty corridors of St Ignatius', was how Sister Maureen could have possibly failed to realize that it was precisely because she, Joy Freeman, *did* worry that she was academically sound, popular with students and respected by her colleagues. Joy felt herself swell with pleasure at the praise. But she worried too much! Nonsense. Everybody worried. If you didn't worry, nothing would ever get done. I mean, she argued with herself as she located her Micra in the car park and wondered where her keys were, I mean, how can you live at the end of the twentieth century and *not* worry? Tell me that, Sister.

First there are the big worries – the environment, the collapse of the world banking system, killer bugs (I'm telling you, Sister, read the *Guardian* any day) – and then everyday life is so complex – bills to pay and remembering the day's meetings and lesson plans and organizing a social life and income-tax forms (all of that, Sister). Worrying is the glue that holds it all together. (Joy was enjoying herself. She made the most wonderful speeches to Sister Maureen when she wasn't there. She had composed many such speeches when lying awake in bed.) And it's not just that, Sister, Joy continued. (Sister looked at her, astonished, impressed, delighted.) Just as you said, worrying *is* caring. Worrying is loving. It's what we do when we want to step into someone else's shoes and walk around in them. Joy paused. That was a familiar thought. *To Kill a Mockingbird*? Possibly. She recognized that, as an English teacher, her mind was littered with quotations which reared their little heads at all sorts of inconvenient times. Worrying is empathy, she continued, starting the ignition. (Was there enough petrol? Probably not.) Worrying is what we do to stop us being selfish!

It occurred to Joy with satisfaction that she would be

wrong, morally wrong, to stop worrying. Sister was mistaken. Joy's only error was that she *showed* that she worried. All she had to do was to pretend not to worry. She would lounge about in the staff room occasionally and smile a lot in the corridors. She could be as cool as Peter Worthington if she tried. Anything, if it meant actually being head of department, which stood not within the prospect of belief, no more than to be – Peter Worthington! He would certainly apply too. They would be rivals, the price of the success of one being the total defeat of the other.

That was something to think about, as was Betty's leaving, possible promotion, Sister's strange request – it was all too much. She would get straight home and tell Michael immediately. He would understand, Joy thought. He was a teacher too. A maths teacher, at one of the local comprehensives. He, more than anyone, would know if it was true that she worried too much.

Joy thought lovingly of Michael, her partner. It was easier to think lovingly of him when he wasn't there. Michael as an idea, a concept, was always more attractive than Michael, the real thing. Joy asked herself if he worried as much as she did. Probably not. His problem was stress. As he often told her, he was Stressed Out. It was a label he enjoyed applying to himself. Stress, he told her, didn't just come from having too much to do. You could suffer from stress if you had too little to do, if you were undervalued at work. Michael was undervalued at work. No chance of promotion as his head of department was young. No extra allowances on offer because of threatened funding cuts. It was the stress caused by lack of responsibility that made him tired all the time, he'd told her. So Joy decided that she wouldn't make too much of a fuss about the promotion angle of Sister Maureen's interview. She would save that for her mother. She would just check with Michael whether she worried too much.

Joy parked her car in front of the garage as Michael's car was already inside. She noticed the metallic doors needed painting. She turned off the engine and checked she'd taken the car out of gear and put the handbrake on tightly enough, as the drive was on a slight slope. She pulled the handbrake up as far as it would go. Just now, she thought, when things had begun to go so well (promotion!), she didn't want the car rolling down the drive and smashing into passing traffic, or careering into a small child innocently playing on a bike.

Joy got out of the car, locked it, checked she had locked it, looked in the passenger window to check that side was locked too and opened the front door. Joy listened for Michael. There was no sound. She put her head round the door of the living room. The newspaper lay where it had fallen, and their coffee mugs had not been taken in to the kitchen. The red figures on the video clock twitched insanely. The kitchen was deserted too, their lunch things still lying in the sink. Joy looked out into the garden, which consisted of a small area of overgrown lawn, and some untidy bushes she and Michael had planted several years ago and then ignored. No one there.

Suddenly, from nowhere, Joy remembered reading about cases of women coming home and finding their partners dead, hanging from ceilings, strangled, having indulged in acts of auto-eroticism. A picture of Michael, choking, swinging from the doorway, flashed into her mind. These women *thought* their men were perfectly normal, and yet . . . If Michael was upstairs working, Joy thought, her adrenalin racing, he would have the radio on for the cricket, but there was just this uncanny silence . . .

Joy mounted the stairs anxiously. The door to the rear bedroom, which was his study, was open, and Joy could see immediately that he wasn't there. Some folders lay on his desk but his computer screen was dark and blank. Dead. Joy bit her lip. The bathroom door was open. No one in there. Joy caught a glimpse of her face in the bathroom mirror and was struck by its resemblance to a painting she'd once seen – what was it? – yes! Munch's *The Scream*. She looked just like the figure in that.

The bedroom was at the front of the semi. The door was ajar. Joy pushed it open and stopped as she saw Michael, in his tartan socks and boxer shorts, spread-eagled on his front on the bed. He was snoring gently, his face to one side on the pillow. Relief flooded her. Normally, she detested the catarrhal snoring that kept her awake at night, but now she loved it; it was proof he was alive. She sat down at the foot of the bed and contemplated him. She was thoroughly familiar with the fact that he was unattractive and she was immune to the comments of friends such as Lesley. Surely if it was politically correct for women not to have to ape the supermodels, men should be allowed their minor imperfections too. Lots of men were short. Many lost their hair early, the receding chin wasn't Michael's fault and nor were the large ears. And it certainly wasn't his fault that he wasn't Jewish. That was Joy's mother's major objection to Michael.

Joy considered that, sleeping, he really wasn't too bad after all. She told herself that his main virtue, the best thing about him, the reason why they were living together, was that she could trust him. He'd never leave her. That was one thing she didn't have to worry about.

Michael raised a hand to his face and rubbed his nose. With the other hand he reached below to scratch himself. He was waking up. He opened his eyes, caught sight of Joy and started.

'What the . . .? What're you doing here?'

'Sorry,' Joy said. 'Did I wake you?'

'No, no. I was just . . . resting. I couldn't work. Thought I'd clear my head.' Michael rolled on to his back and watched Joy.

'I saw Sister Maureen,' she said cautiously. Her fingers played with the counterpane on the bed. 'Michael. Do you think I worry too much?'

'No,' he replied, with a matter of fact air.

'You don't? Are you sure?'

'I'm sure.'

'Because Sister said she thought I worried too much. What do you think she means?'

'Draw the curtains,' Michael said.

'Why . . . ?' Joy began, looked down and noticed the bump in his boxer shorts and knew why. But not now, please not now, in the middle of the afternoon, and with Sister's revelation to worry about.

'You're gorgeous, you know that?' Michael said, sitting up.

Flattered by his comment, she felt obliged to do something to please him, so she moved over to the curtains and pulled them to. A soft light filtered through into the shadowy room.

'Come here,' Michael insisted.

Joy paused indecisively. It had been kind of Michael to say she didn't worry but really, she didn't feel like sex right now. She'd only been in Sister's study half an hour ago. She breathed deeply. Ought she to tell him right out that she didn't want to make love? No. It was easier to go through with it than explain why she wasn't in the mood. She turned, and there was Michael standing by the side of the bed, naked, his penis bobbing about like some red, wrinkled, alien life-force, like something Steven Spielberg might have thought up. Suddenly she wanted to laugh, but suppressed the thought. Michael came up to her, stood behind her and pressed himself close against her back. Help, Joy thought, I don't want to take my clothes off. Sister Maureen's face appeared in her inner vision. Lucky Sister. Joy could see the attraction of Holy Orders.

Michael began to nuzzle her neck, and little prickles shot through her shoulders like needles. She could feel the wet where he had been kissing her. With every advance he made, when the snake-like arm came round her front and latched on to a breast, she became more detached. She hoped she wouldn't get a stain on the back of her jeans, the way he was rubbing against her.

It was at that moment that a new thought occurred to Joy. Was she frigid? Most women, surely, would jump at the thought of sex in the afternoon (except Sister Maureen and her mother). Lesley liked sex at any time, although she wouldn't thank you for Michael. What was wrong with Joy that she should feel so unsexy? Michael took Joy's hand, brought it behind her and placed it on his penis. Joy stared into the velvet pile of the curtain and saw how the colour varied with the density, and listened to the cries of the children playing outside on their bikes. She wondered again whether she ought to say that she didn't want to make love, but feared he'd react badly to the rejection. Instead her hand tightened around his penis in a vice-like grip.

Please God, she prayed, I know this is a bad time to talk to you, but can we make a bargain? If you can get me out of this, I promise to read up all the articles I can on female frigidity, I'll go to *shul* both days of Rosh Hashanah, I'll even invite David to stay, as well as my mother. Just do something.

Michael began to fumble with the button on her jeans. It was then that the telephone rang. There *is* a God, Joy concluded.

'I'll answer it,' Joy volunteered.

In response, Michael placed his hand over Joy's hand on his penis.

'You don't have to,' he panted. 'The answering machine's on.'

Joy cursed modern technology. She heard the click of the machine and the commencement of the message.

'Joy? It's only me. I'm bored, and I wondered if you had any news.'

Joy could feel Michael's erection dwindle. Thanks, Mum, she said to herself.

'Are you sleeping better? Did you know Uncle Barney is trying new water tablets? Did I tell you I'm considering double glazing? Are you taking the selenium I told you about? Because I worry about you, you know.' Click.

Joy turned to face Michael. 'Uncle Barney's on new water tablets,' she said. 'For his blood pressure. He's got diabetes too, that's the problem. Look, I'd better ring her back. I don't like to think of her alone in the house, not if she's bored.'

Joy kissed the top of Michael's head, which was an inch or two below hers, and thanked him for being so understanding. She pushed aside the thought that Michael might be worried she didn't fancy him. That worry was swallowed up by a greater worry. Her mother's voice didn't sound quite right. There had been a new note of peevishness. There had been pauses and half-suppressed sighs. Joy wondered if she was hiding something. Why ring in the middle of the afternoon, when long-distance calls are twice as expensive, unless there was something wrong? Something more serious than Uncle Barney's water tablets! Joy ran down to the hall and dialled her mother's number.

'Mum?'

'Joy?'

'Are you all right?'

'Are *you* all right?'

'Oh, *I'm* all right,' Joy said. 'I got your message. Are you sure you're all right?'

'I'm all right!' Her tone was sharper, and Joy relaxed. She was probably all right after all. Ruth Freeman continued. 'Where were you when I rang? Have you been at college? I thought term didn't start for a few days.'

'No, you're right. But Sister asked to see me. Betty – you know Betty, my head of department –'

'I like Betty – ' Joy's mother interjected.

'That's right. Betty – she's retiring, and Sister called me in to suggest that I apply for her job. She said I'd make a very strong candidate.'

'Really?' Her mother was pleased and excited. Joy caught the emotion and it doubled her own satisfaction.

'Yes! It's excellent news for me. You know it's what I've always wanted – my own department. You know I told you – it's not the money, though that would be very welcome, but to be responsible for policy, for the other staff . . . except . . . except – Mum?' Joy careered to a halt. 'Mum. Do you think I worry too much? Sister Maureen said she thought I did.'

'It's natural to worry.'

'Yes, that's what I thought.' Joy decided that what her mother was saying now made more sense than Sister Maureen's comments earlier.

'If you didn't worry, you wouldn't be a good teacher.'

Joy loved her mother for saying what she believed herself. She experienced a glow of contentment at the thought that she and her mother were so close. She never truly understood those families where daughters never visited their mothers, or complained about them. She and her mother were – well, they were best friends. Partly, she knew, it was because her father had died when she was small, and David, her younger brother, was a full four years her junior and had been protected from a lot of things. She, Joy, had had to be her mother's companion, her confidante, her friend. David was –

'I've had a phone call from David,' Ruth continued.

Joy held the receiver more tightly. She lifted her eyebrows in a gesture of contempt. She spoke to her mother three or four times a week; David rang her once in a blue moon. But David was the original boy wonder, he who could do nothing wrong. Joy was barely able to collude in this pantomime of David's perfection, but did so, for her mother's sake.

'How nice,' she said.

'We were discussing Rosh Hashanah.'

Joy tensed again. Mum was coming to her for Rosh Hashanah. If David had dared to invite Mum to

Bournemouth, where he managed his kosher hotel, and if she had accepted . . .

'David has made a very kind offer.'

'Oh yes?' Joy said.

'He can't come to me in London as he's not taking the time off work. He says he feels guilty and so he said he'd pay for my fare to you.'

Joy understood immediately. He was making absolutely sure that Mum didn't think of visiting him for Rosh Hashanah. However, the truth was that she wanted her mother anyway, and the offer was a generous one. David, for once, had been considerate and fair.

'That's great, Mum. I was hoping you'd come here as it's easier for me, as I'll be back at college by then. Deborah mentioned we should go to *shul* with her and Howard. We could –'

'And, do you know, he's paying for me to fly to you!'

'Fly?' Joy echoed. How could he do this to her? David knew Joy was terrified of flying. So terrified, in fact, that her terror engulfed anyone she cared about who was foolhardy enough to fly, especially and most particularly her mother. David had probably saved up the air miles and pulled this stunt just to rile her.

'Are you sure you want to fly?' Joy asked her mother carefully. 'It only takes two and a half hours by train and by the time you've gone all the way to Heathrow and taken a bus from Ringway –'

'But he's sent me the ticket already.'

'I can't pick you up from Ringway, Mum.'

'I can get a bus. We'll manage.'

Joy decided it was time to tell her mother the truth. 'Mum – look – I don't really like to think of you flying.'

Joy's mother laughed. 'It's only a fifty-minute journey. And I could be on a train which has a head-on collision.'

The truth of that struck Joy forcibly. It had been some time since there was a serious rail crash; it was about time for one. There were no seat-belts in trains. Joy was filled with a leaden despair. She would have to let her mother fly. She pushed to one side her own memories of flying; the icy panic, rushing to the loo as soon as the seat-belt lights were switched off, the terror of looking down and seeing the earth falling away.

'OK,' Joy said miserably. It was all David's fault. She imagined the scene after the mid-air collision, at the funeral, when David would come towards her, weeping openly, sobbing that he was entirely to blame. Joy believed she might find it in her to be magnanimous then. She would talk about fate and hug him tightly, but nothing she could ever say would eradicate the guilt from his heart. She felt quite emotional.

Ruth Freeman spoke for a bit longer, about Uncle Barney, and the *shul* social group. Joy listened impatiently. She needed her mother's reassurance.

'I don't worry too much, do I?' Joy asked.

'Are you sure Sister Maureen isn't anti-Semitic?' Ruth responded obliquely.

'I'm sure. She likes Jews.'

'So *she's* never worried?'

Joy could tell from her mother's tone that she did not like her daughter being criticized. In fact, thought Joy, I don't like me being criticized either. So then, why did Sister comment about her worrying? Perhaps, after all, it was to prepare her for not getting the promotion. A chilling thought.

Joy finished the conversation with a heavy heart. As

she replaced the receiver Michael thudded down the stairs, an envelope in his hands.

'This came for you earlier,' he said. 'I took it up to my room by mistake. It doesn't look important.'

It didn't, Joy thought. The address label came from a mailing list. It was a toss-up whether to throw it away or open it out of curiosity. Curiosity won. Joy opened the envelope and stared in horror at the contents.

A circular from the doctor's surgery. Her last Well Woman check was three years ago, and she was to ring the clinic to arrange an appointment.

Joy swallowed hard. Three years, was it? It seemed like yesterday. Her lips were dry. Since Michael wasn't around she quickly checked her breast for lumps, although she'd checked them that morning in the shower. But what if a lump was so deep that you couldn't feel it? And how could you tell the difference between a lump that was supposed to be there and one that wasn't? Relax, she commanded herself. She told herself that the Well Woman check was preventative medicine. But to prevent *what?* That was the point.

The nurse donned plastic gloves and inserted her hands into Joy, who lay, legs apart, on the examination table. Joy watched her face. Her eyebrows drew together. 'There's something . . .' she murmured . . . 'a sort of lump. How long was it since your last smear? Three years? That's strange. I think I'd like Doctor to see you. If you can just hold on . . .'

No, Joy thought, it won't be like that. The examination will be routine. I'll ring the surgery a few weeks later. *Joy Freeman? Yes, the results are in. I'll just check the list. Freeman, Freeman, Freeman. Ah, there we are. Ah! Oh dear. Yes, there's an abnormality. If you could make an appointment with Doctor.*

Joy felt quite shaky although she knew it was completely irrational. She hated any sort of medical test. Whatever it was for she assumed that she'd got it. With the Well Woman check it wasn't the embarrassment of the internal; it was what the nurse might find. Joy wondered if she should ring her mother again for support, but she knew Michael would be livid at the size of the phone bill. On the other hand, the day had been enormously stressful. There was Sister's criticism, her mother flying, and now this.

Joy's back slid down against the wall and she sat on the floor. There was a creeping feeling along her veins. She felt like a child again, head bowed, knowing what the teacher said was true. She was a worrier. Not just an ordinary worrier or an everyday anxious person. No, a contender for the Nobel Prize for Worrying. Fear was her middle name.

Sister Maureen had pointed out to her what could be hers if she could change. Could she change? Was it possible? Joy thought back over her life, recognizing that its pattern had been a lurch from one anticipated disaster that didn't happen to another. She had passed her A-levels after all. Despite the anonymously penned letter to the teen magazine she did get a boyfriend. Several, in fact. Her mother didn't die from the hysterectomy. She did get her place at university. The deal on the house didn't fall through. Amazing! Yet she'd wasted years and years thinking through the *what if*s, the *just suppose*s. She counted all the diseases she hadn't got yet.

Was it possible to be different? Could she be like Lesley? Lesley was one of the vice-principals at college – bold, fearless and independent. She didn't even need to live with a man. Did Lesley wake up each morning and count up the bad things that could happen? No way. Was Les afraid of sex? Absolutely not; she positively craved it. Why, Joy thought, if she could conquer her fears, she needn't even stop at head of department. She could be vice-principal too. Or better. And if she didn't worry all the time, then she could actually begin to enjoy life.

That thought, for some reason, struck her as dangerous. Perhaps she wouldn't give up worrying just yet. Tomorrow would do. Or next week. In the meantime, she could speak to Lesley. That was safe. Yes, she would speak to Lesley.

CHAPTER TWO

Term had officially begun. As Joy locked her car in the half-full college car park she decided that it must have felt just like this in 1939 during the Phoney War. The college had opened, the staff had taken up arms and yet the buildings and grounds were quiet and deserted: the students weren't due in for another few days. The present peace was an illusion. An illusion maintained, she thought, by the first item on the agenda today – the staff Mass. Then there was meeting after meeting – enrolment procedures, staff news – masses of information to assimilate. Joy's head began to throb. Then she cheered up. Today was the day she would be able to speak to Lesley.

Joy entered college and grinned at Sam, the caretaker, who responded with a Neanderthal grunt. From him, that counted as a greeting. He gave off an aroma of stale cigarette smoke and wood chippings. She passed him, clutching her briefcase and a fresh jar of coffee, and made her way through the high-ceilinged corridors of the main building, glancing at the lonely statue of St Thomas More suspended above the picture rail. Grey lockers stood like silent sentries along the walls. Joy dodged past cleaning machines and inhaled the smell of polish. She mounted the stairs to the English department, grasped the cool, clammy banister and hoped that Betty would already be in the office.

She was in luck. As she approached the small book-lined room that overlooked the car park she heard the sound of voices. One male, one female. Betty was standing by the glass cabinet when Joy entered, and with her was Peter Worthington. Betty, Joy noticed, had dressed with her usual disregard for fashion and colour coordination, in a tight mustard cardigan buttoned up to the top, a black and white dog-tooth skirt, jade green stockings and trainers. The trainers were Betty's way of saying that today wasn't a teaching day and one could afford to be casual. Pete provided a stunning contrast. His tight cream trousers were immaculately pressed, his short-sleeved checked shirt crisp and fresh. He looked tanned and relaxed. Betty seemed pleased about something.

'Peter's been very industrious,' she informed Joy, beaming with pride. She handed her a sheaf of typed notes in clear binding. The title page of the first read 'Scheme of Work – Year 12 – Language'. As Joy felt the weight of them in her hand it occurred to her that these were Pete's schemes of work for all the classes he taught, and that the bastard had had them professionally typed and bound. Never before, in the history of the English department . . .

'Isn't he a good boy?' Betty said. 'I'm thinking, if the substance of everyone else's schemes of work is similar, we could all save ourselves trouble by adopting Peter's. I can file them for the inspection –'

'If you like,' Peter said, 'I'll get them photocopied first so each one of us can have our own personal copy.'

'But here are *my* schemes of work,' Joy said, feverishly hunting in her briefcase for her own handwritten notes. Damn! There was no way she was going to teach according to Pete's schemes. What kind of conspiracy was going on? And she had spent ages thinking carefully through every aspect of this year's teaching – lesson plans, essay and assignment titles – and *that* was why she had not presented hers so beautifully – because she had spent so long making sure they were absolutely right, and –

'Peter's been skiing this summer,' Betty continued.

'Skiing? In summer?' Joy questioned. She was one of those people who couldn't see the point of skiing at any time. Joy and her mother believed that the only reason anyone would want to propel himself down a snow-covered mountain at top speed would be to kill himself.

'There is some snow, if you know where to look for it,' Peter remarked.

'Did you go with friends?' Joy asked, curious about her colleague's private life. Peter's reserve was a constant irritant to her.

'I went alone,' Peter said briefly. He glanced at his watch. 'I've got to see Sister before Mass,' he added mysteriously, and departed. Joy returned to the question of the schemes of work. She couldn't possibly adopt Peter's. His teaching style and whole approach were so utterly different to hers.

'I can't follow Pete's schemes of work,' she said. 'For one thing, I haven't seen them yet, and I spent all summer worrying about how to approach *The Winter's Tale* so the students wouldn't be put off by the pastoral element. And Pete's method of tackling the language course-work –'

Betty interrupted. 'When I said we should adopt Peter's schemes, I didn't say you had to use them to teach by.'

Joy frowned. What did Betty mean?

She explained. 'The Further Education Funding Council in its infinite wisdom has declared that we must have schemes of work or else we can't have any money, and Peter, bless his heart, has provided us with beautiful schemes of work. Good. Now we can get on with teaching, which is what we are here to do.'

'Yes, but what if when the inspectors come they have Peter's scheme of work and come into my lesson and discover I'm teaching something different. Betty, this is dangerous!'

Betty gave an inscrutable smile. As much as she loved Betty, Joy was annoyed. If Betty was retiring she could afford to take this attitude. By the time of the inspection she'd be gone and living with her sister in the Lake District, communing with nature and keeping chickens, no doubt. It was all very well for Betty to regard the FEFC with high disdain, but Joy would be left to pick up the pieces. As head of department? Joy vowed there and then to type up her schemes of work that evening, with Technicolor illustrations if need be, and to present them to Betty tomorrow so that they could be filed along with Peter's. There might be time to work on them after sorting through the enrolment documents and going for the Well Woman check. The muscles in Joy's stomach tightened. She had almost forgotten. It was at twenty past six that night. It said so on the little green card. Depending on what the nurse found tonight, Joy thought, *she* might not be around for the inspection either. Joy, she told herself, think of something else, quickly. So Joy focused on Betty, on her owl-like glasses and unruly greying hair. She wondered if, now they were alone, Betty would mention her impending retirement. Or whether she had already spoken to Peter?

'Shall we go to Mass?' Betty suggested. Joy checked her watch and realized that they only had a few moments to get across to the chapel. She nodded her assent, and they left the office.

*

28

After entering the chapel, Joy lingered and took a seat at the back. Betty pressed forward, greeting other members of the college staff, and sat in the front row. Being one of the practising Catholics, she always took Communion. Joy picked up from her chair the duplicated sheet with the order of service on it and began to peruse it. Then she felt a friendly touch on her shoulder and turned round.

'Lesley!' Joy exclaimed, delighted to see her.

'Come and see me later,' Lesley whispered, and moved away to take her place by Bruce O'Connor, one of the other vice-principals. Joy felt better immediately. Her affection for Lesley was deeply rooted. She knew it was an attraction of opposites. Whereas Joy saw her own life as a wayward horse that refused the commands of the reins and threatened to gallop away with her, Lesley was most definitely in control, right up there with Boadicea. Joy stole a sidelong glance at Lesley, who was dressed like a thrusting female politician, tailored Jaeger suit, short skirt but not too short – just enough to give a hint of shapely leg – and a Liberty scarf arranged with artful carelessness around her shoulders. That was Lesley's work persona. At home, Joy knew, Les was completely different. Perhaps that was the secret of her success.

From her vantage point at the back of the chapel, Joy watched the rest of the staff assemble. The head of science arrived, looking as harassed as if term were already halfway over. Mary from Business Studies came in with Fran from the office. Peter Worthington was chaffing Pauline from Modern Languages. Finally, all Joy could see was backs of heads and shirt-clad shoulders. At the front of the chapel Father Davidson was conferring with

Sister Maureen. It was most definitely the start of the new school year.

Joy's eyes strayed to the vaulting on the chapel ceiling and then to the crucifix on the wall above the altar. There was a mute reproach in the humble droop of Christ's head. Joy knew it was addressed to her. She was an alien. She was Jewish. What on earth was she doing here?

Dear God, she thought, addressing him as if she were writing a letter, you know jolly well why I'm here. I don't like teaching younger children because I don't have any empathy with them – even Debbie's children – and apart from the tertiary, which is huge and soulless, St Ignatius' was my only option. And surely, from your point of view, being in a Catholic chapel is better than nothing?

At this point Joy wondered if God was really Jewish after all. She'd always assumed that He was. But what if He wasn't? What if the Muslims were right? Or even the Hindus? Or perhaps the Greeks had got it right from the beginning, and even now Zeus was laughing at her from the top of Mount Olympus, and the three Fates, over some nectar and ambrosia, were sitting down discussing what to do with Joy next. And Joy remembered her Well Woman check for the second time.

Holy Mary, mother of God, Joy prayed, I know that you probably never had to undergo a Well Woman check and I can see why you chose Immaculate Conception, but please help. Please don't let them find anything. I promise faithfully that if I'm OK I'll stop worrying, I'll even try to like David and I'll work hard at my sex life.

Damn! Joy thought to herself. The Virgin Mary never had sex. Perhaps she'd have been better off after all with a Greek god – Aphrodite, say. Or on the other hand, she wondered, perhaps somewhere in the Catholic sainthood there was a St Gynaecologia. It sounded likely. A crucifix in one hand and a speculum in the other.

'*My brothers and sisters, to prepare ourselves to celebrate the sacred mysteries, let us call to mind our sins,*' Father Davidson intoned, and his soothing, velvety voice obtruded upon Joy's reverie.

Obediently she tried to enumerate her sins. Was drinking half a bottle of wine last night a sin? Joy was grateful she was mercifully free of sins of the flesh just then. So much for herself. Joy stole another glance at Lesley. What about Lesley's sins? Lesley's face was impassive. She was an atheist, Joy remembered, and this prevented her from ever becoming principal, although that didn't seem to bother her. Les wasn't exactly an adulteress, although she did have a lively sex life. Her latest was Rennie, a sculptor from Edinburgh, who descended on her occasionally, or perhaps, Joy thought, playing around with words in her English teacher's way, it would be more correct to say *ascended* her. Or rather, from Lesley's lurid accounts, more often than not *she* ascended *him*.

Joy reprimanded herself for thinking of sex in the middle of Mass. During any religious service she veered from reading the prayers and feelingly gushingly sentimental to mind-wandering and trespassing on all sorts of inappropriate areas. When she was smaller she had imagined God as some High Court judge who watched her and wrote down in a record book every occasion on which her mind strayed. She believed that when she died all these misdemeanours would be read aloud to her. It was a worrying thought.

Joy observed the stream of people leaving their chairs and approaching the altar to take Communion. She was curious about the host. Did it taste nice? It looked dry and difficult to swallow. What if you couldn't swallow it and choked? At least you'd go straight to heaven, she imagined.

Joy brought her thoughts back to the present and joined in the reading of the prayer after Communion, which was about young people.

That they may go forward with confidence and hope; That they may learn to live with life's uncertainties and fears.

We pray for all young people that they may love and understand their parents, conserving what they find good in the past, bettering that which wrong.

Joy wondered about the grammar of that last phrase. Ought there to be a verb there? Joy thought about the new English language A-level syllabus and whether it would be an idea to prepare a session on Correctness from the eighteenth century to the present day.

Might it come up in the exam? Had they done enough on language acquisition? On gender in the media? Ought she to repeat some of the course-work? Had Peter put anything new in his language scheme of work that she didn't know about? She didn't quite trust Peter, and there was every chance that he had also been told about Betty's retirement . . .

Joy realized the staff had begun to sing the final hymn and she made herself join in. Communal singing always cheered her, and she decided there was a lot to be said for Catholicism. Except for the ban on birth control, of course. Particularly in the light of the predicted population explosion. Joy pictured to herself a planet as full of people as a crowded tube train. This might be the way the world was going to end. Everyone rotting away, shoulder to shoulder. Yet Joy remembered reading only yesterday in the *Guardian* that the high levels of pseudo-female hormones in the water supply were affecting men's sperm count, so they couldn't father as many children, which meant that there wouldn't be a population explosion after all. The two would cancel each other out. Joy offered a silent prayer of thanks to St Gynaecologia, or possibly St Testosteronia, and prepared to go to the staff meeting.

Joy decided college was worse without the students. By half past three her head was vibrating painfully with the overload of information received. Sister Maureen had emphasized that the impending inspection should not put any pressure on the staff at all; all they had to do was carry on with their jobs as efficiently as ever. Joy counted, and noted that she mentioned the inspection fifteen times during her staff address. She spoke of the strategic plan and the necessity for positive UCAS reports and deadlines and value-added scores. No teacher, Joy thought to herself, certainly not her, nor Lesley, nor even Plato or Socrates, could hope to get it all right. Perhaps she would invest in shares for paracetamol and retire on the profits. If stress was a killer Joy reckoned she'd be dead before the practice nurse could get to her tonight.

Lesley's office door was ajar. Joy saw that Lesley herself was standing in front of her filing cabinet looking for some papers. The vice-principal sensed someone was watching her and turned swiftly. Her face relaxed into a smile as she saw it was Joy.

'Come in,' Lesley said, 'and close the door. This can wait. It's great to see you.'

Lesley's office was tiny. It contained a large, elderly desk stacked high with plastic trays full of papers, a tall reclining chair behind it for Lesley, the filing cabinet, some shelving and a rickety wooden chair. Joy lowered herself on to that and watched her friend return to her desk.

She had never meant to befriend the vice-principal. Yet early in her days at St Ignatius' she had been surprised at how much she had enjoyed the brief conversations she'd had with Lesley Wright. First, there was the discovery that they shared a sense of humour; then there were the unmistakable signals that Lesley actually *liked* Joy and sought out her company; finally, as the two women drew closer, came Lesley's willingness to impart confidences to Joy. Joy was hugely flattered, but better still, here was yet another older woman to admire, to be mothered by. Secretly she knew she was addicted to being mothered. There was her own mother, pre-eminent, of course, and then Sister Maureen, and her cousin Deborah (although they were the same age) and Lesley. All these wiser, experienced women who threw a lantern across her dark path.

'Well,' began Lesley, 'how goes it?'

Joy hardly knew where to begin. Were those tears beginning to swell inside her? She forced them back. She concentrated hard on the water-colour of Heptonstall churchyard which hung on Lesley's wall – Les had painted that herself – the geography textbooks, the net curtains on the windows, anything but Lesley's solicitous face.

'Is anything wrong?' Lesley asked.

Carefully Joy began to unpack her shopping bag of woes.

'I have to go for my Well Woman check tonight – it's mostly that – but also I'm scared I might be frigid – and my mother's *flying* to Manchester – I've been having pains in my stomach all day – and a headache – and Sister Maureen has told me I've got to stop worrying. I know you think I'm crying,' Joy said, hastily brushing aside the tear or two that had escaped, 'but I'm not. It's just a spontaneous overflow of powerful feelings. I've been bottling this up all day.'

'Vintage misery,' said Lesley dryly. 'Château Freeman, 1995.'

'I have drunk,' Joy said, 'and seen the spider.'

Lesley looked at her oddly. Joy realized that Les, a geographer, was not as intimate with *The Winter's Tale* as she was and would not appreciate the reference to Leontes' neurotic behaviour, however deft the allusion. But thinking about Shakespeare cheered Joy up. It always did.

Lesley straightened some files on her desk and spoke again, a smile playing round her lips.

'Let's take these things one by one. Regarding the Well Woman check, provided you had your last smear three years ago it's very unlikely you've developed anything fatal.'

'Yes, I know,' Joy interrupted. 'But it's not 100 per cent definite, is it? You just said "very unlikely".'

'Nothing's definite,' Lesley said.

Joy thought briefly how infinitely wide was that hair's-breadth gap between unlikely and definite, and how in it resided all her fears.

'As for going off sex,' Les continued, 'who can blame you if the only sex you have is with Michael?'

Joy was expecting that riposte. She mentally made a note that she would have to approach someone else about her libido problem.

'Next, provided your mother is flying to Manchester in

35

an aeroplane and not by flapping her arms, you have little to worry about there. Your stomach pains and headache are almost certainly caused by the return to college, as well as the fact that you've been worrying. And regarding Sister Maureen's advice –' Here Lesley paused. Joy waited breathlessly.

'I know a little about this. Sister is absolutely right in thinking you'd be an excellent candidate for Betty's job, and I respect her for telling you. And I think she might be right about you worrying too much.'

Joy nodded slowly. Lesley regarded her narrowly.

'Can't you just stop worrying?' she suggested.

'Stop?' echoed Joy.

'Mm, stop. If you catch yourself worrying, just think of something else. The shopping, the gas bill, a sunny beach, anything – except the worry.'

Joy decided this was an interesting idea.

'No,' she said.

'Why not?' Lesley asked.

Joy gave her best Semitic shrug. How could she possibly explain to logical, sensible Lesley her profound conviction that worrying actually prevents things going wrong. Joy knew that if she imagined her mother expiring in an air crash, it was a guarantee that in fact she wouldn't. She knew that if she relaxed her vigilance for just a moment, if she lulled herself into a sense of false security, that's when the engines would fail or lightning would strike.

'If you really want to stop worrying,' Lesley continued, 'there are things you can do.'

Joy made herself listen, remembering her earlier decision to abstain from worry.

'Some people try relaxation exercises or meditation.

Or deep breathing – that's supposed to have a calming effect. Or yoga.'

'Is that what you do?' Joy asked her.

'Me?'

'You never seem to worry, Les. Why is that?'

Lesley half closed her eyes in thought. Her reply, when it came, was unhelpful.

'It's just me, I suppose. I don't dwell on things.'

'Surely there are some things that make you anxious,' Joy persisted. If Lesley admitted that she worried sometimes too, Joy would feel less of a fool. But on the other hand, if Lesley *was* a worrier, then she wouldn't be able to help Joy. Why was life always so bloody complicated?

'If I am feeling a little nervous,' Lesley continued, 'say, for example, when another person looks at one of my paintings for the first time and is about to deliver an opinion, then I just act as if I'm confident – even though I might not be.'

'Like Deborah Kerr in *The King and I*!' Joy announced.

'*The King and I*?'

'Whenever she feels afraid, she holds her head erect and whistles a happy tune so nobody will suspect she's afraid – I think that's how it goes.'

'Yes, like that,' Lesley laughed. 'Why don't you try it?' Lesley wanted to change the subject. She felt it was morbid to talk too much about negative emotions. A sense of discomfort assailed her. So she brought her thoughts back to Joy, sitting here in front of her, looking for all the world like a student in need of help with some course-work. Now, if Joy was in advice-taking mode, Lesley decided, there was one piece of advice which she knew would be in Joy's best interest.

'I know another way you can help yourself – by broadening your horizons,' Lesley said, feeling her way carefully.

'I don't go in much for travelling,' Joy said.

'I was talking about metaphorical horizons,' said Lesley. 'Male horizons.' Lesley saw that Joy looked uneasy. Perhaps she had moved too quickly. Possibly it was too soon to say that, as far as she was concerned, it was Michael who held Joy back. Being allied to a man like that, she believed, damaged Joy's self-esteem. Low self-esteem, she calculated, in her precise mathematical fashion, led to anxiety, a feeling of not being able to cope. Lesley began to flick through her internal file of available men. Surely there would be someone for Joy.

'Enough about me,' Joy said. 'Sometimes I get heartily fed up with myself. How about you? How's Rennie?'

'Rennie?' Lesley chuckled to herself. 'Rennie's fine. I've been helping him with his modelling.'

'What? You've been posing for him?' Rennie exhibited his work in a craft shop in the Piece Hall in Halifax.

'No; he's been posing for me.'

'For you?' Joy was confused.

'It was something he's always wanted to do. Rennie has an interest in fertility rites. We made a plaster cast of his penis. The main problem was maintaining the erection. I had to –'

There was a knock at the door, followed almost immediately by Sister Maureen's head. Lesley did not turn a hair. She was vice-principal once again rather than vice queen.

'May I have a word?' Sister asked her.

Joy rose hastily and assured Sister that she was just on her way out.

Walking down the corridor to collect her things from the English office, she felt cheated. She had been certain that Lesley was going to be able to tell her how to stop worrying, but she had said nothing, nothing that seemed to be of any use. On the contrary – now Joy was beginning to feel more inadequate about her love life than ever. Whereas she was only too happy never to recall her fumblings with Michael, here was Lesley setting down *her* love life in concrete, as it were. Fancy having your own phallic symbol, Joy thought. (It would be useful in English lessons, it occurred to her. Now look, everyone – *this* is a phallic symbol. P – h – a . . .)

Joy smiled ruefully to herself. She had a real problem, there was no doubt about it. Modern women were supposed to enjoy sex. The magazines she read were full of it. All over the country, the world, women were reaching orgasm when she couldn't even reach the bedroom. There was even the time she told Michael that her jeans' zip had stuck. Was she frigid? And if she was, who should she talk to? Most absolutely not her mother. Deborah? No. Perhaps the practice nurse tonight might know something about frigidity. Because if I'm able to solve my libido problems, then perhaps I could stop worrying. Maybe it was all that sex that made Lesley able to cope with the pressures of being a vice-principal.

I wonder what they're going to use it for, Joy thought to herself, locking the empty English office, her mind still playing on Lesley's clay penis. A paperweight? A cosh in case of burglars? Would Rennie really want to exhibit it? All the way to the car Joy thought about this. Was she suffering from penis envy? Another thing to worry about.

CHAPTER THREE

Joy took a deep breath and paused before she pushed on the bar that would open the door of the general practice and gain her entry to the waiting room. There! She felt better already. Another deep breath. And now for some positive thinking. She, Joy Freeman, was an enviably confident, serene young woman and the practice nurse would discover that there was nothing wrong with her. And even if there was, she would be so brimful of poise, confidence and serenity that she wouldn't mind. Another deep breath. Now for it.

Like a character in a play, she walked over to the receptionist and delivered her lines. 'I'm Joy Freeman,' she said. 'I have an appointment at the Well Woman clinic.' Was that applause? No – just the sound of the rain beating on the window. No matter. She deserved applause. She was good, bloody good.

Imagining the eyes of the other patients upon her, she moved to a seat by the pile of magazines and sat down. Now it was time for the happy tune. She pursed her lips. She'd been practising 'Oh, What a Beautiful Morning' from *Oklahoma!* Yet as she began to whistle softly she realized she was competing with a tape playing in the background, filling the air with relaxing Celtic New Age music, and it prevented her from holding the tune. Never mind, Joy thought. I'm so confident I don't need a tune.

This was easy, Joy thought. Les was right. Provided you act as if you're not scared, you don't feel scared. She let her eyes rove around the surgery. There was the obligatory aquarium, with goldfish swimming aimlessly under tiny bridges and around plastic ferns. There were some paintings of the Lake District. There was a blackboard informing patients that they *must* inform the surgery if they were unable to keep appointments, as other patients might want them. It was all quite restful.

A buzzer sounded. Joy jumped involuntarily.

'Mrs Cohen, room three,' announced the receptionist.

Thank God it was not her turn! She glanced at Mrs Cohen. She didn't look very well. There were dark circles around her eyes and she moved as if she was in pain. Joy felt a tremor of fear on her behalf. What if the woman was going in to the doctor's surgery only to be told that the constant pain in her stomach was serious, that the tests at the hospital indicated she only had months to live – and as the doctor told her this, he couldn't maintain eye contact with her, and she said, 'My family, Doctor, how can I tell my family?' Joy felt her eyes fill with tears.

She tried to hum 'Oh, What a Beautiful Morning' but it sounded like a funeral dirge. She stopped. She would distract herself by reading a magazine. Joy reached to her left and withdrew one from the stack. She read the letters on the front pages about the funny things that the readers' grandchildren had said, and how to fill old tights with cat litter so they'd act as an odour absorber. She flicked through a few more pages of knitting patterns and celebrity interviews. Then she saw it: 'Ovarian cancer, the silent killer. She thought she was suffering from PMT, but the doctor told her otherwise. The fatal disease that has no symptoms.'

PMT? I have that. No symptoms? That's me too, I have no symptoms. Do I have ovarian cancer? It was possible. Anything was possible. She closed the magazine

41

gently and attempted to hum a cheerful tune. Joy took some more audible, deep breaths.

'Chest infection, is it?' asked the elderly man sitting next to her.

'No, no,' said Joy, glad of the chance of some conversation. 'No, just a check-up.'

'Good idea to have a check-up,' wheezed the old man. 'You never know what they might find.'

'Well, I . . .'

'You can never be too careful about your health. That's what I always say. It's what I told my wife. She passed away three years ago.'

Joy decided that conversation might not be such a good idea. Hunting through the magazine pile again she found an upmarket glossy. That was more her style. She scanned the pages, looking for something frivolous. Here was an article on stress; Joy felt drawn to read it. It listed significant life events and gave them a stress rating. It said that even good things cause stress, and that stress causes illness. So, Joy reasoned, even if she was promoted she might get ill. She closed that magazine too. Best not to change anything. Lesley was wrong about her needing to find a new interest.

Damn! She had forgotten to be her new, serene self! She reminded herself that she wasn't worried about anything. She was positively looking forward to her chat with the practice nurse. Her stomach, which contracted and sent a wave of nausea through her, informed her otherwise. Traitor, Joy whispered to it. Raindrops on roses, she told herself, and whiskers on kittens. Bright copper kettles . . . how did the rest of it go? Something about brown paper packages? Did snowflakes come into it?

The buzzer went again. Joy tensed. When she heard

her name her stomach leapt again, as if it had a life of its own. Joy jumped up as if she had been shot.

'Room one,' the receptionist announced.

Joy's face assumed a rictus grin as she made her way towards the warren of consulting rooms. If she couldn't do anything else, at least she would look happy.

She rapped loudly with her knuckles on the closed door.

'Come in,' said the nurse.

Looking ahead of her, Joy saw the examination bed with its layer of white paper like a huge kitchen towel, the white cupboards, the sink with its large tap, the colourful children's paintings on the wall contrasting with the white sterility of the consulting room. The nurse sat at a desk by a computer screen. In her white coat, and with her sleek dark hair pushed behind her ears, she looked the picture of brisk efficiency. Joy noticed, too, that around her neck was a star of David. The name on her lapel badge read 'Nurse Abrams'. She was evidently Jewish, too, which was not surprising, as the general practice lay in the heart of the north Manchester Jewish community.

Joy took the seat she was offered and focused on the nurse's face, on her brown, rather protuberant eyes, her full mouth, her scrubbed, clean skin. She seemed quite friendly. Joy caught sight of the file on her desk. It had Joy's name on it: it was her medical file. On the bottom was printed 'date of death' and 'cause of death'. One day someone was going to have to fill that in. Joy's stomach gave another leap.

'Right, Joy,' the nurse began. 'First, we just need to go through a few questions. The usual sort of thing,' she said reassuringly. Joy relaxed a fraction and began to talk about her general health, flattered by the nurse's apparent interest in her replies. I like her, thought Joy. I like the way she smiles and nods as if everything's OK, as if everything's as she expects it to be.

'Good, good,' Sister Abrams said, and put down her pen. 'Is there anything you want to ask me?'

Aha! Here was an opportunity to postpone that dreadful moment when she would have to get up on the examination table. Besides, she liked Nurse Abrams. She seemed – well – maternal.

'Have you been here long?' Joy asked. 'Not that I come to the surgery much, but I don't remember seeing you.'

'You're right,' Sister Abrams agreed cheerfully. 'We've only just moved to Manchester, from Leeds. Daniel's working for a Manchester firm of accountants. I was lucky to find this job, as it's part time, so I'm combining this with my other line of work.'

'Which is?' Joy asked her, glad to find her so communicative.

'Counselling. I trained with Relate initially, but I've moved out into a number of other areas. Sometimes I get referrals from the surgery, but I advertise too. I do stress counselling, bereavement counselling –'

Joy made a suitably solemn face.

'But my favourite area is relationship problems. It's educational but very gruelling emotionally. It certainly makes you examine your own marriage.'

'So you're married,' Joy prompted her.

'Oh yes. With two children. We've just started the elder at the grammar school.'

'I'm a teacher,' Joy announced. She had hopes of prolonging this conversation indefinitely.

'Where?'

'St Ignatius' – a sixth form college.'

'Oh, so you're Catholic. I thought . . .'

'No, I'm Jewish. You don't have to be Catholic to work there.'

'I never realized. Now, if you don't mind slipping out of your clothes.'

The sudden request jolted Joy, but obediently she disappeared behind the screen with its ironic pattern of jolly sprigs of flowers. Clumsily she removed her jeans, her blouse, all the while clinging on to Sister Abrams's chatter like a drowning sailor to a raft.

'It's been quite a transition for Abbie, starting at the grammar school as well as moving house. We think she's coped very well. We sat down last night and I encouraged her to tell me about her feelings – we do that a lot, you know. I was pleased that Abbie told me she was scared. Admitting it helps you to come to terms with it, don't you think? Acknowledging a problem is the first important step in the journey to overcoming it.'

Trembling, Joy lay herself on the examination table and saw how the polystyrene tiles on the ceiling were yellowing slightly, and how the one on the extreme left-hand side was becoming damp and had worked itself loose. The tiles had little dimpled indentations in them. Joy tried to count the tiles to still the beating of her heart.

Nurse Abrams pushed the screen to one side and approached Joy. She was silent now. Joy lay immobile on the table as Sister Abrams's cool fingers probed her right breast, searching for something. The time for happy tunes had long since passed. Without saying a word, the nurse moved round the base of the bed, came to Joy's other side and began to press her fingers into Joy's left breast. One down, one to go, Joy thought. She tried to think of something else but the whole of her universe was composed of Sister Abrams's cool, probing fingers, and her left breast.

The nurse stopped. 'Nothing to worry about there,' she said.

Joy realized that she'd passed. Her breasts were fine! She filled with love for Sister Abrams. She was an excellent nurse, professional, efficient, a real asset to the surgery. How glad Joy was that Sister Abrams had left Leeds for Manchester! She watched her move over to the sink, where she donned some plastic gloves. Joy guessed what was coming next.

Nurse Abrams had started chatting again. She was saying something about it being hard to let her daughter travel all that way to school alone, but it was important to let go early on. That she had to trust her daughter now. Joy shut her eyes and tried to pretend she was somewhere else, but she couldn't even think of anywhere else to be. The nurse explained to Joy what she was about to do and asked her to raise her knees and part them. Then Joy was aware of a series of intensely uncomfortable sensations, followed by a sharp pain, which was almost immediately over.

'Everything seems fine down there too,' the nurse said. 'Just ring the surgery in a couple of weeks to check the result of the smear. Don't worry if you're asked for a recall; it's only for batch testing. And even if there is an abnormality, it'll be easily treatable at this stage.'

Joy was thrilled. This was wonderful news. 'So I won't die?' she asked.

'Not of a smear test.' The nurse laughed.

Joy felt like a prisoner in a Hollywood melodrama who has just been given a reprieve. She had neither breast

46

cancer nor cervical cancer (probably). It was almost worth all the worry beforehand to feel so good now it was all over. Suddenly all of life seemed pregnant with possibilities.

One very distinct possibility occurred to Joy now. God had not only saved her for another year or two, but He'd also provided her with a Well Woman nurse who was a counsellor. A Relate counsellor. Who might even know a thing or two about female frigidity. Moreover, Joy was certain that she and Sister Abrams had established a rapport. The nurse seemed about her age. More importantly, because she'd only just moved to north Manchester, she wouldn't know anyone Joy knew. Joy decided her recovery from anxiety and frigidity would start here.

'I'm not married,' Joy said suddenly.

The nurse, who was washing her hands at the sink, turned round, wondering what had brought on this revelation.

'But I am in a long-term relationship,' Joy continued. 'It's like being married. Same sort of problems, I guess.'

'Absolutely,' said Nurse Abrams, glad to be talking about counselling again. 'Any form of committed relationship presents challenges.'

'Like when one finds one goes off sex for a while?' Joy suggested, very impersonally.

'Is that your problem?' asked the nurse.

Joy flushed and nodded. Nurse Abrams turned and smiled at her, obviously in her element, as Joy had hoped.

'This is much more common than people realize. You're brave to mention it. In even the most loving long-term relationships there's a cooling-off period, when your feelings change from passion to something more

enduring. For lots of couples, when sex becomes legitim-
ate, some excitement fades.'

Joy was impressed. All this sounded true. This was
possibly why she didn't fancy Michael any more.

'Or sometimes there are underlying problems in the
relationship that affect the sexual side.'

'But what if you're sure there aren't?' asked Joy.

'If you're sure, perhaps you need to experiment a little.
Some couples find their sex lives have got into a routine.
Some couples use game-playing or fantasy as a way out.
Look, would you like me to give you my card? You could
always book me for a session.'

Joy thanked her, took the card and glanced at the address, which looked familiar. Nurse Abrams lived on the
same street as her cousin Deborah. Knowing that put Joy
off a consultation, not that she was seriously thinking of
seeing a counsellor anyway. Yet it was interesting what
she had said – experiment, fantasize, play games. What
games? Monopoly? Dingbats? Lesley was obviously on
the right lines with her clay model of Rennie's phallus.

Joy said goodbye to the nurse and thanked her profusely. She left the surgery and walked out into a clear,
crisp evening, the sky for once free of clouds and richly
blue as the day transformed itself into night. The world
was a safe and wonderful place. There really was nothing
to worry about after all. Joy paused by her car and drank
a deep draught of the cool evening air. Experiment. Is
that how you do it? Fantasize? Play games? Tonight, Joy
decided, she would revitalize her sex life. And if she could
do that, she could do anything!

Still buoyed along by her euphoria, Joy unlocked her
front door and noticed the light was on in the lounge. She

entered, and there was Michael. He'd moved one of the armchairs right in front of the TV screen as he was playing Sonic the Hedgehog on his megadrive. Joy paused. She knew he was easily irritated when she disturbed him playing Sonic. Perhaps that ought to be the fantasy. Joy tried to see herself dressed up as a little blue hedgehog, chasing through the Marble Garden zone. Somehow, it didn't have erotic appeal. After a few minutes, Michael pressed the pause button and turned round to look at Joy.

'OK?' he said.

'Yeah,' Joy confirmed. 'They couldn't find anything wrong.'

'Good,' he said, and carried on with the game.

Joy sat herself down on the settee and deliberated her next move. She was certain she wanted to try some sex. Receiving a clean bill of health had left her feeling confident about her body. So what did she do now? Turn off the megadrive and take off her clothes? No: they must fantasize, play games. Joy realized she had to get her mind focused on sex. She needed to get herself more fully in the mood. Sister Abrams was right. Familiarity was a great killer of passion. She stood over the armchair where Michael was furiously clicking the control pad. Looking at his sandy, thinning hair with its scattering of dandruff and the maroon Fred Perry T-shirt he refused to throw away, Joy felt she knew him ever so well. That was why it was so hard to get excited.

The best thing to do, Joy realized, was to have a bath. That would relax her. To make doubly sure it would do the trick, she went over to the wall unit and extracted the bottle of Gordon's gin from behind the cherry brandy they kept for Joy's mother, and took it into the kitchen. Joy found a clean glass, poured a large measure into it and topped it up with some tonic from the fridge. Carefully she ascended the stairs, taking a sip from the generously filled glass to prevent any spillages.

Now, this was decadent, lying back in a mass of bubbles, sipping at a gin and tonic. Joy was pleased with herself. She let herself enjoy the way the heat of the water dissipated the thoughts in her brain so that whatever she thought about, she was unable to reach any conclusion. She felt deliciously muzzy. She decided she should do something about the bathroom; she would get lots of plants and put them on the shelf above the bath. She ought to clear that shelf. At the moment there were old razors of Michael's and dead bottles of aftershave and three empty containers of Flash bathroom cleaner on it. Joy wondered why there were five toothbrushes by the sink when there were only two of them, but she didn't care.

Now, Joy thought, now was the time to think about sex. The trouble was, her mind refused to lock on that either. Instead she began to have an imaginary conversation with someone, Lesley, or Sister Abrams. *I love Michael, and ours is a mature relationship because we let each other do our own thing.* And when we first met he was lovely. He was the most persistent boyfriend I'd ever had. He followed me around, and it was so flattering. Once we'd started our relationship he was completely reliable – I mean, if I called on him unannounced he'd always be in his room, watching telly. And I knew he fancied me because he was always wanting to make love. It was so reassuring.

Joy tried to remember the first time she and Michael had made love, but couldn't. Did she enjoy it then, in the early stages? She really couldn't remember and took another sip of the gin and tonic. Sometimes when she was very drunk she lost her inhibitions. That was a phrase of her mother's. When Joy was younger she'd actually thought that Inhibitions was a sort of underwear, like liberty bodices or pantie girdles. 'Be careful not to lose your inhibitions,' Joy's mother had told her. Joy admitted to herself she was a bit of a prude. It was all her mother's doing. Her mother said it was a good thing for a girl to be a prude; it was a form of protection. She had told her daughter the facts of life, after much nagging, when she was ten. Joy had refused to believe her, and so her mother had drawn a diagram on a piece of paper from the shopping-list pad. When they'd finished with it Ruth tore it up in tiny bits and threw it away in case David should see it. An unnecessary precaution – that night Joy had repeated to him everything her mother had told her.

Joy remembered now a time when she was still at school – she must have been about fifteen – when she was at a party and slow-danced with a boy called Tom. He had blond hair and he wasn't Jewish. All night they were playing the Law Enforcers album, the one that stayed in the charts for ages. Tom had kissed her for a long time as they danced, and she remembered quite vividly the melting feeling in her solar plexus, and the way her knees lost their strength, and the way she clung to him and wanted more. Whatever happened to him? She had never seen him again. She remembered instead the Law Enforcers album and their lead singer, Tom Quinn. A coincidence that he was called Tom too. He was beautiful. Long, almost feminine hair contrasting with that masculine jaw-line. Joy had loved him for ages. She'd plastered her bedroom wall with his posters. Almost coincidentally, when she'd lost interest in him, he'd faded into obscurity.

Either it was the gin, or the memories, but there was that melty feeling again. Joy caught her breath. She was in the mood! Now, what did the nurse say? Experiment, play games, fantasize. Joy instructed herself to think of Michael and to place him in a fantasy. But what fantasy? She regretted not having read Nancy Friday. She told herself she was a teacher. Perhaps authority was what turned her on. Perhaps she wanted to dress as a dominatrix, in leathers, with a whip, and Michael to be on his knees at her feet. Like in Madonna's *Erotica* video. A voice told Joy that Neurotica was more appropriate in her case. The vision dissolved. What about food? Once she'd confiscated a soft-porn mag in college which had a picture of a naked woman covered in custard. What a waste of custard! Refusing to give up, she thought of the Häagen-Dazs advertisement. No good. Food always reminded her of her mother.

Joy realized she was losing her excitement. She had to make herself think about sex again. Perhaps she should dress in black stockings and high heels? Possibly, but she didn't have any. Did she want Michael to dress in black stockings and high heels? No. Then, as always, English literature came to her rescue. Shakespeare's *Antony and Cleopatra*. That was erotic. 'Let's have one other gaudy night . . . Let Rome in Tiber melt . . . The barge she sat in, like a burnished throne, burned on the water . . .' Water. Joy had told the upper sixth, and they had all written it down, that Shakespeare used water as an image of sexual passion. Water. Currents of emotion. Borne away on seas of ecstasy. Waves of sensation. Wet with desire.

Eureka! Joy decided that they would make love in the bath.

She shouted loudly for Michael. There was no reply. She shouted again.

'What?' came the reply.

'Come here!'

At first there was no response. Then Joy could hear a few creaking sounds and the banging of footsteps on the stairs. She began to worry. What if he wasn't in the mood? Except that was highly doubtful; it wasn't *Michael*'s libido that was in question. Michael was always ready for it.

'Where are you?' he asked, just outside the bathroom door.

'In here,' Joy said.

Michael opened the door and stared. Joy watched his mouth move slowly into a smile.

'You can join me if you want,' she said.

In response, Michael pulled off his Fred Perry, threw it behind him, unzipped his trousers, wriggled out of them and shoved them in a corner of the bathroom. Joy could tell that Michael needed a bath, or perhaps that was the scent of male excitement. Wasn't that supposed to turn a woman on? Joy wondered briefly why it didn't work on her. One sock off, then the other. Down with the boxer shorts. Michael was sporting a jaunty erection. Joy was always amazed at the speed with which he became aroused.

She brought her knees up to make room for him in the bath. Michael eased himself in, but this did not prevent the excess water from gushing over the side of the bath on to the bathroom carpet. Joy hoped it wouldn't soak through to the hall ceiling as she was fairly certain that the bath was directly over the light fittings. Then they would probably be electrocuted. When she didn't turn up for college the next morning Sister would send a search party and a young policeman would fling open the bathroom door and find them both nude and dead in the bath.

While she was thinking this, Michael took some soap and began to wash her breasts. Joy's first thought was that she'd already washed them, and then she realized that the sensation of being washed was strangely familiar. The taps were pressing sharply into her back. Yes! That was it! Michael's movements reminded her of being washed by her mother. A dangerous, non-arousing thought. She repeated her invocation: Let's have one other gaudy night. Then, full of determination, Joy reached down to take hold of Michael's penis. It occurred to her not for the first time how strange it must be to be a man and to have all your equipment hanging outside. In a way, there would be a lot less to worry about. Joy moved her hand to the base of his penis and felt his balls. It was her guess that Michael didn't check them regularly. That was despite her lectures on the advisability of going to the Well Man clinic and her reassurances that testicular cancer was easily treatable in the early stages. She felt carefully to see if there were any lumps or bumps.

Then Michael lunged on top of her and more water spilled over the sides. Joy was puzzled as to how they were actually going to do it in the bath. If he were to lay down on top of her she would drown. She glanced over the side of the bath to estimate how much space there was on the bathroom carpet. Not a lot. If they were to do it there, her head would either be stuck under the towel rail or beneath the toilet. It was time to exit the bathroom. Joy whispered to Michael that they should move on somewhere else, and so they clambered wetly out of the bath. On the landing Michael began to kiss Joy again, but for some reason his kisses tasted of soap. Turning and hastily rubbing her mouth, she suggested they move into the bedroom.

Once in there, Michael pushed Joy down on to the bedroom floor. She was lying parallel with the bed and under it she could see one of Michael's grey socks. So it was *there*. She'd had the other grey sock on top of the tumble-drier in the utility room for weeks and she'd been certain that the other one had got itself caught in the corner of a duvet cover. She was glad to have found it. Then Joy was aware of a series of intensely uncomfortable sensations, followed by a sharp sigh from Michael. Perhaps because they were both wet, thought Joy, it hurt more than usual.

Michael lay panting on top of her. Joy lay back, not certain what to think. She had done it, and that was good. She hoped the damp patch on the carpet would dry without leaving a stain. There was a kind of squelch as Michael levered himself up and withdrew. His dressing gown was on the bed, and he put it on. He stood there looking indecisive.

'All right?' Joy said to him.

'Yeah,' he said. 'Is it OK if I go downstairs? I was in the middle of this game . . .'

'Go on,' Joy said, mildly. She watched him leave and soon, floating into the bedroom, came the jingly sounds of Sonic the Hedgehog. Joy was reluctant to get up just yet. She congratulated herself on succeeding in having sex on only one large gin and tonic.

Yet she had to admit it still wasn't all right. It wasn't like she'd read in the magazines. It had been something she'd tolerated rather than enjoyed. Like a Victorian lady, she'd laid back and thought of – not England, but – socks. What was wrong with her? Perhaps there really are two different sorts of woman – whores and virgins – and Lesley and everybody else belonged to the first sort, and she and her mother and Sister Maureen belonged to the second.

The faint music stopped; Michael must have finished his game. Joy listened to him running up the stairs. She hoped to heaven he didn't want a repeat performance. He appeared in the doorway, his dressing gown tied loosely around him, revealing a hairy tummy and a flaccid penis. There was something apologetic in his stance, something sheepish. Joy pulled herself up and sat back on her heels.

'Sorry,' Michael said.

Joy was touched. He'd realized he was wrong to go down to play on the megadrive. It was a start. Or better still, he'd known she was unsatisfied. There was hope yet.

'It's all right,' Joy said, pleased.

'I'm sure you won't get pregnant,' Michael explained. 'It's the first time I've forgotten to put one on. I just got worked up, seeing you in the bath like that.'

Joy's mind was moving very, very slowly, reluctant to accept this new reality. Put what on? Pregnant . . .?

'You forgot the condom?' she suggested. As she said it, she realized it was true. Michael had not put on a condom. Their farce in the bathroom had prevented her from reminding him about birth control, as she usually did. And once in the bedroom she had just wanted to get the whole performance over and done with.

'Like I said, sorry,' Michael repeated.

Oh my God! Now, even now, Michael's sperm could be sailing up my fallopian tubes and meeting a fat little egg – no, it was unthinkable! If she had a baby and was unmarried, she could never be head of department at St Ignatius'. She probably wouldn't even have a job at St Ignatius'. So she would have to get married; she would have to marry Michael. As if someone had turned on a light switch in a darkened room, Joy knew absolutely and finally that she did not want to marry Michael. Not only that, she never wanted to have sex with him again.

But what about the baby, if there was a baby?

Now she really did have something to worry about.

CHAPTER FOUR

At certain times in the academic year the hall in St Ignatius' was covered with the blue plastic sheeting stored in the basement and the indoor netball court was lost to view. In came the caretaker and his henchmen with single desks and hard plastic chairs and laid them out in rows. In January and June this was a harbinger of examinations; in September it signified the enrolment of new students.

Already the senior staff and heads of department were milling around, consulting with each other, preparing themselves for the steady flow of students, who would shortly be entering through the swing doors, each clutching a card with their GCSE results written on for all to see and looking round anxiously to find out where they had to go. Meanwhile the office staff stood by the stage, laying out upon it sheafs of papers, and Lesley Wright, vice-principal, directed where the different piles should go. Betty Forster, in her blue pinafore dress and purple blouse, watched the proceedings.

Joy could see them from the desk at which she sat, biting the side of her cheek. Normally she would have gone to join them, made some pleasantries about enrolment, how the whole procedure felt like children playing shop, selling courses rather than groceries. *Yes, we have a lovely, new, improved English language A-level, easily divided into modules including new topics such as gender and society. The price? All you need are five GCSEs at grade C or above, including English language and literature!* Today Joy felt incapable of good-humoured banter. Today she was glad that she was alone, because she needed time to think things through yet again.

Firstly, it *was* possible she wasn't pregnant. She sat very still to see if she could feel anything growing inside her. She couldn't tell. If only, if only she'd been on the Pill. But then, her father had died of a heart attack in his early forties, and she was terrified of following in his footsteps. The Pill carried a slight risk of thrombosis, so the Pill was out. Why, oh why, hadn't she used the cap or even that new Femidom? Anything but trust Michael. This mess was all her fault.

She realized she was getting nowhere and pulled her attention back to the hall, where the first few new students were beginning to trickle in and queue at Bruce O'Connor's table. They looked younger every year. It was possible that in sixteen years' time a son or daughter of hers might be walking through those very doors, the very one that was rapidly multiplying its cells in her womb right now. A dreadful thought. She felt faintly nauseous. Was that morning sickness? If only she hadn't had sex last night. If only she hadn't been distracted by that sock. If only she'd done what her mother did ten years ago and had her womb removed to stop having to worry about it.

Joy knew self-pity was wrong. Instead she thought she would try to be like Lesley and decide calmly and rationally what to do about it. Abortion? Joy believed passionately in a woman's right to choose, but for herself, she would choose passionately not to have an abortion. Just the thought alone was frightening; equally frightening, however, was the thought of giving birth to the baby and having to look after it. If she did decide to have the baby, ought she to marry Michael, misgivings notwithstanding?

Sister Maureen entered the hall, smiling benignly at the new students, stopping to talk to one or two of them as the queen might on a royal visit. Sister Maureen. Joy immediately began to smile. It was absolutely vital that Sister shouldn't suspect she was worrying. She looked down at the pamphlets on her desk describing the A-level courses on offer and read them, still smiling. Sister Maureen glanced at Joy and wondered briefly what there was in the course descriptions that amused Joy Freeman so much? A misprint? Perhaps she should go and see.

The third possibility, Joy knew, was the morning after pill. She realized she knew very little about that. Betty had a Burmese cat once who was on heat and bit through four layers of cardboard placed over the cat flap to get herself impregnated by the local tom. She had a morning after pill. But what happened when you took it? Did it give you cramps or make you sick? Joy realized her mother would be in Manchester in a few days and, if she was noticeably ill, Mum might guess what she was up to. Unthinkable. Could I wait until she's gone? And if I did, and the embryo had started its precarious little existence, would the morning after pill be tantamount to abortion? Ought she to wait? Her period was due in two days.

Joy forgot to smile. Why was it all this worrying hadn't produced anything like a solution? She'd gone round and round in circles, all night, all morning. But there was Sister Maureen bearing down upon her. Joy beamed at no one in particular.

'You seem cheerful this morning, Joy.'

'Oh, yes, Sister. Very cheerful. Not worried at all.'

'Good. Ah, look. I think you have a customer.'

The head of science, looking as overworked as ever,

and with a young lad by his side, was coming over to Joy's desk. Sister Maureen retreated.

'This is Philip,' explained the head of science. 'Can you have a few words with him? He's interested in English literature.'

Joy was glad to be distracted from her reverie. She quickly glanced at the boy in front of her. His acne was remarkably bad. His hair was shaved close to his head, army style, and his pale blue eyes held a silent colloquy with Joy's desk. Joy realized it was up to her to break the silence.

'Can I see your registration card?' she asked him. Using her calm professional voice soothed her. She concentrated on the matter in hand. Philip's GCSE results were patchy, with Bs in Eng. lit., biology and religious knowledge. Consequently, those were his choices for A-level. Joy tried hard to think what he could do with that combination. Chaplain in a zoo, perhaps? College policy was to accept anyone with five Cs, and Joy knew she couldn't quibble with a B in Eng. lit.

'Why do you want to do English?' Joy asked him, hoping to discover some enthusiasm for the subject.

'Got a B in it,' the lad said. Self-expression was obviously a problem for him, Joy thought.

'Did you enjoy English at GCSE?' she asked him.

''S all right.' From a northerner, that could be praise indeed.

'Which set texts did you study?'

'*A Taste of Honey*,' he muttered. Then, deciding it was incumbent upon him to sound as if he liked it, he burst into loquaciousness. 'You know, that play about that girl and her Mum, and how she gets pregnant and the father leaves her and that.'

'Yes, yes,' Joy said hastily. 'No Shakespeare?'

He shook his head. Joy explained that he would have to read some Shakespeare and carefully described the set texts, while the young lad looked blankly at her.

'So are you still interested?' she enquired, suggesting by her tone that it would be perfectly all right if he wasn't.

'Yeah, I am,' Philip said.

Well, Joy thought, he'd be a challenge, no doubt about that. She wondered if you could get pregnant just before a period. Was it a fertile time? Joy realized that she wasn't sure when her fertile times were and wished she'd paid more attention to the magazine articles she'd read on the subject. Then it struck her forcibly that she loved her job and she loved St Ignatius' and the very last thing she wanted to happen was for her to leave. She swelled with misery. Then Lesley appeared, with a mother and daughter in tow. They were introduced and took the two seats opposite Joy. Snapping shut her box of woe, she began again.

Joy congratulated the girl on an impressive set of GCSE results, and her mother explained that they were very surprised, *very* surprised, not that they thought she couldn't do it, but she'd told them that she didn't think she'd passed more than three, and you could imagine their faces when she came into the car outside school – the Mini – it was before they got their new Corsa – and she told them both she'd got three As and two A stars, and her dad were right chuffed, he was, and said she could have some money to go away for a few days with Karen, which was good of him, because . . .

Joy remembered how, as soon as she'd discovered that he'd forgotten the condom, she'd run to the bathroom and scrubbed herself thoroughly. Would that have helped? Perhaps if she married Michael now, next week, say, she might be able to keep her job. But that would mean keeping Michael too.

She went to a play, didn't you, Katy? What was it? 'Cats'. That were it. She likes the theatre, she does, well, we all do. We saw Deirdre Barlow off 'Coronation Street' in the Rochdale Asda! And I've taken our Katy to the library since she were that small. She's read all the classics, 'Jane Eyre', 'Oliver Twist', 'Kane and Abel', haven't you, pet? And I always say . . .

Joy was certain it wasn't her imagination. There was a strange sensation around her womb, a tightness. Something was going on there. Strange to think that by this time it was already a boy or a girl. If it was a boy, ought she to have him circumcised? The unkindest cut of all. And yet Joy's mother would be inconsolable if it wasn't done, and Joy wondered how she herself would feel, given that the baby would be Jewish, despite Michael's input. Another thought struck her. If she didn't marry Michael she'd be a single mother, and she'd get blamed for all society's ills, and . . .

She goes up to her bedroom and we don't hear a peep, and I don't even need to ask, Have you done your homework? because she's that well organized, she helped run the tuck shop at her old school, and when she was a Brownie, she . . .

Yes, there was certainly something growing in her womb.

Well, thank you, Miss Freeman, for being so nice. Katy's friend is in your class and she says your lessons are ever so interesting. Katy hopes she gets you. Bye!

The last comment lacerated Joy. She loved it when someone said she was interesting – it was her favourite compliment. But what use was it now when her teaching career was virtually at an end? Panic and self-pity jostled inside her for supremacy.

She passed the rest of the first hour in a stupor. She processed students on automatic pilot – demure girls with excellent GCSE results, gangly boys embarrassed by everything, the occasional child who'd read more than the set texts – meanwhile, Joy felt as if she were drowning. It flashed across her mind that the morning after pill was probably the best option, except if Sister Maureen knew she'd consider it to be murder, and more than anything, Joy wanted to have Sister Maureen's approval. More than that, she wanted to be good and she wanted her life to be simple and certain. Why was it never either of those things?

Joy realized that the noise in the hall had abated. Students and staff had drifted into the canteen for coffee. Joy knew that if she continued sitting at her desk she would be left entirely alone, and isolation did not appeal to her. Anything to save her from her thoughts. So she rose and, leaving her pamphlets on her desk as a sort of territorial marker, she left the gym and stopped at the Ladies.

On entering, she caught a glimpse of her reflection in the mirror. Her Aunt Miriam said you could tell from someone's face if they were pregnant. Joy scanned her own. She looked wan, her eyes were puffy and her curly hair was dishevelled and lifeless. What did that mean?

She opened the door of the cubicle and wondered what it was like to have a baby. How much did it hurt? Did it hurt more than toothache? Could you compare? There were so many things that could go wrong with childbirth, it just didn't bear thinking about, yet how could you stop yourself thinking about it? Joy felt tears pricking at her eyes. She told herself grimly that there would be plenty of time for tears later. She stood up, and wiped herself.

What was that? What was that reddish stain? Joy's heart bounded in her chest. It was her period! She checked again – it was possible that her desperation had made her hallucinate. It was most definitely her period. So she wasn't pregnant after all, not if she was having a period. Joy sat down again, eagerly searching for her tampons and praising God simultaneously. Her life was beginning all over again.

It seemed to Joy, as she washed her hands in the sink outside, that everything around her was transfigured. Light poured in through the coloured glass in the skylight and dyed her fingers orange and red and green, like a rainbow. Like a promise from God that He wouldn't do this to her again. Joy knew she ought to promise something in return. Guiltily she realized that her pledge to stop worrying had been well and truly broken. At least she hadn't *told* anyone what she'd been thinking – if she had, she would have seemed a proper fool. 'God', she said, looking up, 'I'm sorry. I really won't worry again, not now. Not when there isn't anything to worry about. And I'll do something about Michael.'

What that something might be Joy left in abeyance. For now, she bounced out of the Ladies, too high to sit and drink coffee with her colleagues and unable to trust herself not to announce in a loud voice to the assembled staff, 'I'm not pregnant!' Instead Joy turned back to the hall to return to her work station. To her surprise, she saw someone sitting in the seat facing hers, apparently waiting for her return. Someone in a green combat jacket three sizes too big and with a mass of matted hennaed hair. As Joy took her seat again she saw that her

65

interviewee was a she, a girl whose lips were stained a deep scarlet and who had a small silver ring through the right side of her nose. Her eyes were outlined with kohl and held Joy's with a startling directness.

'Hi!' she said. 'I'm Lucy. I shouldn't really be here today because I'm M for Marshall, but you're the English teacher, aren't you?'

Joy grinned at her to give herself time to recover her composure. Lucy Marshall wasn't a typical new recruit at all. She looked as if she'd drifted in from the street; Joy had seen girls like her hanging around some of the less salubrious pubs in town, and wondered about their lives. Perhaps this Lucy Marshall was one of those girls. Joy was conscious of feeling a sudden strong interest in her and knew dimly that it was because of the euphoria derived from her recent reprieve from motherhood. A mist had lifted, and the world was Technicolor again. This Lucy Marshall was part of that.

'Do you have a record card, Lucy?'

Joy realized she was still grinning, but this time it was because she was happy. Lucy grinned back, as if the two of them were sharing a huge joke.

'Yeah,' she said, and handed over a rather dog-eared card. Joy scanned it quickly. She had an A star in English literature as well as As in English language, art and chemistry. The rest were Cs. She was sixteen and had come from St Mary's, one of the college's feeder schools. Joy stole a glance at her again. Behind the heavy, daring make-up was a young girl's face, eyes bright and inquisitive, skin fresh and clear.

'These are good results,' Joy said. 'Apart from English, what else do you hope to do at A-level?'

'Art,' she said. 'And theatre studies. And I'm going to

learn the drums.' She lifted a hand to brush away some stray hair from her forehead and Joy could see her fingernails had been painted black. She wondered if Sister Maureen had met her yet.

'Are you a Goth?' Joy ventured. Were there Goths any more? Joy hoped she wasn't showing her ignorance in her attempt to be friendly. She was. Lucy's eyebrows rose in surprise.

'I'm not anything,' she said. 'I was Generation X last year but I've finished with that. It's sad to follow someone else's style.'

'Do you read much, Lucy?'

'What, books?'

Joy suppressed a sigh. For one moment she had thought Lucy might be different from the others. Clearly she had never got further than the pages of *Melody Maker*.

'Yes, books,' Joy repeated.

Lucy screwed up her eyes and thought. 'Jack Kerouac, J. D. Salinger and Sylvia Plath. Does she count, because she's mainly a poet? Charlotte Brontë. Terry Pratchett. Oscar Wilde especially. And Stephen King. Do you like them?'

'They're quite a mixture.'

'Oh, all right. Who are your favourite authors, then?'

Joy was stumped. Even though she was an English teacher, she'd been so busy in the last year or two keeping up with changes in record-keeping and new government initiatives that she'd not read anything exciting for ages. Not to seem outdone, she brought out an old favourite.

'George Eliot,' she said.

'I think I've heard of him.'

'He was a she,' Joy said delicately.

'Cool! That sounds interesting.'

Joy coughed slightly. 'And Shakespeare,' she added.

'Yeah. All English teachers like Shakespeare. Is it true or do you just pretend? I read an article in one of the Sunday papers that said that Shakespeare's overrated – the middle classes showing off, like.'

'George Bernard Shaw said much the same thing,' Joy commented.

'Was he a woman too?'

Joy laughed. 'No. But he had problems with women. He probably had an Oedipus complex.'

'I know what that is,' Lucy announced. Joy was aware now of Betty hovering close to her with another student, but she wished her away. 'It's when you love your mother too much. If you're a boy. I don't think girls can get it. My Dad got me this cartoon guide to Freud. And one to Marx. I'd quite like to be a Marxist but no one else is now, are they? Except my Dad.'

Joy glanced down at her record card. There was a tick in the box to indicate she came from a single-parent family. Apparently she lived with her father. In the occupation box, it said 'Lecturer in Social Studies'. Joy was curious about her mother but she didn't want to upset her by asking anything too personal.

'What do you vote?' Lucy asked. 'I bet you're Labour. Most teachers are, these days. My Dad says the Labour party isn't left enough for him. Do you fancy Tony Blair? I don't. I prefer Robin Cook. He's cute. Let me guess what your type is. I know! I bet you fancy Jonathon Porritt!'

Joy felt as if she were the one who was being interviewed. She tried to regain the initiative. 'What are your interests outside school?' she asked.

'Right,' said Lucy, warming to her subject. 'I club it in town and I want to learn to ride a bike, a Harley–Davidson, and I write poetry and I want to be a performance poet one day. That's why I need to learn the drums – because you have to have a sense of rhythm. But at the moment we're thinking of starting a band. Girls only. I've given up relationships with lads for now. It's sad to have a steady boyfriend.'

Joy suddenly felt scared for Lucy. For all her orange hair and scarlet lipstick, this Lucy Marshall was a motherless sixteen year old allowed to go to the clubs in Manchester. She may even have been offered drugs! It was even possible that her high spirits now were caused by amphetamines. She was planning to learn to ride a motorbike, which was extremely dangerous. Her appearance, veering on the sluttish, was bound to attract the wrong sort of boy. Or man. She was outrageous and vulnerable and at risk all at the same time. Joy found herself wishing desperately that she would end up in her A-level group. She knew Lucy needed watching carefully and she felt some kind of pull towards her. This girl needed someone to worry about her. Joy decided she would have a word with Betty. Meanwhile, there was something else she felt compelled to ask her.

'Did it hurt, having your nose pierced?'

'No. It was done very quick, like. In the beginning it was funny, 'cause you could feel something in your nose. And you keep catching it out of the corner of your eye. But I'm used to it now.'

'Weren't you worried that the needle wasn't clean or that the hole might go septic?'

'No,' she said. 'Why? Do you want to get yours done? I

can tell you somewhere to go. In the Corn Exchange, there's –'

At that point Betty did interrupt, bringing with her a short, plumpish lad who looked no older than fourteen. Lucy understood her time was up. As she rose, Joy realized that the aroma of stale cigarette smoke she had been conscious of had emanated from Lucy.

'*Ciao,*' said Lucy. 'I like you, Miss Freeman. I hope you're going to be my teacher. And you don't have to worry about getting your nose pierced. It's like one, two, three and it's over. Sorry!' she said to Betty, and Lucy strode out towards the hall door.

Betty exchanged a glance with Joy, but they were unable to say anything as the boy had taken Lucy's seat and was looking around him expectantly. Joy felt invigorated, as if she had just drunk a strong cup of coffee. Lucy had said that she liked her! As her mother would say, perhaps all this was meant. Joy decided there and then that she would watch over Lucy. Lucy would be her special charge.

Joy smiled brilliantly at the boy in front of her, who looked startled at her apparent enthusiasm.

'Now why do *you* want to do English?' Joy asked him.

CHAPTER FIVE

It was Thursday afternoon, and Miss Freeman's upper sixth English literature group was having its Shakespeare lesson. Joy was perched on the edge of the teacher's table, one leg swinging to a steady rhythm, her arms slicing the air as if she could enforce understanding by sleight of hand alone. The group of twelve or so seventeen-year-olds sat behind desks which lined three sides of the room. Some took notes; others leaned back in their chairs and observed their teacher's indefatigable enthusiasm. It cheered them. At least *she* liked *The Winter's Tale*; none of them had been able to understand it when they read it in the holidays. Miss Freeman, they noted, didn't seem to mind their ignorance. She seemed relentlessly cheerful today, more than usually cheerful. This was encouraging. With a bit of luck, she'd forget to set them an essay.

Emma wondered, as she doodled aimlessly in the margin, why Miss Freeman was in such a good mood. Had she had sex last night? There was a rumour Miss Freeman had a boyfriend, and she for one believed it; Freeman was one of the younger teachers and would be quite good-looking if she took more care with her appearance, like wearing make-up sometimes. Andrew saw Miss Freeman but was conscious only of that fuzzy feeling that meant he'd had too many pints last night, but it was the only way he could get to spend time with his dad. Karen wondered if she had time after college to pop to the shops to get a birthday card for Susan and also some more lip balm from the Body Shop, and would that leave her time to get the tea on for Mum *and* to get out early for babysitting? Kieran couldn't decide whether to risk listening to his Walkman to check on the cricket.

'And of course the other difficulty is with Leontes' sudden jealousy. There's no reason for it – we just have to accept it. It's completely unfounded. But once this obsession has taken root – this idea that his wife and best friend are having an affair – it controls him completely.'

Emma began to listen. So that was what the play was about.

'Just imagining the affair was enough for Leontes. Once it had happened in his head, it was as good as fact for him.'

Subliminally, Joy realized that she had left the group behind. How could she make them see, make them empathize with Leontes, this bunch of seventeen-year-olds whose experience of love was confined to gropes at parties and the problem page of *More* magazine. 'Thinking makes it so!' she announced. 'Do you remember that from *Hamlet*?'

Karen frowned and wrinkled her nose. Why was Miss Freeman muddling up the set texts? Karen had found it hard enough not writing Polonius for Polixenes and Laertes for Leontes. The trouble with Shakespeare was that he couldn't think of new names, he didn't have any imagination.

'Imagination!' Joy declared. 'Leontes' flaw was that he was cursed with too vivid an imagination. Do any of you suffer from that? Perhaps you don't experience jealousy as such, but let's think of something else.'

Her class, sensing a diversion, began to pay attention.

'Have you ever imagined something happening and then convinced yourself it's true?' Joy felt she was on the verge of making them understand. This was exciting. This was what she loved about teaching, that click, that sudden moment of comprehension. In the heat of the chase after knowledge, she'd even forgotten that her mother was flying to Manchester this very afternoon. She congratulated herself on that fact.

'So, have you? Imagined something, and then believed in it?'

'Like Father Christmas?' Karen suggested, knowing it was wrong and hoping for once it wasn't.

'Kind of like Father Christmas,' Joy said. 'Except I really mean something you don't want to believe in. For a child, it might be the monster you think is hiding at the foot of your bed. Whenever you look to see if it's there, it hides again. But it comes out when you get back under the covers.'

'Yeah, I did that,' Jamie said.

'When we're bigger,' Joy continued, excited now, 'we get neurotic about other things. Look – here's an example from my life. My mother's flying to Manchester today. From London,' she added, conversationally. 'Now, if I imagine the plane crashing and I picture her with her arms braced against the impact and the other passengers screaming and losing control, while my mother mutters a prayer and thinks that now her life is almost over –'

The class was spellbound. This was much better than Shakespeare.

'Well, then you see, I'm imagining it, and it's as if it's happening.' Joy's voice trailed away. It could happen. There could be a crash. She shivered. Wouldn't it be a coincidence if just now, just at this very minute, her mother's plane started its spiralling downward descent? Please God, no . . .

Emma tried to think if she ever imagined bad things happening. What if Ste was to leave her? Could she imagine that? Could she imagine him leaving a note in her file saying it was all over? That would be terrible. Andrew imagined his dad getting that job in Belfast and his mam saying he couldn't have the fare money to go and see him. Karen thought how awful it would be if she didn't get the grades she needed for college, and she ended up without anything, without A-levels, without a job. Kieran decided he had to know how England was doing and quickly inserted the earphones in his ears. And Miss Freeman turned to gaze out of the window.

She turned back, brushing tears out of her eyes that she hoped no one would see. Joy noticed her class looked rather solemn. Did they feel sorry for her? She grinned and decided she would try to prove to them she was quite all right.

'But the only thing you've got to worry about is the essay I'm going to set you.' There were loud groans and mock sighs. Take down this title: Examine the development of Leontes' obsession with Hermione's infidelity – 'Kieran!'

The small dark boy in the corner of the room hastily removed his earphones and was conscious of an embarrassed heat flooding his face.

'Bring it here, Kieran.' Joy's voice was weary. She didn't like having to reprimand the students. They were, after all, young adults, but when they behaved like children . . . A black Walkman was placed in her hand. The class waited with bated breath to see what the teacher was going to do.

Joy put on the earphones herself to hear what Kieran was listening to. Expecting some rave or jungle music she was initially surprised to hear the soporific tones of the Test match commentator.

'Atherton's beginning the innings, Miss,' Kieran said, sadly.

'Without you,' Joy commented, and went to sit behind the teacher's desk. An idea was forming in her mind. 'There's thirty minutes left of the lesson,' she told her class. 'Why don't you make a start on the essay? Begin a rough plan. OK?'

It wasn't so much that she was worried that there really had been a mid-air collision; it was more in the way of re-assurance that there hadn't been one. Listening to the news and discovering that nothing had happened except for an interest rate rise would help her to stop worrying. The news was in five minutes. Joy inserted the earphones and began to listen. Her class wouldn't mind. She would pass the whole thing off at the end of the lesson as a teacher's idea of a joke. But what if there really had been an air crash?

Atherton is walking out to the crease to begin the innings. The rain seems to be holding off . . .

Joy became aware of a figure at the window of the door to the classroom. She turned slowly to see who it was. Sister Maureen. She looked serious. Joy thought immediately of the scene in *David Copperfield* when David is taken out of his lesson so Mrs Creakle can tell him his mother has died. Was that why Sister had come to the classroom? Or was Sister looking serious because Joy was listening to the radio while her class were talking amongst themselves? Blushing furiously and cursing herself, she removed the earphones and stood up. Now all the students were silent, and watching her.

'Carry on with your work quietly,' Joy said, and

gestured to Sister that she would speak to her outside the classroom.

'It's not what you think,' Joy explained, laughing to cover her embarrassment. 'It wasn't the Test match. It's just that my mother's flying from Heathrow today, and I . . .'

Joy looked into Sister's face. Her pale blue eyes gave nothing away. The slight tightening of her lips was either a smile or faint irritation.

'. . . I wanted to check that Mum was all right, that nothing had happened to the flight, and . . .'

Sister Maureen raised her eyebrows in an admonitory fashion.

'. . . really it was just that. I mean, I don't even understand cricket.'

'Atherton's just begun to bat,' Sister said, 'and the rain's holding off.'

Joy loved Sister Maureen for that.

'So you're still worrying,' Sister said.

'No!' Joy declared. 'Kieran's Walkman tempted me. I'm not worrying. I'm not even going to worry about the upper sixth,' Joy said brightly, and her gaze travelled, with Sister Maureen's, to the classroom window. The group had stopped working and were chatting in twos and threes. Emma was brushing her hair, and another Walkman had materialized, and both Kieran and Craig were listening to it. Karen and Leanne were comparing notes.

'Leanne needs to see me for her mock interview,' Sister said. 'I think she's forgotten the appointment, so I came to get her myself.'

At that moment Leanne put her hand to her mouth in horror, left her desk and appeared outside the classroom.

She and Sister made their way down the corridor while Joy returned to her class.

'Silence!' she said as she entered.

She needed silence. She needed to think. Ever since Sister's challenge that Joy should stop worrying she had done nothing but worry. Now Sister had caught her at it, fair and square. Why on earth did she do it? Was she as mad as Leontes? Would she even believe the oracle if it told her her mother was safe? Probably not. What was wrong with her?

Joy saw her propensity for worry as some sort of disease, or a cloud, a kind of internal weather, that drifted across her vision and made everything dark and fraught. Even when she didn't want to worry, she worried. Was all this anxiety some sort of mental illness? That in itself was a worrying thought. Joy could not believe it. Here she was worrying about worrying. Now she could hardly suppress the desire to laugh. The bell cut across her rising hysteria.

The class was galvanized into action, collected its files and left the room in a huddle. Joy picked up her bag and books and made her way to the staff room. She checked her pigeon-hole. In it was a scribbled note from Fran in the office: 'Your mother rang from Ringway to say she's arrived safely.' Joy loved her mother for knowing how much she worried. Joy then wondered whether it was her mother who made her worry. This was a new thought. On one hand, her mother encouraged her to worry; on the other hand, living with a man she no longer loved destroyed her self-esteem. What hope was there for her?

Plenty, thought Joy, as she resolutely collected her things in preparation for leaving college. Tomorrow was

Rosh Hashanah, and the first day of the rest of her worry-free life.

Joy made her way to Domestic Arrivals and scanned the waiting figures there. As her eyes caught sight of her mother, everyone else blurred out of focus, and she saw only that well-loved, short, plump figure in its navy coat (bought in the sales at Lewis's three years ago), and the large brown leather suitcase which had accompanied her on every journey she had ever undertaken. Joy eagerly made her way towards her, anxiously hoping her mother didn't look any older, waiting excitedly for her mother to see her and for her face to light up, as it always did.

It did now. Joy and Ruth Freeman hugged each other, each relishing the contact with each other's body. Then they parted to examine each other. Joy noticed that her mother had let her hair grey just above her ears and was surprised that when she had had it set, she hadn't asked Irene to colour it again. She was pleased that her mother was wearing make-up, and the blue silk scarf she had bought her mother from Kendal's for her last birthday looked well. Ruth examined Joy. She hadn't put on weight, which was good. She looked tired and was probably working too hard; there was no colour in her face. The brown jacket she had flung on was falling off one shoulder, and Ruth resisted an urge to straighten it, knowing it would irritate Joy. But that pallor! Something was wrong.

'Are you all right?' Ruth asked, noticing the little lines around her daughter's eyes.

'I'm fine,' Joy asserted, smiling to prove it.

'You look pale.'

'I suppose I was a bit fraught during your flight. And

it's that time of month.' Joy lowered her voice to say that in case her mother thought she ought not to mention periods in public. She picked up her mother's suitcase and tilted it so she could pull it along the concourse on its wheels. Together they walked towards the car park.

'Tomorrow you can have a rest,' Ruth announced. 'And by the way, what are we doing for Rosh Hashanah?'

'Deborah rang,' Joy told her mother. 'She's invited us both to go with them to their *shul* and then have lunch at their house.'

Deborah was Joy's first cousin, her only other relative to live in Manchester. This was because Gants Hill-born Debbie had married Howard, a Mancunian, who ran a wholesale ladies'-clothing business and had settled in Whitefield, producing two children, Hayleigh and Josh.

'That sounds nice,' Ruth admitted, as Joy tried to remember where in the car park she had left the car. 'It won't be too much for her?'

'No, Mum. You know Debs loves entertaining. She sounded excited about having us all over. You know Barney and Miriam are there too.' Ruth knew that, and was pleased. Barney was her younger brother, and she was uncritically fond of him. Miriam wasn't too bad for a sister-in-law.

Joy saw her Micra parked by the ticket machine. When she reached it, she opened the boot and hoisted her mother's case inside. Then Joy unlocked the passenger door for her mother who, adjusting her coat, settled herself in the car. Only then did Joy enter too.

'So you're well,' Ruth said, as the engine started.

'Yes!' Joy declared emphatically. 'Perfectly.' She was glad to be able to tell her mother this. 'In fact, I had a Well

Woman check yesterday, and the nurse gave me a clean bill of health.'

There was a pause. Ruth wondered why Joy was telling her that. Was it a smokescreen? Why had she gone for a Well Woman check at all? Was there a symptom Joy had hidden from her? She would call her bluff immediately.

'You're lying,' Joy's mother said.

'No, honestly. Why should I lie?' Joy wound down the window and inserted her parking ticket into the machine.

'Because you don't want me to worry,' said Ruth.

'The truth is I'm fine.'

'Yes, but have you had the result of the smear yet?'

'No, but even if it is abnormal, it's treatable, you know.'

'So it might be abnormal.'

'No, I didn't say that. I'm sure it won't be.' If Joy hadn't been concentrating on taking the right exit from the roundabout, she would have taken a hand off the steering wheel and crossed her fingers. She had tempted fate. Her mother, unencumbered, did cross her fingers. Ruth decided to change the subject.

'And Michael. Is he well?'

'Fine,' said Joy laconically.

'Is he taking the day off tomorrow?'

'Come on, Mum, you know he's not Jewish.'

'It would be nice,' she said. Joy smiled to herself. The last thing her mother would want was Michael's company all day. Her comment was just a reminder that Michael wasn't Jewish and therefore wasn't suitable, and probably didn't love her enough to take the day off work in her honour. Joy debated whether to tell her mother that she was feeling less settled with Michael. It was certainly tempting. Except telling her was another step forward on the road to taking some sort of action, and that was scary.

In addition, how could she possibly explain the sequence of events that led to her realization that Michael was the wrong man for her? She did not relish talking to her mother about sex. To Ruth, Joy knew, sex was a bodily function on a par with micturition and excretion. It was something necessary that you did in private, it was faintly disgusting, but it had to be tolerated if you wanted children. Joy considered how, whenever a bedroom scene on television was getting torrid, her mother would sigh loudly at the idiocy of the human condition, leave the room and put the kettle on. Joy decided to move to another subject.

'How's the family?'

'David is working too hard and he's not sleeping properly. I reminded him about your father.' At the word 'father', Joy flinched. 'So Davy promised me he'd have a few days away from the hotel now the season is nearly over. They think Miriam might have a prolapse, but you'll be seeing her tomorrow so you can talk about that over lunch.' Ruth paused. 'And I had a letter from your Aunty Faye.'

Joy experienced a flicker of interest. Aunty Faye was the black sheep of the family. She was her mother's elder sister and had moved to New York when Joy was tiny. At that time her grandmother, so the story went, was in and out of hospital, and in between times the sisters were trying to care for her at home. It had never been clear to Joy whether Aunty Faye had simply had enough or genuinely couldn't cope, but she'd chosen that time to announce her engagement to Uncle Benjy. Uncle Benjy was a New Yorker; his father ran a furniture business that would one day be his; Faye and Benjy left the country before Joy's grandmother died. Joy had grown up knowing that Faye was a byword for irresponsibility. Over the years Ruth's attitude to Faye had softened, but only slightly. The correct expression to assume when speaking of Aunty Faye was to suck in your lips with disdain, but simultaneously to suggest some remote pity for her, as if there was bound to be some form of divine retribution for her lack of natural affection.

Ruth Freeman gave a little cough. 'Faye and Benjy are fine.' Joy had often thought that relations with Aunty Faye would have been better if she'd had the sense to be ill occasionally. Then Ruth could have worried about her.

'Sshh,' Joy said, as they moved on to the motorway slip-road. She wanted to concentrate on the flow of traffic. Out of the corner of her eye Joy saw her mother grip on to the bar on the side of the door. She was staring straight ahead of her. A transit van flashed Joy and so she moved on to the inside lane and raised her hand in gratitude.

'What did you do that for?' Joy's mother snapped.

'I was thanking him for letting me in,' Joy explained.

Ruth sat up stiffly, her senses alert for danger.

'It's frantic at college,' Joy began. 'The good A-level results last year means we've had an influx of students who would otherwise have gone to the tertiary, and some of the chemistry groups are –'

'Concentrate, Joy. Look, you're going over sixty miles an hour. You're too near that lorry.'

Joy dropped her speed. She wasn't in a particular hurry. She was enjoying having her mother with her. It was perfectly understandable that her mother should feel nervous when Joy was driving. To her, Joy knew, she would always be somewhere around fourteen. That knowledge made Joy feel young now, and it was a comfortable feeling. For a moment she felt it was presumptuous of her to drive, to have a real job, to be living with a man.

'How's work?' Joy asked her mother. As she asked the question she visualized her mother sitting at her word processor in the solicitor's office, where she was employed part time.

'So so,' she replied. 'Doreen is having trouble with her daughter, who's never home before three in the morning. It's brought on her asthma. Mr Bergman's mother has shingles. At her age, I wouldn't fancy it. I brought some chicken with me.'

Joy reflected that her mother always brought chicken with her.

'Because I don't like the way you do it,' Ruth added. She always said that too, Joy remembered. She smiled to herself as they left the motorway.

'I thought we could have some cold chicken tonight if you have some salad, and perhaps tomorrow as well, if Deborah doesn't feed us properly. Mind you, she knows how to cater. You, on the other hand, have always been hopeless with food. Hopeless. I don't know where I went wrong. Remember when I taught you to peel potatoes and you brought the knife towards you instead of away from you and sliced right through your thumb?' Joy remembered. It was the last time she was ever allowed in the kitchen. 'David had to ring the doctor and you were screaming blue murder and I held your hand under the cold tap. How old was he? Five? I had to shout to him to tell him what to say while I held your hand under the water. I thought you'd need stitches. Then when the doctor . . .'

Ruth's narrative wove in and out of Joy's mind like a familiar, favourite refrain. It was the 'when you sliced your thumb' story. There was also the 'when I first let you choose your own clothes and you came back with that pink monstrosity' story. And the 'when you panicked over your physics exam and I stayed up all night learning with you' story. Joy's childhood was her mother's personal fund of folklore with which she entertained all comers, like a Yiddishe Scheherazade. Joy reflected that her mother knew how to tell a story.

Was it her mother who made her worry? If it was, it was also her mother who made her feel safe and loved and important. They would have a cosy evening. Michael was out at a parents' evening and he wouldn't be back until late, as a group of them went out for a drink afterwards. It would just be Joy and her Mum. They'd chat and laugh and eat the *kichels* Joy had bought specially. At the thought of that, Joy glowed with happiness and smiled to herself as the car was swallowed up by the busy Manchester streets.

CHAPTER SIX

The *shul* was packed. Joy had never seen so many people all at once under one roof, unless she made an exception of the Royal Exchange's recent production of *Hamlet*, which was full to bursting with sixth-formers from all over Manchester. Then, she had sat up in the gallery and found she was watching the audience as much as she was watching the play. The same was true this Rosh Hashanah. For the rabbi and the men on the *bimah*, wrapped up in their prayer shawls and the intricacies of ancient Hebrew, prayer seemed to be a private affair. It didn't reach out to Joy, marooned above them in an ocean of women.

Still, it was soothing to watch the swaying movements of the men *davening* and impressive to see the massed white and blue of the prayer shawls covering expensive *yomtov* suits. Around her she could hear the soft susurration of women whispering and the rustle of designer costumes, and she breathed in an atmosphere rich with currents of expensive perfume that met and mingled in the warm air. There were two hours of this to go. It was nice, in a way, not to have to do anything, but just to be there, her mother on one side of her and Deborah and her family on the other.

Joy looked down at the fat blue prayer-book she was holding, saw the yellowing thumbprint in the inner margin and tried to imagine how many Jews, most far more devout than she was, had stood where she now stood, mouthing these words, praying with conviction.

She felt guilty, and tried to follow the service, but the unwieldy English translation was almost as meaningless to her as the Hebrew lettering on the opposite page.

Much of it, she decided, was about telling God how wonderful He was. Which, if He was omniscient, He would know anyway. And this being Rosh Hashanah, the congregation had to ask God to forgive it for all the wrong things it did last year. The prayer-book contained a sort of check-list of sins. Joy skimmed through it and decided she didn't come out that badly. Except she was beginning to see that her sins weren't the traditionally colourful ones such as murder, adultery and defrauding large financial institutions; her sin was simply that she worried too much, and that she had possibly – only possibly – ended up with the wrong man. So all she had to do was stop worrying and do something about Michael. Something. She wasn't sure what, yet.

So she looked up for inspiration. Through the high windows above the gallery the sunlight was broken up by the dust motes in the air. Joy's attention wandered again. She admired the women around her, with their immaculately coiffeured hair and their hats that toned perfectly with the owners' beautifully tailored suits. She knew that her cousin Deborah, standing by her side, could compete with the best of them. She looked delicious in a cream two-piece suit with a brushed-silk blouse in a rich brown of precisely the same shade as the ribbon around her wide-brimmed hat. Joy looked down sadly at her green interview suit and was conscious of her dowdy black beret. What had her mother said to her that morning? *Well, I suppose you'll do.*

However, Joy knew she had no problem with the way Jewish women overdressed for *shul*. She reckoned it was a cunning method of revenging themselves upon the men who had consigned them to the gallery, where they would not be a distraction. OK, Joy imagined them thinking, you want a distraction? Sure, we can distract. Collectively they were a blaze of colour and sensuousness. Joy wished she could be like them.

It then occurred to her that she wasn't Jewish enough. Perhaps if she hadn't drifted from her roots, going out with non-Jewish boys, avoiding the Jewish Society at university and teaching in a Catholic college, she wouldn't suffer from this permanent anxiety about anything and everything. She would know her place. She would know what to believe. She would know the rules she had to stick to – here they were, here in this prayer-book. She would have a husband who was an accountant or a doctor or a lawyer and she could have lots of babies and join the *shul*'s Ladies' Guild and help on a Wednesday afternoon with teas for the blind and train to be a counsellor. On Thursdays she would make *gefilte* fish and she would lie about how much she spent on dresses. Like Deborah.

Joy glanced at her enviously. Her life was full of comforting certainties. She had a lovely house in Whitefield with a large through-lounge and a kitchen-diner with a wipe-clean ceramic hob and a double sink, so if ever she wanted to become more *frum*, she could. She had Howard, who was good-looking but worked very hard. Except she didn't seem to mind that; it was what she'd been brought up to expect. Everything had turned out as Deborah had expected. Here she was now, with Hayleigh and Josh, turning the pages of a Thomas the Tank Engine book with a quiet confidence that was bred of inner peace. She was even possessed of a sixth sense. She'd guessed Joy was thinking of her and reached over to squeeze her hand.

Yes, two beautiful children, and there was Howard in the main body of the *shul*, brow creased in concentration, attempting to follow the gyrations of the Hebrew. His father stood next to him, a short man with a surprising quantity of white hair, making him look positively venerable. As she beheld him, Joy allowed herself, for just one moment, to have *the* dangerous thought: What would her father have looked like if he had been standing in *shul* today? There was that sharp pang that accompanied her thoughts about her father. As a child she had stood in the gallery in her local *shul* and looked down with her mother, knowing there was no one there who belonged to them. She was five, she'd come downstairs in the morning – and it was all over. She'd worn pyjamas with little sprigs of blue and white flowers. She'd come into the kitchen and her mother was crying, and Uncle Barney was standing over her and it had all happened in the night and Joy had slept through it. She didn't have a father any more. A cold wind swept through her universe and she could feel it now, whipping around her legs, stealing inside her, stirring up that familiar panic.

If it was bad for her, it must have been even more dreadful for her mother. Just seven years married to a dearly loved husband, and then everything was suddenly over. Joy knew she was selfishly glad her mother had never remarried. It was proof that her father was irreplaceable. Had he lived, had he been there for them, everything would be different now. Yet Joy's imagination failed her as she tried to imagine the difference a father's presence would make. To help her, she looked down at the men again, saw Howard, and Howard's father, whose *tallit* was slipping off his shoulders, and watched him adjust it. Then Howard turned to the man on his other side and muttered a few words. He was someone Joy did not know. He had a tidy black beard, a noticeably Semitic nose and wore a traditional blue and white *yarmulke*. Then he looked up at the gallery, his eyes met Joy's, and he smiled. Why did he do that? Joy decided he had mistaken her for someone else and felt embarrassed for him, so she blushed. He continued to gaze at her. Was there something funny about her? Was that why he was smiling at her? She looked down at the prayer-book and stole another glance at him, but now he was following the prayers, yet a smile still played on his lips.

Joy nudged Deborah.

'Who's that sitting next to Howard?'

'Lawrence Weiner, his cousin,' Deborah said. 'He's nice.'

Ah! So it had been Deborah he had been smiling at! Her mother dug her sharply in the ribs.

'Joy – what's that?'

She pointed at the seat in front of them. There was a Sainsbury's carrier bag beneath it with something inside it. Joy didn't know what it was, but she knew what her mother was thinking. On *Yomtov*, you're not supposed to carry anything. No self-respecting Jewish woman would carry a bag to *shul* on *Yomtov* – she'd leave it in the car like everyone else. Joy had read the notices plastered all over *shul* that there was a security alert. Joy's mother had located a suspicious package.

Joy's heart pounded furiously.

'What shall we do?' she asked her mother.

'Shall we tell someone?'

But what if it was nothing? Should she and her mother

start a mass exodus of the whole congregation on Rosh Hashanah? Everyone would panic, and the incident would be bound to make the front pages of the *Jewish Telegraph*. But on the other hand, if it really was a bomb and they did nothing, then they would be responsible for the deaths of over 400 Jews in the worst atrocity in England since the Middle Ages. Joy's skin began to prickle.

Everyone stood. Then the flat, piercing note of the *shofar* rang through the *shul*. Best not to do anything until the rabbi had finished. Joy tried to listen carefully, to find out if the package was ticking, but all she could hear, once again, was the strange, quavering wail of the ram's horn. She swallowed hard and glanced at her mother, whose eyes were fixed on the carrier bag.

'Do something,' she whispered.

The congregation sat again. Then the carrier bag was slowly lifted from view by the woman in front. Joy could see her taking something from it to hand to the child who was with her.

'It's all right,' Joy whispered to her mother, who she could see was shaking. Joy realized she was shaking too. That was understandable. The package could have been a bomb. If most Jews are neurotic, there are good reasons for it, Joy thought in self-defence. Worrying on behalf of other people doesn't count, she informed God. I bet you do it all the time. And I am going to give up worrying on my own account. So there!

Thinking perhaps that wasn't the right way to talk to God, and feeling the need for some fresh air, Joy decided she would leave the *shul* for a while.

'I'm just going outside,' she told her mother. 'Are you all right?'

'Are *you* all right?' her mother asked Joy.

'Yes, but I'd like some fresh air.'

'You look pale,' Ruth said.

Replaying their favourite conversation helped Joy to feel normal again. Wanting some company, she mentioned to Deborah that she was going outside for a few moments and saw a look of interest pass across her cousin's face.

'I'll come with you,' Deborah mouthed, in a stage whisper.

Joy waited at the end of the row of seats while Deborah asked her children if they wanted to come with Mummy or stay with their grandmothers. During that brief interval, Joy glanced down once more to where the men were. Howard's cousin was looking at her again, she was sure of it. It was one of those looks that you gave someone when you were pretending that you weren't looking at them but you were. A suspicion began to grow in Joy's mind, which rapidly gathered force as she watched her cousin shepherd her daughter and son along the row of seats. She was glad Debbie had offered to come outside with her. They clearly needed to talk.

Joy, Deborah, Hayleigh and Josh made their way down the stone stairs, the children skittering in front, glad to be able to move their limbs again. Deborah's heels clacked noisily as they made their descent. In the lobby outside the main *shul* a few men and women were talking, and a uniformed security guard stood at the entrance. Deborah ushered her children into the Ladies, and Joy followed. Near the rail of coats was an elderly settee and, still feeling rather shaky, Joy sat down.

'Are you feeling all right?' Deborah asked.

'It's nothing.' Joy laughed dismissively as a preface to what she was going to say. 'It's just that Mum and I thought we saw a bomb. It turned out to be someone's carrier bag. Really, I don't know what got into us!'

'Ah, well, you can't be too careful,' Deborah said, as she smoothed her skirt and straightened her jacket.

'True,' Joy agreed, and began to think carefully about how to phrase her next comment. She watched her cousin move to a heavy, old-fashioned mirror. The gilt of its frame had come off in places. In a businesslike manner, Deborah took a lipstick from her pocket and began to apply it. The cloakroom was shady and quiet. Joy decided this was as good a place as any.

'Deborah. Howard's cousin has been staring at me.'

'Now why would he want to do that?' observed Deborah, from between lips stretched to receive the lipstick.

'I think you probably know why.'

'Me?' asked Deborah, turning now, and looking innocently at Joy.

Joy coughed. 'It is a truth universally acknowledged that a single Jewish man in possession of a good fortune must be in want of a wife. No – don't tell me. This – who is he? – Lawrence something or other – is the single man, and I'm your choice of candidate for the role of wife, even though there's a slight encumbrance in the shape of Michael.'

'Lawrence is *nice*!' Deborah cited in her defence.

'There isn't such a word as "nice",' Joy said automatically, as if she were addressing a student. 'And it certainly isn't "nice" for me to betray Michael. But I'll do it anyway.'

'Look,' Deborah began. 'You're thirty-one, you're wasted on Michael, he never comes round to see us –'

'I said I'll play along with you this time.'

Deborah's eyes widened with astonishment and pleasure.

'You mean you'll meet Lawrence?'

'I don't think I have any choice.'

'Actually you haven't. Lawrence is coming to lunch too.'

Excited, Deborah sat down by Joy on the settee. For years and years it had been her dearest wish to pair Joy off with someone more suitable than Michael. Why, she'd even lain awake in bed and listed to herself all the single men she knew in Prestwich and Whitefield who might like Joy. Often she'd fall asleep by selecting one and imagining Joy involved in a passionate romance with him, and how they thanked her with tears in their eyes for introducing them, and the wedding, and Joy and whoever-it-was under the *chuppah*, and Hayleigh as bridesmaid, and Josh as page-boy. They would look so adorable and she would *kvell* with pride.

'Aren't you getting on well with Michael?' Deborah asked with concern – but her eyes danced.

Joy bowed her head to avoid eye contact with her cousin. 'Something happened, and I realized I don't want to spend the rest of my life with him. So I'm at a bit of a crossroads. I'm not quite sure what to do next.'

'What happened?' Deborah asked eagerly.

'It turned out to be nothing in the end,' Joy said demurely. 'So it doesn't matter.'

'I'm glad, whatever it was,' Deborah said decisively. 'He's not right for you, Joy. We all think – Howard, me, your mother, my mother – we all think you can do better than Michael.'

'I know,' said Joy sadly. 'But I just can't leave him.' There. The thought was out.

Hayleigh and Josh were washing their hands at the sink and giggling. A small old lady came into the cloakroom, saw Joy and Deborah and complained about the temperature in *shul*.

'Why can't you leave him?' Deborah persisted.

This was what Joy had been asking herself. 'Well, firstly, the house is my house and, if we finish, he'll have nowhere to live. Secondly, it isn't fair, because I haven't tried to talk to him yet to see if we can mend things. And thirdly . . .'

'And thirdly what?'

Joy decided to speak the truth. 'I'm not sure if I want to live on my own.' She thought of burglars, of escaped criminals, of the central heating breaking down.

Deborah bit her lip, deep in thought. Joy knew that Deborah would think of something. Even when they were teenagers, she had been the most brilliant strategist when it came to boys.

'I can understand you not wanting to live by yourself. I wouldn't want to either. So all the more reason to meet Lawrence now and get to know him. Then perhaps . . .'

'Then perhaps I can move seamlessly from one to the other?' Joy suggested incredulously.

Deborah shrugged.

'Debs! That's almost adultery!'

For a moment, Joy thought, her cousin looked sheepish, but not that sheepish.

'Look, I'm not going to push Lawrence at you. But he's very clever – like you!' Deborah believed sincerely in flattery. 'He has a philosophy degree. You'll get on fabulously. And it's not adultery because you're not married and you've decided to leave Michael anyway.'

'I'm only thinking about leaving him,' Joy said in her

pedantic voice, which she hoped would cover her increasing nervousness. Until she had told Debbie her relationship with Michael was over, she hadn't realized it was. It was as if the words had come before the thought. That was strange. Joy had always been careful in the past to think everything through before it happened. Her new resolve was most definitely strange, and frightening. How was she going to finish with Michael? How could she do it without hurting his feelings?

'You must think about leaving him,' Deborah said urgently. 'It's not just that he isn't Jewish. I'm not your mother. But he's mean to you. Remember when you saved so he could follow his football team to Europe? You didn't have a holiday that year, did you? I was appalled. And you have nothing in common with him. You told me once you never discuss books with him, or go with him to the theatre. Lawrence, on the other hand, has a season ticket for the Royal Exchange.'

'Shut up,' Joy said.

'I won't,' Deborah said. 'It's time you went out with a *nice* man!'

'Shut up,' Joy repeated. She felt uncomfortable. She had a suspicion Debbie might be right. If 'nice' in this context meant considerate and delicate and generous and decent, then Michael probably wasn't nice. She'd believed that a good relationship was built on tolerance, and she'd tolerated his little ways, such as looking in her purse for money and leaving her short, such as throwing tea bags in the sink, which clogged up the drain, such as forgetting to pull the chain after he'd been to the toilet. She'd just assumed all men were like that. Perhaps, Joy thought, she might even enjoy sex with a nice man.

Hayleigh came over and sat herself on Joy's lap,

effectively putting an end to the conversation. She informed Joy confidentially that she'd been helping Mummy butter the bridge rolls and Mummy had made a cheesecake and Josh had wet his shoes in the toilet.

Joy listened with only half her attention to this childish prattle. Why hadn't she realized until this very moment how bad her relationship with Michael had become? What had been wrong with her that she couldn't admit all this negative stuff until now? She began to wonder if this denial could be a form of mental illness – the onset of Alzheimer's? – until she realized she was worrying again and commanded herself to stop.

Josh was tugging at his mother's jacket. 'I want to go home now.'

'No, honey,' Deborah explained. 'We've got to go back upstairs for a little bit longer, and then we'll all go back home for lunch – Joshy and Hayleigh and Mummy and Daddy and both your grandmas and grandads and Aunty Joy and Uncle Lawrence!'

It sounds like we're a couple already, Joy thought.

CHAPTER SEVEN

Everyone stood back as Howard unlocked the front door.

'Go in, go in,' he insisted.

Joy followed Deborah into the house. Her first thought was that it was lucky she didn't suffer from hay fever. There were flowers everywhere, on the shelf by the window, in a huge vase on the floor, and a small spray on the telephone table; but just as Joy was about to look further to see if they were real or not, Howard obscured her view, masking the telephone. There was friendly chaos as everyone helped each other with coats, Uncle Barney squeezed all the ladies and the children danced up and down with excitement. Deborah appeared, already in an apron, and whooshed everyone into the lounge, the double doors of which stood open, ready to receive the company. Howard remained by the telephone. His eyes met his wife's apologetically.

'Got to make a phone call,' he explained.

Joy watched Deborah's face. Her expression was inscrutable. Howard lived and breathed work, Joy knew. Since not all of his employees were Jewish, it was possible that his firm was open that day and Howard had remembered something he needed to tell them, or simply wanted to check up on them. Was Deborah annoyed? It was impossible to say.

Joy turned and entered the lounge, and immediately her mouth watered. Along the wall facing her was a large, extended table, groaning with food. There were plates of bridge rolls with cream cheese, with salmon, with egg, with chopped herring; there were mushroom vol-au-vents, tiny balls of chopped and fried fish, bowls of salad; there were strips of vegetables and pitta bread next to a bowl of hummus, decorated with home-made falafel; there were nuts, crisps, an aubergine dip, fresh salmon wrapped in lattice pastry; there were plates, serviettes, forks. That was just the first course. Joy looked in the mirror above the table and saw reflected in it Deborah's kitchen table, where there were gâteaux, honey cake, cheesecake, *kichels* and a trifle. Deborah was thrusting things in the microwave while Hayleigh stood by the sink drinking from her cup.

Joy felt someone prod her arm. It was her mother.

'Very nice!' Ruth murmured appreciatively.

Hypocrite, thought Joy to herself. In fact, her mother was a tiny eater. But the point about food, according to Ruth Freeman, was that there had to be a lot of it. She measured the success of catering ventures by the amount of food left over at the end. The more left over, the better the meal. Joy reckoned Deborah was going to score very highly indeed. There were only ten assembled, but this lunch could have fed the whole *shul*.

When Howard came in he opened the drinks cabinet and started to pour drinks for those who wanted them. Simultaneously, Deborah appeared, holding aloft in her oven-gloved hands a plate of hot mushroom *blintzes*. There was more commotion at the door as other people began to arrive. Aware that Lawrence might be one of them, Joy immediately bent down to talk to Josh, who had just been released from the hugs and kisses of his maternal grandmother.

'Do you want me to help you fill your plate, Joshy?' Joy asked him, seeing him gaze abstractedly at the food. The boy nodded, and Joy moved round the table with him, discussing what was on it.

'I want crisps,' Josh said.

Joy took a handful of crisps and deposited it on his plate.

'Do you want some bridge rolls?' she asked him.

He shook his head vigorously. 'Jus' crisps.' He was about to take his plate out of the lounge and into the sitting room, where the television lived, but was stopped by his father, who turned him round to face the company, to be spotted by Aunty Miriam, who again planted a big kiss on both of his cheeks, leaving two lipstick imprints.

Joy was amused. She remembered having to suffer the same indignities. No one else had entered the lounge, so Joy decided to join her mother and Uncle Barney. They were talking animatedly, despite the fact they had only seen each other a few days ago. Meeting in Manchester was something different, and added spice to their conversation. Joy would not interrupt. Instead she started on her mushroom *blintz* and marvelled at the immaculate beauty of Deborah's home. However did she manage? How did she stop the children having accidents and spoiling the beautiful pale-grey carpet? How come the furniture looked as if it had come straight from the showroom?

Then more people came into the lounge – strangers, Joy realized. Not Lawrence – and she surprised herself by the twinge of disappointment she experienced. She scanned the new arrivals – two pretty but overdressed young girls; a man with receding hair and granny specs and a woman who was powerfully familiar. Joy wondered where she could have seen her before. The trouble with being a teacher was that so many people knew her whom she could not remember – students, students' parents, other teachers from courses and meetings. This particular woman had dark, bobbed hair, a clean complexion and slightly protuberant, kind eyes. Looking at her and trying to place her, Joy suddenly felt herself getting anxious for no apparent reason. What was the connection? She seemed painfully, intimately familiar.

Her identity flashed upon Joy. It was the nurse – Sister Abrams – here, in Deborah's lounge, with her mother, her relations and a prospective boyfriend. Sister Abrams – a woman who had prodded her breasts and felt inside her vagina! Joy felt herself turn scarlet. She saw Sister Abrams smile at her in recognition. There was no hiding-place. Joy smiled back, and Sister Abrams advanced upon her.

'Weren't you in the clinic a few days ago?' she asked.

'Yes. That was me,' announced Joy. 'Joy Freeman. The smear test.'

'Are you a friend of Deborah's?' she began.

'She's my cousin,' Joy explained.

'She's my neighbour,' said Sister Abrams. 'I live a few doors away. My Anna and Rebecca play with Hayleigh. Rebecca is in the same class as Hayleigh. It was very kind of Deborah to invite us all. My family is in Leeds and so we couldn't –'

'I know,' Joy interrupted, remembering their conversation in the clinic. Did the nurse know if her smear result had come through? Was it good etiquette to ask?

'Call me Sharon,' Sister Abrams continued. 'I'm so glad there's someone I know here. Look, there are my two girls – over by the food. That's Daniel – over there talking to Howard. My husband.'

There was a pause. Joy knew how she was meant to fill it. She was to introduce her man. Sister Abrams – Sharon – had heard all about how Joy intended to revive her flagging love life and assumed her boyfriend would be here right now. Joy considered explaining that Michael wasn't Jewish, and that she'd tried her advice and it hadn't worked. No, she couldn't face that. That was when she saw Lawrence enter.

'That's Lawrence,' Joy said casually. Sorry God, Joy thought to herself. It's not exactly a lie, is it? There *was* Lawrence. As deceptions go, it hardly registered on the Richter scale.

'He looks nice,' Sharon said, in a stage whisper.

'I don't suppose . . .' Joy began, hoping to introduce the subject of the smear results. It would be so good to know if everything was negative.

Then her mother arrived. Joy felt obliged to make the necessary introductions.

'My mother, Sharon. Mum, this is Sharon Abrams,' Joy said, and added, 'Deborah's neighbour.'

'I met Joy at the Well Woman clinic,' Sharon said brightly. 'I'm the nurse there.'

Damn! Why did she have to say that?

'A nurse!' Ruth said, immediately interested. Her eyes lit up. She guided Sharon by her elbow into a corner. Joy wondered why. It crossed her mind that her mother might have a health problem that she was keeping from her, to stop her worrying about it. She must explain to her mother that she'd given up worrying and then perhaps her mother could tell Joy what it was she was worried about, which would save her worrying! Joy followed Sharon and her mother. She had to know what they were talking about.

'So you're sure,' Ruth said to Sharon, 'that Joy really did seem healthy to you?'

'Very healthy.'

'Are you sure?'

'Absolutely sure.'

'Because at one time she suffered from cervical erosion . . .'

Joy moved away to the food. What was this? Didn't her mother trust her? How embarrassing to make the insides of her body the theme of a lunch-time conversation. Why not invite Aunty Miriam over too? And everyone else! Ask the nurse to give an illustrated slide-show of her birth canal – why not?

Joy realized she was feeling fraught. Family do's always made her feel this way. Time to eat. She joined Howard in filling her plate with whatever came to hand, chopped and fried, bridge rolls, anything.

'Work all right?' Howard asked her.

'Great.'

'Try the salmon,' he said.

Joy helped herself to the salmon.

'And your business?'

Howard grimaced. 'I can't afford to be off both today and tomorrow. But what can you do?'

Deborah had put some straight-backed chairs along the sides of the lounge, and Joy chose one to sit on. As she did so, her cousin came to join her.

'Well,' said Deborah, 'what do you think of him at close quarters?'

For a moment Joy didn't understand the question. Then she followed Deborah's eyes to Lawrence, standing by the buffet, helping his elderly mother fill her plate. His navy pinstripe suit seemed a little too big for him.

His beard made him look vaguely rabbinical. She wasn't sure whether she fancied him exactly, but he looked very nice.

'Nice,' Joy said.

Deborah beamed happily. She loved matchmaking. Joy knew that when her cousin read the local paper, she turned straight to the Lonely Hearts column to try to pair up the ads.

'So do you think you'll –'

'Enough about him for now,' Joy stopped her. 'Congratulations on a splendid lunch. Did you do it yourself?'

'Over a week or so. I prepared most of it while the kids were at school and put it in the freezer.'

'Even then, Debbie, it's –' Joy swept her hand to indicate the whole room. 'It's fantastic. And the house is beautiful and you look gorgeous.'

Deborah basked in Joy's praise. Words like Joy's made it all worthwhile. Little wavelets of bliss lapped in her veins.

'So, come on, what's your secret? I couldn't begin to do all this.'

'I don't know,' said Deborah. She felt as if she were making an Oscar acceptance speech. 'Naturally the children are very good mostly and Howard knows when to leave me alone. But you work, Joy. It's different for me. I have the time.'

'So you have time to do everything and you don't worry,' Joy mused aloud.

'Mmmm,' agreed Deborah, picking up a carrot baton and dipping it in some hummus. It was a signal for a lull in the conversation. Joy watched her mother leave Sharon and rejoin Uncle Barney. Sharon and Lawrence were next to each other by the bridge rolls, and began to talk.

★

'So you're Joy's – ?' Sharon asked. Ought she to say boyfriend, lover, cohabitee? She'd forgotten what word Joy had used.

'Yes,' Lawrence said, and shuffled awkwardly. His hand trembled as he held a small glass of sherry.

Sharon regarded him. She could see the trouble now. He was unusually retiring and inhibited. His body language shouted passivity. That was why their sex life had got into a rut. A shame, as he was attractive, and a nice man too. Ought she to tell him to take an assertiveness course? That would help Joy.

'You are?' Lawrence asked.

'Sharon Abrams. A neighbour of Debbie's. I'm a trained counsellor.'

'That must be very interesting.'

There were beads of perspiration forming on Lawrence's brow. Sharon felt a rush of sympathy for him. Was there anything she could do to help? Here was this poor man, and his anxious partner, unable to have the kind of relationship they deserved.

'I like Joy,' Sharon began. 'And I can see why you're suited. It's because both of you – I hope you don't mind me saying this – both of you are the anxious type. Not a bad thing. Provided you step out of that occasionally. I told Joy to try game-playing, fantasy. She seemed keen on the idea. She's the imaginative sort, you see. Worriers often are. So I advised her to use fantasy. It's very liberating.'

'I see,' said Lawrence, swallowing what was left of his sherry in one gulp. 'Excuse me,' he said, heading in the direction of the drinks cabinet.

Sharon wondered if she might have said too much. No, no, she hadn't. She wasn't one of those counsellors who just sat there listening and taking a fat fee at the end. She was a practical kind of counsellor. She believed in helping things along a bit. And you can't counsel couples without speaking to both of them, she told herself as she took a mouthful of salmon en croûte and resolved to ask Deborah for the recipe.

As Joy ate, she observed Lawrence talking to Sharon. Deborah added a commentary.

'As I told you, he has a philosophy degree.' She stopped talking to swallow some food. 'He's been living in Glasgow for a while doing some sort of teaching, but he's back here now living with his mother, Aunty Doris. Can you see her over by the piano? With the emerald suit? He's taking exams in insurance, I think. You can't earn money studying philosophy. As for his love life, he's had girlfriends, but nothing long-lasting. He's in his late thirties. Howard says –'

Deborah's briefing was interrupted by a shriek from Hayleigh. The women turned instantly, to see a mess of bridge rolls and crisps on the carpet.

'Josh pushed me!' she screamed.

Deborah had moved at the speed of light. Already she was scooping up food and calling for someone to get a cloth. Aunty Miriam bustled to the kitchen. Joy prepared to stand up and help, but could see that too many people were trying to scrub the carpet and comfort Hayleigh. Instead she sat down again. Before she knew it, Lawrence had joined her. She stopped eating.

'Shall I introduce myself?' he asked. Out of the corner of her eye Joy saw that he reddened. Thank God he was embarrassed too.

'I know who you are,' Joy mumbled.

'Lawrence Weiner.'

'I'm Joy Freeman.'

'I know,' Lawrence said. He cleared his throat. 'I'm ready if you are.'

Joy was mystified. Ready for what?

'It's difficult to establish the existence of reality as incontrovertible fact. Who's to say we don't create our own reality? I say, we're not here in Debbie's lounge. I say, we're sitting under a palm tree on a Caribbean island. Which? St Lucia? What's your favourite drink?'

'Gin,' Joy said. Was he telling a joke?

'There's a large gin on the table in front of you. I have a Pernod. The sky is a clear, rich blue and the sand a golden yellow. The waiter comes over with a mouth-watering selection of seafood – do you eat seafood?'

'Well, I know I shouldn't, but –'

'Good. So do I. Some seafood. A steel band strikes up behind us as the sun sinks slowly behind the horizon. I explain to you that the reason we're here is because of a huge inheritance from a distant relation who always believed in my talent to get on in life. I point to the helicopter that's landing on a distant beach and tell you it's mine, and ask you if you'd like to cruise in the skies while I get to know more about you.'

'Not a helicopter,' Joy said firmly.

'A luxury yacht?'

'If you have a good, reliable crew.'

'The best. With certificates to prove it.'

'I would need to see the certificates,' Joy insisted.

'You do, and you're satisfied. I take your hand and help you on to the yacht. Now it's your turn.'

Turn for what? Joy thought, literally all at sea. She watched Lawrence take out a handkerchief from his jacket pocket and wipe his forehead. He did look rather red. But why talk about yachts on the Caribbean? Was he trying to make a philosophical point?

'So what do *you* want to happen?' he continued.

'What do I want to happen? I don't know, but I can tell you what's going to happen. I'm going to have to introduce you to my mother.' Joy could see Ruth picking her way towards them, her face alight with interest.

Ruth sat down on Lawrence's other side. She also seemed flushed, and for a moment Joy wondered if she could be developing a fever, until she saw the large glass of cherry brandy in her mother's hand.

'This is Lawrence Weiner,' Joy explained. 'Howard's cousin.'

'Pleased to meet you,' Ruth said, with an arch smile.

'And you,' Lawrence said.

'I came over,' Joy's mother said, adopting a confidential tone, 'because I was talking to Barney and trying to remember the name of the dustman – you know – the only one you'd let come in the house.'

Joy shrugged, and fought a feeling of foreboding. Ruth laughed, and placed her hand on Lawrence's.

'Now, I was reminding Barney, when Joy was a little girl, she'd never let any strange man into the house. We never had any groceries delivered because she was scared of the grocer's man; she screamed at the gas-man, but there was one dustman – was it Ted? Or Bill? Maybe it was Bill. Anyway, just this one dustman. He took his time to win her trust, you see. When I gave him a tip at Christmas, he gave the money straight back to her. He liked her. So you see, she wasn't an easy child. She was frightened of public toilets. She thought they were dirty. So I'd take her shopping, and when we'd been out for an hour or so she'd want to go, and after a while she'd want to go so badly she'd stand there in the middle of the High Street with her legs crossed refusing to move, but when I suggested the Ladies she'd scream, and we'd end up having to traipse all the way back home again.' Ruth Freeman laughed fondly at the memory.

Joy could not believe all this was happening. Even though she couldn't really think of getting to know Lawrence before dealing with Michael, she burnt with shame at her mother's account of her childhood. The worst of it was, it was all true. All of it. Up until she opened her mouth, there had been just the slightest possibility that Lawrence might think she was normal. But now he knew that she was scared of strange men and opening her bladder. If Lawrence had even a nodding acquaintance with Freud he would recognize in her the original Ice Maiden. Joy knew she couldn't sit there one moment longer.

'Excuse me,' she murmured. 'I promised Debbie I'd help her in the kitchen.'

Joy knew it wasn't so much Deborah she wanted to see as the kitchen. It seemed a haven of sanity right now. Nothing much happened in kitchens except the preparation of food. In fact, when she reached the kitchen, Deborah was there, slicing gâteaux, and Sharon was with her, sitting on a stool, leaning on the breakfast bar.

'Deborah,' Joy announced. 'It's all gone horrendously wrong. You're going to kill me.'

'What's gone wrong?' asked Deborah, holding the cake knife in mid-air, looking for all the world like a would-be assassin.

'Lawrence is what's gone wrong. I mean, how come this guy passed your vetting procedure? All he can talk about is his imaginary yacht on the Caribbean. And as if that wasn't enough, along comes Mum, high on cherry brandy, and she regales him with stories of my misspent youth!'

'But you didn't misspend your youth,' Deborah reminded her.

'I mean she's going through each of my childhood neuroses and obsessions.'

Deborah's face lit up. 'Has she told him the story about you reading the symptoms of diphtheria in the clinic and being convinced you'd got it for months?'

'She'll get on to that.'

Deborah put her hand to her mouth to stop herself laughing but, encouraged by Joy's droll expression, she allowed herself a giggle or two.

'As soon as he sat down by me he was off into this fantasy about a seafood salad on St Lucia! Mad or what?'

'That doesn't sound like Lawrence,' Deborah said, calming down. 'Normally he's quite hesitant and sweet. That's why I thought you'd both get along so well together. Just promise me you'll go out with him once.'

'How can I?' Joy said, pulling up a stool for herself. 'You forget I still have Michael.'

'But you said at *shul* . . .'

'Who is Michael?' asked Sharon, in a small voice.

'My boyfriend,' explained Joy.

'But you said –'

'Ah,' said Joy. 'Did I give you the impression that Lawrence was my boyfriend?'

'Who is Lawrence?' asked Sharon.

'Her *shidduch*,' said Deborah.

'So he was the one I suggested fantasy to? Oh, no! Joy – I'm so sorry! I thought he was your boyfriend. What have

I done? This is dreadful of me!' Sharon was beside herself with embarrassment.

'No, no, I misled you. It's entirely my fault,' Joy insisted.

'I'm so sorry!'

'Please will somebody tell me what on earth is going on?' demanded Deborah, hating the feeling of being on the outside.

'Me. I will,' said Joy. Suddenly she was filled with the euphoria that came with abject confession. She wanted to admit and explain everything. Was this the effect of her Catholic work environment, or Rosh Hashanah? 'I met Sharon at the Well Woman clinic and I asked her how to improve my love life. With Michael. Because it hadn't been . . . I hadn't been . . . That was where the fantasy came in. So we did make love and Michael forgot to use a condom and I thought I was pregnant, and that made me realize I didn't want Michael any more. So that was why I told you, Debbie, I'd meet Lawrence. And when Sharon came in I was embarrassed that Michael wasn't with me and I pretended that Lawrence was Michael – do you follow all that?'

'So you're going to finish with Michael?' asked Deborah breathlessly.

'I didn't say I was going to finish with him,' Joy reminded her.

'I'm so sorry,' wailed Sharon.

'No, don't be. I like it when people make mistakes. It means I have permission to make mistakes too.'

'But that fantasy thing wasn't all! I told Lawrence you were the anxious type.'

'Hey,' said Joy, impressed. 'How did you know that? I've only met you once.'

This compliment on her professional expertise served to cheer Sharon. 'I can tell,' she said.

'That's right,' joined in Deborah, who had temporarily ceased from her cake-cutting. 'Ever since she was a child, Joy's been anxious. It's why she's never got married!' she concluded in an illogical flourish.

'Is your anxiety a problem for you?' asked Sharon, wearing her counsellor's expression. Putting on that wise, listening air restored her confidence in herself.

All this attention intoxicated Joy. 'Yes,' she said, 'it's a problem all right. What I was going to tell you, Debs, was that I'm applying for head of department at college, and Sister's suggested to me that my chances would be greater if I worried less. I want to worry less, but sometimes I just can't help it. It's like a compulsion, like some kind of black beast that comes and sits on my shoulder and whispers disasters in my ear.'

Joy was pleased with herself. That sounded very poetic. It was true, too. She waited with bated breath to see what Sharon and Debbie would deem the solution to be.

Sharon nodded. 'That's interesting, that you should see it as some kind of compulsion. Like alcoholism, you mean. Or overeating.'

Joy thought not. She quite liked drinking and eating but didn't enjoy worrying one bit. She decided nevertheless to remain quiet.

'It's illogical to worry!' declared Debbie. 'If you spend all your time worrying and the thing turns out OK, then you've been miserable for nothing. If it turns out bad, then you're twice as miserable.' Deborah looked pleased with herself.

'When you catch yourself worrying,' Sharon said,

'reprimand yourself, or think of something nice in place of the worry, like a red rose or ... or ... a lemon cheesecake,' she said, seeing that one was in front of her.

'Tell yourself you're being silly!' chimed in Deborah.

'Learn transcendental meditation.'

'Stop it!' said Joy, feeling nettled but not quite realizing why. 'Sometimes there are things I *have* to worry about. Michael, for instance.'

'You want to end your relationship?' Sharon sounded sympathetic. 'Just make sure you establish rules around listening to each other properly, and then things will take their course.'

'He's not right for her,' Deborah added.

'Don't either of you ever worry?' Joy interrupted. She was feeling cornered.

There was a silence. Each woman thought carefully. Sharon spoke first.

'Naturally I have concerns, but my work as a counsellor has helped me to deal with them. If anything bothers me unduly, I force myself to cope with it. Escape or cope – there are only two options. Or I talk the problem over with Daniel – that usually helps.'

Deborah nodded in agreement. 'Yes,' she said. 'Telling your husband. That helps. And I think having someone to love stops you worrying. You don't think about your own concerns so much.'

'Yes,' said Sharon. 'Love sends fear away. And we have our children too. Maybe that's why we don't worry as much as you.'

What were they saying? That she was a selfish, twitchy old spinster? Joy was hurt and angry and consequently lost for words. Yet as much as she wanted to accuse them of insensitivity, she knew they meant well. She drew a deep breath.

Just at that moment, the door was thrown open and Josh appeared. 'Mum, can I watch telly now?'

'No, Joshy. You know too much television is bad for you. Play an educational game on the computer, but mind it's educational! Have you finished your lunch already?'

'Yeah.'

'What did you have?'

'Crisps.'

'And what else?'

'Jus' crisps. Aunty Joy said I could.' Josh turned and scampered away. Deborah's face was ashen.

'What does he mean, "just crisps"? There's no protein in crisps. He can't just have crisps for lunch. Oh God, Joy. You know he never eats properly! You should have forced him to have some salmon at least. I knew I should have made some sweetcorn – it's the only vegetable he eats. Of course he eats frankfurters, but I couldn't mix the milk with the meat, with it being *Yomtov*, and so he's had no lunch! You know he's one of the smallest boys in class. What if he doesn't grow? I read that growth hormones give you mad cow disease, but if we don't give him growth hormones he'll be smaller than all the girls of his age and he'll never get married.'

'I know how you feel,' said Sharon. 'When Anna was a toddler, she'd only eat chips. I was beside myself. But now she's stopped eating chips and I hope she isn't secretly going on a diet. They get anorexia earlier and earlier these days.'

'You don't think Josh is anorectic?' gasped Deborah.

'He's still too young. But Anna is going through the stage where her peer-group opinion is dominant. And do you know what? She wants to go shopping alone with her friends! Without any adult! What do I say? If I let her go and something bad happens, like she meets a drunk-driver, or a pickpocket, I'll never forgive myself, but if I don't let her go, am I being over-protective?'

Joy coughed to draw attention to herself.

'You know what the trouble with you two is? You both worry too much.'

'We can't help it,' said Sharon. 'You'd worry too, if you had children.'

Once the cakes had been placed on the table and everyone had been served with their tea, Joy felt free to sit down again. She realized she was exhausted – too tired, in fact, to worry about anything. That meant that now was the best moment to clear things up with Lawrence. He was sitting alone on a sofa at the far end of the through lounge with a cup of tea on his lap. No time like the present, Joy thought.

She took the seat by him. 'I've just come over to ask you not to believe all the things you've heard about me today. My mother has a selective memory.'

Lawrence chuckled to himself. 'Wait till you hear my mother on how I had to walk all the way round each lamppost backwards and forwards on the way to and from school, even when I was late.'

'Did you?' Joy was interested. 'Because you thought something bad would happen if you didn't?'

'Of course.'

'Of course,' Joy echoed. 'And about that fantasy business. It was a case of mistaken identity. Sharon thought –

no, it was just a practical joke. Sharon is a bit of a practical joker.'

'Don't apologize. Actually, I enjoyed it. It beats talking about what we both do and where we both live and how neither of us ever expected to be involved in a *shidduch*.'

'True,' Joy said. She decided she liked Lawrence's smile. It was the kind of smile that sought approval before it allowed itself to blossom into a fully fledged, no-holds-barred smile. Close up he wasn't good-looking. His skin was pitted, and obviously his beard was meant to cover the traces of teenage acne. His large nose had a slightly comic air. But Deborah was right. He was nice.

'OK,' he said. 'Let's continue with the fantasy. We'll scale it down this time. Imagine I invite you for a meal. You can choose anywhere in town for a romantic dinner for two. Tell me where it would be.'

'Is this really a fantasy or are you actually asking me out?'

'Whichever you want it to be.'

'You are asking me out, aren't you?'

'I could be,' Lawrence said.

Joy thought she detected a note of uncertainty. It was becoming, in a way, but first she had to put him straight about Michael. She didn't want there to be any more misunderstandings.

'I can't go out with you,' she said, a little wistfully.

Lawrence visibly deflated. As she watched the energy go out of him Joy felt a sudden kinship with Vlad the Impaler on a particularly bad day. She was a vicious tyrant.

'I thought we were getting on well,' Lawrence remarked.

'We were. We are.'

'But still you don't want to have dinner with me.'

'I didn't say I didn't want to. I can't.'

Joy decided for that moment to say no more. She was worried about what would happen if Lawrence got dragged in to the end of her relationship with Michael. Yet looking at Lawrence now, she guessed she might have delivered a terminal blow to his self-esteem. He looked at her ruefully.

'I'm sorry,' he said. 'I hate these introductions. I get very anxious beforehand and I've been too insistent, haven't I? I'm afraid I've put you in an embarrassing position.'

'No, no!' Joy was filled with remorse. 'It's my fault. I should have explained. I'm still involved with someone else. But we're going our separate ways.' As she said that, Joy crossed her fingers behind her back. 'Because of him, I don't feel I can see you.'

Lawrence nodded resignedly. Suddenly Joy was scared he didn't believe her. It was possible Lawrence thought she'd said this so she didn't have to meet him again. He would go home thoroughly depressed. His Rosh Hashanah would be in ruins. It would be all her fault. She knew she had to retract.

'I don't feel I can see you *yet*. But in a few days, maybe things will be sorted out. I'll give you my number at college. I'll take your number too. Yes?'

The cloud passed from his face. 'Yes,' he said. Then he frowned momentarily. 'You're not doing this because you feel sorry for me?'

'No,' Joy said. 'I like you.'

'I like you too,' he said. 'And before I book the restaurant, I'll make a point of checking out the Ladies, and only if I think they meet your exacting standards –'

'Shut up,' Joy said, but smiled.

★

It was four o'clock. The company, exclaiming at the time, and thanking Deborah profusely, rose, found their coats, hugged each other and shouted for the children. Joy decided, searching for her handbag, that it had not been such a bad lunch after all. In fact she was experiencing a profound reluctance to go home. She knew why. Home meant Michael, and it was hard to believe how fast events were moving. Why, a few days ago she thought she still loved him. Now she knew she didn't.

Yet until her mother went back to London, she couldn't possibly commence the talk that would result in – whatever it would result in. Three whole days of pretending everything was normal. At all costs her mother must be protected from a scene. Three nightmarish days, and the worst thing was, she couldn't even allow herself to worry about it.

CHAPTER EIGHT

The weekend, so far, had been uneventful. Michael had spent Friday night investigating the properties of commercially produced lager at the local, used Saturday morning to recover in bed, then went out to town to buy some jeans – a sort of consolation present for having to put up with Joy's mum. He returned at six, watched telly while Joy and Ruth ate the evening meal, then put an old James Bond film in the video while the women washed up and talked in the kitchen. Michael did not feel at all guilty; Ruth was *Joy's* mother, she had come to see Joy, and it was best to leave them to it.

Although this philosophy of Michael's had distressed Joy in the past, it came as a blessed relief to her now. There had been hardly any need to talk to him all weekend. That was lucky, as she had not even been able to look at him directly. There was no actual need to look at him now, either, as he wasn't there. He was approximately eight feet above her, still in bed, where she had left him a couple of hours ago. Joy, unable to sleep, had come downstairs to start on some marking, and Ruth had joined her and was sitting now in an easy chair, glancing at the contents of the *Sunday Express*.

Yes, everything was deceptively peaceful. Just the rustle of the newspaper and the distant barking of a dog from the street. Except the peace did not reach into Joy's soul, the state of which rather resembled a war-torn republic.

It was D-Day, she had thought to herself, as she awoke

that morning, immediately alert and conscious of her resolution to broach matters with Michael that very evening. D-Day. D for deliverance – or would it be D for disaster? As she left the bed, careful not to touch Michael, who lay there snoring softly, she felt her dislike of him spread through her like a virus.

She trod to the bathroom with guilty steps. Here she was, a Guy Fawkes plotting to blow up Michael, and neither he nor her mother had a clue of her intentions. That her mother didn't know, she was glad. The one thing she could feel proud of was that her mother would go home tonight before her showdown with Michael. In a few days she would be presented with a *fait accompli. Michael and I have decided to go our separate ways.* What a lovely euphemism! The main thing, she reminded herself virtuously, was not to upset her mother.

That much she could achieve. What she was less certain about was whether she could avoid upsetting Michael. Ideally, she would prefer him to take it gallantly, showing some emotion but accepting their break-up with heroic resignation. The only problem with that, she thought to herself as she gazed out of the window, was that if he did, she might be tempted to take him back again, as Adela did with Ronnie in the beginning of *A Passage to India.*

Fat chance of that, she concluded. It was far more likely that Michael would make a scene. He would accuse her of cruelty. She would deserve it too. She had lain awake all night composing farewell speeches to him while he had snored there innocently. Like Deborah, he would accuse her of selfishness, and the worst of it was, it would be thoroughly deserved. Her head continued to throb. The Nurofen Plus weren't working.

She started involuntarily as her mother spoke.

'He sleeps a lot, doesn't he?' she remarked, the *Sunday Express* evidently failing to hold her interest.

'Oh, yes,' Joy said quickly. Had her mother guessed? Ought she to tell her after all? No, it would be mean. Yes, it would be such a relief.

'Mind you, it's just as well,' said Ruth.

There! She had guessed. The temptation to tell her mother nearly overwhelmed Joy. Yet to do so, she knew, would compound her treachery. It would be two against one. That wasn't a fair fight. She reminded herself she had a pile of essays to mark. She would get on with those.

In this essay I am going to write about the ways in which Shakespeare makes Act Three, Scene Two dramatically effective. At the beginning of Act Three, Scene Two . . .

The handwriting was difficult to read, and Joy's vision became entangled in the loops and confusions of Helen Chadderton's calligraphy. Whether Joy was cruel or kind to Michael tonight, the point was, how would he react? Was it possible to guess? To predict? Joy believed she knew Michael well – too well – but how could she be sure that his phlegmatic approach to life would be maintained in the face of losing her?

Would he become violent? She couldn't rule this out. Most murders of women were committed by men known to the victim. How many of them were done by men whose partners were attempting to give them the push? How could she be sure he wouldn't get violent? Look how aggressively he played Sonic the Hedgehog! All that cursing, that vile language when he lost a life! Joy imagined Michael standing over her, his fist raised. Next scene: Joy hastily flinging a few essential items into a suitcase. Act Three, Scene Two: Joy scurrying out of the house, on her way to the women's refuge.

Surely he wouldn't be violent? In all the time she'd known him, he'd never been involved in a fight. He wasn't one for direct action. Perhaps his revenge would be indirect? Poison? No – she was being silly. Or humiliation. He'd come in to college on Monday morning demanding to see Sister Maureen and begging her to intercede. Or he'd burst into her lower sixth language group and get down on his knees, pleading for her to take him back.

Joy, Joy, she told herself, you're being over-dramatic. Dramatically effective. It won't happen like that; it'll happen like this. You'll explain gently to him how you thought the relationship had reached an impasse, how it was time for you both to extend your circle of friends and think about new horizons, and . . . and . . . Michael will agree, and look down at the table, and haltingly explain that he was glad you'd brought the whole thing up because he was meaning to tell you about this woman at work he'd been seeing for some time.

Joy wondered if she could handle that. *So*, came an accusatory voice, *how do you think he'll feel on hearing you want to finish with him!* Not so wonderful. What if he can't cope with the rejection? Suicide rates for young males were on the increase – it said so in all the papers. The pain in her temples tightened. Her headache was more intense than usual. Could it be a brain tumour? She smiled at the irony. There she was, planning to ditch Michael, and it wouldn't be necessary after all. God would do it for her. Somehow it cheered her to think of a brain tumour; it was a familiar sort of worry, unlike the prospect of leaving Michael.

Now to the truth. What was really scaring her, the

thing she was trying not to think about, was that if she did succeed in finishing with Michael he would leave her and she would be alone. There, it was out. She would be alone. Alone, alone, all all alone, alone on a wide, wide sea. Suddenly the lounge felt chilly. Better to have somebody than nobody.

Then she looked at her mother, frowning in concentration as she studied the crossword. Her mother knew how to live alone, and now, facing the prospect herself, Joy was lost in admiration. Her mother had suffered the death of a husband she'd loved dearly, and her two children leaving home and was still relatively cheerful. Her mother was a tower of strength. Her mother was the most obvious, the best person to talk to about her fears of giving up Michael. Joy yearned for the exquisite relief of being able to share her feelings.

'Mum,' she said.

Ruth looked up from her paper.

'I want to tell you something.'

'You're not pregnant?' Ruth exclaimed.

'Oh no, nothing like that.'

No, thought Joy, I shan't tell her. I mustn't be dependent on my mother's approval. I shall do this alone. A girl's gotta do what a girl's gotta do.

'So tell me,' Ruth said.

'I'm thinking of finishing with Michael.'

There. It was out. How wonderful to have said it!

Ruth thought, 'At last!', but understood her role as mother too well to tell her daughter so. She remained silent, nodded, but in that nod there was an implied permission as well as an acknowledgement that she had understood.

'I'm doing the right thing, aren't I?'

'If it's what you want to do,' Ruth said with a studied neutrality.

'I thought I'd talk to him tonight – after you've gone.'

'Look,' said Ruth, 'if you want to speak to him now, I'll go out for a walk.' Did she sound too eager? Possibly. This was the best news she'd heard for a long time.

'No, no, Mum. Tonight will do. Stay with me now. I feel a bit –' Just then the women heard heavy footsteps cross the landing and the toilet door bang shut. Like two conspirators, they were suddenly silent. Joy froze with embarrassment as they both listened to the loud torrent of urine hitting the toilet bowl. After an eternity the toilet flushed, and the house shook to it. Michael then turned on the taps, and the plumbing creaked into action.

'Forget I told you, Mum. I'll talk to him tonight. I'm sorry if you feel awkward for the rest of the day. Please try not to worry.'

'Worry!' exclaimed Ruth enigmatically.

Bang, bang, bang down the stairs. Michael appeared at the lounge door, still unshaven, in his blue T-shirt and new jeans.

'Tell you what,' he said to Joy and Ruth. 'We'll go out for lunch. If you can afford it.' He directed that last comment at Ruth. 'Seeing as it's your last day.' Then he vanished into the kitchen for some coffee.

Joy and her mother exchanged guilty glances. Joy wondered why Michael was being so nice. Had he guessed? What ought they to do? Joy reckoned that if they owed him anything, they owed him lunch. It was the least they could do. It would be the last lunch they would all have together. The Last Lunch. It didn't have quite the same ring as the Last Supper, but a Judas would be there all the same, except this time her name was Joy.

★

As they approached the Heaton Arms, Michael slowed down and indicated that he was turning into the car park. Joy thought that he could have chosen somewhere better than the Heaton Arms. It was one of those large, sprawling, detached pubs, situated on the rise of a hill, that do family lunches on Sundays – kids eat for free – with a jukebox that pounded heavily in one corner. A banner was flying in the grounds announcing 'Happy Meals!' Joy had been there on a few occasions with Michael, but it was the last place she would have thought of taking her mother. Pub culture was alien to Ruth. Apart from the occasional cherry brandy on *simchas* she was a stranger to alcohol. As a child Joy was never warned against pubs and booze simply because neither played any part in her mother's life at all.

For that reason Ruth seemed perfectly happy getting out of the car and even seemed impressed at the size of the Heaton Arms. The weather was chilly, and there was a fine drizzle that made them all want to hurry into the interior of the pub.

As soon as they got in they were enveloped by heat and noise. There was the babble of conversation, an aroma of roast beef, Wet Wet Wet on the jukebox, and children running from table to table. Joy glanced at her mother in her tightly buttoned navy coat and ached for her. She guessed she was feeling completely out of place.

Michael cheerfully gestured to a table by the window, which admittedly had no one sitting there, but was cluttered with old plates and the detritus of someone else's coffee. Joy took her mother there and quickly removed the cups and plates. Ruth took off her coat, folding it carefully, and placed it over a spare chair. She gave Joy a small smile and sat down, picking up the Sunday lunch menu. Joy noticed a family at the table next to them, two little girls in matching flowery T-shirts and leggings, a mother with an elaborate hair-do and a balding man in a pink pullover.

Michael returned from the bar with a pint of lager for himself, a glass of house white for Joy and an orange juice for Ruth. On glancing at the menu he announced he was going for the works – a full roast-beef dinner.

'Just like Joy doesn't make,' he quipped.

To Joy the menu was just a meaningless jumble of words. She wasn't in the least bit hungry. Just then, food was an absurd concept to her. Her mother didn't seem too hungry either.

'Is it possible just to have a sandwich?' she asked.

Joy saw that it was, and mother and daughter each selected a tuna and mayonnaise. Michael seemed quite happy with that and, informed of their choices, made his way over to the food counter to speak to the waitresses. Joy took a sip of her wine. It was too sweet and left a cloying after-taste. She wasn't sure that she would be able to drink it. She watched Michael as he placed the order, and contemplated the back of his shell-suit jacket – the green and purple one – and the way it didn't quite meet his denims. Ruth reached over and patted Joy's hand, in a gesture of silent support.

Michael returned to the table, pulled out his chair and sat down heavily.

'Makes a change, doesn't it?' he commented.

Joy and Ruth nodded. There was a silence that was noticeable despite the jaunty dance music emanating from the jukebox.

'How's work?' Michael asked Ruth, pleased with himself for initiating some conversation.

'All right,' Joy's mother said.

'You'll be retiring soon,' he said. 'When are you going to be sixty?'

'Next year.'

'Joining the wrinklies, eh?' he joked. Joy thought he seemed in rather a good mood.

There was another lull in the conversation. Joy's stomach felt as tight and dry as a walnut. Michael sipped at his beer abstractedly.

'I'm thinking of moving on from my job,' he informed Ruth. 'I expect Joy's told you. No hopes of promotion at my place. I'll wait till Joy gets her job as head of department. Then I'll have a break, put myself on the supply list, look around a bit.'

Joy wondered if she was actually going to be physically sick. Scared of having a panic attack, she felt the urgent need to move. She saw the Ladies on the other side of the room and excused herself. She pushed open the door with its little drawing of a lady with a parasol and inhaled a whiff of stale tobacco and cheap scent. The hand-drier, situated next to a machine dispensing condoms, whirred noisily. Joy decided she was not going to be ill after all. She waited a few moments, then splashed some cold water on her face. As a tired-looking woman with dyed blond hair came in, she went out.

As she crossed the crowded pub to rejoin her mother and Michael, she could see immediately that her mother looked more ill at ease than ever. She wondered what Michael had been saying to her now. Ruth shot her an urgent look. Was her mother feeling ill? The atmosphere was hot and smoky, and Joy was sure it wasn't good for her. Michael, on the other hand, was trying and failing to suppress a grin. He looked mightily pleased with himself.

As Joy sat down she could see that her mother was tapping the finger of one of her hands against a finger of the other, repeatedly. Why was she doing that? Joy had never seen her perform that particular mannerism before. Was this the beginning of Parkinson's disease? Joy looked at her quizzically. Ruth seemed alarmed. Joy watched her strange gesture again. She continued to tap the fourth finger of her left hand. What was she saying? That it was time to go? That she was suffering from cramp in her fingers? Michael still wore that insane grin. Ruth Freeman rose.

'I must visit the Ladies too,' she said.

'I'll go with you,' Joy added.

Joy felt Michael's restraining hand.

'She's fine,' he said. 'Stay here.'

'No.'

'I tell you, she's fine. She wants us to be alone.'

By now Joy's mother was halfway to the Ladies. Joy didn't believe Michael for one minute. Something was up. He drained his pint and looked at her. He seemed pleased about something, yet at the same time uncharacteristically coy.

'I think I surprised your mother,' he said.

'Did you?' Joy was being cool.

'I told her we were getting married.'

'That would have surprised her,' Joy said. 'Did she realize it was a joke?'

'Nope,' he said.

'When she comes back you can tell her. She doesn't have much of a sense of humour.'

'It wasn't a joke,' Michael said. 'I've decided to marry you.'

'You've decided,' Joy echoed, flatly.

'Yeah. It was when we forgot that condom. I got

thinking. What if you are pregnant? We'd have to get married. Anyway, it's not so bad getting married. We'd get a lot of wedding presents. Otherwise, it'll be the same as now, I reckon. The way I figure it, if you had a brat, I could stay at home and look after it.'

Michael as a New Man? Joy was astonished. The unthinkable had happened.

'Yeah. It's a brilliant plan. You've got the bigger income, right? And I'm completely pissed off with school. Bloody fifth-years.'

'So you want us to get married and me to have a baby so you can escape the fifth-years?'

'Well, not exactly.' Here Michael looked embarrassed. 'I love you too.'

Michael's selfishness gave Joy the courage to speak. Besides, she knew she had to say something now. Things weren't going according to plan.

'No!' she shouted. There was silence from the family at the next table.

Now Michael looked puzzled.

'I'm sorry, Michael. I'm sorry for shouting. Oh God, how can I say this? I don't think I want to get married. But it's not that. I was going to tell you that I was thinking of –' Joy could proceed no further. The word 'finishing' seemed so final. 'I was thinking of discussing it all with you,' she concluded lamely.

'We can leave it till the end of the academic year if you want.' Michael seemed unbothered.

'I mean, I don't want to get married.'

'You want to have a kid without getting married?'

'I don't want to get married and I don't want to have a kid!' Joy knew she was speaking loudly but Michael was being deliberately obtuse.

'I don't understand,' he said. The smile had gone from his face. Joy felt as if she were balancing on the edge of a precipice. 'Why don't you want to get married?' he asked.

'I'm not sure we're right for each other.' The pub floor seemed to rock under Joy's feet as she said this.

'Yes we are,' Michael said.

'No we're not.'

'Yes we are.'

This was rapidly descending to the level of panto-mime. Joy realized she had to try to become more sophisticated.

'No, no. I think . . . there's a failure to communicate. We don't talk to each other any more.'

'We're talking now.'

'No, we're not – we're arguing.'

'You started it!'

'No I didn't.'

'Oh yes you did!'

'Stop it, Michael! All I'm saying here is that I think we need to think about our relationship.' Joy desperately hoped that he would guess what she was driving at.

'I've thought about it. I think we should get married.'

'But I don't.'

'Christ!' he exclaimed. 'We're getting nowhere.'

Then, out of the corner of her eye, Joy saw her mother returning from the Ladies. She looked agitated. Joy decided to smile brightly so her mother would believe she wasn't too upset. Ruth took her seat again at the table, with the innate authority of a high court judge. Michael looked at her as if the whole muddle was her fault.

'She won't marry me!' he said accusingly to Ruth.

'I can't help that,' said Ruth, diplomatically. 'It's up to Joy.'

Joy was silent, waiting to see what would happen next.

'But I don't get this,' Michael said. 'We've been living together for three years. I took it for granted we'd get married. What else was I supposed to think?'

'Perhaps she was trying to decide if she wanted to marry you,' Ruth said.

'What more does she want? We get on well. We don't argue. I've been faithful.' The family at the next table was rapt with attention. This was better than *EastEnders*.

'There's more than *that* to a relationship,' Joy's mother declared.

Michael looked bemused. Joy knew that her mother was referring to sex and wondered at her temerity.

'Shut up!' Michael said to her. 'Let Joy speak for herself.'

His rudeness to her mother gave Joy strength. 'The truth is,' she began, 'I've been thinking of –' she coughed, 'changing our relationship. We haven't been happy for some time.'

'I've been happy,' said Michael.

'Well, I haven't. I'm serious, Michael. I can't marry you. In fact, I was thinking of –' Joy found she couldn't bring out the words. *I want to finish with you.* Dare she say it? The tables on both sides of them were silent now.

'I want to finish with you,' Joy said, and took a deep breath, as she hadn't been breathing properly for some time. There, it had been said. The guillotine had fallen. Joy felt curiously detached and relieved. She hadn't meant all this to happen now, in this way, and she was worried about her mother, but perhaps it was all for the best that it happened like this. Michael had been rude and insensitive and deserved a comeuppance. Joy took a sip of her wine, which was lukewarm now. It made her feel sick.

'Why?' asked Michael. 'Why do you want to finish with me?'

That was when the waitress came over with their meal. 'Who's for the roast beef?' she enquired perkily.

Joy pointed to Michael. The waitress placed the plate down in front of him. The beef was as pink as his face. The Yorkshire pudding looked sad and deflated. The waitress scurried away and returned with two frightening tuna sandwiches with a limp salad garnish. Happy Meals? They should be sued under the Trade Descriptions Act.

Ruth rose from her seat again. 'I'm going to the Ladies,' she said.

'Are you sure you're all right?' Joy demanded.

'Yes, yes. Don't worry about me.'

Joy wasn't convinced, but let her go.

'Why do you want to finish with me?' persisted Michael. 'I don't want to finish with you. Tell me why.'

There seemed to be an unearthly hush in the pub. Even the jukebox had stopped to listen. Joy lifted her glass of wine and stared at the Boddington's beer mat that had curled with embarrassment in front of her.

'Well, we don't talk to each other . . . And you know, the rest of it.' Joy meant sex but, like her mother, couldn't bring herself to use the word. 'It's just . . . that we lead different lives. You with your computer and your megadrive, and me with college and literature. It's just sterile, if you see what I mean.'

These were terrible accusations, Joy knew. Did she have the courage to look up at Michael to see how he had taken them? She did. He sat very, very still. Clearly her words had made an impact. Michael actually looked as if he was thinking.

'You mean we're drifting apart,' he said slowly.

Hooray! He understood. He would accept the inevitability of their break-up.

'All right,' Michael said. 'Here's what I'll do. I'll sell the megadrive. I'll put an ad in the *Manchester Evening News*. I reckon I can get £100 if I throw in the games. And I don't mind working on our sex life.' Joy did not like his sly grin. 'We'll get one of those videos like *The Lovers' Guide* – yeah! – we'll do that. I'll talk to you when I come in at night. I'll ask you about your day and you can ask me about mine. That should do it.'

Joy was horrified. It sounded like a living hell. Then Michael reached out and grabbed her hand.

'Look, I don't even mind if I have to sell it for less than a hundred. I love you. I can't live without you.'

Joy squirmed. His emotional outpourings revolted her, but how could she reject them? Michael gazed across the table at her with a puppy-like devotion.

'You're right, Joy. A woman needs more attention than I've been giving you. I can change. I'm going to start now. I'll pay for this meal, even your Mum's. Just don't leave me. I need you.'

Joy began to panic. This was awful. She was suffocating in his good intentions. Gone was the oxygen that gave her courage.

'Just tell me what you want me to do and I'll do it,' Michael said imploringly.

What would the people on the next table think if she were to turn that offer down? Wasn't it every woman's dream? A man who could change, who would do anything she wanted? Joy began to feel that she didn't know *what* she wanted any more. Michael gone – what would that be like? She realized she wasn't even sure where the fuse-box was. Would she ever find another man? She was all of thirty-one. She could end up living alone in her little house, so neurotic she'd not get the promotion to head of department, and losing everything – job, man, happiness. Or, if she accepted Michael's promise to change – and who said he couldn't change? People can change! Alcoholics become sober! Oprah Winfrey lost all that weight! If Michael changed, and talked more, and wasn't so mean, and went with her to the theatre, and was nice to her mother, and woke up early on the weekends, and helped more in the house, and took more care of his appearance and personal habits, and restrained himself sexually – if he did all that, perhaps her feelings could change too. She really ought to give him a fair trial.

'We'll see,' Joy said. She knew it was a climb-down.

'Oh, Joy!' whispered Michael. She wished he would stop being so sentimental. She decided to tell him.

'Stop being so sentimental.'

Michael grinned at her foolishly. 'Sorry,' he said. Joy could tell from his face that he knew he'd won.

Joy removed her hand from his and gave him a weak smile. She watched him shake the bottle of tomato ketchup on the table, open it and pour a generous slug on his potatoes. A wave of nausea washed over Joy. She decided to go and see if her mother was all right. As she passed the adjoining table, the man in the pink pullover whispered, 'Good on yer, lass!' Did she imagine it, or did his wife shake her head in disagreement? Impossible to know.

Impossible to know, too, if she had done the right thing. Was she kind and fair to give Michael a second chance? Or was she just a plain coward, yellow through and through? She thought she might know the answer to that. What would her mother think? Another question Joy preferred not to answer. And what about Lawrence? Joy realized with a pang she would be unable to go out with him now.

She paused as she placed her hand on the doorknob of the Ladies. She didn't want to have to face her mother at the moment. She didn't have the energy to explain or justify her actions. She felt the walls of the pub closing in on her, and the heat and smoke constricted her lungs. She knew she had to get some fresh air.

Joy pushed her way out into the courtyard in front of the pub. The drizzle had solidified into proper rain, drumming on to the concrete, and cars rushed along the main road in front of her, sending up showers of spray. A heavy blanket of cloud pressed in from above. There was no escape.

What was it Sharon had said? That you either cope or escape? I shall cope, thought Joy, and turned back into the pub.

CHAPTER NINE

Michael whistled as he did the washing-up. Joy could hear his whistling from where she sat in the lounge, hastily ticking the Shakespeare essays, writing 'good' occasionally and hoping it was appropriate. Michael, she considered ruefully, deserved ten out of ten for effort. He'd come with her when she'd dropped her mum off at the station, had offered to make dinner, was washing up now and had been relentlessly and overwhelmingly cheerful. She really didn't know if she could take it.

Worst of all was his new found talkativeness. Unpractised in the art of conversation, Michael approached verbal encounters with the finesse of an amateur chat-show host. *So tell me, Joy, what are your views on the royal family, then? What d'you think of the National Lottery, then? Anything else you want to talk to me about, eh?* Gaining confidence, he'd moved on to introducing more personal, intimate subjects that affected them both exclusively. Ought they to decorate the spare room? Could they afford a satellite dish? Shouldn't they think seriously about taking out insurance policies on each other, because you never know what might happen.

Since most of Joy's mental efforts were designed to stop her thinking about what might happen, she suggested to Michael that it would be nice to watch some TV instead of just chatting idly. She assured him several times she really did want to watch TV, and after he'd switched on the set, he came to join her on the sofa, put his arm around her shoulders and snuggled up. Joy could not prevent herself freezing. What ought she to do now? Moving away from him would make her the guilty party. Putting up with it was unthinkable.

'I'll ring Mum now,' she said. 'See if she's got home safely. And I need to speak to Lesley. I have to ask her something.'

'Don't be long,' Michael said.

Joy spent another restless night. Every so often she felt a hot, proprietorial arm coming over her side and she did not have the heart to move it away. Lying there in the dark, she wondered if it was possible to learn to love someone bit by bit, like you learned cookery or car mechanics. There ought to be some sort of self-help book, written by an enthusiastic American. *Learning to Love Him Again*: 'It *is* possible to restore the shine to your relationship. Take a soft cloth and rub vigorously for several minutes . . .'

She woke with a start. Michael was standing over her holding a cup of tea.

'It's morning,' he said. He placed the tea on the bedside table and stood there waiting to be thanked. Thank him Joy did, despite the fact he'd forgotten she drank only coffee in the morning. She took it to the bathroom with her and guiltily threw it down the sink.

Grinning like the Cheshire Cat, Michael stood in the kitchen. 'Did you sleep well?' he enquired. 'Was your tea all right? Do you want the paper? I've got an idea – why don't we meet up for lunch today? Shall I put on some toast for you?'

I didn't expect the Spanish Inquisition, Joy thought, but she answered Michael civilly enough. She refused the lunch date, claiming a departmental meeting, and asked if it would be all right if she had dinner with Lesley that evening. Michael looked crestfallen.

'She begged me,' Joy explained. Lucky she wasn't Pinocchio, else her nose would have grown another few inches.

'It takes two, Joy,' Michael admonished.

Bastard, thought Joy. 'I know,' she said, 'but it's been arranged a long time.'

'First I've heard of it,' Michael mumbled, as he moved away to make some more tea.

Pleading an early staff briefing, Joy left the house and emerged into the fresh morning air. It was a blessed relief to her. This new Michael, this considerate, loving, thoughtful Michael, was ten times worse than the old variety. And the worst of it was, as he was getting better and better in every way, her moral stature was steadily shrinking. She had lied to him, had avoided him, had shown herself unable to respond to kindness. A wave of self-hatred threatened to overwhelm her. There was panic mixed in with it too. Whatever was she going to do next?

She remembered her resolution to cope, rather than escape. Then she realized how very wrong she had been. She would escape! She would get to college as soon as she could and she wouldn't give Michael another thought. She would drown herself in work.

When she arrived in the English office it was still dark and deserted. Joy switched on all the lights, and they buzzed, flickered and illuminated the familiar shelves of books, files and piles of essays. Joy felt glad to be there. She stood by the window that overlooked the car park and watched the head of science get out of his Renault, open the boot and then struggle to balance his briefcase and several unwieldy box files.

Thank God for work! Here, in St Ignatius', she didn't have to think about Michael. Indeed, she *shouldn't* be thinking about Michael. Here she had a job to do, an important job. She couldn't afford to be preoccupied with her private affairs. Duty, my dear, she told herself, duty calls. And my duty is to enlighten the young.

On her way to reprographics later that morning Joy asked herself again if Larkin's 'Afternoons' was a wise choice for her new lower sixth group. Larkin always made her nervous. He was an unashamedly bleak poet. On the other hand, 'Afternoons' was straightforward and accessible, and Joy wasn't yet sure how strong the group was. It was better to play safe with something they could all understand. Still, Larkin was depressing. And true. That was the worst of it. How could you deny that life was a process of loss? And what did it all mean? Suddenly gripped by a flash of existentialist *angst*, Joy tried to change the current of her thoughts.

Anyway, she told herself, it was more important to give the group a poem they had the confidence to talk about. For most of the kids who passed through her hands poetry was a foreign language. Or, worse than that, it was a torture sadistically invented by English examiners. Why else would someone write poetry?

Clutching the photocopied sheets of 'Afternoons', Joy walked along the corridor, passing the area under the fire-escape stairs where students were allowed to smoke and shorten their lives. They lounged around, drab in their uniform of denim jeans and grunge-inspired, frayed pullovers. Joy glanced into the canteen, where more students sat drinking coffee, and looked over bulging files. Ahead of her she saw Peter Worthington talking to Bruce O'Connor. They seemed to be sharing some sort of joke. Peter's Paul Smith trousers looked new to Joy, as did his

Jigsaw jumper. Was he trying to be noticed? Joy remembered being told on her teachers' training course that teachers should only be conspicuous by their smartness. Peter was certainly that.

No time to think about Peter now. The new lower sixth group would already be in E2. Joy was filled with a pleasant anticipation. New students to meet, and a chance to reinvent herself as the funny, knowledgeable Miss Freeman, English teacher, always in control. To her, teaching was performance, and a chance to escape from being her fearful self. Today it was more welcome than ever.

Her spirits rose as she approached the classroom. She hoped her new group was going to be talkative. She'd had new A-level groups before where no one would utter a word. Fear of exposure paralysed them. She'd walked into classrooms where the atmosphere resembled nothing so much as a male impotence clinic. Not that I would know, Joy thought to herself, smiling. The important thing, she reminded herself, was to get them talking. She hoped Philip Larkin would help her.

When she entered the classroom it was already full. New sixth-formers are always punctual. She knew that only lasted a week or so. Riding on a surge of adrenalin, Joy placed her books and papers down on the desk in front of her and surveyed the students. Her eyes were drawn immediately to the girl with spiky orange hair. The orange was dazzling. Had she meant to dye it that colour, or was this the result of an experiment gone wrong? And why did the girl look so familiar? I know, Joy realized. It's Lucy, the girl I interviewed. The would-be drummer and performance poet. She's in my group after all! Joy was delighted.

The rest of the group was much as she expected. Boys

sat on one side of the room and girls on the other. The girls for the most part looked demure and studious, hair tied back with wide bands or slides, with brand-new files in front of them on the tables. The boys looked more awkward and embarrassed than the girls, perhaps because there were only three of them. As Joy called out their names from her register and they answered, she could sense each student's self-consciousness.

'And I'm Miss Freeman,' Joy concluded, in a friendly but brisk way.

'OK,' she said. 'I expect you're all terrified, and feeling that now you're real students at a sixth form college we're going to want you to be brilliantly clever and full of insight and to read every classic ever written and write four essays a week.' She paused. 'Well, you're right.' The group looked uneasy. 'We might want that, but we're not going to get it. You'll turn out like every other new lower sixth, not understanding half of what goes on, worried that your essays are rubbish, worried that nobody likes you or thinks you're clever and hiding your copy of *Viz* in the Dickens novel I told you to read.' Some laughter now. 'But don't worry. If you work hard, in two years' time you'll be sitting behind a new set of desks in your university or college feeling just as terrified and inadequate all over again.' There were more smiles. Joy was pleased with herself. She'd pinpointed their fears precisely. That was something she was good at.

'Take a look at this,' she then said, passing 'Afternoons' around the group. 'It's a poem.' Joy sensed some apprehension. 'Don't worry – it won't bite. It's quite tame and it likes children.' Some of the girls laughed. 'I don't expect you to understand it all – it's just a starting point to get you talking. Do you read much poetry?' Joy enquired generally.

No response. Joy knew that meant that no one read any poetry. After a pause one girl, who'd introduced herself as Rachel, said she'd done some poems at her old school, and then there was some nodding in the group. There was a general consensus that this was a good answer.

'Anyone read poetry for fun?' Joy suggested.

The group looked embarrassed for Joy. Reading poetry for fun struck them as an unnatural aberration, something only English teachers would do. Joy glanced at Lucy. She seemed to be examining her fingernails.

'Except this poem isn't exactly funny.' Joy stopped because she didn't want to influence their reactions. 'Let me read it to you.'

'Summer is fading . . .'

Joy went on to describe in Larkin's dry words how schoolgirls become young mothers burdened by washing, children and deadening routines.

'Something is pushing them
To the side of their own lives.'

Joy didn't speak for a while. She waited and hoped the group was collecting its responses. As for her, she felt momentarily depressed. Larkin was right. A horrible inevitability governed all our lives. There *was* no escape.

'Bollocks,' came a voice.

It was Lucy. The word shocked Joy, but her instinct told her not to react. She knew the eyes of the class were upon her.

'Bollocks?' she repeated, a deliberate note of enquiry in her voice.

'Yeah, well, it is bollocks. Sexist bollocks. Look, he's talking about women as if, like, they're entirely passive. Like they're trees or something. Shedding their leaves. That's not true.'

Joy was excited by this challenge. Her role as teacher was to oppose Lucy.

'There's a sense in which it is true. Women do grow older and must give way to the demands of others. We all think it's going to be different when we're younger, but . . .' Joy stopped herself just in time. She didn't want to be too gloomy.

'Yeah, but that Larkin, I've read about him. He didn't like women, did he? Like, he had all these dirty pictures stashed away in the library, and he was screwing everything in skirts. But he looked like Eric Morecambe. That was the funny thing.'

The whole group was staring at Lucy now but she seemed unconcerned.

'Have you read the Larkin biography?' Joy asked her.

'Only what was in the papers, and my dad pointed out stuff. He wrote this poem, didn't he, saying books are a load of crap? And there was that other poem, the one about his parents –'

'Which we'll pass on for now,' Joy said smoothly. *They fuck you up, your mum and dad.* She thought quickly. If the class insisted on knowing what Lucy was going to say, she could always substitute the word 'muck' as the sense was the same. But the rest of the group seemed stunned by Lucy's revelations about Larkin. Joy tried to reclaim the lesson.

'Now look again at the poem. Why do you think Larkin uses the word "hollows" in the fifth line to describe the mothers' afternoons? Richard?'

'Sorry, Miss.'

'Katy?'

'Does "hollow" mean empty?'

'Yes!' exclaimed Joy, a touch too enthusiastically. 'So what does that tell you about the mothers' afternoons?'

'That they were empty?' asked Katy, with the hesitation of a nervous tightrope walker.

'Absolutely. Are there any other meanings for the word "hollow"? Neil?'

'Like when you've got nothing inside.'

'Could be. Now go on,' Joy said, trying to draw him out. Neil cleared his throat and continued gruffly. 'Is it that they've got nothing inside after having their children?'

'Almost,' Joy conceded, knowing that he was talking rubbish but unwilling to destroy his confidence at this early stage. 'Any one else? What else do you think of when you see the word "hollow"?' She wanted them to get the connection between hollows in fields, which are depressions too. She waited patiently. She knew she would have to answer her own question.

'A hollow can be a sort of depression. Literally speaking, but also metaphorically. A metaphor is a comparison,' Joy added, remembering her class was new to college. 'So the word echoes the mothers' state of mind.'

'I don't think we should be reading this,' Lucy said.

'Why?' Joy asked quickly, sensing a confrontation. She trembled; she disliked any sort of scene and, moreover, she liked Lucy and wanted Lucy to like her.

'Because, look, he's saying that there's no point in living because everyone gets older and dies. Silly bugger,' she concluded.

Joy cut in swiftly. 'Language!' she warned. 'But Lucy,

basically he's right. We all get older and die. How can you deny that?' Joy badly wanted her to deny it. It seemed vital that she should.

'Is that what you think, Miss? That life's pointless?'

Joy shrugged ambiguously.

'I don't,' Lucy said. 'It's how you choose to live that gives your life meaning, and I'm going to do a lot with my life. I'm not going to sit in a library surrounded with soft porn!'

The boys looked at her as if to suggest that that wasn't such a bad idea. Joy asked herself what she was doing with her life and felt uneasy. Like Larkin, she was a coward. With effort, she brought her attention back to the lesson.

'Larkin needed deprivation in order to be able to write,' she said, stating literary criticism's clichés.

'More fool him,' Lucy said. 'He could have had a lot more fun, if he wasn't so scared of death and everything. So what if he was the poet laureate? Poet laureates are allowed to have fun, so Sir John Betjeman watched *Coronation Street*.'

'We did Betjeman,' Rachel said proudly. 'In this poem he went shooting with his Dad and he shot him or something.'

'No, no.' Joy stopped her, and explained.

When the bell rang to signal break Joy hadn't quite finished going over the poem. She asked the group to write up what they'd established and watched them file out in the direction of the nearest drinks machine. Lucy gathered her books with a deliberate slowness. Joy hoped she was lingering because she wanted to talk to her. She waited until the room was empty.

'You know a lot about Larkin,' Joy said.

'He's kind of interesting. But I still think he's wrong,' she added, with an aggressive but becoming tilt of her chin.

'Does your dad read poetry?' Joy prompted her.

'He used to. But now he just reads the *Guardian* and the *New Statesman* and sighs a lot.'

Joy knew why. She'd stopped the *Guardian* some time ago. The newspaper convinced her she was absolutely right to worry. There was Aids, poverty and famine in Africa, trouble-spots all over the world, no hope of stemming the hole in the ozone layer, no effective controls on the ex-USSR's nuclear arsenal, no end to the rise of fundamentalism, and no one fit to govern Britain or America. No wonder Lucy's father sighed a lot.

'My Dad's a socialist. Still!' Lucy exclaimed. 'And he's proud of it. I tell him he's a fool. He says I sound like my mum.'

'Do you see your mum?' Joy asked delicately, hoping this was not a painful question.

'Not a lot. She married again and she's gone to live in Stirling. She's got babies.'

Lucy spoke as if this were a disease. Joy nodded sympathetically.

'So, yeah, I live with my dad.' Lucy grinned. Joy guessed it was out of bravado. It must be terrible to live without a mother, Joy thought. Losing a mother must be the worst thing that could happen to anyone.

'You know you were talking about reading poetry before,' Lucy pursued. 'Well, I read poetry.' Joy was flattered. Lucy wanted to please her. 'My favourite poet is Oscar Wilde. You know, *The Ballad of Reading Gaol*. I can't believe he was imprisoned just for being gay. Like, the Victorians were so *sad*!'

'Hypocrites, too,' Joy added. 'Wilde really only sinned in their eyes because he flaunted what he did.'

'Good for him,' said Lucy.

'But it was his downfall. He'd have been better off using some discretion.'

Lucy shook her head vehemently. 'No – he was the winner. He was real.' Then she changed the subject. 'I didn't start reading properly – I could read, of course – but I never read a grown-up book until last year, 'cause I was pissed off with school and kept getting into trouble, and Dad wrote me notes saying I had migraines and I stayed at home and read a lot, so that's why I want to do English. I'm sorry for swearing today. I hope it didn't upset you.'

'I've heard worse,' Joy said.

'Have you?' Lucy asked. 'What?'

'That's not the sort of English I'm here to teach you.' Lucy laughed, and gave a toothy grin that made her seem very young.

'I'd better go now,' she said. 'I'm dying for a fag.' With that, she left.

Joy realized she felt rather exhilarated. She was bursting to tell the rest of the department about Lucy, and so she ran along the corridor to the English office. Everyone was there, and Joy was pleased to see that someone had filled her mug with coffee, and it stood waiting for her at her desk. She murmured her thanks and lifted the mug to her lips. As she did so, she became aware that she had interrupted something; there was a strained silence. Had they been talking about her? Was there some bad news? No: Betty was smiling, albeit awkwardly, and Peter seemed perfectly relaxed, as did the others.

'Now you're *all* here,' Betty began, 'I can say what I

was going to say.' Joy guessed immediately what that was. She was going to announce her retirement. What with Michael and her mother and everything else, Betty had completely slipped her mind. 'Sister told me this morning the governors have agreed to let me have early retirement from July,' she concluded.

Joy could see Betty's hand was shaking as she sipped her tea. Betty disliked talking about herself and there was some exposure even in the announcement of her retirement.

'As you know,' she said, 'it was what I wanted, and there's an end to it. Is anyone else short of copies of *The Merchant of Venice*?'

Joy wondered what Betty would do without St Ignatius'. Presently it filled her life. She hoped fervently that she wouldn't get ill. Joy had read or heard of so many cases where workers retire and then have a heart attack and so never get to enjoy or even experience –

'What on earth are we going to do without you, Betty?' Peter asked, shaking his head in mock despair.

'You'll survive,' she said.

Joy reckoned that that wasn't what Peter meant. He was attempting to enquire about the succession. Someone was going to have to replace Betty, and it was quite reasonable for Peter to suppose that he was in with a chance. Joy knew there was little to choose between them. On one hand, Joy was several years older than Peter and considerably more experienced. On the other, Peter had been at St Ignatius' a year longer than Joy and so, technically, Peter was Joy's superior. This idea struck Joy with a new force. Was he her superior? His dress sense was immaculate – he certainly looked her superior. His notes and files were more organized, more up-to-date than hers. His cool, detached, capable approach to life contrasted markedly with her neurotic obsessions. How would the senior-management team view them both? Lesley apart, they were all male. They talked football all day long, and in fact it was Peter who'd started the fantasy league in the staff room. Joy wondered how she could have even dared to hope that the head of department post might be hers.

'Will you be staying in the area?' Peter asked Betty, pushing a stray strand of hair from his perfectly chiselled forehead.

'My sister has a cottage just north of Windermere, and I'm going to join her there, assuming I can sell my house. I'm hoping to work some days in a small second-hand bookshop in the village, to give me something to do. My sister has a friend who was looking for some help.'

Joy felt a twinge of envy. Perhaps she'd let her come and stay and –

'Has Sister decided what's happening to the department?' Peter asked.

Joy was suddenly alert.

'There'll be interviews,' Betty said, ambiguously.

Peter nodded slowly. Joy watched him from the corner of her eye. If an interview were to be be held, 'twere well it were done quickly. The whole department – Fiona and Bev and George as well – would suffer from the suspense. Was it going to be a race between herself and Peter? And was she too full of the milk of human kindness to catch the nearest way? Was Peter smiling, and smiling, and being a villain? What if Peter Worthington became head of department?

Joy, Joy, she berated herself gently. You're worrying again. Don't do it. Peter's only ambitions are sartorial, and you know it. *Relax.* Joy attempted to draw a deep, relaxing breath, which ended in a nervous cough.

Everyone seemed glad when Fran from the office arrived with a sheaf of papers. She handed them to Peter, who looked momentarily puzzled, and then his face cleared. Joy guessed he'd been having yet more notes typed up for his students.

'I think there's enough,' Fran said. 'There's usually about sixty kids on the adventure weekend, so I've printed out a hundred letters to be on the safe side.' She bustled away.

Joy glanced quickly at the letters. They were the annual invitations for students to spend three days in the Lake District with Sid, the head of P.E., and a few other foolhardy teachers, canoeing, abseiling, rock climbing, and performing various other activities which basically entailed them risking their lives while getting very wet and cold. Joy knew the P.E. department claimed this developed management skills, but as she had once said to Sid, she'd never known of board meetings that convened halfway up a rock face with the M.D. and executives strung out in a line, joined by brightly coloured harnesses. But what was Peter doing with the letters?

'I'm leading the holiday this year,' he explained to the department. 'Sid Nelson's having an op on his knee, and he's not going.'

Leading the expedition? Joy was alarmed. Peter had never even gone on the adventure weekend before, let alone taken charge of it. Here was her proof that Peter was absolutely serious about becoming head of department. He was demonstrating his leadership potential. And where? On the peaks of the Lake District, while she, Joy, couldn't even climb on to a chair without checking each leg was securely fixed to the ground. He had found the best possible way of upstaging her. Joy remembered last year, when she'd taken a party to the theatre to see *A View from the Bridge* and she couldn't even sit with them when she'd discovered the ticket she'd allotted herself was in the upper circle. Peter was aiming for the top, in every sense of the word, and the one thing Joy didn't have was a head for heights.

Lesley did, Joy thought to herself, as she dropped into second gear to pull her car up the steep incline to Lesley's village, which nestled on the tops of the West Yorkshire moors. Yet as the car protested by pushing forward ever more slowly, Joy felt her spirits lifting. Lesley's place spelt freedom, a whole night of freedom. Naturally when she had got home and told Michael that Les had asked if Joy could spend the night with her so she could take her into college in the morning, as her car needed to spend a day in the garage, Michael was crestfallen, to say the least. Then he had kissed her tenderly and let her go. She'd got in the car, switched on the old Law Enforcers tape she had bought herself as a secret indulgence, turned the volume up high and joined the M62 in good spirits. So what if she was escaping – it felt fantastic.

The cottage door opened to reveal Lesley in full cooking mode – red and white apron tied tightly round her waist, with a Kitchen Devil in one hand. Lesley's kitchen was tiny – in fact it used to be the coal-hole for the cottage when genuine eighteenth-century weavers lived there. Some years ago Lesley had renovated it to become a tiny, bare kitchen, painting over the rough stones in gleaming white. There was only room for a cooker, a sink, some open shelving and a spice rack, and for decoration Lesley had put up a poster depicting some brightly coloured vegetables. Standing there, Joy felt there was barely room for her.

Lesley continued to chop at a cucumber.

'All M&S, I'm afraid. No time to cook today.'

Joy was relieved. Food was not Lesley's thing. She was one of those people who simply ate to live, just refuelling herself at certain intervals. Joy could remember occasions when she had eaten with her friend, and she had become so interested in the conversation she had forgotten to finish her meal. As a Jew, Joy found this decidedly odd.

'Here, Joy,' Lesley said. 'Take the salad next door. I'll get the quiche out of the oven.'

Joy took the wooden salad bowl into Lesley's other room, the only other downstairs room. Les had pulled out the gate-legged table from its usual position under the open staircase and had put some table mats upon it, adorned with pictures of fat tabby cats. Joy orientated herself. It was good to be away from her habitual haunts and here instead in Lesley's cottage, with its low dark beams and its tastefully arranged wall lighting. The wooden floor was elegant, but chilly. Lesley's cats evidently thought so, as both of them had settled on the rug in front of the wood-burning stove. Around the walls were water-colours that Lesley had painted herself, and Joy recognized the music that filled the room as Shostakovich.

Joy knew that the affection she felt for Lesley was laced with admiration. Here was a woman who had made a life, a home for herself, a career, without a man, without anyone, and lived alone, out in the wilds, without the comforts and security of the city, and wasn't lonely and didn't worry. Lesley's self-sufficiency was both a reproach and an incentive to Joy – it was possible to be independent, to be your own woman. This was clearly the thing to which she should aspire. Joy imagined herself living next door to Lesley, in a similarly designed cottage, sitting in front of a similar stove, sipping a drink while perusing some essays. Could she? Would she dare?

'Da-da!' Lesley sang, as she entered carrying the quiche aloft, and placed it on the table. 'Walnut and broccoli, I think, or salmon and broccoli, it doesn't matter. I've put the wine you brought in the freezer, so we'll start on mine.'

Lesley dashed back to the kitchen to rescue the new potatoes from the simmering water, and as she drained them she knew she was glad to be busy. She resolved to be extra cheerful tonight, to prove to herself how little he meant to her, or rather, how well able she was to cope with the inevitable difficulties of open relationships. Joy was bound to ask about Rennie, she knew. Really, she thought, there was precious little to say.

'How's Rennie?' Joy asked, as she lifted a forkful of quiche to her mouth.

'Fine,' said Lesley.

'Did you see him this weekend?' pursued Joy. It was nice when someone talked while you were eating dinner, and Lesley's stories about Rennie fascinated her.

'No. We were both busy.'

'Doing what?' persisted Joy.

'I was working on the value-added results. Rennie was away.'

'Oh. Does he often go away?'

'Exhibitions. Fairs. Besides,' Lesley said briskly, 'I wouldn't want him around me all the time.'

'I know what you mean!' agreed Joy. 'I'd find it much

easier to cope with Michael if I only saw him occasionally – say on his birthday.'

Lesley laughed. 'Do I detect an awakening here?'

'You do,' admitted Joy. She saw how Lesley's face brightened.

'So you're going to finish with him!' Lesley didn't think it was worth hiding her pleasure.

'I tried to finish with him yesterday afternoon,' Joy said demurely.

'Tried?' questioned Les.

'Tried. And failed.'

'Badly?'

'Grade U. Unclassified. The consequence is that he loves me more than ever, and I can't stand it.'

'So try again. If at first you don't succeed –'

'Give up,' Joy said. 'It's the best way I know to avoid failure. Works every time.' Just then Joy didn't want to dwell on Michael, nor expose the details of her ineptness to Lesley.

'But, Les, listen. I've met another man.'

'Tell me about him!'

'Don't get too excited. Lawrence is a *shidduch*, a match, arranged for me by my cousin Deborah.'

'So are you playing at home or away?'

'Neither at present. I'm not altogether sure about him. He's older than me, more Jewish-looking than Moses, and the worst of it is, he's a worrier too.'

'All the better for you to worry with . . .'

'No, I'm not sure,' Joy said. The quiche was soggy in the middle, and she pushed it to one side of her plate. 'And anyway, there's Michael.'

'I should have thought that Michael was the biggest incentive for you to see this man.'

153

'I can't be unfaithful,' Joy said primly.

'Many people are,' Lesley commented, and thought for a moment of one of them.

Joy was silent. She was hoping that Les would push her into seeing Lawrence. Sitting here in Lesley's cottage, anything seemed possible. It seemed perfectly reasonable to go out with Lawrence and to finish with Michael. It was just that she needed a little encouragement.

'So what shall I do?' Joy prompted Lesley.

'Investigate. Experiment. See this man, this Lawrence. Go out with him, go back to his place. Get to know him. Start with an intimate exchange of your worries, and then go on to an intimate exchange –'

'Les! No, seriously, I was thinking of ringing him up at work. But it's all got to be very hush hush. I don't want Michael to know, and also Lawrence is living with his mother. I'll meet him in town for a meal or the theatre or something.'

'Hmm.' Lesley stroked her chin. 'Sounds very formal. You can bring him back here, you know.'

'To meet you?'

'No, I shan't be here.'

'Lesley! I hope you're not suggesting that I'd do anything improper on a first date.'

'I'm not suggesting that you would; I'm suggesting that you do.'

'Lesley, he's Jewish!'

'So are you.'

'Even worse!'

'So how do Jews get babies?'

'You bring them back from the delicatessen like everything else.'

'No, I mean it, Joy. Have the freedom of my cottage. If

you want to get to know this man, you'll need to be alone together. And you'll need a relaxed atmosphere if both of you are going to be terrified.'

Joy smiled to herself. There was something in what Lesley said. Lesley's cottage was cosy and private, and certainly conducive to getting things on the right footing. She was certain that, like her, Lawrence wouldn't want to start anything on a first date. It struck her then that she felt safe with Lawrence; it was an inspiring thought. Joy proceeded to fill Lesley in on the details of her weekend. She thought she'd wait for the dessert to introduce the subject of Peter Worthington and her vaulting ambition, but when she realized there wasn't going to be any dessert, she refilled her glass with the Entre Deux Mers and began.

'Do you know if Peter Worthington is applying for head of department too?' It was possible that Les would know.

Les shrugged; she looked faintly surprised. 'I don't know. I shouldn't think so. I would have thought . . .'

Her voice trailed away.

'What would you have thought?'

'Oh, that he wouldn't be interested. That he wouldn't need –'

'He *is* interested. Listen: He's had his schemes of work bound professionally, he's been sucking up to Betty, he seems to have bought a whole new wardrobe and he's leading the adventure weekend!'

'I know; Sid's having an operation on his knee.'

'Yes, but don't you see? Usually Peter spends his holidays travelling. I'm sure he mentioned he was going to Venice or somewhere. And here he is giving up part of his half-term to climb mountains and sleep in a youth hostel in the Lakes. Why do that unless you're trying to impress Sister?'

'I concede it's possible. I must say I'm a little surprised. But it shouldn't put you off applying. You're a much stronger candidate academically, and when Betty was off with her gall-bladder, you more or less ran the department single-handedly.'

'Yes, but don't you see? Peter's going to prove himself in the one area where I'm weakest. Joy the Worrier versus Peter the Undaunted. Which one would you pick to lead the English department of St Ignatius' into the twenty-first century? No, don't laugh, Les!'

'OK, so perhaps it's true. Perhaps you do need to prove yourself. Checkmate him. Offer to go on the adventure weekend too. It might do you the world of good.'

'What?' Joy's spine turned to ice.

'I know Maisie's keen to drop out. You'll enjoy yourself. I went once. It was fun.'

'No, not for me. You see, I have a real fear of heights. A bad one. I've also heard they make you abseil. I couldn't canoe because I can't swim. And I have a fear of wide-open spaces, apart from the fact I'm out of condition.'

'Joy, you don't have to do all those things. The centre leaders see to the activities. You only try what appeals to you. Do it, go on.'

'No.'

'OK. Do something else. Take a school trip abroad – Sister was saying to me just the other day we ought to take the kids to Poland, establish some links there. You and me, we'll go together.'

'I'm scared of flying,' Joy reminded her.

Lesley shook her head and took a sip of wine. Joy started to feel rather foolish. She began to see how her fears were stopping her from getting what she wanted. She remembered once watching a mime artist pretending to be in an invisible cage, feeling round the interior with the flat of his hand. That was her, inside that invisible box. A sort of womb with a view.

'All your problems are connected,' Lesley said.

'What do you mean?'

'This worrying – it's just another form of fear. Fear of the future. I think you're going to have to face your fears head on. Do the things that scare you. Then you won't be worried any more.'

'I think it's normal to worry,' Joy challenged. 'Everyone worries about something. I bet you worry about Rennie when he's away.'

'No, I don't,' Lesley cut in swiftly. 'You see, he's not everything to me. Of course sex is very important but then, so's work, and so's my family, and my painting and sketching. If I have a problem in one part of my life, there's another part which is fine. I compartmentalize.'

'Ha! So the only difference between us is that you won't risk everything, and I won't risk anything. But I bet you worry about work. Every teacher does. There's the marking and the pressure of exam results and the form-filling and the funding and –'

'I only ever think about one thing at a time,' Lesley explained.

'You only ever think about one thing,' Joy corrected her.

Lesley laughed. 'Recently thinking's all I've been doing?'

'Why?'

'Rennie has other commitments.' Joy picked up the ambiguity, and decided to press Les further.

'Is he faithful to you?'

'While he's with me, he's faithful to me – God! Joy, you make him sound like a puppy. He's an extremely attractive and charismatic sculptor, and I'm absolutely realistic and rather smitten. And the sex is out of this world. Enough of me. I want to know what you're going to do to conquer your fear.'

'Which fear?' Joy quipped. 'Take your pick. There's my fear of heights, of illness, flying, failure, satellites breaking up over Manchester –'

'Go on the adventure weekend,' Lesley persisted.

Joy considered. It was a whole weekend away from Michael. If it was true that the centre leaders ran the activities and she could just watch it might not be such a bad idea. Then there was Wordsworth and Coleridge to think about – perhaps she'd take a break-away group to look round Dove Cottage and Grasmere . . .

'I might,' she said.

Lesley continued to think. Joy could almost hear her mind clicking and whirring.

'You could try a stress-management course, though that's not really about fear as such. Fear,' said Lesley ruminatively. 'Fear. Of course, you'd never get funding for it, but you could always try the Fear of Flying course at Manchester Airport.'

'What's that?' Joy enquired. 'A crash course?'

'Don't be silly. It's just an idea. If you can learn not to be scared of one thing, perhaps you can apply it to all the others.'

'You mean I can learn not to be scared?'

'I should think so.'

Joy looked at her watch. 'Don't you think we ought to go to bed? College in the morning.'

'True,' said Lesley. She yawned, and looked over at her two cats, who had not budged from their vantage point in front of the stove.

'It's too cold to put them out,' she remarked. 'The problem is, the spare bedroom door doesn't shut fully. They might disturb you in the night. No, look, you have my bed. Caesar's bound to start yowling about five in the morning, and Napoleon has a habit of spraying.'

'No, it's all right,' Joy protested feebly. In fact she didn't fancy the company of the cats.

'Sleep in my bed – I insist. From the sound of it, you need a good night's rest.' Joy was inclined to agree with her.

And so it was that Joy sat on the edge of Lesley's bed, pulling on her pyjamas and thinking that, yes, she would go on a Fear of Flying course, and she would go on the adventure weekend too. And she would take control of her life, and see Lawrence, and confront Michael again quite soon, and do all of these things not today, of course, but tomorrow. Well, not tomorrow, because tomorrow was Tuesday and she taught all day without any free periods, and she wouldn't have any time. Wednesday, perhaps, or Thursday. On the weekend she would ring up the airport. Joy yawned. She went to turn on Lesley's bedside lamp so she could read a little. What was that by the side of the lamp? A modern sculpture? Something of Rennie's? Yes, it was something of Rennie's. Something rather personal. Joy blanched in horror. Lesley had been telling the truth – it was a terracotta phallus, and it was nine inches long at the very least. Surely he wasn't as big as that? Joy guessed he'd probably added a bit before he put it in the oven. Most men would. Fancy Lesley keeping it on her bedside table! Perhaps it was her way of making sure she had a part of Rennie close at hand. And what a part! Joy found herself wishing Les wasn't going to come into the bedroom to wish her good night. What would she say then? What a lovely phallus! Mind you, it would be useful if an intruder came in the night. Just one glimpse would make him blush with inferiority.

Joy felt awkwardly self-conscious. There was no way she could go to sleep with it staring at her like that. Neither could she pick it up and put it on the floor. That was too embarrassing to contemplate. Ought she to hang something over it? Her blouse?

No. She would just have to ignore it, she decided, as she slipped into bed and lay there, her eyes wide open. She realized she'd never been in Lesley's bedroom before. All over the walls were sketches and paintings that Les had done, a drawing of a cathedral, a water-colour of some hills and some life drawings, one particularly large one, of a naked man with – thank God! – his hand coyly covering his nether regions. Joy wondered if that was Rennie too? Except he seemed too young for Rennie; the Scottish sculptor was apparently in his fifties. Joy examined the face of the model to see if he looked ashamed of what he was doing. His expression seemed abstracted. Joy frowned to herself. Didn't she know him from somewhere? Yes – she was sure of it. The trouble was, seeing him out of context like that made it impossible to place him.

For a minute, she thought he looked like Peter Worthington.

She laughed at herself. She was obsessed with Peter Worthington. She looked at the drawing again. There was no doubt – the model bore an uncanny resemblance to Peter Worthington. She would point this out to Lesley

in the morning. Unless, she thought, it really was Peter
. . . Impossible, she thought. You're mad. When you look
at the drawing in the morning, it will be nothing like him.
You're over-imaginative, Joy told herself, and settled
herself for sleep.

CHAPTER TEN

The idea of learning to conquer fear had interested Joy profoundly. She was a teacher and she knew it was possible to learn anything, given time, patience, strong motivation and a good teacher. Lesley, as usual, had been right. Nervously Joy had approached Maisie in the staff room to mention she'd heard that there might be a place on the adventure weekend for another female member of staff. Maisie had been delighted. It was only the work of a moment for Joy to be enrolled in that band of intrepid tutors who were off to the Lake District at half-term. Had she imagined that Peter had looked somewhat disconcerted? Or was it just surprise?

That was her first step. She had made a commitment, and it felt unexpectedly good. Encouraged by her success, she rifled through the Yellow Pages by the staff phone and looked up Manchester Airport. A few phone calls later she had ascertained the existence of a Fear of Flying course and had actually asked for a form to be sent to her at her home address. She really couldn't believe she was doing this! Amazing! She had completed step two. Like a toddler, she was beginning to walk alone for the first time.

Now for the third step. A phone call to Lawrence, just to say she'd be interested in seeing him again. Her fingers hovered over the dial. Ought she? What about Michael? Perhaps step three ought to be saying farewell to Michael. Then she would be clear to attempt step four. Yet telling Michael the truth about her feelings was more alarming than ringing up Lawrence, and really ought to be step four. There was no one to consult about this sticky procedural point in the staff room and really, she couldn't pester Lesley again. Then, not for the first time that day, she became aware of that nagging ache at the back of her mouth. I probably need a filling, Joy thought absently. I ought to ring the dentist.

That was it. That was step three. A visit to the dentist. It was far, far easier than tackling Michael or Lawrence. The dentist was commonly held to be a fear-inducing experience; Uncle Barney, for example, puts off going to the dentist for ages and ages and comes out white and shaking from the surgery. That decided her. She would ring the dentist. Joy did not pause to examine the fact that she quite enjoyed visiting the dentist; her dentist was Howard's brother-in-law, and a more genial, friendly man you couldn't hope to meet. She checked his number in her address book and dialled.

His name was over the shared entrance to the surgery: Martin Wiseman. Joy reflected that he sounded like a character from *The Pilgrim's Progress*. If that was so, it showed she was already making progress on her own little voyage away from fear. She was about to meet Mr Wiseman.

With some anticipation, she mounted the steps to the surgery. She tensed only slightly at the antiseptic smell and, sitting in the waiting area, wondered why she'd never been particularly frightened of the dentist. She didn't have to seek far for the answer. Generally speaking, you couldn't die from going to the dentist, unless he was careless and you contracted HIV, or there was a bubble of air in the syringe when he injected you. Even

Joy accepted that the possibility of either of these happening was remote. The worst thing a dentist could do to you was remove a tooth.

Martin Wiseman appeared in the waiting area and beamed when he saw Joy, welcoming her warmly. He was a tall man, easily over six foot, and big-boned too. Joy had often wondered why it was that he'd become a dentist, choosing to work in the smallest space possible. Perhaps it was a way of denying his size.

Within moments Joy was lying back in the chair, staring into a light directly above her eyes, her hands clasped tightly on her stomach. She held her mouth open as widely as she could. Martin Wiseman quickly scanned her teeth, while the radio played a familiar song softly in the background. It was the Law Enforcers. So this is growing up, she thought. Songs you thrill and dance to when you're young are background music when you're prostrate on the dentist's chair with rotten teeth.

'Mmmm,' murmured Martin, 'I can see where the problem is.'

Joy wasn't absolutely sure whether to close her mouth so she could reply to this gnomic utterance. She boldly decided to do so.

'What is it?'

'There's a swelling on your gum. I'm not even sure if an X-ray would tell us what's going on in there.'

Oh my God, thought Joy, it's not cancer?

'What is it?' she asked again, this time vibrato.

'Some sort of root infection. Have you been run down lately?'

'No – yes, I mean, there's been lots of stress.'

'I'll take an X-ray to help us decide what to do. I'm reluctant to take invasive action at this stage. Teeth are people, you know. You must treat them with respect. You're not pregnant, are you?'

'Oh, no,' Joy said, with some pleasure.

'Right.' Martin positioned the X-ray camera over Joy's tooth and moved outside the surgery to activate the machine.

Ha! It's psychosomatic, Joy thought. All this trouble with Michael – it's caused a root infection.

Martin returned. 'It'll take a few moments for the X-ray to develop. Excuse me,' he said. And Joy was left on her own.

No doubt about it, Michael was making her ill. He was a pain in the mouth. That was the connection. All those stressful evenings, with Michael coming in to her study, or interrupting *Coronation Street* with his eternal 'let's talk'. But even when she did narrate some incident from college he seemed to switch off and count the minutes until it was his turn to say something, and then bored her with a long speech on Manchester United's chances in the European Cup. Then he'd look pleased with himself, and his eyes would stray to the TV, where there was a pale square of carpet where the megadrive had been. He'd sold that to one of his fifth-years at school.

Or he would come over to her and put his arm around her shoulders in a matey hug. She would try not to flinch. Or he would kiss her ear lobe, her skin would prickle with distaste, and he would say, 'We're getting on a lot better, aren't we?'

Really, lying here in the dentist's chair was preferable. No doubt about it, Michael was her root infection.

Martin Wiseman returned, holding her X-ray on a plastic spine. Joy sat up so she could see it.

'Look at that dark area there. That's the infection. But, as I thought, there's no real indication what's causing it.'

'What are you going to do?' asked Joy.

'Root-canal treatment is a possibility.'

Joy didn't like the sound of that. Canals, bridges – why was it that dental work was so reminiscent of large-scale engineering?

'But I think I'd prefer to tread gently. Can you take antibiotics?'

'Yes!' said Joy eagerly.

'That might clear it up. There's no point in drastic action yet. Softly, softly, that's my motto.'

How right he was, Joy thought. Mr Wise Man had spoken. Despite the torrent of dislike for Michael that was overwhelming her she would tread softly, softly. No need to do anything yet. She would just continue to avoid him.

'I think I'd better see you again in ten days or so,' Martin continued. He paused and smiled at her, indicating a change of subject.

'So, how are you? How's your mother?'

'Fine!' Joy declared.

'And have you seen Howard and Deborah recently?'

'We were there at Rosh Hashanah. And I'm going over this Friday night. I do that every month.'

'And was Howard all right?'

'Yes,' said Joy, puzzled. 'Except he seemed a bit preoccupied.'

'Yes, that's what Lynne and I have noticed. Frankly, we're a little bit worried about him. Something's up. And for some reason, he's not talking about it.'

Joy felt guilty. She had been so wrapped up in her own concerns she hadn't noticed that Howard had problems too. And what could they be?

'I'll watch him carefully,' she assured Martin.

Was there something seriously wrong with her cousins, Joy wondered as she brushed her hair in front of her bedroom mirror. The idea had haunted her all day. She'd remembered Howard's furtive phone calls on Rosh Hashanah. Who could he have called?

Now, however, her problem was telling Michael that she was going out alone again, this time to Howard and Deborah's for Friday-night supper. When she came downstairs he was sitting in the lounge reading the sports pages of the *Manchester Evening News*.

'It's my night for seeing Deborah,' Joy explained. 'I did mention it earlier in the week.'

Michael placed the paper carefully down by his side.

'Oh, right. Thought I might come with you.'

Joy was horrified, and astonished too. Up to now Michael had always avoided Deborah and Howard, saying that they didn't like him, which was true, and that he had nothing in common with them, which was also true. He had been so steadfast in this opinion that Deborah had stopped inviting him. Joy didn't know what to do now.

'Are you sure? It's a proper *Shabbat* dinner, and I know Deborah has things she wants to talk to me about. Women's problems!' Joy announced, slamming down the portcullis.

'Don't you want me to go with you?' Michael whined.

'It's just that I think you might feel out of place.' She was flailing wildly.

'Not with you there, I won't.'

'Look, Michael, I need to have a life of my own. We both do.'

'We also need a life together.'

Joy could feel a sweat breaking out. 'Look, I know what. I'll . . . I'll come home early and we can watch a video. Get a video. Something good.'

'What?' he asked, sounding somewhat mollified.

'Oh, I don't know. Not James Bond or Clint Eastwood. Oh, I don't know. Something a bit more educational.' Educational wasn't the word she meant. It was the first word that came into her head. At all costs, she must end this conversation. Michael, however, was backing down.

'All right then,' he said. 'Leave it to me. I know what you like. Just don't come home too late.'

'All right,' Joy conceded, and turned to get her coat, which was lying over the banister.

'Love you,' he said.

'Yes,' said Joy.

Martin Wiseman was right. There was an atmosphere. Howard had a far-off look in his eyes and was picking at his food, despite the fact that Deborah's chicken was as succulent and flavoursome as ever. The children seemed restless, and Deborah distracted. Joy was glad that she had stopped worrying on her own account. It was clearly her role to cheer the others up. This she could do. She decided to be as bright and entertaining as possible.

'And so,' she concluded, 'I've decided to learn bit by bit to conquer my fears. Ask Martin. I bet I was the most relaxed patient he'd had all day.'

'But you didn't have any treatment,' Deborah commented.

'No difference,' Joy announced. 'Waiting to hear what's wrong is often worse than the treatment itself!'

'And you're really going on an adventure weekend?'

'Absolutely,' said Joy, helping herself to more chicken, stuffing and potatoes.

The telephone rang, and Joy noted how Howard seemed to shoot out of his chair.

'Me, me!' shouted Hayleigh. Before anyone could stop her, she ran to the hall to answer the phone. She returned a few moments later, unconcerned.

'Who was it?' Deborah asked.

'Wrong number,' Hayleigh said.

'What did they say?' persisted Deborah, curious.

'I said 774 9310 and she said, oh sorry, it's the wrong number, and I said, do you want Mummy, and she said no.'

Joy watched Howard's face. Why was he avoiding eye contact with everyone? A horrible suspicion was beginning to dawn on her. At all events Deborah must not share it. Joy knew she must divert her attention.

'So, what are your plans for the weekend?'

'We were thinking of taking the children ice-skating.'

'Yes!' shouted Hayleigh, punching the air with her fist. Josh copied her.

'That's nice,' Joy said brightly. 'It must be fun, ice-skating.'

'Why don't you come with?' Deborah asked her.

'Yes!' from both children this time.

'Ah no,' said Joy. 'Ice-skating isn't my thing. I can't skate,' she explained to the children.

'It's easy,' Deborah said. 'I bet you're scared.'

'No, I'm not!'

'Prove it. Come with us. I know what. I'll invite Lawrence too. Did you know, you made a strong impression on him, Joy? He really *liked* you. What was it Lawrence said to you, Howard?'

'What?' said Howard.

'About Joy. What did Lawrence say about Joy?'

'He really liked you,' repeated Howard, winking at Joy.

For a moment, Joy decided that her growing suspicions were unfounded. Like the old joke says, the only sort of affair her cousin Howard would have was one that needed outside caterers.

Deborah continued. 'Yes, come with us on Sunday. Meet him again. I just know you're right for each other.'

Secretly Joy thought this was a rather splendid idea. Another day apart from Michael and a chance to get to know Lawrence better in a non-intimate setting. This appealed to her more than Lesley's plan that she should get to know Lawrence in the biblical sense. What's more, not *everyone* who went skating broke a leg. And if she fell, and a skater sliced through her fingers with his skates, there'd be plenty of ice around to wrap her fingers in so that the microsurgeon could sew them back on again.

'Please come, Aunty Joy. You can watch me!' begged Hayleigh.

'All right,' Joy conceded. She was glad she'd agreed. Everyone looked a bit brighter. This campaign of hers to face her fears head on was certainly paying dividends.

'Torvill and Dean, here I come!' she quipped. Joy glanced at Deborah to see how her joke had been received. Deborah seemed not to have heard it. There were lines of tension on her brow, and she was biting her bottom lip. Joy looked at Howard, who had stopped eating and seemed to be thinking about something, or someone, Joy assumed. Only the children seemed normal.

Joy swallowed hard. She thought to herself that she really ought to go home now; she'd promised Michael she'd be home early; she could do no good here because she knew it was never wise to interfere in other people's affairs. Affairs! Howard! Who ever would have thought it! For one thing, how did he have the time? And what a consummate hypocrite to be able to sit there at the Friday-night table, while his bit on the side coolly rang him at home and spoke to his daughter! Joy's head was full of exclamation marks.

Deborah rose. 'Since everyone's finished eating, I might as well clear up.'

Joy looked around the table. It was true. The knives and forks were still. She got up too and began to carry plates and cutlery into the kitchen. There was quite a lot of food left over. Joy wasn't sure whether to draw Deborah's attention to this or just quietly to scrape the plates into the bin. Once Deborah and Joy were both in the kitchen, however, Deborah shut the door. Her face bore testimony to both grief and anger. Joy tensed herself. It was coming now.

'Have you noticed?' Deborah asked her.

Joy gave an imperceptible nod.

'He didn't eat anything. He was picking at his food. He couldn't meet my eyes. And when I try to talk to him, he slinks away. Joy, it's been going on for months. I'm at my wit's end.'

Joy's eyes widened with horror. This was worse than she thought.

'But, look, I've been thinking, can you talk to him? Perhaps he'd take it better from you, being an outsider, so to speak. He listens to you, I know.'

Joy was about to say that she couldn't, that she wouldn't, but then how could she abandon Deborah in what was going to be the worst time of her life?

'What do you want me to say?' Joy was hoarse.

'Oh, whatever you think fit. Point out the consequences to him. Tell him how unhappy he makes me. No – don't say that. I don't want him to feel guilty.'

'You don't?'

'Oh no, that will make it worse. But listen, what do you think of this? I had another idea. I'll tell the rabbi about it – he's very approachable. Perhaps he'll give him a special dispensation.'

'I don't . . .'

'Then we can go for a meal at McDonald's. Joy – the only meat he'll eat is a Big Mac! I don't know if it's me and my cooking he's rejecting, or whether he doesn't want to be Jewish. But if he doesn't eat meat he's missing out on essential vitamins. No wonder he's slow with his reading!'

'You mean Josh,' Joy said to her.

'Of course I mean Josh. Why is he doing it? You're a teacher – you tell me.' Deborah paused. 'I'm sorry, Joy. I'm sorry for offloading this on you. But you always understand me so well.' Deborah began to scrape the plates. 'It's not easy being a mother these days. What with junk food, drugs, unemployment and shoes that don't fit properly, you never have a moment's peace. Sometimes I envy you, Joy, being single. No, no. I don't mean that. I'd never wish my family away. But until you're a mother, you don't know what it is to worry. I know you have problems with men, Joy, but men are easy, men you can deal with. Wait until you have children.'

Normally, in the theatre, Joy enjoyed dramatic irony as much as the next person. Here, in her cousin's kitchen, it lacerated her like a knife. Deborah's children were the least of her worries. It wasn't Josh's lack of appetite that

172

should be worrying her, but the fact that Howard's was all too gross. Deborah, arch-manipulator of men, was being outmanoeuvred.

Joy could hardly contain her rage at Howard and her pity for Deborah. Yet she knew, being addicted to problem pages in magazines, that one must never interfere between husband and wife. What the agony aunts didn't tell you was how to find the strength to say nothing and watch your cousin being abused. Whatever happened, she would stand by Deborah and the children.

'Howard's going to get the children ready for bed now,' Deborah said. 'I'll make coffee, and we can all have a chat.'

'No!' Joy said. 'I mean, I promised Michael I'd be home early. I did.'

'Ring him. Tell him you're staying longer.'

'No, I can't do that. Not tonight. Not if I'm going out with you on Sunday. I really had better go.'

Deborah saw the justice of that and, having secured permission for a retreat, Joy began her farewells. The relief she felt at escaping from the hotbed of passions that was her cousins' house was tempered by trepidation at having to spend the rest of the evening with Michael. At least, she thought, she'd had the wisdom to suggest a video. That would keep him quiet.

At the front door she hugged Deborah closely and hoped her cousin didn't pick up on the intense sympathy in the embrace. Poor, poor Deborah! Joy resolved to worry about her all weekend. Because worrying about *other* people didn't count.

As Joy drew to a halt outside her own house, she could see a thin line of light shining through where the curtains didn't quite meet up. Michael was waiting for her. She would have to endure the evening. Casting aside thoughts of Deborah, to be resumed as soon as possible, she unlocked her front door and entered the hall. She took off her coat and hung it on the banister. She placed her handbag at the foot of the stairs so she wouldn't forget to take it up to bed with her. Gingerly she pushed the door to the lounge open. Michael was slumped in the armchair with a can of Boddington's by his side. For a moment Joy prayed that he had fallen asleep. It was possible. But as he heard her movements he turned his head and smiled at her, without moving his body.

'Hi,' Joy said.

'You're back,' said Michael. 'D'you want a drink?'

Joy thought that wasn't such a bad idea.

'I bought you some wine from the off-licence,' Michael announced. 'It's in the fridge. I'll set the video up.'

Joy made her way to the kitchen and opened the fridge. There was a bottle of Liebfraumilch. Better than nothing, she thought, and proceeded to open it. She wondered what tape Michael had hired. She hoped it was something with Kevin Costner in. Taking her glass of wine, she re-entered the lounge, where Michael was bent over by the video, his sweatshirt riding up to expose the cleavage of his bottom.

'You'll like this,' Michael said. 'I've seen it once already.'

'What is it?' Joy asked, settling back on the settee.

Michael returned to his armchair. '*The Lovers' Guide*,' he said. 'No, don't look like that. You said you wanted something educational! I thought it would help us to . . .'

She saw Michael searching for the right word. A four-letter one might do, she thought.

'. . . communicate better,' he ended. 'It was you who said we were having problems. Anyway, it's a laugh. I've seen it once – it's a laugh. Go on, watch it!'

Joy hesitated. It was the last thing she wanted to watch, but Michael did seem so very keen. She had to admit she was curious too.

'Shall I put it straight in?' Michael asked. Joy realized he meant the video.

'OK.' She watched Michael open a packet of Cajun Chicken Hot and Spicy crisps and insert his hand in the packet.

In fact, as the tape began to roll, Joy decided that it might not be too embarrassing after all. The doctor who sat on the table and addressed the viewers was a jolly and reassuring sort of chap, rather like the head of science at college. He had the same persuasive, comforting manner. Joy thought she might even learn something. As Michael had said, it was educational.

The tape cut away to a section entitled 'Sex and Communication'. Michael held the remote control in front of him like a magic wand.

'We'll fast-forward this,' he said.

He stopped when a title came up reading 'Foreplay'. Joy watched a man and a woman kissing, and the jaunty voice-over of the doctor recommended the activity as if it were a particularly effective brand of washing-powder. Suddenly the scene cut away to a man lying naked on a bed. Joy's attention was unwillingly drawn to the erect penis that wobbled uncertainly between his legs.

'You roll the penis like dough between your hands,' the jolly doctor instructed the woman discovered by the camera entering the bedroom. Joy wondered who she was in real life. A soft-porn star? A housewife short on the readies? Now it was the woman's turn. She lay on the bed while the doctor's voice guided the man's hands below her stomach, and she began to squirm with pleasure. Joy squirmed with embarrassment. She sneaked a look at Michael. He was watching it all unsmilingly, his eyes fixed on the screen, his fingers probing the bottom of the packet of crisps.

The next scene was in a smart fitted kitchen. Joy felt quite envious. She wondered how much something like that would cost to have installed. Next, a couple was having a quickie on the work surface. Then, a man and a woman doing the same thing on a beach, with the doctor warning about the way sand transfers itself. Joy watched a woman tie her lover's hands to the bedpost as he simpered pathetically at her. She heard a myriad of voices describe in a variety of local accents what turned them on in bed. Joy felt as if she were leafing through a shopping catalogue of bodies in various poses. Everything that was happening on the screen seemed increasingly remote to her. Yet the video was educational, as Michael had promised. She had learned one thing. Michael had rented the tape to try to heal her ailing libido; he had wasted his time because the illness was terminal.

The tape, having climaxed, wound slowly down through shots of sunsets and bluesy rock 'n' roll. It was over. Joy had kept her promise and hoped to go to bed now. It had been an exhausting evening.

'What d'you think?' Michael asked her huskily.

'Too many characters, not enough plot,' Joy remarked lightly.

Michael chuckled. 'What bit do you want to try?'

Joy was horrified. The tape, she now saw, was the theory. The practical was to follow.

'I thought it would give you some ideas,' Michael said, leaving his armchair and approaching Joy. 'You see, I've been talking more, and now it's your turn to –'

Michael broke off to nuzzle Joy's neck with his wet mouth. The stubble on his chin grazed her.

'Relax,' he said to her. 'You heard what they said.'

'Not now,' Joy panted. 'I'm not in the mood.'

'Let me put you in the mood,' he said, his hands straying down her stomach.

Joy knew she had to put a stop to this. She wriggled away from him.

'Deborah and the kids are fine,' she said. 'They've asked me to go ice-skating with them next Sunday. Debbie made a lovely apple strudel. She does her own filo pastry. It takes ages. You roll –'

The penis in your hands like dough. The doctor's voice taunted Joy. As she was talking, Michael was undressing. Sweatshirt, jeans, boxer shorts, all were discarded on the lounge carpet.

'Skating?' Michael echoed. 'Right. I'm coming with you. I used to skate and I'm good at it.'

'No!'

'Yes. We must do more things together. We'll start now.' Michael was fully naked, and panting.

'Excuse me,' Joy said. 'I need the bathroom.'

She sprang up from the settee and left the lounge, stepping over her handbag and taking the stairs two at a time. She was possessed by the knowledge that she could not make love with Michael, not now, not ever again, and that it was her cowardice that had got her in this position.

She stood on the landing, undecided where to take refuge.

'Joy!' she heard Michael call from below. 'Joy! What are you doing up there?'

She listened, breathless, as he left the lounge and made for the stairs.

'Joy? Christ! What the hell?' This was accompanied by a series of thumps and a yell from Michael which Joy guessed would wake up all the neighbours. Curious, she peered over the banister. Michael was sitting at the bottom of the stairs clutching his foot. He was entirely naked.

'What's happened?' Joy asked from her vantage point.

'I've tripped over your fucking handbag.'

'Have you hurt yourself?' Joy asked unnecessarily.

'My bloody toe,' he moaned, rocking in agony.

Joy ventured down the stairs. Michael was still clasping his foot, and she noticed that his erection had dwindled to nothing.

'What happened?' she asked again.

'I caught my toe in your bloody handbag strap,' he said. Joy watched as he removed his hand from his foot, and she could see that already his little toe was red and inflamed.

'What do you think you've done to it?'

Michael clutched his toe again and grimaced as pain coursed through him.

'Have you broken it?' Joy enquired. She experienced a curious mixture of elation and guilt.

'Broken it?' The idea seemed to appeal to him. 'Yeah, I reckon it's broken. Must be. You know what this'll mean. I'll have to be off school for a while.' Did Joy imagine it, or was he cheering up? 'Probably till half-term. Oh, Jesus!' he groaned, but with some equanimity.

'Are you cold sitting there?' Joy asked. 'Shall I get you your dressing-gown?'

Michael nodded his assent. Joy returned upstairs and went to the bedroom. Unkindly, she paused, and sat on the edge of the bed taking a moment or two for herself before she descended to attend to the pain-wracked, shivering Michael. She blessed her handbag and whichever deity had prompted her to place it just where she did. Diana, goddess of chastity? Then she was struck by a new thought. If his toe was broken, and he had to move around on crutches and couldn't even get to school, how could she possibly finish with him? It would be unthinkably cruel. She would be reviled by all who knew her. Did she place her handbag at the foot of the stairs because she secretly wanted Michael to stay? Or did she want him dead? Whichever, she was well and truly stuck with him now. Michael, the abominable toe-man.

Joy picked up his musty-smelling maroon dressing-gown from where it had slid off his chair. Its anaesthetic fumes almost suffocated her as she made her way downstairs.

CHAPTER ELEVEN

Joy was annoyed with herself for having told the English department about Michael's toe. They were full of sympathy for him. Every morning Betty, Peter and the others made solicitous enquiries. *Is it any better? What did the doctor say?* Joy reflected that they did not have to live with Michael's Academy Award-winning performance of *A Man in Pain*. She, as supporting actress, spent her evenings scurrying around, bringing him drinks, food, newspapers, finding the remote control, while he sighed, groaned and gave her a running commentary on the twinges he experienced, or the agony it caused him to place any pressure on the toe.

It was morning break now, and the department, congregated in the English office, would be caught up in the minutiae of life at St Ignatius'. As Joy approached the English office, she could see that Betty and Peter were already there, and Bruce O'Connor was with them. Entering the small room and checking the kettle to see if it was still hot, she tried to tune in to their conversation.

'Just below her right shoulder-blade,' Bruce said. 'A black rose. Encased in what looks like barbed wire.'

'I'll have a word with her,' Peter said.

'I'd be grateful,' Bruce continued. 'I concede it's a difficult one. Officially students can dress how they please, but there's the college ethos to remember, and Sister and I feel a tattoo isn't really appropriate.'

'I'll pass that on,' Peter repeated.

'Otherwise, next thing we know, we'll be in for an

epidemic of body piercing – rings through the eyebrows, the tongues – anything goes these days. Perverted, that's what I call it.'

'Come on now, Bruce.' Betty's tone was admonitory. 'The girl's probably only stuck the tattoo on. It's a moment's work to get it off again.'

Joy wondered, first, how Betty had come to know about removable tattoos, and second, which student was under discussion.

'As I said, Bruce, I'll have a word with Lucy Marshall,' Peter remarked again. 'The tattoo contravenes the dress code.'

'And you'll also speak to her about the missing work for Jane Thomson, won't you? Jane says she's not at all serious about her music A-level. Let me know if there are any difficulties.'

Bruce prepared to leave. Joy stopped him.

'Is Lucy in trouble?'

'Not exactly, but she's one to watch. She's been flashing this tattoo at all the male staff and won't hand in work.'

'But she's completed everything on time for me,' Joy insisted, 'and it's been bloody good.' There, that's telling him, she thought.

'Me too,' said Peter. Lucy was in the A-level group they both shared, and she was in Peter's tutor group too. Joy found herself wishing that she had pastoral repons-ibility for Lucy. Perhaps Peter would feel uncomfortable speaking to Lucy about her tattoo. Ought she to offer to speak to her?

'Look, I know Lucy,' Joy announced. 'I've spoken to her a couple of times after lessons. If you prefer, Peter, I'll have a word with her about the tattoo. It might be better coming from a woman.'

'That's OK with me,' Peter said, quite cool. Not for the first time, Joy found herself wondering what he was thinking. Peter had always been a closed book to her.

'Whichever of you speaks to her is fine by me,' Bruce conceded. 'Just mention the missing music too. Point out to her it's not worth the trouble, that sort of thing. Must be off. If you come with me now, Betty, I'll show you the correspondence we've had from the board.'

Betty rose, and she and Bruce left the English office. Joy found herself alone with Peter, both of them just starting on their coffee. Not normally one to be tongue-tied, Joy always found herself uncharacteristically awkward with Peter. He was naturally quiet and reserved; as a result Joy felt compelled to fill up all the silences, but had difficulty in thinking of anything to say.

'You don't mind me speaking to Lucy, do you?' she began.

'No, that's fine.'

'Perhaps I shouldn't have butted in. It's just that I rather like her. She's such a change from the other kids – it's not just that she's brighter, which she is, but she doesn't mind speaking up for herself, and she's so open, don't you find?'

Damn! That was definitely the wrong thing for her to say. Peter would think she was covertly insulting him, he who was anything but open.

'I do hope her openness doesn't get her into trouble,' Joy continued. 'It can be a danger, especially in a young girl.' Peter didn't seem to react. Joy took a deep breath. 'Do you know, she can recite chunks of *The Ballad of Reading Gaol* and she's thinking of setting it to music.'

'Interesting,' Peter said.

Lucy seemed to be the wrong subject. What wasn't?

Joy knew that Peter was very keen on football and had a season ticket for United, but she knew little about the game and preferred to avoid it. She reflected how little she knew about Peter. He lived alone, or at least he never mentioned anyone living with him, although he saw a lot of his mother – a widow, like hers. He belonged to some health-club in town and was thinking of taking up Thai boxing. The students said they saw him with a very attractive woman once, in a Manchester club, but he'd never mentioned her at work. What characterized him most was his love of privacy. That was what made him so difficult to talk to. Joy tensed in the silence that seemed to enfold them. Then she had an idea. They could talk about Betty. They both liked Betty.

'Betty seems a lot happier since she's handed in her notice, don't you think? More relaxed, even though she still has a year to go. I think the idea of living in the Lake District and selling books is just wonderful, absolutely right for her. Ha! The Lake District! Just three weeks to go. Are you all prepared?'

Peter nodded his assent.

'I'm not. I'm not sure what to take with me. The last time I did anything sporty was at school and even then I spent more time in the last couple of years getting out of games than doing them.'

Damn, damn, damn! She'd done it again. Peter would wonder why she'd volunteered to take Maisie's place if she hated sport. She had to cover for herself.

'So I'm desperately unfit and I thought the adventure weekend would do me good. And I'm going ice-skating on Sunday. With my cousins and their two children. Howard has a fashion business in town, but Deborah doesn't work.'

Joy knew why she was wittering on so inconsequentially. There *was* a reason why the silences between herself and Peter were so painful. Yet Joy was not going to mention her ambition to be head of department to Peter, and she guessed Peter would not refer to his ambition either. She was wrong. After another pause Peter gazed out of the window and remarked, 'Are you applying for head of department?'

Joy was caught unawares, but recovered herself. 'Are you?' It was a tense moment.

'I haven't decided yet,' Peter said. 'Have you seen the notice in the staff room?' Joy hadn't. She listened intently. 'Sister's asking for internal applications, but somehow I don't think the interview will be just a cosy chat. Rumour has it she'll have a governor or two in with her. I expect they'll want details of budgeting, how we can increase revenue by attracting more students, that sort of thing.'

'An English department isn't a business!' Joy exclaimed, appalled.

'It is these days,' Peter continued. 'Education's all about money now. It's the way things are going. You've got to be on the ball. Total Quality Management. Value-added Results. Investing in People. That's what you've got to know about.'

Peter's tone was one of deliberate neutrality, and Joy couldn't make out whether he agreed with these developments or shared her dislike of the dehumanization of education. Or, worse still, was he parading his knowledge of business jargon to make her feel inadequate? She immediately dismissed the thought as unworthy of her. It was one thing to go all out for a job; another to make enemies of your rivals. At all costs she would stop herself thinking unkind thoughts about Peter. She reminded herself he had not yet said if he was applying. Macbeth was ambitious, she told herself, and look what happened to him. But Peter Worthington was a step on which I must fall down, or else o'er-leap. Then Joy thought of Michael's toe and smiled. Suddenly Peter spoke.

'You ought to apply,' he said.

Joy swiftly returned the compliment. 'So should you.'

'It's an idea,' Peter mused. 'Just for the experience of the interview, if nothing else.'

'So will you apply?' Joy felt she had to know.

'Would you mind if I did?'

'No, no, of course not!' Joy hoped Peter didn't think she was protesting too much.

Peter grinned in a friendly way, and Joy momentarily melted. He hadn't smiled at her quite like that before, and it embarrassed her, as they were alone in the English office. It occurred to her that as good-looking as Peter was – and he was good-looking, very – she had never actually asked herself whether she fancied him. She did now. No, she didn't fancy him. He was too young, for one thing. And his looks were just too perfect, too carefully presented for her taste. Just as well, really. Fancying Peter was a complication she could do without.

The bell rang, and at that signal both Peter and Joy began to collect their books for the next session. Remembering she was teaching out of the English block, Joy began to hurry and, bidding farewell to Peter, she stepped lightly down the stairs and hastened along the main corridor. She saw Lesley coming towards her and they exchanged a greeting.

'All right?' Joy asked her. They stopped outside the

canteen, which was empty now, the only noise being the clatter of pans from the distant recesses of the kitchens.

'Fine,' Lesley said. 'And how's Michael's –'

'Stop it!' Joy declared. 'This is a toe-free zone.'

Lesley smiled. 'One good thing is that he won't be able to go ice-skating with you. Remember, just say the word, and my house is at your command.'

Joy thought that Lesley sounded like the wrong sort of fairy godmother. Since watching that video, she reflected, the idea of sex with anyone seemed faintly ridiculous. All week Joy had been relishing the aura of chastity that emanated from the high ceilings of the main corridor and the devotional pictures on the pale-green walls of St Ignatius'. Then she recalled what else she wanted to tell Lesley.

'Peter *is* thinking of applying for head of department!'

'Is he?' Lesley said carelessly.

'For the experience, he says.'

'Fair enough,' she commented.

Joy felt cheated. Lesley was being the fair-minded vice-principal, just when she wanted her to be her best friend, rooting for her against all comers. Why couldn't she be totally unprofessional for once? But Lesley exercised complete control over herself and her reactions. Joy envied her. Imagine being able not to allow one idea in your head that shouldn't be there. How on earth did anybody manage to do that?

'Good morning, Joy,' came a familiar voice, with its Irish lilt. It was Sister Maureen. Joy turned and smiled.

'I hear your boyfriend's injured his foot,' she remarked with concern. 'I do hope he's not in too much pain.'

Joy wished she had the *chutzpah* to inform her that

Michael was the pain, rather than his foot, but let the moment pass.

'And Bruce tells me you're going to have a few words with Lucy Marshall. I'm pleased about that.' Joy sensed that was a cryptic remark and wondered what lay behind it.

'And I'm expecting your application,' she said, wagging her finger at Joy.

Joy was thrilled. That was tantamount to positive encouragement. Toes aside, life was looking up.

'I'm working on my worrying, Sister,' Joy enthused. 'That's why I'm going on the adventure weekend, and I've applied for a place on a Fear of Flying course!'

'I know,' Sister said. Joy looked at Lesley; but her expression was absolutely inscrutable.

'Good, good,' Sister said and, glancing up at a portrait of the Madonna and Child that hung above their heads, she made her way back to her study.

Joy had spent most of her day on Lucy's trail, but had finally succeeded in tracking her down at the Drama Studio and arranged to see her at the end of the day in E1. Joy was there now, nursing a cup of coffee, her ears alert for the sound of footsteps that would herald Lucy's arrival. It intrigued her that Lucy was sporting a tattoo. Had she really gone to a tattoo parlour to have it done? Or was it, as Betty had suggested, simply a removable one? Without fully knowing why, Joy hoped it was for real.

Joy heard the clunk of army boots ascending the stairs and braced herself for Lucy's appearance. Today she was wearing a short black pinafore dress evidently from a second-hand shop, a combat jacket with sewn-on patches, and her hair was now icy platinum-blonde. Yet her wide smile lacked any trace of self-consciousness or sophistication.

'Come in, Lucy,' Joy said. 'Would you like a coffee?'

'Yeah, all right.'

'I'll make you one. There's a kettle in the English office.'

'Hey, cool!'

Joy left Lucy for a moment and enjoyed the sensation of contravening one of St Ignatius' unwritten rules – that there should be a decorous distance kept between the teachers and the taught. It had often occurred to Joy that despite the officially chummy relationship between staff and students in college, students were never supposed to share staff facilities or address their teachers by their first names. It was as if they were natives in some colonized country and the staff were the white supremacists, with the staff room as a sort of whites-only club. Instinctively Joy felt that her discussion with Lucy about the tattoo might be more fruitful if it took place in an adult atmosphere.

She brought the coffee back into the classroom. Lucy was sitting on a table, looking out over the roofs of the town and the yard of Hartfield's Garage, full of dismembered cars and overalled mechanics.

'I know why you want to see me, Miss Freeman,' Lucy remarked, sipping at her coffee. 'It's my tattoo, isn't it?'

'You guessed,' said Joy.

'Yeah, well, it wasn't difficult. Every lesson I've been in today, it's like, all the teachers staring at my shoulder and looking away and, like, checking it's still there.' Lucy laughed. Evidently that was the effect it was meant to have.

'I haven't seen it,' Joy reminded her.

Lucy slipped off her combat jacket and, adjusting the strap on her dress, revealed a black rose on the curve of her freckled shoulder.

'It hurt like hell,' she said, 'but it was worth it.'

'You mean it's real?'

'Yeah! I had it done because I'm in a band, you know, now. Me and some other girls. Like a kind of post-feminist band. We're called Pussy Galore.'

'You mustn't call yourselves that!' Joy tried to disguise the fact that she was taken aback.

'Why? Has someone already used that name?'

Joy chose her words carefully. 'Uh, don't you think it's inviting sexist comment?'

'Yeah, it's meant to. Y'see, it's ironic. Like you said in the lesson. Saying stuff that you don't mean. Writers do it. Writers do it with irony!'

Joy tried not to laugh, and to bring Lucy back to the subject under discussion.

'Is the tattoo ironic?' she asked.

'No. It's sexy. Don't you think?'

'Perhaps that's why it's not quite right for college,' Joy suggested mildly. 'Mr Worthington and I –'

'Does he like it?' Lucy interjected.

'He thinks the same as I do,' Joy cut in. 'That you ought not to exhibit it.'

'I saw him looking at it in class today,' Lucy said, a hint of devilry in her voice.

Joy began to feel a little uncomfortable, and became more stern.

'Which proves my point. It's distracting. Therefore not suitable for a work environment. You'll have to keep it covered up.'

'Do you like it, Miss Freeman?' Lucy asked, a note of appeal in her voice.

Yes, thought Joy. I do like it, and I wish I had one too. Except I'd never have the courage because one, it hurts; two, people might pass comment; three, you might catch something from dirty needles. The last thought struck Joy forcibly.

'Were the needles clean?' she asked Lucy.

'Oh yeah, I know the bloke who did it.'

'Well, I suppose no harm's done.' Joy realized her last comment was decidedly uncharitable. Worse than uncharitable; she sounded exactly like the sort of mean, repressed, sixty-something woman who'd taught her when she was at school, the sort she vowed she'd never become. Where was all her prudery leading her?

'Actually, Lucy, I do rather like it. It's different. Just as long as you don't go and have HATE stencilled on your knuckles.' There, that was better.

Lucy grinned. 'I knew you'd understand.' She loved Miss Freeman. She was dead friendly and made you laugh in lessons. And you could talk to her. And she didn't let you down. In this gush of enthusiasm for her teacher, Lucy decided to make a concession.

'I will cover it up, then. I see what you mean.'

Joy grinned conspiratorially at her. 'And while you're in this reasonable mood, I have to tell you I've been commissioned to mention the slight matter of the missing music work.'

Lucy's face fell, then almost immediately she recovered her composure. 'I lent the books.'

'No, you didn't,' Joy said, smelling an untruth.

Lucy crossed, then uncrossed her ankles. 'Well, it's boring.'

'Makes no difference. You've still got to do it.'

'Why?'

'Because you're doing Music A-level and if you don't work, you're wasting your time. And you won't get into a decent higher education course.'

'But I don't want to. I want to have a band like Courtney Love's.'

'Then Music A-level is going to be the most relevant thing you do.'

'Oh, boll – sorry. A-level is all dead music and counterpoint and, anyway, when they interview me for *Melody Maker* they're not going to say, have you got music A-level? No? Oh, sorry, go home then. Are they?'

'No, but it's something to fall back on.'

'So I've got to spend all my time doing stuff I don't like in case something bad happens?'

'Well, yes.'

Lucy laughed. 'What a silly way to live!' She checked out Miss Freeman. She looked uncomfortable. Lucy immediately felt contrite. She had this habit, she knew, of disappointing people. But she didn't want to disappoint Miss Freeman, no way.

'I'm sorry,' she said, her eyes lowered. 'I was being cheeky. I know I should do the music. I'll catch up, honest.'

'Good,' said Joy, still feeling rather thrown.

'I'm a handful, aren't I?' Lucy remarked, half proud, half not.

'Makes life more interesting.'

Joy felt the need to cover the growing liking she was feeling for this girl. She hardly knew why. If Lucy had been older, like Lesley or Deborah (poor Deborah!), she would have named the feeling admiration. Since she was younger, it had to be something different. Envy?

They finished their coffees companionably, and Lucy explained that it was her turn to make tea tonight, and she'd better be off. As Joy went back into the English office to wash the mugs, Lucy stood outside, chatting about this and that, apparently reluctant to go. Not as much as I am, thought Joy. She visualized Michael at home, his foot balanced on the pouffe, the whinging, the demands. Cut! she instructed herself. She listened instead to Lucy's account of her band's practice last night as she threw some essays and texts into her briefcase. Together they left the English block, with Lucy still chatting by Joy's side.

Automatically Joy looked up at the garish painting of the Madonna and Child above the picture rail. Ha! That was the feeling she had for Lucy. Not admiration, no. Nor envy. For the first time her maternal impulses had been roused. She was Lucy's mother-substitute! It's obvious, she told herself. Just think. A sixteen-year-old girl, no mother at home – a father was not the same thing at all – clearly her desire to spend time with her English teacher was a cry for attention. Joy felt moved and flattered. She wanted desperately to live up to this new role. She felt quite proud as they walked into the entrance lobby, and hoped the secretaries would notice the two of them.

Then Lucy stopped by a large black box, flung her rucksack down on the floor, embraced the box with both arms and tried unsuccessfully to lift it.

'Shit!'

'Lucy!' Joy admonished her. 'What are you trying to do?'

'It's the amp for our practice tonight. Liam brought it

for us to lend but he had a car and I thought I could get it home on the bus. But it's too heavy. Shit!'

'I'll give you a lift,' Joy volunteered. 'You live in Radcliffe, don't you? It's on my way.'

'That's brill,' Lucy said. Joy thought she saw the heads of the secretaries, watching as she and Lucy lifted the amplifier and carried it out like two criminals heisting a safe. Joy had to admit she was enjoying herself.

The amp lay on the back seat of the car, and Lucy strapped herself in as if she was perfectly accustomed to travelling in Joy's car. She asked if Joy minded her having a ciggie.

'It's all right,' Joy said, surprised at herself. Normally she didn't like people smoking in her car because of the dangers of passive smoking. She turned out of college on to the main road, where a steady flow of traffic was heading into Manchester.

'It should be easy to get gigs,' Lucy explained. 'Once we've got the hang of the guitars a bit better. But we don't have to be brilliant or anything. That's the whole point really. Like, men's rhythm is different to women's rhythm. It's, like, we have a different time thing. Like, we come in when we're ready. With blokes, it's like, bang, bang, bang, know what I mean?'

Joy thought she did.

'You know, like the Raincoats. They were ace. We go to gigs in town sometimes and go backstage afterwards cos Kelly knows some of the lads. You get mixed up with the groupies. It's a laugh.'

'Be careful, Lucy,' Joy couldn't help herself saying. Lucy was only sixteen.

'Oh, *we* don't do anything. Except we might go on to a club. Last Saturday it was brill. Me and Kelly and these two lads were clubbing, and we got pissed off with it all, all those posers and stuff, and they said, come down the canal, and we'd had a few drinks, and so we thought we'd go. Right, well, there's this thing like a lock going across the canal, and this lad said, he bet I couldn't walk across it with my eyes shut. So I said, all right, and I began to walk, and they began calling out, no, to the right, and stuff like that, and I got all mixed up.' Lucy laughed at the memory.

Joy imagined herself in Lucy's position. It sounded terrifying.

'But you were all right?' Joy asked.

'Oh no! I lost my footing and fell in. Jesus Christ, it was freezing! I swam to the side and Ricky lifted me out. I was sopping wet. So I took my dress off and Phil gave me his jacket, but when we got into this taxi the back seat was soaked through by the time I left. It was good down by the canal. It was all dead black and spooky. So when I got home I didn't go to bed but I sat down and wrote this song about a girl who tried to kill herself by jumping into the canal.'

Joy knew she was not concentrating on her driving. Did Lucy have a death-wish? Was that the reason behind the tattoo, the missing music, the leap into the canal? She was just the sort of girl who'd take drugs, too. Did she know that one Ecstasy tablet could kill you? Did she know about the dangers of dehydration? Was it Joy's role to tell her?

'Right,' Lucy said suddenly. 'Just after the church. Then the second on the left – yeah – here – now it's that house on the left, opposite the white car.'

Joy drew to a halt outside a reasonably well-maintained terraced house. Someone had paved over the small front garden, although weeds were showing through the cracks. Lucy freed herself from the restraint of the seat-belt and opened the door. Joy followed her, and together they hefted the amplifier into the yard and stood it upright against the front door while Lucy hunted for her keys in the rucksack. Eventually she extracted a large purple purse with a daisy painted on the front and opened it, taking out a key. Joy deduced that her father wasn't in yet. A sleek black cat arrived at their feet and insinuated himself around Lucy's ankles.

'That's Trotsky,' Lucy explained.

The door opened, and the cat shot in and vanished. Joy helped Lucy to shunt the amp into the short hall, and then she prepared to depart.

'Stay and have a coffee,' said Lucy.

'I've just had one,' Joy reminded her. She wished she hadn't. She would have rather liked to have stayed and seen the interior of Lucy's house.

'Well, I want one. There's no one here except the cat, and I get lonely. Or is there anyone expecting you at home?'

One thought of Michael decided Joy. 'I'll stay for a short time,' she conceded.

Lucy led her into the one downstairs room, a square sitting room with a brick-built fireplace, an armchair, one green sofa that had seen better days, and papers and magazines scattered around the frayed Indian carpet. The kitchen was beyond the sitting room. It was small and messy, with a saucepan on the stove, and the breakfast things were still not washed up. Joy moved some newspapers from the sofa, eased herself down and felt the ancient springs creak beneath her. Lucy busied herself in the kitchen with the coffee.

'I like coffee,' she shouted to Joy. 'It gives me a buzz. Like speed.'

Joy flinched. Perhaps she was taking drugs. Ought she to say something? It was difficult being a substitute mother.

Lucy returned, her coffee in a mug that Joy recognized from a petrol-company promotion some years ago. She sat on the floor opposite Joy and grinned with pleasure.

'I've never been friends with a teacher before,' she said.

'We are human,' Joy said.

'Well, *you* are. I don't know about the others. The teachers at my old school were really tight. They didn't like me, but then, I was always, like, cheeking them. Once I –'

Lucy stopped. Both Lucy and Joy could hear the sounds of the front door being opened.

'That's Dad,' Lucy remarked.

In a few moments Lucy's dad appeared, a man in a brown corduroy jacket, with a bulging briefcase. He looked taken aback to see Joy.

'Hi, Dad,' Lucy said. 'You're early. This is Miss Freeman from St Ignatius'. She helped me bring the amp back.'

'Nice of you,' he said gruffly. He wore thick, black-rimmed spectacles which gave him a beatnik air, which wasn't diminished by his unkempt, grizzled beard. Joy watched him look through into the kitchen.

'Bloody hell, Luce. You haven't washed up!'

'Your turn,' she said sweetly. 'It's Wednesday. Men!' she said, addressing herself to Joy.

'I don't know how you put up with her cheek!' Lucy's dad addressed himself to Joy, but he didn't sound particularly angry. 'Go on,' he said to Lucy, 'get your old dad some coffee.'

Meanwhile he took his position on the armchair opposite Joy, and his eyes followed Lucy to the kitchen.

'There's no problem, is there? You've not come here to kick her out?'

'Far from it!' Joy declared. 'She's a very talented girl. She's going to do exceptionally well in English.'

'She's not thick, is she? I wanted her to do politics A-level. She's got the brain for it. But she's bloody apathetic, like all of them these days. I teach at the City University. Name's Dave. Dave Marshall. Do you find that? Kids not interested in what's going on around them any more?'

'Well, I –'

'Because they're not. Even Luce here, and God knows I've tried my hardest to get her involved. I've said to her, go and flog some copies of the *Socialist Worker*. Will she heck as like.'

Lucy returned with another mug of coffee. 'You're dead right I won't,' she said, appealing to Joy as if to some sort of jury. 'I've got better things to do. And he's a fine one to talk. Look at him! He sits there blaming me for doing nothing but all he ever does is talk, talk, talk. Analyses why the Labour party got derailed in the seventies, explains why Blair's not a true socialist – well, what good does that do?'

'It's not meant to do any bloody good,' he told her. 'It's up to you now, the next generation. But, like I said, you're apathetic. And you know whose fault that is? Bloody Thatcher's! She made greed respectable, that's what it was. She made selfishness respectable. So kids like Luce aren't interested in what's around them, only in them-selves. It's bad news. Y'see, once the oil runs out, then it'll hit all these kids – no more affluent Western lifestyle for them. You mark my words. There'll be a scramble for the available riches, and all these apathetic non-politicized kids won't know how to fight back. So we'll end up with a Haitian-style economy with a ridiculous wealth gap, and yob culture. Give it twenty or thirty years, at the most. Unless there's a nuclear accident first. Might not even make the millennium.'

Joy shivered. No wonder Lucy had a death-wish if this was what she had to put up with every night. Yet she seemed quite unaffected, sitting on the floor playing with the cat, who had just come into the room. Joy wasn't unaffected. Dave Marshall was talking about the end of the civilized world as we know it. Little tremblings of fear assailed her.

'My dad's talking out of his backside!' announced Lucy. Joy glanced at Dave, who seemed cheered by this obscenity. 'He's only peeved because they never made him prime minister. If he really believed all the stuff he came out with, he'd top himself!'

Dave Marshall sipped serenely at his coffee. How could someone seem so composed while predicting the breakdown of society? Surely one ought to be terrified? Joy was. Permanently. She tried not to think about the future too much. It was all the uncertainty. She was only really comfortable when she thought she knew what was going to happen next. For the first time she realized that was why she always read the ends of novels first – just to check there was going to be a happy ending.

'Anyway,' Lucy persisted. '*He* doesn't know what's going to happen in the future. No one knows what's going to happen in the future. Anyway, there's no such thing as the future. Or the past, not when you think about it. There's only now. Which I mean to enjoy.'

'Listen to her!' Dave Marshall demanded. 'No sense of responsibility. No backbone. These are the kids who've had it too easy. They've never had to struggle, not like us. At her age I was out working, and having to go to night school. She arses around all day having A-levels handed to her on a plate.' Joy could tell by the complacent looks of both father and daughter that this sort of heckling was their bread and butter. But Dave had cast aspersions on St Ignatius', and Joy felt honour bound to defend it.

'We hardly hand them A-levels on a plate. I wish it was that easy. And we have our own ways of toughening them up. There's our outward-bound course in Keswick in three weeks, for example.'

'Are you going on that, Luce?'

'It's too late. You had to bring back the form last week.'

'This outward-bound course –' Dave addressed himself to Joy. 'This course. What is it? Abseiling? Canoeing? Rock climbing? Assault courses?'

'That's right,' Joy assented.

'Sounds just the thing. You ought to be on that, Luce.'

'It's not really me,' she said to the cat.

'Go on, Luce. I'll fork out for it. I'd like to see you abseiling.'

'Oh Dad, give over!'

'Scared, are you? Frightened of getting your feet wet?'

'Oh, it's not that!'

Joy sensed a defensiveness in Lucy's voice and decided to support her. 'It's all right to be scared. I'm going and I'm petrified!'

Both Dave and Lucy stopped to look at her. Embarrassed, Joy pressed on. 'But, look, if you do decide to go,

Lucy, I'm sure it's not too late. I'll have a word with Mr Worthington and see if we can fit you in.'

'I thought it was up to Mr Nelson?' Lucy enquired.

'No. He has a bad knee. Mr Worthington's taking the expedition.'

'Oh good. Yeah, well, you can ask him if you like. Are you satisfied?' she said to Dave.

He chortled in merriment.

Joy was alarmed. She saw that flash of interest when she mentioned Peter Worthington. Surely Lucy didn't ... Just because she, Joy, didn't fancy him didn't mean ... In fact, there were only twelve years between Lucy and Peter. Was the tattoo meant for Peter? Was that why she was trying so hard at her A-level English?

For the first time Joy was glad she was going to Keswick. Lucy definitely needed watching. Her father was gaily sending her on an adventure holiday, blissfully unaware of what kind of adventure holiday it might prove to be. It's lucky, thought Joy, that I've given up worrying on my own account. Other people keep you pretty busy!

CHAPTER TWELVE

'Are you nervous?' asked Deborah, as she and Joy approached the ice-rink.

'About what?' Joy asked, very coolly. Did she mean the skating, meeting Lawrence again, or living with the knowledge that Howard was cheating on her cousin?

'The skating,' Deborah said cheerfully.

'That,' Joy said, 'is the least of my worries.'

In fact the closer she got to the ice-rink, the less apprehensive she felt about taking to the ice. Hundreds of people went skating every day, and few of them were involved in fatal accidents. True, she might fall over, but if she fell over very, very carefully, she might not hurt herself too much. At present she was more concerned about her appearance. Deborah had warned her it would be cold on the rink, and so Joy had hunted through the downstairs cupboard trying to find an attractive yet practical outer garment. All she had was an ankle-length black coat that smelt of mothballs and a number of jackets she used for work. She had been reduced to pilfering Michael's bright-blue nylon anorak. There was a contrast, to say the least, between her and Deborah, who wore an elegant fur-trimmed winter coat. Behind them strolled Howard with the children.

'There's Lawrence!' cried Deborah.

Joy could see him now, standing on the steps by the entrance to the ice-rink. Once again she was struck by his resemblance to a picture of Moses she remembered from her childhood illustrated Old Testament. Moses in tidy denims with a soft velour navy jacket. Ought she to mention the resemblance to him? Perhaps not. Although flattering in the spiritual sense, it was a bit of a passion-killer. Lawrence greeted them all warmly, and Deborah's bubbly enthusiasm smoothed any awkwardness. She shooed them all into the foyer, past groups of gawky adolescents and a party of small children.

Howard queued at the ticket booth, with Josh by his side.

'Do you like skating?' Lawrence enquired of Joy.

'I don't really know. I've never skated before.'

'Nor have I!'

'Well, that makes two of us!'

Joy cringed at the banality of the conversation. She flashed a glance at Deborah, who she hoped would help them out.

'It's ever so easy!' Deborah announced. 'Even the children can do it. Hayleigh's been to ever so many skating parties, and Josh is amazing on the ice. And don't be embarrassed if you take a tumble. All beginners do. To be honest,' Deborah confided, 'the children will be disappointed if you don't!'

Joy tried to smile. In front of them, Howard had moved away from the ticket kiosk and waved at them to join him. Joy walked towards the entrance to the rink and peered inside. A blast of cold air chilled her. Then she focused on the men, women and children wrapped in brightly coloured scarves and coats, gliding effortlessly in large circles on the ice. The rink was noisy with the shouts of the skaters and the throb of the music over the loudspeakers. Everyone seemed to be having fun and, really, skating looked very easy. Joy felt encouraged.

She entered, picked her way over the puddles on the floor and joined the queue at the skate-hire booth. Joy realized that doing something so outside of her routine was having a positive effect on her. It was almost possible to forget about her other concerns. Almost possible to forget about the knock on the door yesterday morning, opening it to a delivery man from Dixon's bringing a CD Megadrive, and Michael's whining insistence that he was bored, not being able to walk, and Joy could use it too, and so could the children when they had children, and when she got promoted they wouldn't notice the expense. Michael was one reason why Joy was all the more determined to enjoy herself today.

The skates were fiendishly difficult to lace. Joy was grateful when Deborah came over, after finishing with the children, and knelt by her feet, tugging each lace tightly over the hooks on either side.

'I need to speak to you,' Deborah whispered. Joy could hardly make out what she was saying because of the hubbub on the rink. 'We're bound to have a chance later. It's about –'

Lawrence materialized at their side, preventing any further disclosures. In some ways, Joy thought, it would be a relief to get it over with. Waiting for Deborah's marriage to collapse felt like living next door to a nuclear reactor.

'There we are!' said Deborah. 'Now try to stand.'

Joy did. To her delight she found it was perfectly possible to balance on the skates. The blades were narrow, but not too narrow. She enjoyed the sensation of being a couple of inches taller. As she made her way to the rink, she felt Lawrence's hand at her elbow, and she liked his gallantry. It was so unlike Michael.

Both Joy and Lawrence paused by the side of the ice-rink to watch the other skaters. Everyone seemed to be enjoying themselves, and skating looked to be a simple, natural activity. People swept past them gracefully like ballet dancers. Hayleigh slipped through the entrance in front of them and began to skate self-consciously near them, looking to see if her uncle and aunt were watching. Joy and Lawrence applauded her loudly, and she disappeared into the throng of skaters.

'Do you think we can do it?' Lawrence asked Joy. The question seemed profound.

'I think we should have a try,' Joy remarked.

'After you,' said Lawrence.

So this was it. Holding on to the rail, Joy placed her right foot on the ice. Yes, it did feel slippery. She kept a tight hold on the rail and, supporting all her weight on her arms, she brought her left foot over to join her right foot. She was standing on the ice and grinned in triumph at Lawrence. Following her movements, Lawrence manoeuvred himself to the rail on the other side of the entrance and stood there uncertainly.

'I'll see if I can move,' Joy mouthed to Lawrence.

Her hands gripped the rail hard, she lifted her right foot and placed it a little in front of her left foot. Success. Then she moved her left foot to meet it. It was like learning to walk all over again. She repeated the sequence of movements. Yes, it was actually possible to move on the ice. This struck Joy as being significant too. She looked behind her. Lawrence was still clasping the rail, a good few feet away.

Joy stopped to give him the chance to catch her up. He stepped out boldly, lurched into a terrifying slide, and saved himself by colliding with her. Joy held herself steady on the rail so she could take the impact of the collision.

So there he was, right up against her. The intimacy was shocking, but not unpleasant. He smelled nicely of aftershave and apologized, laughing. As he attempted to detach himself from Joy, there was an unexpected ripping, crunching sound. Joy wondered what on earth it could be. She looked down. The velcro of her anorak had attached itself to the velour of Lawrence's jacket. They had adhered together. Joy detached herself gently, not wanting to hurt Lawrence's jacket or his feelings.

'Look, it's easy!' she announced. 'You just sort of march. Watch me.' She set off along the ice, still clutching the rail, plodding heavily. In fact, it was fun. Also holding the rail, Lawrence followed her. Then they met an obstacle. An elderly man was holding on to the portion of the rail they were approaching. Joy wondered about the etiquette of the situation. If he was a beginner too, they should really walk around him. If he wasn't, he should move for them. But was he a beginner?

Then the gentleman, seeing Joy approach, moved out into the centre of the rink to allow her to continue her circuit. Joy gave him a smile of thanks and then watched with horror as he lost his footing and slid to the ice on his behind. My fault, thought Joy, thinking she ought to assist him but not knowing how. Fortunately, the man seemed more amused than anything. The fall had certainly brought some colour to the veins on his cheeks, and his silvery-yellow hair seemed a little ruffled. Once on his feet he smoothed his hair down, wrapped his tartan scarf round his neck again, smiled at Joy and returned to the rail.

Just then Deborah, Howard and the children arrived,

and the children insisted Joy watch what they could do. Howard stood by her side and yawned.

'Tired?' she said to him.

'Not been sleeping much,' he said.

How brazen of him, Joy thought. At that moment Deborah glided over to her.

'I need to talk,' she said. 'You don't mind leaving Lawrence for a moment?'

'Not at all,' Joy said. So this was it. In a way, it was a relief.

There were damp benches around the perimeter of the rink, and Joy and Deborah took a seat on the opposite side to Lawrence, Howard and the children. Joy was glad to take the weight off her feet. The skates were rubbing against her ankles.

'Joy,' Deborah began, 'something awful's happened.'

'Tell me,' Joy said.

'It's Josh. His teacher asked to speak to me on Friday. He's been picking fights with other boys.'

Josh again. Was her cousin wilfully blinding herself?

'Joy, honestly, I was devastated. At first I couldn't believe it! You know how gentle Josh is; I thought Miss Greenberg had taken against him. But it really is true. He picks fights at playtime. I've spoken to him, but how do you know if a six-year-old is understanding you?'

There was Josh, skating with his dark little head slightly in front of him, as if it was propelling him forward.

'I'm sure he understands you,' Joy said.

'Oh, I hope so! But what is worrying me now is why he started. I asked him if he was being bullied, and he says he isn't, and I wondered if it was Cynthia Finegold's little boy who'd been provoking him and –'

Joy momentarily switched off from Deborah's

narrative. Other people's worries can be rather tire-some, she thought, guiltily. Her eyes strayed to Lawrence, still clinging to the sides. If he wasn't exactly good-looking he was comfortable-looking, and perhaps that –

'. . . then I began to wonder if it was his lack of height, and he felt he had to prove himself to the other boys. So I mentioned this to Sharon – you remember Sharon, who was at my Rosh Hashanah lunch – and she said it might be that, but not to worry because Josh had a good role model in Howard, but what she doesn't know is that Howard has been spending less and less time at home –'

Now Joy began to listen. Her heart beat fast.

'– I know he has to work hard, but it's been getting worse lately, and a few evenings he's missed Josh's bath-time – and then I read an article in a magazine about absent fathers and the harm they can do – and I told Howard, and he was very cross, and said I didn't realize the pressure he was under –'

From whom? Joy patted Deborah's gloved hand sym-pathetically. So she had noticed after all. It would only be a short time now before the penny dropped.

'Aunty Joy!' came a voice. 'I want to skate with you. Please!'

It was Hayleigh.

'I'm talking to Mummy,' Joy said, very seriously.

'No, it's all right, you go.' Deborah said. 'It's really Howard I should be talking to. I'll have a word with him later.'

Joy made her way back to the ice and edged on to the rink once again. She began to move very slowly, still holding on to the sides.

'No, look, Aunty Joy, you can go round holding my hand. It's quite safe!'

Dare I? thought Joy.

'Please! I'm very good.'

There was Lawrence, watching her. The temptation to impress him was irresistible. Joy took Hayleigh's hand and began to plod along the ice. She found it was perfectly possible to use the small girl to balance. She began to plod with more pronounced steps and increased her pace.

'Well done, Aunty Joy! That's very good.'

Joy filled with pride.

'The only thing is, Aunty, you're not really skating. You're walking. To skate properly you've got to push your skate behind you. Look!'

Hayleigh detached herself from Joy's vice-like grip and gave a brief demonstration.

'Like this?' Joy said, attempting a short slide.

'Yes, yes!'

Joy was elated. At last, a physical activity she could do. This was going to be the first of many happy hours at the ice-rink. Ought she to consider getting a season ticket? She felt Lawrence's gaze upon her and skated towards him with brio. So quickly that she didn't have time to work out exactly how it happened, her right leg slid away from her, and her body followed. The ice came up and smacked her for her presumption. Joy landed at Lawrence's feet and, in her desperation, pulled herself up by his legs. Thank God he looked concerned rather than amused.

'Are you all right? Do want to sit down?'

Joy did want to sit down, and Lawrence escorted her off the ice. Her hip felt as if it might well be bruised; at least, she thought, she wasn't post-menopausal and needn't fear osteoporosis. Yet.

In a few moments she was seated on a bench again, this time sipping from a polystyrene cup of frothy hot chocolate. Lawrence was by her side. Together they watched the other skaters. They saw Deborah glide by at Howard's side, neither speaking.

It was then that Joy formed a desperate resolution. She was Deborah's cousin; Lawrence was Howard's cousin. To voice her concerns about their marriage to Lawrence was keeping it in the family, so to speak. The more she thought about this, the wiser it seemed. Lawrence could, if necessary, speak to Howard. Even if he didn't do that, at least she could share the burden of her anxiety with him. Possibly not the best way to start a relationship, but just now Deborah's affairs seemed more important than hers. Or should that be Howard's affairs?

'Lawrence?' Joy faltered.

'Yes?'

'I've been worried about Debbie and Howard. And I think I know what's wrong.'

'I know too. But what can I do?' He paused and bit nervously at a nail. I've been pushing Howard to tell Debbie all about it, but he refuses. He still thinks that, given time, he'll get through it. I've said to him that his best chance is to involve Debbie too, get her support and just come clean. I know she'll understand. It could happen to anyone.'

Joy was winded by the shock. Lawrence knew about the affair, and more or less approved! Involve Debbie? The man was utterly amoral. Affairs could just happen to anyone? He made them sound like the common cold. She paused to give herself time to compose a sufficiently withering reply.

'In any case, he'll have to get her signature if they're

going to remortgage the house. It is possible that with a cash injection the business can be kick-started again. Sometimes it can be an advantage to declare bankruptcy. In fact, I'm optimistic. Howard's done everything he can, making economies, replacing full-timers with part-timers, everything but tell his wife. He's so worried about how she'll react.'

'You mean his business is in trouble?'

'He's been there most evenings this week. I've been with him. We've started to –'

'And Deborah doesn't know this?'

'As I said –'

'Excuse me,' Joy said to Lawrence, and staggered to her feet. Deborah had nothing to worry about after all! The silly man, thinking he was protecting her by saying nothing. In fact, she was probably worried sick, fearing all sorts of things, as Joy had been herself. It was absolutely vital that Deborah should know the truth and know it now.

Joy grasped the rail by the entrance and swung herself on to the rink. Where were Howard and Deborah? She surveyed the gaily coloured throng that swept by her. There they were, near the centre of the rink. She set out determinedly. Plod, plod, plod. She couldn't decide whether to speak to both of them at once, or just to instruct Howard to talk to Debbie. Perhaps the second might be better. Who was that coming towards her, coming rapidly towards her? He seemed familiar. It was that man in the tartan scarf, with the silvered yellow hair and the veiny cheeks.

This time she got a much better view of him, as within moments he was lying on top of her and staring, alarmed, into her eyes.

'We can't go on meeting like this!' Joy gasped.

He apologized profusely and rolled off her, assured her he was fine, and then apologized again. In a moment Howard and Deborah were there, followed by Hayleigh, Josh and a rink attendant. Once the fuss had died down, Joy, rather shaken, held tightly on to Howard's arm.

'Isn't Lawrence enough for your insatiable appetite?' he joked.

'Howard, listen. You're going to tell Deborah about your business problems and you're going to tell her now. Otherwise I will.'

'No, no; it'll spoil the afternoon.'

'Coward!' Hypocrite that I am, Joy thought.

'But the children are here.'

'Lawrence and I will look after them. Hayleigh? Josh?' The children followed her automatically, as she was using her schoolteacher voice, honed by years of experience to ensure immediate obedience. Grabbing tightly on to Hayleigh's hand, Josh trailing them, they left the rink.

Lawrence was standing at the side to meet them.

'We're looking after the children,' Joy explained. 'Howard and Debbie are having a little talk.'

'Aunty Joy?' piped up Josh.

'Mmm?'

'Can I have a burger? They're selling burgers. With cheese on!'

Hayleigh intervened. 'Oh, Josh, you know you're not supposed to eat burgers! They're not *kosher*! Aunty Joy – he mustn't have a burger!' Her voice dripped with moral indignation.

'Do you want one too?' Joy asked.

'Yes, please.'

Joy fished for her purse in her anorak pocket and

extracted a five-pound note. 'Here. Get a burger each, and a drink and anything else you fancy. Just don't bother Mummy or Daddy. OK?'

The children vanished almost instantaneously.

'Well done!' Lawrence reached over and squeezed Joy's hand. 'I wish I could be as decisive as you.'

'Me? Decisive?' Joy laughed. 'I can make decisions for other people, but just don't ask me to decide something for myself.'

'No, you were brave. *I* should have forced Howard to say something. Instead I've been sleepless with worry.'

'Sleepless? Try Night Nurse. Just take a small dose before bedtime and it should put you out like a light.'

'I've tried it. It doesn't work for me,' he said.

'No, it doesn't work for me either.'

For the first time their eyes met, and they smiled. Well, one thing's for certain, Joy thought. We've got quite a lot in common.

The children had finally finished eating. Lawrence collected together all the burger wrappers and paper cups to take them to the bins. Joy focused on the skaters on the rink, trying to pick out the figures of Deborah and Howard, but with no success. They had been gone so long that Joy was certain Howard had spoken; what wasn't so certain was Deborah's reaction. Although Joy was fairly sure that Debbie's love of problem-solving would help her cope with the shock, it was also possible that Debbie had reacted badly. She thought she knew her cousin, but then, how well does anyone ever know anyone?

'Aunty Joy! We want to go back on the ice now,' Hayleigh commanded.

'Go on, then,' Joy told her.

'No, we want you to come with us. It's more fun with you.'

'Tell you what, I'll ask Uncle Lawrence to take you. He's a lot of fun!' Joy spoke brightly and loudly so the returning Lawrence could hear her.

'Hayleigh and Josh want you to take them back on the ice.'

Within a few minutes Lawrence was gripping the rails tightly again, while the children amused themselves by pretending to be human cannon-balls and hurling themselves at him, as he stood there tensely, withstanding the blows and buffets of outrageous fortune. Joy smiled to herself.

Any person seeing them now would assume that Hayleigh and Josh were Lawrence's children, that he was their father. That same person, noticing Joy gazing fondly at the children, would have her down as their mother. And so it could turn out. In a few years' time there they would be at the ice-rink again. This time, Lawrence and Joy would be there with their own offspring.

Joy could imagine it all. A few months' courtship, and then Lawrence would present her with an engagement ring, nestling in a blue-velvet box. Joy imagined her mother's pleasure on hearing the news. It would give her a whole new lease of life. All of a sudden she would have a wedding to plan for – caterers to hire, a hall to choose, clothes to buy, a guest list to be drawn up – a proper wedding. Joy imagined being the centre of attention, all eyes upon her as she stood under the *chuppah*, just as Debbie had on her wedding day. Then how long? Six months, a year? Joy would ring her mother with the news that she was pregnant. Ruth's happiness would be indescribable. Fast-forward nine months – Ruth would be a grandmother! Joy melted at the thought of her mother reaching into the hospital crib and tenderly picking up that precious scrap of humanity. Joy brushed a tear from her eye.

Would it be a girl or a boy? Would it be like her or like Lawrence? Yes – the baby might be of a philosophical bent, like its father, unable to reach decisions, or, like her, it might worry a lot, the sort of baby that screams at bathtime, and screams when it's laid in its cot, and screams when you try to feed it, and screams when you don't try to feed it. Joy had been that sort of baby, her mother had told her. And what kind of father would Lawrence turn out to be? Why was it that no other woman had snapped him up? Did he have some dark secret that not even Debbie had fathomed?

He might be unable to father children. Ought she to ask him about his sperm count? He might be addicted to a secret vice. Joy vaguely remembered her mother telling her that there was a gambling streak in Howard's family. Now there was a thought! She could see it all now. She would be returning home, having taken baby to play in the park. Two strange men would be on her doorstep, shaven heads, brash manners, flashy, expensive suits. Loan sharks. *Are you Mrs Weiner? There's the small matter of the £2,000 your husband owes us – and that's only the interest.* Joy imagined herself holding on to the stroller for support, and baby, sensing the catastrophe, setting up an unearthly howl. Joy looked at Lawrence standing there on the ice. She hated him. What kind of monster would do that to his young family?

She jumped as a hand was placed on her shoulder. It was Howard. He looked happy.

'It's OK,' he said.

Deborah was there behind him, more cheerful than she had been for some time.

'Joy,' she said, 'would you say I was a good cook?'

'Is the Pope a Catholic?' Joy replied.

'Good enough to cook for others?'

'It's a privilege for others to eat your food!'

'So, do you think I could make money doing it?' Deborah continued, her face glowing.

'Indubitably.'

'Listen! This is what I've – we've – decided. Howard will remortgage the house. Meanwhile, I'm going to take a course on how to run a small business, and then I'm going to get cooking – strictly *kosher* – and I'm going to deliver too. But not for functions – not to begin with. I'll cook for domestic occasions, birthday parties, family dinners, traditional Friday-night suppers, intimate dinners for two. Just imagine it! Someone comes to your door with a surprise gourmet meal for you to eat. It beats a birthday balloon. And –'

Josh came up to her, pulling at her coat. 'Mummy, I falled over,' he whimpered.

'Shut up, Josh! As I was saying, Joy, I could advertise in the local Jewish press and perhaps get someone to do a feature on me. We could distribute leaflets. And then we could –'

Deborah had turned up trumps again. Joy decided that if Jewish women shared one characteristic, that characteristic was resourcefulness. What's more, she realized, Debbie needed a challenge. So much so, she had invented problems with her children that weren't there, expressly so she could solve them. Thank God she had a real problem now.

Joy pulled Josh on to her lap and rubbed his leg. She told him everything was going to be all right and, for once, she meant it.

CHAPTER THIRTEEN

Joy fumbled with the zip of her anorak, unable to slot it together to fasten it. This pause before departure gave Deborah the opportunity she was waiting for.

'Oh, dear! Just look at the time! We must get the children back home and feed them, and bathe them, and we'll never manage all of that if we have to drop Joy off too. Lawrence! Would you be an absolute darling and take Joy home for us? It's just that the children have school in the morning, and Howard and I have a thousand and one things to do.'

That was pretty transparent, Joy thought to herself with a resigned amusement. In fact, she was rather pleased. The idea of spending some time with Lawrence, getting acquainted just a little more deeply, was not an unappealing prospect. She was glad to see that Lawrence eagerly assented to Deborah's proposition and, before too long, he was guiding her over to his car, a not-so-young baby Volvo, unlocking the passenger door and holding it open while she climbed inside. Joy couldn't remember the last time someone had done that for her. Michael had probably never done it, ever.

Lawrence joined the A56 and headed north. Settling at a steady thirty-five miles an hour, he cleared his throat, and spoke. 'Do you have to go straight home?'

'No,' said Joy.

'Are you hungry?' he continued.

'I thought you'd never ask.'

Lawrence's face brightened. 'We'll go out to eat,' he

declared. 'My treat, I insist. You deserve it. So what's it to be? Chinese? Indian? French? Middle Eastern? Italian?'

'You didn't say you were throwing in a world cruise.'

'No, no, I want you to decide.'

'What do *you* like eating?' Joy asked Lawrence.

'I'm easy. It's up to you where we go.'

'Oh, Italian,' Joy announced. She liked pizzas, and a pizzeria would sidestep the problem of whether to eat *kosher*. Lawrence mentioned a place he'd been to once or twice close to the Town Hall, and Joy said she'd heard of it and had always wanted to go there.

It had been a fine day, and as the evening closed in the skies intensified their colour to a rich indigo. Joy and Lawrence entered a city which seemed not to have shaken off its Sunday-afternoon torpor. The roads were reasonably quiet, and even the buildings seemed visibly relaxed. Lawrence parked by an empty meter in a side street and got out quickly in order to open Joy's door. I could get used to this, she thought.

They walked side by side to the pizzeria. Lawrence was slightly hunched, his head thrust forward.

'When I last spoke to Deborah I asked her if you were involved with someone else, and I couldn't get a straight answer from her. Are you otherwise engaged?'

'Not for much longer,' Joy said, assuming a confidence she wished she had. 'The relationship's as good as over. Really, I am free.'

'So am I,' said Lawrence.

Joy was glad they'd got that one over with. In between two tall office buildings Joy saw the neon sign reading 'Trattoria Napoli', and hastened towards it. Lawrence reached it first. He opened the door for her, and they descended a short staircase into a marble-floored restaurant, where several Italian-looking waiters had congregated by a small bar. One detached himself from the group, welcomed Joy and Lawrence, found them a table, and pulled a chair out for Joy. She sat.

'Will you excuse me for a few moments?' Lawrence asked.

And he was gone. Joy felt quite composed. At first she looked round the restaurant at the lurid paintings of Naples and the Chianti bottles on the shelves. She glanced at the few other diners, sharing their intimacy for one brief instant. Her eyes rested lingeringly on the dessert trolley as she tried to make out if they had any cheesecake. Then she began to wonder what Lawrence might be doing. At first she had assumed he'd gone to the Gents. But he had been gone so long! She remembered a story her mother had told her once about a friend who had been taken out by a man after a tea dance and was abandoned in the cinema by him, on the pretence of him going to spend a penny. No, impossible! The sensible voice in her head, which had been getting stronger recently, suggested he had a nervous tummy. Just as she did on certain occasions. She would be sympathetic in manner when he returned, but would not mention it, in case it embarrassed him.

Just as the waiter appeared with two large plastic menu-cards, Lawrence rejoined her at the table, looking much more cheerful. He said nothing, but picked up the menu with gusto and began to read through it.

The pleasure of choosing food calmed them. Both seized on the melon to begin with, Joy selected a pizza and Lawrence, hovering between a calzone pizza and a mushroom tagliatelle, opted for the tagliatelle. They ordered a Frascati and before too long, as the restaurant was not very busy, the waiter had appeared with their bottle and, the neck wrapped in a napkin, poured some wine for both of them.

'Here's to . . .' Lawrence faltered. Would it be presumptuous of him to say 'us'?

'To Deborah and Howard's new venture!' Joy concluded.

'Yes, yes!' They drank. The wine was cool, crisp and delicious. Joy could feel it affecting her right away.

'This is going to be fun!' she declared.

'Thank you,' Lawrence said. 'I love your optimism. You're very nice, and I appreciate it. I have to say that I find these getting-to-know-you occasions slightly terrifying.'

'But nothing bad can happen,' Joy assured him. She meant it too. They were on the ground, young and healthy. Nothing, therefore, could possibly go wrong. She watched Lawrence drain his glass and hoped the alcohol wouldn't upset his stomach further.

'You're right. Nothing bad can happen. That's very true. So let's talk about something else. Let's talk about you. Tell me about your job, or your hobbies, or whatever.'

Joy began to talk about college in a desultory sort of way and explained how she'd drifted into teaching after university. It had seemed safer than trying to get a job in an increasingly competitive market. But, in fact, when she had first stepped into a classroom, she had found the experience electrifying. She had found she could pretend to be another person – authoritative, witty, self-assured. If she believed in this other person enough, then the kids did too. The melon was laced with port, was mouth-watering, and Joy realized she was quite hungry. She bit into the soft, yielding flesh of the melon and enjoyed the contrast of the innocent sweetness of the fruit with the sinful bite of the alcohol.

Lawrence asked about her mother, and they talked family for a bit. His detailed questions delighted Joy. Lawrence was the first man she had ever met who seemed interested in her mother! Returning the compliment, she enquired about his. A widow too, she lived alone off Kings Road, was pleased that Lawrence had come to live with her again and fussed around him, which he put up with, as it gave her a lot of pleasure.

The waiter returned and refilled their glasses. Joy began to fizz and sparkle. Looking at Lawrence now, he really wasn't so bad. His brown eyes were kind and intelligent, and the air of biblical wisdom conferred by his beard was not unbecoming. Besides, Joy knew better than to judge by appearances.

'Tell me about you now,' she said to him. 'I want to hear everything.'

His eyes met hers for a moment with a half-shy, half-gratified smile. And then the waiter arrived with their meals, producing them with as much panache as a magician withdrawing a rabbit from a top hat. As he came at them again with the pepper mill, Joy was momentarily reminded of Lesley's bedroom sculpture. The waiter applied a frosting of parmesan cheese to Lawrence's tagliatelle, and then, sad that he could do no more, he retreated to the bar. Joy began to cut into her pizza. It was very good. It was some time since she'd had such an authentic, well-cooked pizza, the dough light, crispy and a perfect complement to the rich mozzarella and the salty tang of the anchovies and olives.

'Where shall I begin? You know I studied philosophy at

university. I enjoyed that. So I spent four years worrying about the existence of God and the meaning of life, and then I realized my real problem was going to be getting a job. Compared to that, the existence of God was a walk-over. First, I taught evening classes, but I couldn't make a living at it. I didn't want my mother to have to support me, so I left home and worked for a time in a sales department – menswear – to try to make some money. But I was no good. I never earned any commission because I empathized too much with the indecisive customers. So I went back to college and began to study psychiatry, but that only showed me how much I had to worry about. In the end Howard insisted I work at something down to earth, and that's why I'm taking my insurance exams in a few months.'

'But won't insurance make you worry more because you have to keep calculating risks, and trying to predict what the bad things are that can happen?' Joy asked, and cut into her pizza again.

Lawrence was silent as he wound some tagliatelle around his fork and watched the sauce drip back on to his plate.

'I hadn't thought of that,' he said bleakly.

Joy felt a rush of pity for him. Here was a man who actually worried more than she did. She felt self-assured, bold, heroic in comparison.

'No, ignore me. I'm sure you'll be fine. Insurance is a great idea. This pizza is delicious.'

'Perhaps I should have ordered one,' said Lawrence.

'Your tagliatelle looks scrumptious too. Can I try some?' Joy reached over and hooked some with her fork. Taking food from his plate seemed unforgivably provocative. She could hardly believe that it was she, Joy, doing this. The tagliatelle was good too, and she assured Lawrence that it was.

'I can see why Deborah wanted us to meet,' Joy said. 'We're two of a kind. I worry too. Not so much because I can't make up my mind, but because I'm generally scared of things. Or in other words, I'm a coward! But I'm working on it. I'm taking myself off on an adventure holiday and going on a Fear of Flying course.'

Lawrence carefully put down his knife and fork. 'That's very interesting. I'm working on my worrying too.' He glanced around the restaurant, as if he were about to impart some sensitive information. 'I belong to a twelve-step group – you know – based on Alcholics Anonymous – to control my obsessive worrying. I have to learn to live one day at a time and to hand my worries over. We meet once a week.'

'Fascinating!' said Joy. 'And does it work?'

'I'm optimistic,' Lawrence said. 'But on the other hand –'

'So tell me, you have group meetings and confess all your worries?'

'Yes, and I have a sponsor. It was him I rang when I came in to the restaurant with you. That's why I was away so long. I needed an extra boost.'

'Because of me?'

'Absolutely because of you. The anxiety I have about my career is nothing compared to my anxiety about women. Or rather, how to initiate and sustain a relationship with a woman. For example, what do you want of me? Do you want me to seduce you tonight? Am I to book a hotel room? Which hotel? Or do you just want a good-night kiss? Or do I do nothing, and let you make all the running?'

'Oh, Lawrence!' Joy laid down her knife and fork too. 'This is the nineties! You can ask women what they want now. You don't have to try to play guessing games.'

'All right. Do you want me to make a pass at you, or don't you want me to make a pass at you?'

'What do *you* want to do?'

'Pass,' said Lawrence.

Joy could see that Lawrence was a master of ambiguity, but then, he was a philosophy graduate. At that moment it occurred to her that she could never have had a conversation like this with Michael. Maybe here, in this pizzeria, she was meeting her destiny. Here was a match made in heaven. She and Lawrence were clearly kindred spirits. Worriers United. He, who could never make up his mind, and she, with her suitcase full of fears, of spiral staircases, of worms, of the thinning of the ozone layer, of exterior lifts, of an alarming new virus that decimates the whole of Manchester. Enough of that. She would think about Lawrence, this eminently suitable man sitting opposite her now. Joy wondered for the first time what Lawrence would be like in bed. And would she like to go to bed with him? At the moment the question was academic. Nevertheless, it needed an answer.

Joy regarded him carefully as he selected a tiramisu from the sweet trolley. His large hands had a thin layer of dark hair. Did she find that attractive? He certainly wouldn't be a forceful lover. He would ask her permission, no doubt, for whatever he wanted to do. She would have to guide him. Joy tried to imagine him without his jacket, tie and shirt, but the cheesecake she was eating melted in her mouth and she stopped to luxuriate in the sensation of all that creaminess and sweetness.

'Mmmm,' she sighed, trying to indicate the extent of her pleasure to Lawrence.

'Is it good? Are you enjoying it?'

'Out of this world!'

'Would you like some more? Waiter!' He gave brief instructions to the Italian, who swiftly cut some more. Joy had not quite finished her first portion.

'Over there,' she indicated a space on the table. 'Yes, that's it. That's just the spot!'

'Mmmm . . . aaah!' she said, as she licked the spoon and pulled over her second plate. 'I'm insatiable. How was yours?'

'Nice. I have a partiality for tiramisu.' Lawrence was smiling at her now, much more confident than he had been all evening. 'I'm so glad we decided to come here.'

'I'm enjoying myself too.'

'I haven't enjoyed myself so much for a very long time.'

Joy felt some pressure around her ankle. Was that Lawrence's foot? Was he making his first move? She couldn't quite finish her cheesecake and put down her fork. Now he reached over the table and took her hand.

'Thank you, Joy.'

'What for?' Joy's heart began to pound in her chest. Lawrence liked her! Things really were going to progress further! She would do what she could to help matters. She grasped his hand tightly, and they stayed like that, immobile, for a few moments.

'Shall we go now?' Lawrence asked, huskily. 'I have an idea. We could –'

Suddenly another Italian arrived at their table. Joy and Lawrence started guiltily, releasing each other's hands.

'Excuse me,' said the stranger. 'Are you Miss Freeman?'

'Yes?' A flash of panic assailed Joy. Was something wrong?

'I knew it! It is Miss Freeman. Do you remember me? I am Maria Lippi's father. No? You taught my daughter English. At St Ignatius'. You were her favourite teacher. It is Miss Freeman!' he called in the direction of the kitchen. A plump, red-faced woman looked out of the kitchen and clapped her hands in pleasure.

'Miss Freeman, we are proud to have you here. Maria will be so glad. You know, she is engaged now? I am the manager here, and the father of her fiancé owns the business and is opening a high-class restaurant in Sale! Maria did so well in her English. She is upstairs now. Carlo – call her!'

'It's true,' whispered Joy to Lawrence. 'I taught Maria three years ago.'

A slim, elegant girl emerged from a back room. 'Hello,' she said, and blushed.

'Hello, Maria,' said Joy, in her schoolteacher voice. 'Congratulations on your engagement.'

Maria's mother emerged from the kitchen, and soon the family had congregated around the table.

'My daughter's English teacher!' announced Mr Lippi to the waiters.

Joy signalled an apology to Lawrence with her eyes. He grinned foolishly.

'Occupational hazard,' she whispered.

Finally they emerged from the restaurant, Lawrence's attempts to pay for the meal having been in vain. Joy felt guilty. Just as Lawrence had summoned the confidence to become more intimate, he had been thwarted by a well-meaning mafioso. There was obviously some divine plan to keep her pure, and the Lippis, like the good Catholics they were, were part of it. So she owed it to Lawrence to try to resurrect a more romantic atmosphere, despite the fact she was feeling uncomfortably full. Two pieces of cheesecake really were excessive. Perhaps if she walked it off, she would feel better, more like whatever Lawrence had in mind. Besides, it was still quite early, and she had no desire at all to return home.

'Shall we go for a walk?' Joy suggested. 'It's a fine evening.'

'A very good idea,' said Lawrence.

They walked away from the street where the car was parked, and Lawrence slipped his arm around Joy's waist. She immediately nestled closer to him, partly out of politeness, partly from a desire to experiment. It occurred to her that she felt comfortable with him. Was that a good sign?

They walked by the Town Hall and spoke of Victorian architecture, the Victorian novel, cultural relativism, modern rock music. Lawrence confessed that he still listened to his Pink Floyd albums, and Joy admitted to her partiality for the Law Enforcers. She began to get used to the rhythm of Lawrence's walking and his physical closeness. She tried to imagine what it would be like if he turned and kissed her. She was sure she could respond, and with some enthusiasm. Was he going to try? Time spent with Lawrence was full of uncertainties.

They passed down a side street that led to Deansgate. Lawrence squeezed her more tightly. Damn that cheesecake, she thought. The street was not so well lit; the darkness and the quietness enveloped them and increased their sense of their own importance. They were alone in the universe, man and woman, held together under a spell.

Joy looked across the street and saw a building that looked suspiciously like a synagogue.

'Surely that's not a *shul*?' she asked.

Lawrence explained that it was Manchester Reform Synagogue, and that he had been to a *Bat Mitzvah* there once. Joy was interested.

'Let's have a look,' Lawrence said, and crossed the street with her.

A *shul* right in the centre of the city. Joy was fascinated.

'Come here,' Lawrence suggested to her.

She walked with him around the side of the building, so that they were off the street and sheltered by a brick wall. It was then that Lawrence drew Joy towards him and pressed his lips against hers. Joy yielded to the pressure of his lips and shut her eyes tightly to avoid the sight of the *shul*, the presence of which robbed Lawrence's kiss of all its eroticism. Being kissed by a man the spitting image of Moses by the side of a *shul* wasn't sexy; it was *kosher*. Joy felt as if she were being kissed by Uncle Barney.

She wriggled out of Lawrence's embrace. 'Not here,' she said.

Lawrence apologized profusely. He knew it was too soon, he had misread the signals, he had not meant to upset her. Joy realized she had probably put him back light-years in his twelve-step group. He'd need at least an hour alone with his sponsor to work through this rejection. There was nothing for it. Hoping God was otherwise engaged, like, for example, sorting out the Middle East, she lunged at Lawrence and kissed him fully on his mouth, prising it open with her tongue and hoping the cheesecake wouldn't repeat. He responded by rubbing her back, just that way her mother used to when she'd had hiccups. As she kissed him she felt one hand tentatively move to the side, and he began to rub the front of her anorak, approximately where her right breast was. She felt nothing; Michael's anorak masked all sensation.

What was she going to do? What if the rabbi came out? Surely Lawrence wasn't going to seduce her here in the street?

There were suddenly some raucous chants and shouts. From the pub opposite some young lads emerged, and immediately Joy and Lawrence jumped apart. Thank God, Joy thought, and looked up at the *shul* appreciatively.

They made their way back to Lawrence's car. Joy tried to assess what had happened. Ought she to proceed further with Lawrence, this time on an empty stomach and far away from any religious institution? She thought of the offer of Lesley's house. There was never any food at Lesley's house, and she was an atheist to boot! She ought to give it a try. She'd never met anyone as well suited to her as Lawrence, and an inner voice (her mother's?) told her it might be worth persevering.

'I'll drive you home,' Lawrence said, when they reached his car.

Joy was about to thank him, when she thought of Michael. He would be sitting in the lounge waiting up for her. She would have to explain her situation to Lawrence, and she didn't want to.

'I'll go back to Debbie's,' she announced brightly. 'Just take me there.'

On arrival at Deborah's, Joy explained that the

children would be asleep, and that she had better just creep in alone. Lawrence understood. He bent towards her and gave her another tender kiss. Joy stood by Deborah's drive, waving him off.

Once the sound of the car's engine had faded, Joy turned and proceeded to walk. Her house was only about fifteen minutes on foot from Deborah's and, provided she kept to the main road, she didn't expect to come to any harm.

The walk gave her time to think. Lawrence was evidently interested in her. She owed it to herself to be bloody, bold and resolute, and to pursue this relationship. Which, she reminded herself, would also mean finishing with Michael. It came to her clearly, then, as she walked by the side of a brightly lit garage, that despite Michael's toe, despite the ugliness of the scene that would follow, she had to end her relationship with Michael now. It occurred to her that Michael was her own personal albatross, which she had been wearing round her neck, like the Ancient Mariner, for years and years. It had begun to smell rather badly. She would go home and cast him from her. Or at least tell him that his attempts to change were not enough and that they would have to find a new future apart. Yes! That was a good phrase! She would use that!

Her pace quickened as more and more phrases arrived unannounced in her head. *It's no use . . . we're holding each other back . . . we need a new challenge . . . it's over, Michael, can't you see? . . . God knows, I've tried . . .*

There was her front door. Home already! Joy took a deep breath, like an actress standing in the wings, hearing her cue and about to walk on to the stage. She unlocked the door. The light in the lounge and the electronic tinkling from the TV indicated that Michael was playing on the CD megadrive.

'Michael?' she said. It was a few moments before he turned to speak to her.

'Still in one piece, then?' he quipped.

Joy remarked that she was. 'Michael,' she repeated, her throat dry. She realized that all of the phrases that had come to her aid on the walk home had scattered like leaves in the wind.

'It's over,' she muttered, trying the words out and getting ready to repeat them when Michael paused the megadrive to turn and confront her.

Michael paused the megadrive and turned.

'Oh, by the way. Your brother David rang. He wouldn't tell me what it was. I think he said there was some bad news about your mother.'

CHAPTER FOURTEEN

Bad news. Those were the two words Joy dreaded most. Yet how infinitely worse they were made by the addition of the next three – *about your mother*. Bad news about her mother. Joy's skin turned to ice. She both wanted to know immediately what the news was, to face the worst, to plumb the bottom of the black depths of chaos, and also not to know, to hide her head in the sand, ostrich-like, and pretend nothing had happened, that Michael had not spoken those fateful words. *Bad news about your mother*.

'What bad news?' There was a hysterical edge to her voice.

'Hold your horses,' said Michael. 'How should I know? David wouldn't tell me, would he? Said to ring him back at your mother's.'

What was David doing at her mother's? Had he been called there by a doctor? Why didn't her mother ring? Was she ill, or worse? This time, there couldn't possibly be an innocent explanation. Her fingers trembling, Joy dialled her mother's number. She felt very, very cold.

There was ringing and then a click as her mother's phone was answered. She praised God as she heard her mother's voice – at least Ruth was still alive!

'Hello?' Ruth asked, in that suspicious voice she reserved for answering the telephone, deliberately calculated to throw all obscene callers off their stride.

'It's Joy. What's wrong?'

'Joy, it's late!' There was a strong reprimand in her mother's voice. 'You had me worried.'

'Michael said David phoned with some bad news.'

'It could have waited till tomorrow,' Ruth said.

Why, Joy thought, wasn't she saying what was wrong?

'Tell me the bad news,' Joy insisted. She heard her mother laugh bitterly.

'I was on my way to bed,' she said. 'David's here, you know. He's on a course. He's staying with me all week! He's out in the West End now. When you rang, I thought something had happened to him.'

'Mum, please tell me what the bad news is!'

'The bad news?' she repeated, as if she had temporarily laid it on one side and subsequently forgotten it. 'Oh, it's just that on Friday Mr Bergman told me that he wants me to retire.' She gave a long, expressive sigh. It contained regret for the foolishness of Mr Bergman, infinite patience for her daughter and her neuroticism, and a wry acceptance of the ways of the world.

'So that's all the bad news?' Joy demanded, incredulous.

'What do you mean, "That's all the bad news"? Isn't that bad enough for you?'

'Yes, yes,' Joy said quickly, 'it's terrible.'

'I should say it's terrible. There are hardly any local part-time jobs, and the ones that there are go to younger women. I've given the best years of my life to that firm. I'm not pretending I'm not upset.'

'But why did David ring me to tell me this? Why couldn't you have rung?'

'I didn't want to bother you. But I suppose I'd been bottling it up. When I told David, I was a bit weepy. Poor lamb, he panicked. You know what men are like,' she said, indulgently. 'And he had to go out. He was meeting someone.'

233

'Are you very upset?' Joy asked Ruth.

'Yes, Joy, I am.'

Joy wondered what she could do to cheer her mother up. There was no point in taking revenge on Bergman, sweet as that might be. She had an idea, and the more she thought of it, the more it appealed to her.

'Look. It's half-term next week. I'll come down for a few days, and we can discuss what to do.'

'Joy! How lovely. If you can come next Saturday, David will still be here, and I can have you both together!'

'Well, all right.'

'I feel better already!'

Joy, on replacing the receiver, did not feel better. The after-effects of her panic had left her feeling drained and depressed. But at least her mother was all right. All she wanted to do now was to go to bed. She did not have the strength to talk to Michael tonight, and now that she had promised her mother to visit over half-term, it would be possible to postpone a showdown with Michael until after the adventure holiday, which was on the final week-end of the half-term break. At the moment, all she craved was peace.

As much as the escape from Michael was an attractive prospect, spending time with her brother was not. David made her feel guilty. They ought to be closer, she knew it. On one hand, it was understandable that they should have grown apart, with David living in Bournemouth and herself in Manchester. On the other, she was perfectly aware that she often thought of ringing him to see how he was, but decided that she wouldn't because of the effort involved, the immense effort of bridging the gap that had developed between them, David, the hotel manager, with his canny business mind, and she, Joy, a teacher who cared only for people and books. And what else is there to care about? Yet she owed it to her mother to be nice to David. And she would be. They would all play happy families.

Joy popped her head into the lounge and told Michael she was going to bed. She noticed that he didn't even stop to ask her what was wrong with her mother. Lawrence would have done. He would have panicked with her. The thought was reassuring and, accompanied by it, Joy mounted the stairs to bed.

Now that Joy was almost at the end of the M1, she felt an unalloyed pleasure at coming back to London for a few days. The vastness of the capital made her feel safe, and she still recognized it as her real home. She bivouacked in Manchester with Michael; she had been born and brought up in London. Yet that was just a half-conscious thought. More immediate was the pleasant realization that her mother would be the ideal audience to hear and respond to her plans for her forthcoming interview for head of department. Sister Maureen had informed her yesterday that the interview dates had been set for three weeks after the return to college. That soon! So she had been thinking through a departmental policy to present to Sister and whoever else might be there and trying to formulate some appropriate expressions to couch it in all the way down the M6 and M1, ignoring the Law Enforcers tape that was playing in the background.

Now, even thoughts of the interview were dispersed from her mind as she left the roundabout and approached Gants Hill. Joy smiled to herself. It looked as *kosher* as ever. Even the houses seemed Jewish. It wasn't her imagination – they really did. Almost as if they had been circumcised. Which in a way they had been. Every member of Joy's family had knocked through the lounge and dining room to make one spacious room. The dividing wall as foreskin. An interesting idea – perhaps she would share it with Lawrence. A right turn, a left turn, and then Joy was in the road that was more familiar than any other place on earth. Home.

Home for Joy was a small, white-painted semi with a courtyard in front, which Ruth had had paved over so she wouldn't have the bother of keeping a garden tidy. Net curtains hung demurely behind the lounge windows. Joy found a parking space and with rising excitement took her case from the boot and made for her front door, happy in the certainty that her mother would be waiting for her.

Ruth answered the doorbell immediately, and Joy put down her case to hug her. As she put her arms around her she tried to gauge if she had lost weight with all that worry over Bergman's, but she seemed more or less the same. Joy then gave herself up to the delicious preliminaries of arriving home. She opened her case then and there in the hall, brought out a book she'd bought as a present for Ruth and gave it to her. She made her way to the kitchen and began to browse comfortably in the pantry to see what food her mother had got in for her, and regaled Ruth with the details of her journey while coffee was prepared.

'So where's David?' Joy asked, her mouth full of chocolate digestive.

'Shopping,' Ruth said. 'He needed a new suit. He's gone to Romford.'

Joy was pleased about that. It would be nice to have her mother to herself for a while. She watched Ruth put the coffee and biscuits on the Tel Aviv tray and take them through into the lounge. Joy followed. She noticed a pair of David's shoes by the settee and a folded copy of *GQ* on the coffee-table, open at an article about pension plans. Joy moved the magazine to the floor and pushed the shoes under the television before settling herself down on the settee. Ruth, as usual, took the armchair.

There was no need for Ruth to tell her daughter precisely what had happened that fateful Friday when Bergman had called her into his inner sanctum to tell her that economies and the recession and the need to remain competitive had forced him, unwillingly, to etc., and how the office had reacted, and what Uncle Barney had said and what had happened since, as she had already been through these matters several times on the telephone in the intervening days. But, on the other hand, having Joy here in front of her, Ruth could not resist telling her daughter once again, face to face, what Bergman had said, and what the office had said, as Joy's face was so gratifyingly expressive during the whole recital. Both women agreed that it would be flattering to the vermin of the earth to compare them to Bergman, and that Ruth was a wronged woman.

It was comfortable agreeing with each other, whatever the subject, and equally comfortable for Joy to look around the lounge with its cherished, *haimishe* objects – a cut-glass vase, which was an early anniversary present, and the picture Joy had bought her mother on her fiftieth birthday, of a gipsy caravan with light streaming out of the windows and a black horse stamping outside, looking towards the distant mountains. At the time Joy had thought it rather tacky and wondered why her mother had insisted on getting it. She inhaled the clean, spicy aroma of the house and curled up on the settee that almost seemed to remember the contours of her body. Through the French windows was the familiar horizon of the garden, whispering that everything was the same as ever. Joy bathed in contentment, a contentment that reached out and embraced even her brother.

'I'm looking forward to seeing David,' she said.

'I'm sorry that it won't be for longer. He has to go back to Bournemouth tonight. His girlfriend is flying back from Ibiza, and he's meeting her at the airport.'

'Which girlfriend is this?' Joy asked. She didn't mean the comment to sound unkind, but her brother changed his girlfriends as regularly as his socks.

Ruth shrugged, but smiled at Joy waggishly. The smile conveyed her pleasure at David's exotic love life. Whereas Ruth entertained an abiding hope that Joy would meet a nice man, settle down and have some babies, David acted out her wild side for her. He was allowed – encouraged even – to have a string of girlfriends, live in a hotel and drive an expensive sports car. She worried about him, of course, as any mother would, but he was only young and deserved some fun. When he was small, there wasn't a lot of fun to be had.

Ruth then rose from her armchair, explaining to her daughter that she had something to show her. She made her way to the sideboard, where there was a forest of pictures of David and Joy. She picked up an airmail envelope, held it aloft for a moment, then took the envelope back to her chair and took out the contents.

'From your Aunty Faye,' Ruth explained in business-like tones. 'She decided to write.'

'How is she?' Joy asked.

'So so.' Joy was able to translate. Aunty Faye was in the

very pink of health. No one in Ruth's life was permitted to be thoroughly well. It was inviting disaster. 'So so' was safe.

'She says they're thinking of moving to Florida. There's a bit I don't understand. She says she's thinking of getting a retirement condo. That's not what I think it is, Joy?'

'No, no,' Joy hastily assured her. 'It's short for condominium. An apartment complex.'

'And she says here she's going to classes to learn belly-dancing. At her age!'

'Belly-dancing!' Joy exclaimed.

'Belly-dancing,' Ruth said again, enjoying the effect of her disclosure. 'Your Aunty Faye is sixty-four and has started belly-dancing. Who knows what it will do to her internal organs! Apparently the woman who lives upstairs from her was an Egyptian cabaret dancer, would you believe? So Faye has to join in. She's making herself a costume. With sequins.'

'With sequins,' Joy echoed.

'My mother will turn in her grave,' Ruth said. It was one of her favourite expressions. Joy reflected that her grandmother had by now made so many revolutions she was probably permanently dizzy.

'And do you know who Faye bumped into?'

Joy didn't.

'Sammy Liebermann.'

Joy thought she recognized the name. It was one from her childhood, but not one she could readily identify. Because it was from her past, the sound of the name pleased her. *Sammy Liebermann.*

'Who was he?' she asked.

'I've told you about Sammy.' Was her mother

blushing? 'He was an old flame. It was around the time we lived in Clapton Common, before I met your father. He wanted me to go to Israel with him, but I wouldn't leave my mother.'

Joy did remember now. Her mother enjoyed recounting tales of her exes. Joy imagined she would, too, when she was Ruth's age and came to relive her own personal history.

'But what's he doing in New York, if he went to Israel?'

'His wife's father owned a delicatessen in New York. They settled there. She died a few years ago. Faye says he lives in an apartment on the Upper West Side. Whatever that is. There was some function at Faye's *shul* and she recognized him.'

Joy wondered how her mother felt about that. Was Ruth jealous? Would she have liked to have seen this Sammy Liebermann again?

'Would you like to see him again?' Joy asked.

'What would we have in common, Joy? Be sensible. I expect he wears loud clothes and carries a gun!'

Joy wasn't sure that Ruth's sketch of the average American male was entirely accurate, but moved the conversation on without comment. She wanted to tell her mother about Lawrence, and before David returned home. If there was time Joy also wanted to discuss the interview with her and ask her advice on one or two points. With luck, there might even be time to run through what she had planned so far, with Ruth substituting as Sister Maureen. Just at that moment the doorbell rang. Ruth's face lit up.

'That's David,' she announced unnecessarily.

Joy followed her mother to the door. David was there,

ballasted by several shopping bags. He dropped them in the hall prior to hugging Ruth and then hugged Joy. His aftershave was strong and reminded Joy of a proprietary brand of fly-killer.

'What did you get in the end?' Ruth asked him, excited.

'A suit,' David said. 'From Marks and Spencer's. It wasn't quite what I was looking for, but it'll do.' Ruth was already taking it out of the green Marks and Spencer bag and examining it, murmuring her approval.

Joy stood a little way back, forgotten in the excitement, as David brought out some shoes from the Saxone bag and placed the HMV and Debenhams bags on the telephone table. Finally, he turned to Joy.

'Well, sis, how's life treating you?'

'Fine,' Joy said.

Joy decided that David looked well, very well; in fact, his whole appearance exuded affluence. Although his hairline had begun its slow journey to the back of his head, his eyes were still bright and his features mobile. The round glasses he wore conferred upon him the air of an intellectual, while his chin-length curly hair, in its immaculate condition, hinted at a not inconsiderable amount of vanity.

'Poor old Mum,' he said to Joy.

'It's not right,' Joy said. 'After all those years, and she was the most reliable employee he had.'

'The recession has no pity,' he said, turned to the hall mirror, took out a comb from his brown-leather-jacket pocket and began combing his hair.

'I'll hang the suit up for you,' Ruth said. 'I'll get a hanger from my wardrobe. This hanger they gave you isn't strong enough. I must say, I like the stripe. It's very distinguished. And good quality. You can tell it's good quality.'

Ruth scurried upstairs. Joy watched her brother, troubled by the discomforting blend of affection and distaste she experienced. Was she suffering from sibling rivalry, or was David actually quite hard to like? For her mother's sake, as always, Joy swallowed her negative feelings and decided to make the best of things.

'Work OK?' she asked.

'Yep. It's been a great summer. The weather meant that fewer families went abroad. And it's going to be a good autumn too, which is entirely down to me. I had this rather good idea of starting *kosher* mystery weekends, whodunnits, that sort of thing. We've hired crime-writers to plot the stories, and the local rep is supplying actors. The guests are the detectives. Bookings are pouring in. We're planning a *Chanukah* special. Benson had me into his office to congratulate me.'

'Isn't it a wonderful idea?' Ruth echoed, coming down the stairs.

'Yes,' Joy said. She reflected that it had been easier to join her mother in praise of David's achievements when he was younger. Somehow it was different then. Now, he still expected them to be pleased at his achievements. In some ways, he hadn't grown up.

'I've got some chicken left over from last night,' Ruth said. 'I thought I'd make a salad, and you can have it before you go, David. Is that OK for you, Joy?'

'Fine,' Joy said. 'But don't put yourself to any trouble.'

'It's no trouble,' she said. 'It's lovely to have you both together. Just like old times.'

'I'll come and help you.'

'No, Joy. You've not seen David for ages. You both go and sit in the lounge and have a chat.'

Obediently Joy and David entered the lounge. David made for the wall unit where Ruth stored her few bottles of spirits: some cherry brandy, some Tia Maria and a bottle of ouzo that had never been opened, which Barney and Miriam had brought back from Cyprus.

David closed the double doors.

'Forget it,' he said. He remained standing, then strolled over to the bookcase.

'Michael OK?'

'Fine,' Joy said.

'Job all right?'

'I'm very busy right now,' Joy said, deciding to elaborate, as she felt she had been brusque to David in her previous reply. 'I'm preparing for an interview for head of department, and my upper-sixth group this year is struggling, and I'm putting on some extra lessons. That's on top of the heavy timetable I've got this year, and the documentation to get in place for the inspection.'

David laughed. 'I've never spoken to a teacher who doesn't complain how much they've got to do. I was saying to someone the other day that if teachers whined less and just got on with it, they'd get more sympathy from the public.'

'No, that's not fair! We don't whine, and I'm not whining. But the government has made education a political football, and we've been forced to take on board change after change, most of which are jargon-ridden and invented by administrators, not educationalists.'

'There you go – whining again!'

Joy knew he was deliberately riling her. It was a game

243

he played. Winding Joy up. It was fun for him, because it always worked.

'I'm not whining, I'm explaining.'

'All right, then. Explain this to me. If education is so perfect, what systems do you have for getting rid of bad teachers? Go on. You know as well as I do that there are some rotten teachers. I'm not saying you're one. But how do you get rid of them? Do they get the push for not doing their job properly?'

'In some cases, but –'

'Take my hotel. If I find an employee who's letting the side down, I can give him the boot. Now in schools –'

'You can't compare teaching to industry!' Joy was beginning to shout. 'We deal with people, not products.'

'I deal with people too,' David said. 'There's no difference.'

'Yes there is! Your function is to make a profit; mine to educate people.'

'All the more reason to weed out bad teachers. But they can't get the sack, can they? They –'

Ruth popped her head round the door.

'Look at you both! Seeing you together is doing me the world of good! Do you both eat beetroot?'

Flushed, Joy shook her head. David followed. He flexed his hands and examined his fingers. His fingernails were spotless.

'David, we shouldn't be arguing at a time like this,' Joy said placatingly.

'What? Before dinner?'

'No – I mean that Mum has lost her job, and I'm worried about her!' Joy was conscious that she was playing her worry as a trump card.

'I don't think there's any need to worry.' David's voice was distant; he was thinking. True, his mother would miss the income from the solicitor's and might have to supplement her pension by dipping into her savings. Of course, that could only go on so long. Should she ever want to move to some sort of sheltered accommodation or a rest-home, she would have to sell the house, which would be a pity, as it would fetch a tidy sum, and he could do with his share. As, no doubt, could Joy.

I *am* worried, thought Joy petulantly. I'm worried because Mum will be alone all day and she'll become bored and listless and she'll brood and get old before her time. She needs to work. She ought to try to get another job, except that she might be turned down on account of her age and then she'll feel even worse, and more depressed. I'll just have to invite her to stay more often – and so should David.

'Joy?' Ruth sang from the kitchen. 'I need you to help me to lay the table.'

Joy loved her mother's cooking. Ruth wasn't a stylish cook like Debbie; she just prepared chicken the way her own mother had prepared chicken, always bought Tesco's coleslaw and low-calorie potato salad and sliced tomatoes rather than chopped them. Yet Ruth's chicken salad tasted how a chicken salad ought to taste. It was right, somehow. Everyone was silent as they ate; the only noise came from the children who were playing in next door's garden.

Then Ruth put down her knife and fork, and smiled. 'It's almost worth losing my job to have you both here together.'

Ruth watched her children. They had changed; and

they hadn't changed. David still chewed his food at the front of his mouth; Joy had not lost that abstracted look as she ate. They had both turned out well, both turned out as she had hoped. David could look after himself, he had fight. Joy was the one she was close to, which is as it should be. A daughter is a friend for life.

'How much longer have you got at Bergman's?' Joy asked, quickly swallowing her chicken.

'Just four weeks,' Ruth said.

'I think he is so disgusting,' Joy continued. 'Why you? You've been there how many years? Fifteen? It must be nearly fifteen. Why not get rid of one of the younger ones?'

'I think it was something to do with the new computer system. Bergman thinks I wouldn't learn so easily. Maybe he's right.'

'Computers are easy!' Joy declared. 'Bergman is just an ungrateful bastard!'

Ruth raised her eyebrows. She never liked her children to swear. David spoke next.

'Come on, Joy. It's a matter of economic realities. Bergman had to cut back, and Mum was reaching retirement age anyway. From his point of view, it's perfectly reasonable. Younger staff are better at adapting to change; that's something I've learned as a manager.'

'That's not true!' Joy was livid. How dare David not champion his mother! 'I think older people have other qualities that more than compensate. They're less slapdash, they have wisdom.'

'Wisdom!' laughed David. 'Is that what you need to operate a new computer system?'

'Yes,' said Joy, refusing to give in. 'And wisdom is certainly what you need when you're dealing with people.

246

Our head of department, Betty, who's retiring, is loved by everyone because she has wisdom, and –'

'You mean the wisdom to retire,' David cut in, and winked at Ruth.

Ruth remembered how much David and Joy used to enjoy this conversational sparring. It was just like old times. Except this time Ruth felt somewhat aggrieved, without knowing quite why. Perhaps it had something to do with the fact that they were arguing while she had lost her job. It was time to remind them of that.

'Meanwhile,' she said, 'here I am, out of work. And as David says, at my age, who will want me?' Ruth decided to allow herself just this one moment of self-pity.

'I want you!' Joy said immediately, before David could.

'Ah, but you wouldn't want me around you all the time,' Ruth said, in the brave tones of a martyr.

'I would,' Joy said. 'I happen to love you, and I like your company too. I'd be perfectly happy to have you around all the time.'

'That's not a bad idea,' David said suddenly. 'You've always said you liked Manchester, Mum.' He made some rapid calculations. If his mother went to live with Joy, the rent from the Gants Hill house would more than cover her living expenses and, what's more, she wouldn't need a rest-home if Joy looked after her. Then the capital of the house would remain intact.

'Come and stay with me when you finish at Bergman's,' Joy said. It was true, her mother would profit from a change of scene.

'Stay with you?' Ruth echoed.

'It's an excellent idea,' David continued. 'Company for both of you and, who knows, you may even be able to get work up there, Mum. You'll have Debbie and Howard close at hand, and the children –' David couldn't remember their names, and then he had a better thought. '– And if Joy has a baby, you'll be there to help her.'

Joy froze. What did David mean? That her mother should stay with her for ever? Should live with her, permanently? What about Michael? What would he think of that? He'd hate it. Now there was an idea.

Ruth froze. Leave her house and live with Joy? Leave her home and follow her daughter? Give up her independence? But if it was what Joy wanted how could she say no? Joy would think she didn't love her. And if Joy did have a baby . . .

'But there's Michael,' Ruth faltered.

'No, there's not,' Joy said. 'I'm really going to finish with him, as soon as I get home. And I'm seeing another man, a cousin of Howard's. He lives with his mother too.' Joy imagined the mothers getting to know each other, becoming friends. Her initial panic gave way to excitement. 'Mum, we'd have fun. You could join a *shul* near me, meet new people. Did I tell you Debs is starting her own business – perhaps she'll need some help. And I could certainly do with some help!'

She needs me, thought Ruth. And here I was thinking that your children grow up and stop needing you. They never stop needing you. Ruth was thrilled at the discovery, yet a resentment prickled her skin. It was a familiar feeling; it was one she associated with motherhood. Bergman had freed her, and just as she was getting used to it, Joy needed her. So this is what her life was to be – answering the needs of others.

'If you want me, I'll stay,' she said.

'Of course I want you!' said Joy. Her stomach was as jumpy as a Mexican bean. Was it excitement at having her mother to stay? If so, why did she feel she was having difficulty breathing? She remembered Hardy's novel, *Far from the Madding Crowd*, and Gabriel Oak's proposal to Bathsheba. *Whenever I look up, there you'll be, and whenever you look up, there I'll be.* No wonder she refused.

That was different from this. Joy loved her mother and wanted her by her side. Her mother had given up the best years of her life to look after her, and now she would do the same for her. Besides, once they lived together, they wouldn't have to worry about each other any more. And best of all, there was Michael's reaction to consider. Michael would be furious.

'Well, that's settled, then,' said David. 'What's for dessert, Mum?'

CHAPTER FIFTEEN

Joy spent the remainder of her stay with her mother feeling self-consciously good. It was not an unpleasant sensation. Having offered her home to her mother, Joy knew she had done all that a daughter could do – more, in fact. She recalled that self-satisfied glow she'd had when, as a small girl, she'd followed her mother around the house, dusting with the bright orange duster and tidying a mess that wasn't her mess.

This feeling of moral rectitude dissipated as she drove up the M1, back to Manchester. To her mother she had been the dutiful daughter, opening her heart and her home to the woman who had raised her. Yet here she was now, plotting to rid herself of Michael like some modern-day Lucrezia Borgia.

But no, she wouldn't stoop to poison, she thought, as she stared into her cappuccino at the service station. She would have to explain maturely to Michael how his attempts to change had not been enough, how she should have been allowed to finish their relationship that day at the Heaton Arms, how they should have recognized their incompatibility much, much earlier, how he was welcome to take from the house all the items that were his. As far as the house itself was concerned, Joy had no problems; it was in fact hers. Michael paid only a nominal rent to help with the mortgage.

Once again she felt as if an internal fog had lifted. Her clarity of vision almost dazzled her. How could she ever have stood Michael for so long? What had been wrong with her that she could not see it? She pulled her mind back to the present; she needed to decide how to finish with Michael.

She would arrive home, call him into the lounge and deliver her prepared speech. He would plead to be taken back. Joy quailed at the prospect. She hoped she could trust herself to stand firm; vulnerability in anyone excited her pity . . . Or she could ring him now, from the service station. Her eyes drifted to the pay phones. If he was out, she could leave a message on the answering machine. *Joy here. I'm ringing to say that our relationship is finally over. Please move out forthwith*. Tempting, but unutterably cruel. No, she would have to face him, his histrionics, his threats, his grovelling.

Her cappuccino was still too hot to drink. She tried to decide when to speak to him. It was far too dramatic to start a scene as soon as she got back from London, and yet early the next day she was off to the Lake District with college. If she lived that long. Telling him it was over just before bedtime would ensure a sleepless night for both of them. The morning was no good, as Michael always slept late in the holidays. Yet she could not go away pretending that everything between them was fine, not now. That would be deceitful.

It was a pity, Joy thought, as she ventured a sip of the coffee and then wiped the foam from her top lip, that there wasn't a service you could use on these occasions, a sort of kissogram in reverse, a kiss-goodbye-o-gram, in which trained counsellors came round and broke the news gently to the ex-beloved. No – that would be the coward's way out. Almost as bad as writing a letter.

Now there was a thought: she could write a letter. She could leave it in the bedroom when she left for the Lakes.

When he woke he would read it, and she would already be halfway to Keswick. She wouldn't have to face his wrath. He would be able to react in the privacy of his own home, or rather, his ex-home. Not being there, Joy would not be tempted to retract. So what if it was a cowardly thing to do? She was a coward, and although she was attempting to cure herself, she'd never pretended that she was cured already. If letter-writing was what a coward would do, then it was right for Joy.

She left her cappuccino and made for the shop. There were boxes of notelets on sale, but Joy felt it was cruelly inappropriate to send Michael a pretty scene of an English country garden, and then, inside, assassinate his character. The next box, with a couple walking hand in hand across a deserted beach, was even worse. She hunted for the good old Basildon Bond with matching envelopes. She placed her purchases on the counter and guiltily fumbled for her purse.

When she returned to her table, her coffee had been cleared away. It didn't matter. For this letter, she needed her utmost concentration. She sat sucking the top of her pen for ages. This was proving to be even harder to write than UCAS references. *Dear Michael.* Surely 'dear' was hypocritical under the circumstances? *Michael. It's no use. It's over. I know you've tried but our love has died.* Oh God – that's awful – it rhymes! Why was it impossible to write about feelings without sounding like a romantic novelist fallen on hard times? Or a pop lyricist? *Something inside has died and I can't hide . . .* There has to be another way to go about it.

Dear Michael. In vain have I struggled. It will not do. That sounded familiar. Better to try to be original and, best of all, to tell the truth.

Dear Michael, she wrote. *When I was in London I asked my mother to come and live with me. This means that you will probably want to move out. That might be a good idea for all of us. It's sad when a relationship has to end, but I think it will be easier for both of us if we just accept that it's finally over. Thank you for trying to make things better between us: perhaps it's my fault that we haven't made a go of it. I leave it up to you whether you want to go when I'm away, or after I get back . . . Joy.*

She placed the envelope on top of his jeans, which lay across the dressing-table. Michael was hunched under the duvet. Softly Joy walked across the bedroom, picking up her bulging sports bag, and silently closed the door. Her heart was banging against her chest. Soon she was outside, in the fine drizzle which was to accompany the group all the way along the M6, building up in intensity as the coach turned left and made for the centre of the Lake District.

In fact, Joy was glad it was raining. As the clouds thickened, her heart lightened. Surely it was impossible that any of them would be asked to go outside and perform difficult physical feats in the pouring rain? They would all be confined to the hostel and would have to play pool or Patience or read novels. A pleasing prospect.

The coach turned awkwardly into a narrow tree-lined lane, entirely filling the road. Joy trembled at the thought of what would happen if a car came racing towards them. Rearing up in the distance was the panorama of mountain peaks and sweeping hills that surround Keswick. Joy hoped she was not expected to climb any of them. For that reason, she had deliberately brought no footwear suitable for hill-walking; an old pair of Reeboks was all she had. She'd brought only a few spare tops and some extra jeans; this meant she had room for the plasters, paracetamol, high-factor sun creams, bandages, antiseptic wipes and the phial of Bach Flower rescue remedy she'd seen in a Gants Hill health-food shop and which sounded as if it might come in useful.

Slowly the coach edged into another rural lane, ascended an incline behind a row of cottages and drew to a halt. Beyond the cottages Joy could see a long, low, white building, looking rather like an old coach-house, and a sign by it, reading 'Hill Beck Adventure Centre'. So they were here.

Peter Worthington stepped down from the coach and made his way to the front of the building, followed by a straggling line of sixth-formers with rucksacks, sports bags and suitcases. Joy watched Peter greet the man who was evidently in charge of the centre.

'That's Roger Croft,' Laura, the art teacher, explained. 'He owns this place and a couple of other adventure centres. One on the Yorkshire Moors, I think, and one somewhere in Scotland.'

Roger Croft was a tall man with cropped, grizzled hair, partly obscured by a red baseball cap. He was dressed in garish cycling shorts and an expensive-looking scarlet sweatshirt. His legs were tanned and muscular. He entered the building with Peter.

Reunited with their sports bags, Joy and Laura entered the hostel. As Joy had expected, it was basic. In the centre of the building was a lounge not dissimilar to the college students' common-room, with a pool table at one side. There was a dining room with wooden tables and wooden benches. There was a small side room with old easy chairs, which Laura said they used as a staff room. A staircase led upstairs to the dormitories.

'Mainly they have school parties and suchlike here,' Laura continued. She had been on the adventure weekend several years in succession. 'But off-season he does bed and breakfast, short breaks, that kind of thing.'

Joy was puzzled by the mentality of people who chose to go away on holiday specifically to do without the luxuries they had at home. What was the point of it? She followed Laura up the rickety staircase to a small landing with fire doors to the right and the left.

'We're on the first floor,' Laura said. 'That's the women's floor. The men are upstairs. And one of the upstairs dorms is going to have to be for girls too. This year there are more girls than boys with us. Never happened before.'

Joy wondered whether Mr Worthington's presence may have had something to do with that. She'd noticed that Lucy had come to speak to Peter at the service station and had been laughing with him. Unfortunately Joy was too far away to find out what the joke was.

'And here we are!' Laura opened a door on the left, and Joy walked into what seemed to her to be a prison cell. A narrow bed against each wall, a chest of drawers, a sink. That was it.

'Last year I was sharing with three others,' Laura continued. 'We're lucky. There's only one single room and that's on the top floor, so Pete Worthington's got that. Jammy bugger!'

Joy sat down gingerly on a bed. The mattress seemed thin and unwelcoming. Joy doubted she would be able to sleep and hoped that someone had brought some alcohol for a nightcap. Outside the small window of her room a tree was gradually shedding its leaves. She could see some outhouses and a small beck on the perimeter of the grounds. Laura was flinging clothes out of her suitcase and laying them on the bed.

'It's good to get away,' she said. 'I love the Lakes. This year I'm taking a party out sketching, if the weather changes.'

'Can I come with you?' Joy asked immediately. 'I'd love to sketch. Please.'

'You're more than welcome, Joy. But it doesn't work like that. Sid usually puts us all in groups at random. It gets too complicated if everyone chooses what they want to do, and he likes to have staff supervision on all the more dangerous activities. I expect Pete will do the same. You'll have to ask him to see what he's put you on.'

'Do I have to actually *do* the activities?' Joy asked, her mouth dry.

'The kids'll make your life hell if you don't. Half the fun for them is seeing us make complete fools of ourselves.' Laura spoke quite composedly, brushing her long auburn hair in regular, flowing strokes.

'Yes,' said Joy.

Joy pushed away her bowl of Rice Krispies. The idea of a big breakfast, today of all days, was distinctly unappealing. She did not understand how her colleagues and the students could sit there tucking into plates of bacon, eggs, beans and black pudding. She felt faintly nauseous. Predictably, she had slept badly. Accompanied by the sound of Laura's soft breathing, she had taken a torch from her sleeping bag and read until she could read no more. A brisk shower in the morning had woken her up. She had met Peter at the foot of the stairs, his blond hair still damp from the shower, smart as ever in a navy base-ball shirt and tracksuit bottoms, scanning a list.

'Morning, Joy. I've put you with Group D. Assault course in the morning. Abseiling in the afternoon.'

'Abseiling,' Joy echoed, smiling faintly. It was possible this was Peter's idea of a joke.

'Yes, you'll be fine. Roger is your group's instructor. He's the most experienced leader here. He's had an army training.'

The army. Joy shook her head as Laura passed the bacon to her. She was going to go an assault course with an army instructor. And then abseiling. She knew the day would end in her utter and complete humiliation, a hu-miliation all the more devastating because it would be public. What on earth was she, a nice Jewish girl, whose only accomplishment in games lessons at school had been composing inventive excuse notes, doing in a place like this? She felt utterly alien. She realized then that she was essentially an urban creature. The countryside struck her as fundamentally unsafe, and the things she was expected to do in the countryside still less safe. One thing she was pleased about, however, was that she had had the foresight to lie to her mother. As far as Ruth knew, she was taking her A-level group on a reading holi-day, researching Wordsworth and Coleridge.

'You'd better eat something, Joy,' Laura said with con-cern. 'And don't worry. You'll enjoy the assault course. Everyone does.'

Joy watched Lucy rise from her table and come to-wards them.

'Miss Freeman, guess what? I'm in your group. Group D. Isn't that ace? And me and Kelly are dead chuffed be-cause our dorm is with all the lads upstairs. Cool, isn't it?'

'As long as you behave yourself,' Joy said, forcing a smile.

'I know how to behave myself,' Lucy said, with intentional ambiguity. Laura Jessop laughed.

'I think it's nice for the kids to unwind a bit, get to know the staff. Wasn't that Lucy Marshall who has the tattoo?'

'That's her,' Joy said.

'Interesting girl,' said Laura, her mouth full of toast. 'Have you put in for head of department, Joy? You don't mind me asking, do you?'

'No, of course not. Yes, I've applied.'

'And Peter. Is he applying?'

'I expect so.'

'Gosh!' exclaimed Laura. 'That's awkward for you both. When Chris and Steve competed for head of maths, they didn't speak for ages. And here you are on holiday together. But Sister Maureen likes you, everyone thinks that. Even so, I bet you're nervous!'

'Not as nervous as I am about today,' Joy told her.

Both of them were silent as they watched Peter Worthington walk into the dining hall. Evidently he had eaten earlier. Checking off names on his clipboard, he looked every bit the up-and-coming head of department. Meanwhile, Joy was sitting there, unable to eat, a black cloud of anxiety drizzling on her from above. She realized then, as she swallowed her last morsel of toast, that today was going to be decisive. If she ended the day having failed in her own estimation, how could she believe in herself when it came to the interview?

'Peter's very sporty, isn't he?' Laura continued, chatty as ever. He skis, I know, and he belongs to that health club in town, the posh one where you get your own towels, and which has a jacuzzi, doesn't he? He's got a season ticket for United too.'

'Do you know him well?' Joy asked.

'No, not really. Look, I'm going to go now, because we're kayaking and we have to get our life-jackets on. See you later!'

If I survive, thought Joy.

Roger opened a five-barred gate, and the students passed through it and made their way down an uneven footpath, into a valley. Joy waited until they had all passed through and watched Roger fasten the gate.

'It's a good course,' he told her. 'Designed it myself a couple of years ago.' Roger punched the air in front of him, began to jog on the spot and then moved slowly forward in step with Joy. 'It's not a bad life,' he said, 'outdoors most of the time, all this countryside, and challenge. Constant challenge.'

Joy was only half listening. She wondered if it was possible at this late stage to excuse herself from the morning's activities. She could always plead period pains, or pretend to trip over a stone and say she'd hurt her ankle.

'You're doing well so far,' Roger suddenly said to her. 'You haven't pretended to trip and strain your ankle as some of them do. Peter told me this was your first time.'

'Ha ha,' Joy laughed.

'As for me, I've done more assault courses than most people have had hot dinners. Not that assault courses are my thing. Primarily I'm a rock climber. Climbed all over Great Britain, I have. I used to box when I was in the army, then I had an accident. Climbing is safer.'

'Safer? Just you and a rope?' faltered Joy.

'I trust a rope, and if I've got a good climbing partner, I'll try anything.'

'Aren't you ever afraid?' she asked.

Lucy and Kelly had lagged behind to listen to them.

'Not me,' he said, glancing at them.

'You must be frightened of *something*,' Lucy said.

'Girls,' Roger mugged. Lucy and Kelly laughed flirtatiously. Joy looked ahead of her. They had arrived.

The students had massed by another gate, which led into a grove, and they waited while Roger made his way through them and unlocked the gate with a key. On her right Joy could see a complicated arrangement of logs and ropes, connected by planks and platforms. Clearly the idea was to propel yourself from one end to the other by balancing on logs, while holding on to the ropes above. Relief swept through Joy. She had been worrying for nothing after all. The entire system was no more than a foot above the ground.

Her spirits lifted. She joked with the students, looked around her and noticed the lush beauty of the hills that surrounded them. From a rucksack Roger and an assistant brought out a confused mass of straps and buckles.

'These are your safety harnesses,' Roger explained.

Better and better, thought Joy. She watched him demonstrate how to put them on, took the harness offered to her, carefully stepped into the leg openings and asked Lucy to strap her up at the back. Once on, her anorak billowed out in the gaps, and the whole effect was rather as if she were wearing an adult-size nappy. The leg straps cut into her thighs, but Joy was happy to suffer any discomfort in the name of safety.

'You call these lines your cow tails,' Roger went on. He had in his hands some thin ropes with metal fastenings at the ends. 'You attach these to the ropes above as you walk, so if you stumble they'll hold you.' He demonstrated how to move across corners by using one cow tail at a time.

Joy was impressed. Not only was the assault course comfortingly low, but she was to be attached at all times to the equipment. Why, even her mother might like to try this! She joined the line of students eager to test their mettle. She ascended a small ladder to reach the first log. Easy! She attached her cow tails to the rope above and edged herself along. She was doing it! All that fear for nothing! She laughed as she crossed a bridge of planks and rope, which shook as she ran, and soon completed the course. She felt wonderful.

'That's just to get you used to the safety equipment,' Roger said loudly. 'The assault course begins over there.'

What could he mean? Joy looked over to where the instructor was pointing. She saw nothing. Was he joking? She lifted her eyes. There, among the treetops, she could just about discern a similar arrangement of logs, ropes, scramble nets and overhead cables. She craned back her neck. Above her, high up in a tree, was a small platform. The assault course, she could see now, was constructed to take its users across the treetops like young Tarzans. The whole thing was at least thirty foot above the ground. Her nauseous feeling returned.

Roger's assistant had already started to pull himself up the giant-size log ladder that led to the first platform, while some of the students lined up behind him. Lucy and Kelly were watching them from a distance. Roger approached Joy.

'Off you go,' he said.

'No, it's all right,' Joy said hastily. 'I'll just watch.'

'Feeling a bit wobbly?' he asked in gung-ho tones. 'You're as safe as houses up there. Get yourself up the ladder. The view's great from the top. You never achieve anything from the bottom.'

Joy wished he would stop. His persuasions made her feel worse. Macho Roger with his backslapping, hectoring encouragement reminded her of her old gym teacher, who had stood back sadistically as she forced Joy to inch her way up the climbing-frame and laughed when she got stuck. Roger had that same infuriating assumption that, because he could do something, everyone else should be able to.

'I'll go up with you,' he continued. 'There's nothing to be afraid of.'

'Kelly! Kelly! Look who it is!'

Lucy's screaming attracted Joy's attention. She glanced over at her charge, who was waving energetically to an approaching figure. It was Peter Worthington coming to join them. Worse and worse. There was no escape. He would laugh at her for not doing the course, and he'd laugh at her if she did do it.

Lucy gave Peter a half-smile as he let himself into the enclosure.

'Going to have a go, then, sir?'

'Might do,' Peter smiled at her. He turned to Joy. 'No one was left at the centre, and I was spare, so I thought I'd have a spin round the assault course.' Narrowing his eyes, he looked up with confidence at the platforms and zip-lines.

'Damn,' Roger said. ''Fraid you can't. We're out of harnesses.'

'You can have mine!' Joy declared, straining round to unfasten hers as she spoke. 'No, really, it's all right. Please take it. My mother brought me up to do one good turn every day. This is it,' she said brightly, stepping out of the leg loops and handing the equipment to Peter. Peter glanced at Roger and smiled, and with practised ease, Peter got into the harness.

Lucy followed him to the start of the course. Once he had started to climb, Lucy set off in pursuit. Standing on a rise in the grove, Joy followed them with her eyes, her embarrassment at her personal predicament being swallowed up in her fears for Lucy. Was she trying to flirt with Peter? And was Peter responding?

The two of them had reached the top of the ladder and were balanced on a tiny platform. Peter helped Lucy untangle her cow tails. Then he held on to a rope and swung himself across a gap in the trees. Joy was impressed. Lucy stood on the opposite platform, apparently protesting that she couldn't possibly do that. Peter swung her back the rope. Holding on to it tightly, she leapt, and Peter caught her, and for a moment she seemed to cling to him, Joy thought, and he to her. Lucy was giggling quite loudly, and some of the other students were ribbing her in a good-natured way.

The back of her neck aching, Joy watched Peter and Lucy progress along a rope-bridge. Once at the other end, Peter waited for Lucy to join him. Why? Was it a subtle sign in acknowledgement of the way she had singled him out? Ever since arriving in the Lakes, Peter had seemed more confident, as if he were in possession of some secret, some private source of pleasure. There had to be a cause. Now Peter helped Lucy prepare herself for her descent on the zip-line. On one hand, Joy thought, there were only ten years or so between them and, as far as she knew, Peter was single, but then, he was Lucy's teacher, and for him to start any sort of relationship with her would spell the end of his career. If she was going to compete with him to become head of department, she wanted it to be a fair fight. And Lucy, what would become of Lucy?

Lucy screamed with horror and exhilaration as she sped down the zip-line and kicked against the tyre at the end to break her descent. The relationship was bound to end in disaster. Joy wondered if it was too soon to speak to Lucy, or whether she should just continue to be observant. She remembered that there was no other older woman to care for Lucy. She straightened her back imperceptibly as she thought this. Joy knew she might be a physical coward, but she would not be a moral coward. She would rescue Lucy.

The staff and students stood in the courtyard in preparation for the afternoon's activities. The stench of damp trainers billowed from the drying room behind Joy. Roger approached her, dressed now in baggy multicoloured trousers and a waterproof cagoule. Sadist that he was, thought Joy, he seemed to be attracted to her, the masochist. Or was he the bully and she the victim?

'I've had kids here as young as nine or ten,' he informed her, rubbing his large hands, as it was becoming chilly. 'Kids of nine or ten abseiling down the very same cliff we're attempting. They loved it. Kids are great; they're willing to have a go. It builds their character.'

Roger seemed to have a physical energy that crackled beneath his skin, keeping him constantly on the move. He possessed a tautness, a hardness that Joy had always associated with the outdoor type. It acted as a rebuke to her. She wondered if she, who was so different, belonged to a new, de-evolutionized species which was unlearning how to survive. Joy could imagine that if there were to be some cataclysmic ecological catastrophe, men like Roger would manage; she couldn't live for even a day without plenty of hot running water, convenience food and a telephone.

Roger led Group D into a large barn, where the helmets and harnesses were stored. Joy accepted the daffodil-yellow helmet that was proffered her, but privately vowed never to put it on. Since it had been relatively simple to avoid the assault course, it should be equally easy to duck out of abseiling. It was just a matter of picking her moment.

Peter entered the barn. 'Is there room for me in this group?' he asked Roger, who shook his head.

'No helmets left, I'm afraid.'

As Joy went to hold out hers, she was stopped by the look of unmistakable disappointment on Lucy's face. She wished she could have overheard the few words that Lucy whispered to Kelly. It could have been nothing, but then, on the other hand . . .

The ride out to the rocks that lay under Cat Bells was picturesque and, in any other circumstances, Joy would have relished it. Close to here, Beatrix Potter devised the story of Mrs Tiggywinkle. She loved Beatrix Potter almost as much as she did A. A. Milne. Arriving at their destination, a set of slate-walled farm buildings, the party disembarked and followed Roger and two other leaders to a rock-face that rose sharply into the cloud-flecked sky. On its perimeter grew a fringe of trees which masked the rocks from the road. The ground was wet underfoot, and Joy watched her step as she trailed the students in front of her. Lucy was at the rear of the group and, this time, she could be overheard.

'. . . so I arranged to see him later. Yeah, I did! Oh, Miss Freeman. Are you going to abseil? Roger says it's quite safe. He says your harness is attached to a rope and he, like, holds it all the time.'

'We'll see,' Joy said enigmatically. She was less worried

just now about the abseiling than she was about Lucy. Ought she to speak to her now or wait till she could get her alone? She was more and more sure that something needed to be said. Preferably by a teacher who was still in one piece. Abseiling was definitely off for today.

Once they had all assembled at the base of the cliff Roger began to explain procedures and distribute safety harnesses. Joy stood on the edge of the group and debated whether to refuse hers. Unwise. Roger would chaff her again, and this time in front of the students. Better to put one on for now and then lag behind the students. Then, if she left herself until last, there might not be time for her to have a go.

Her safety harness on, she sat on a grey boulder and assessed the cliff-face in front of her. It was high, about forty foot, and almost perpendicular. At the top she could see Roger busying himself with ropes and other tackle. Some students were already scrambling up the hill on the side that gave easy access to the cliff-top. Even that looked somewhat perilous, she decided. Once at the top, all they had to do was lower themselves down the cliff-face. Fairly pointless, of course, but from the bottom of the cliff, descent looked almost possible.

There was the first volunteer now, a lad Joy didn't teach but had seen around college. She watched him peer down the cliff. Then he turned and, with his back towards her, leant backwards, a rope in his hands, and began to walk slowly down the side of the cliff. He was sure-footed and made it seem easy. Just for a moment Joy imagined what it would be like if she were to try. Perhaps she could do it after all. In a moment the boy had reached the ground and began to unfasten the tackle. Joy applauded him, but the faint sound of her clapping was lost in the rush of the breeze, which shook some of the remaining leaves from the surrounding trees.

Then Lucy appeared at the top, her blond hair glinting in the autumn sunlight. Now it was someone she cared for, Joy saw the danger in the activity. What if Lucy were to fall? Could she fall, despite the safety harness? Roger was shouting to Lucy. 'You can do it. Just ease yourself over the edge, let the rope pass through your hands.'

Lucy leant backwards and she too felt her way down the cliff with her feet. The rope swung perilously. Joy's heart was in her mouth. Lower and lower she dropped and then, with a pull on the rope, she was on her feet on solid ground. Amazing!

Lucy ran to her. 'Like, wow, it is so cool! I want to do it again. Come up with me. Don't miss your turn.'

'You have another go. Don't wait for me.'

'Come on, I'm taking you up!' Matily, Lucy linked arms with Joy and marched with her up the hill. Touched by this display of friendship, Joy felt she could hardly break away. Together they ascended the hill that led to the abseiling party. At least, thought Joy, the view should be rather special.

Ahead of them three students, a leader and Roger were at the edge of the cliff, shouting support to Kelly. From a distance it looked as if someone had fallen over and an attempt was being made to rescue them. Joy came up to them, and peered over the edge. There was Kelly's face and a terrifying, stomach-churning drop to the stony ground. Certain she was going to lose her balance, Joy retreated. Her legs were shaking. What on earth was she doing up here? It had all been a terrible mistake. She was going to get herself down immediately.

She turned to climb down the hill. Roger shouted to her.

'Joy! Your turn next!'

'Sorry!' she shouted.

'Come back. You'll never forgive yourself if you don't. You'll always wonder what would have happened if you did try. It's absolutely safe, I promise you.'

Joy knew it was cowardly to continue her retreat down the hill. She retraced her steps back to Roger.

'I just don't want to,' she said.

'OK, but do me a favour. Link yourself up to the rope and get the feel of it in your hands. It might not be as bad as you think.'

'No,' Joy said.

'Go on, Miss Freeman,' said one of the upper sixth.

'She won't do it,' said another.

'She will,' Lucy insisted.

Joy interrupted their argument.

'You can set me up if you want, but don't expect me to abseil.'

'Fair enough,' said Roger, beginning to attach a bright-pink rope to her safety harness, as she stood there in the shelter of a tree that grew close to the edge. Birds wheeled above her. From the lane in the distance she could hear a car engine slowing and stopping. These familiar noises sounded as if they were coming from another world. Joy took the abseiling rope from Roger and held it in her hands. It was cool and smooth, and a red-and-black fleck ran through the beige.

'So I just hold on to this,' she said tentatively.

'Run it through your hands as you're ready to lower yourself, and support yourself with it.'

Joy stood at the edge of the cliff. She knew she was

taking up valuable time, and that the several students who had not yet had a turn were watching her with interest. She turned to face them and took a step or two backwards. Just walking backwards was terrifying. For all she knew she would drop right over the edge of the cliff.

'No,' she said. 'I want to stop.'

'All you have to do is, once you get to the ledge at the end, start to lean backwards,' Roger crooned. 'Just lean and let go.'

'No,' Joy said, panic immobilizing her. She could move neither forward nor back. Her knees continued to shake.

'It's simple,' he insisted. 'Just a little step backwards and you're off.'

The ground seemed to tremble under her feet. Behind her was a forty-foot drop. Her spine turned to ice. In front of her she saw a figure in the distance making his way towards them – another leader, she presumed.

'Joy!' shouted the figure.

His voice was familiar.

'Joy, wait. I've got to talk to you!'

A new shock rocked her. It was Michael. Of all the people in the world, it was Michael. Or was she hallucinating in her terror? What on earth was he doing here? Had he read her letter? He stumbled towards her, looking desperate. A nightmare was upon her.

There was only one thing to do. Holding fast on to the rope, Joy leant backwards and prayed. The sky swung into view. Her head rested on vacancy. She pressed with her feet against the surface of the cliff and was terrified to discover they were useless; she was supporting the whole of her weight on the rope. Above her was sky and a lattice of branches. Below her – she would not think what was below her. People were shouting at the top, but their shouts meant nothing to her. Nothing existed except for her hands, which gripped hold of the rope, and her treacherous feet, which couldn't find purchase on the rock-face. She let more rope pass through her hands and edged down a little further. Never, in her whole life, had she concentrated so fully on what she was doing. She banished her fear; it could not help her now. More rope passed through her hands. She lowered her feet. She was doing it – really abseiling. Her mother would never believe her. No one would believe her. She didn't believe it herself. Joy moved her hands down the rope again, and exultation filled her. She was a bird, she was hovering like a kestrel, slowly lowering herself down a cliff. Then she thought of the drop and turned to ice. *I will not think*, she instructed herself. The rope slid through her hands.

'Brilliant! Oh, Kelly, look at her. Oh, she's ace! She's doing it!'

Lucy's excited cries from the bottom of the cliff seemed to be getting nearer. Not daring to look behind her, Joy continued her journey.

'Nearly, nearly – go on, let your feet go. Oh, that's cool!'

Lucy ran up to Joy and hugged her. It was a moment she would never forget. Tears of triumph and laughter and pure, liquid panic ran down her face. Lucy fumbled to loosen her harness rope.

'Lucy, there's someone up there I don't want to see. My ex-boyfriend.'

'What? That funny-looking bloke in the navy cagoule?'

'Him, yes.'

'Shall we run off and hide?'

Why hide? If Joy could abseil down a cliff, she could

face up to Michael. She looked up the hill and saw him sliding down the hill on his behind. She wanted to laugh, but resisted the impulse.

He came up to her, red-faced and sweating. 'Christ, Joy, I thought you'd kill yourself. What d'you want to go and frighten me like that for?'

'I'm sorry,' she said.

'I got your letter. Your mother can stay. I'll manage. I'm not leaving the house, you know. I've come all the way up here to say this. I still love you.'

Joy took a deep breath. It occurred to her that Lucy, Kelly and a selection of her A-level students were watching them both as if they were the stars in a soap opera. Which, in a way, they were. Joy did not mind. It felt normal to her to have an audience of sixth-formers. In fact, they made her feel better. Besides, nothing could faze her now. Here was a woman who had just abseiled down a cliff. Surely she could make Michael see why they couldn't go on.

'You say you love me,' Joy said, in the neutral, scholarly way she explained Shakespeare in the classroom, 'but really we need to define the word "love". I think in your case you mean that you feel you need me because you don't have the financial or emotional strength to start over again. Love is something different. Love – the best sort of love – has to be mutual – a marriage of true minds.' She was tempted to ask her class if they agreed, and whether they could illustrate this from their own experience. 'Our "love", as you call it, isn't mutual, because for some time I haven't loved you. I'm not sure I ever loved you fully; I lacked the confidence to find someone new, and you were safe, Michael. I wouldn't risk leaving you. Now I am leaving you, and my mother has nothing to do with it. The fact she's coming to live with me is completely irrelevant.'

Lucy put her hand up. 'Please, miss. Why is your mother coming to live with you?'

'A good question. Because she's lost her job and she lives alone. She'll be better off with me.'

'I can't wait to leave *my* mother,' Kelly remarked.

Joy ignored the interruption. 'I know this is hard for you, Michael, and I'm sorry it had to happen like this, so publicly, but it's better that we should be absolutely clear.'

Joy's class nodded. Michael regarded her, and realized that Joy had changed. She wasn't the compliant, eager-to-please girl he'd gratefully shacked up with. He wasn't sure that he liked this new Joy. He wished he could extricate himself from the situation and was uncomfortably aware of the eyes of the students upon him.

'Oh well,' he said, 'if you insist your mother comes to stay, I'm off. I'm not putting up with your mum. You should meet her mum!' he said to the assembled students. 'So it's over, Joy, and I'm sorry if I have to tell you this in front of these kids. But it's over.' He turned and faced their audience, which looked at him in astonishment. Then he addressed Joy again.

'You might be able to abseil down a cliff, Joy Freeman, but you don't have the guts to cut loose from your mother. I've had enough.'

Michael turned and marched down the footpath back to his car.

'It's over,' shouted Joy, and hugged Lucy in her delight.

Chapter Sixteen

Joy folded her arms and held them tightly against herself. It was decidedly chilly. She had come outside to watch the evening game of cricket – staff against students – which was taking place on the small field at the back of the hostel. It would have been more sensible to have stayed in and read a book, but Joy was newly liberated from being sensible. She wanted activity and company. She had already recounted the story of her abseil to Laura, to Peter and to any other member of staff who would listen. She did this partly to convince herself it had really happened. Partly, also, to deflect interest from Michael's surprise appearance. However, she was resigned to the fact that both staff and students would be gossiping about her love life for the rest of the holiday and beyond, but this was a small price to pay for liberation from Michael.

The sky was already darkening. The clocks went back that night, and the next night they would all be back in Manchester. There was the thwack of the ball against the bat, and Joy, like the others, followed the trajectory of the ball over the boundary. Some lads ran after it.

She wished she had someone to talk to. All the staff who were outside were involved in the game. Joy tried to watch, but had never been able to follow cricket. She considered going back into the hostel and ringing Lesley, but the last time she had passed the pay phone a girl had been involved in a long conversation with the boyfriend she had left at home. Perhaps she ought to ring

Lawrence? She smiled to herself. She had conquered one set of physical fears today; she knew that the next step was to tackle another, and that Lawrence was going to be a key player. Now she was free of Michael she had no reason to stall with Lawrence. I know, she thought, enjoying the sensation of plotting, I shall arrange to meet him after the Fear of Flying course. And I shall remind Lesley that she promised to let me have use of her house. She smiled, contemplating her own wickedness. I'm as bad as Lucy, she thought.

Lucy. Now might be a good time to speak to her. She was probably watching the cricket match. Virtually all the students were there. She scanned the figures sitting on the bank. Lucy didn't seem to be among them. Yet there was Kelly, who was laughing with one of the boys from the upper sixth. It was possible, then, that Lucy was in her room. Joy remembered that she was sharing the only girls' dormitory on the boys' floor. Her thoughts were broken up by loud applause and cries from the students. Another member of staff was out. Joy wondered when it would be Peter's turn to bat. He was supposed to be good at cricket.

It wasn't Peter batting now. It was Steve from Biology. She idly scanned the staff bench for Peter. He didn't seem to be there. Joy frowned. Had she seen him at all that evening? Yes – he had eaten with them in the canteen and been more talkative than usual. He had entertained them all with stories of the ghyll-scrambling and the silly boy who'd jumped in a deep pool with his glasses on and had lost them. She looked around her again. Peter was certainly not outside.

No Peter. No Lucy. It was what she had been dreading. They had absconded from the rest of the party and gone somewhere. Joy cradled her forehead in her hands. She was being foolish. Neither of them would take such a risk as to slope off like that – Joy corrected herself – Lucy would! She could sit still no longer. She called over to Kelly, who got to her feet and joined her.

'Where's Lucy?' Joy asked her. No point beating around the bush.

'Lucy?' Kelly said, as if she'd never heard of her before. 'I don't know. Oh, I think she went somewhere with Mr Worthington. Yeah, I saw her go off with him. They went inside.'

'It's all right, Kelly. Thanks.' As blatant as that! Joy was astonished. What was Peter doing? Not only would he lose his job at St Ignatius' – Joy imagined Sister Maureen's wrath and quaked for him – not only would he lose his job there, but he would never get another. Moral turpitude, wasn't that what they called it? And Lucy. Did she know what she was doing? Joy saw her path was now clear. She had to stop them. It was lucky, she reflected, as she strode back into the hostel, that she had been so thoroughly embarrassed in front of the students today. Nothing, absolutely nothing, had the power to embarrass her now. She would find Peter and Lucy and confront them. She had to save them.

She pushed open the back door and entered the lounge. A few lads were playing pool and looked up at her as she came in. Neither Peter nor Lucy was among them. The rest of the lounge was empty. Some empty crisp packets and Coke tins were scattered on the benches, and Joy made a mental note to check they were removed later. She left the lounge and peered round into the dining hall. It was dark. Were they hiding there? The room looked empty. She went back into the entrance lobby and checked the staff area. Empty. There was no light coming from Roger's office either. She hadn't seen him that evening. She guessed he'd gone back to his flat in Keswick.

So Peter and Lucy must be upstairs. Drawing a deep breath, Joy began her ascent of the narrow staircase. She reached the first floor, where the girls' dormitories were. All was silent. She walked the length of the floor, towards the shower area. A couple of the doors were open, revealing no students, just a tumble of suitcases and clothes and boots and toiletries thrown haphazardly on the beds and on the floor. No sound anywhere. Joy turned and made her way back to the staircase, and climbed to the second floor.

The layout of the rooms seemed to be similar. Similar, too, was the silence. All she could hear was the sounds of the cricket from below. There was evidently no one here either. Softly, she glided down the corridor, flinching at the smell of the boys' dirty clothes. That was when she heard the laugh.

For a moment she was reminded of Jane Eyre and the first Mrs Rochester. Except this laugh was neither female, nor insane. It was a man's laugh, and a laugh redolent of sensual pleasure and satisfaction. It came from the end of the corridor. Joy edged forwards a little further. A voice – Peter's voice – said to stop now, that was enough.

Once already that day Joy had told herself not to think of the consequences, but just to act. It had worked for her then. It was going to have to work for her now. Not for her sake, but for Peter's sake and Lucy's sake. She rapped sharply on the door through which she had heard Peter's voice.

'I'm coming in,' she warned.

She opened the door. There was Peter, undressed and in bed. Not alone, either. There were two sets of clothes jumbled together on the floor. The second apparently belonged to Roger, who was sitting, almost entirely naked, on the bed beside Peter.

At first she thought it was all right because Peter wasn't with Lucy after all, and she began to smile with relief. Then she wondered why Peter and Roger had both decided to take their clothes off. As the truth hit her she flooded with a hot embarrassment, worse than anything she had ever experienced in her life. Quickly, in case anyone else was in the corridor, she closed the door behind her and stood there. Peter and Roger stared at her in disbelief.

If only, thought Joy, there was some sort of etiquette to follow on these occasions.

'I'm sorry,' she said after what seemed like an age. 'I thought you were with Lucy. They said you'd gone off with her, and I was worried.'

'Lucy?' echoed Peter.

'I'm sorry, Pete,' Roger said. 'I should have never persuaded you. My fault. I thought everyone would be watching the match.'

'Joy doesn't like cricket,' Peter murmured to Roger.

For a moment Joy contemplated following this conversational link and explaining why cricket jargon had put her off cricket and how she didn't like football much either, except when it was a cup final, but that she was pretty keen on the Olympics. It might defuse the situation. In fact it might be best to act as if nothing untoward had happened. And nothing untoward had happened. Peter and Roger had a perfect right to be lovers. It was Joy, who burst into people's bedrooms as if she were starring in a bedroom farce, who was untoward. Yet as she was about to apologize again, it occurred to her that Peter and Roger probably felt a whole lot worse than she did. The best thing to do, after all, would be to put them at their ease, to proceed as if nothing unusual had happened at all.

She moved some trousers from an upright chair and sat on it. 'My back is ever so stiff,' she said pleasantly. 'I think it must be the abseiling. Using muscles I never knew I had.' She glanced at the two men and blushed. 'I was thinking. Perhaps a few of us could abseil down the side of the sports hall at college for fund-raising – a sponsored abseil. Sister was saying that some extensive work needs to be done to the chapel. I'd be quite happy to organize it. Unless you wanted to, Peter.' Joy didn't want him to think she was trying to compete with him. She continued. 'It's not a bad idea. I'm sure the local press would write it up, and Sister's always on at us to market the college, and this way we could get publicity for St Ignatius' as an institution, the chapel renovations, and the courage of the staff. What do you think, Peter?' she concluded, smiling brightly.

The two men gazed at her in astonishment.

'Yes, you're right. We ought to include the students too, but we might need to get permission slips from their parents. We'd need a first-class instructor – Roger! – could you come down for the day? I'm sure college could fund your expenses and sort out accommodation. Unless you prefer to stay with Peter . . .'

Joy's voice faded away. Everything began to fall into place. Peter was so reserved and inscrutable because he

278

felt he needed to hide his private life. His passion for sport was something he shared with his lover. And Lesley knew – all the time, Lesley knew! And those life sketches in her bedroom – they really were of Peter. And all this time she'd thought of him as cold and distant, when he was nothing of the sort. His meticulous approach to his work – all of it was a cover, so no one would suspect. She had to reassure him.

'Peter, listen. I'm not going to say a word about this to anyone. It's the truth, I promise. I can't apologize enough. I should never have burst in like that.'

'It's OK,' Peter said. 'I know I can trust you.'

'I must go now – see if I can find Lucy. Bye!' Joy sang brightly, closing the door behind her, and for the second time that day the ground rocked under her feet.

The next morning Joy declined to go to Mass at Our Lady and St Charles's. She sat in the small staff room reading a Sunday paper, listening to the rumbling of the coach that was transporting the students down to the church in Keswick. It would be good to have some time to think, or even sleep. Again she had lain awake all night, thinking through the events of the day. Like neon-lit advertisements which constantly recycled their messages, Joy's mind headlined again and again: MICHAEL HAS GONE, I HAVE ABSEILED DOWN A CLIFF, PETER IS GAY.

When Peter appeared at the door of the staff room she was not surprised to see him. It was as if he had never left her. He was dressed in a Barbour jacket and fresh jeans and was wearing a crisp and pleasant aftershave. He smiled at her.

'Coming for a walk?' he asked.

Joy jumped up. 'Yes!' she said.

The path Peter selected zigzagged up by the side of the hostel and climbed steeply until it reached a quiet road. Once at the top Joy had to steady her breathing. On her left the ground fell away steeply, and between the trees she could catch glimpses of water, glittering in the autumn sunlight. As they walked further along the road, she could see the whole of the lake, its surface wrinkled by the ripples lapping at the sides. She increased her pace to keep up with Peter. She guessed he had asked for her company so they could talk and she felt it incumbent on her to provide an opening.

'Is Roger joining us today?' she asked.

'He's down at the church with the students. He's Catholic too. He was a chaplain when he was in the army. When he left he took a job managing a health club. That was where we met. He came into some money and started up Hill Beck, and he's invested in other centres too. When he's in Manchester he lives with me. He has done for the last five years.'

The road began its descent. Peter looked straight ahead of him as he continued to speak.

'I know I shouldn't mind people knowing and in time I would have told you, but it would have taken more courage than I had. It wasn't through me that college started coming to Hill Beck. It was one of those awful coincidences, Sid chancing on this place. I didn't want Sid to find out about Roger and me. That's why I've never come here until this time.'

Joy understood everything. She had also heard Sid make his infamous homophobic remarks. A new irony struck her. All term long she had been worrying unnecessarily, tilting at windmills, when it was Peter who had far more to be worried about. Both of them worrying, and neither of them telling each other.

'Roger has always put pressure on me to come out, so we can be open. I know he's right, but it's just me. I like to keep things quiet. Not because I'm ashamed; I just don't see why people need to know.'

That was a fair point, thought Joy.

'I don't like the idea of being talked about,' he continued.

'You won't be!' Joy declared. 'When the kids get back to college it's going to be Miss Freeman's love life that will be the latest hot gossip.'

Peter laughed. 'It doesn't bother you, does it?'

'Not really. My love life's pretty comic anyway. If it entertains the kids, all well and good.'

'You're brave,' Peter commented.

'Me? Brave? Since we're telling the truth this morning, I'll tell you something. Everyone's been saying to me how brilliant it was, me overcoming my fear of abseiling. But I haven't. I'll be just as terrified if I ever have to do it again. You can't get rid of fear; you just have to learn how to override it.'

'Roger was chuffed you did the abseil. He had you marked out as the fearful type and told me he'd get you down that cliff by any means possible. He didn't plan your boyfriend turning up, though!'

It was Joy's turn to laugh. 'I'm grateful to him. But I still don't think I can really change. I'm a worrier, and that's that. Just like you're gay, I suppose.'

'But I enjoy being gay. Do you enjoy worrying?'

Joy was silent. Peter had scored a direct hit. She decided to change the subject. They skirted the side of a whitewashed cottage with a dog barking in the garden.

281

'I found out what happened to Lucy in the end. She'd sneaked off to the pub with a couple of the lads. Kelly was her cover. She thought it would throw me off Lucy's scent if she said she'd seen Lucy talking to you.' Joy realized this was an awkward subject too. Peter must never know what she had imagined about him. She hunted for another subject. 'So, are you going for head of department? You've never actually told me.'

'I handed in my letter of application to Sister on Friday. Roger was against it; he tells me we don't need the money, and it's true. I'm not too bothered about the outcome. I'd be perfectly happy with you as head of department.'

Joy was flattered. In a rush of gratitude and affection, she interrupted him.

'And I'd be more than happy if you were head of department!'

Peter turned and smiled at her. 'So there's nothing to worry about either way,' he said lightly.

'I'm not worried about the interview,' Joy continued. 'I don't mind performing in public. I worry more about the things I can't control. I'm a control freak!' she shouted into the peaceful Sunday morning.

'Like Roger,' Peter said. 'He's the most physically fearless man I know, but we've never been abroad together. I have to go on holiday on my own.'

'Why's that?' asked Joy.

'He won't fly. He's terrified of aeroplanes. He even drops me off before we get to the airport. Just the sight of the check-in desks makes him panic.'

'Me too! I'm terrified of flying. That's why I've booked myself on a course to get rid of it – my fear of flying. Why doesn't Roger come with me? Look, it's the least I can do, after bursting in on you like that –'

'I'm glad you did,' said Peter. 'In a way, it's a relief.'

Joy hardly heard him.

'And it was Roger who got me down that cliff. I owe him one. He can come with me. We'll take the course together. Then next year you can fly to some coral reef and go snorkelling or something, and take him with you.'

'You're on,' said Peter, and they grinned at each other in happy complicity as they turned on to the main road that would take them back to the hostel.

Peter placed a hand on Joy's shoulder. 'You're a good friend,' he said.

In the distance church bells rang.

CHAPTER SEVENTEEN

Lesley's phone rang.

Joy was used to having stop-start conversations with Lesley. As soon as she made herself comfortable in her friend's office, someone more important would come in, or the phone would ring, or the silhouette of a student would appear outside the frosted-glass door. Tonight she was happy to wait. She was basking in Lesley's approval of her having finally ditched Michael, who had taken the television, video and megadrive with him. Joy thought it was a small price to pay. She had decided not to tell Lesley her plans regarding her mother. There were certain things her friend wouldn't be able to understand. But there was Lawrence to talk about, and Peter and Roger. She was bursting with revelations.

'Yes, Sister. Yes, of course. That's not a problem. Of course. Bye.'

Lesley placed the receiver down with a final little *ping* and a barely suppressed sigh.

'More work?' Joy asked sympathetically. It was after college hours and Sister was still doling out instructions to her vice-principal.

'It's nothing,' Lesley said, brushing her hair back.

Joy considered telling her friend that she was looking weary these days and ought not to work so hard. Except she couldn't do that because Les was one of those people who defined themselves through their work and would be bereft without it. There was Rennie, of course, but as Lesley herself said, Rennie wasn't everything. There was her painting, but that was only a hobby. The painting made Joy think of Peter again.

'Those life drawings in your bedroom – they are of Peter, aren't they?'

'Yes,' Les said, looking steadily at Joy.

'At first I thought they couldn't be, but I've got to know Pete a lot better this weekend, and I can see it's just the sort of thing he might do, be a life model.' This was tricky. Joy suspected Lesley knew about Peter being gay, but didn't want to tell her if she didn't know. However, the temptation proved too great.

'I never realized till this weekend that he was gay!' said Joy.

Lesley nodded and said nothing.

'Did you know?' Joy pursued.

'Yes.'

Lesley knew she sounded abrupt. She disliked discussing such matters in her office in college. It seemed like a betrayal. Her long-standing friendship with Peter and Roger was something she kept separate, separate from her work, from her affair with Rennie, from her friendship with Joy. Compartmentalizing was her insurance policy. If one part of her life should malfunction she could retreat to another. She guessed it was unlikely that all aspects of her life would go wrong at once. If they did, the consequences would be unthinkable. Blackness. Emptiness. She suppressed this spasm of despair and paid attention to Joy. Lesley envied her friend's delight in making connections.

'It explains everything,' Joy continued. 'Why Peter has been so reserved, why he's in two minds about the head of department job. It was the most horrible moment of my life – walking in on Peter and Roger like that.' Lesley stopped tapping her pen on the desk to listen. 'It was taking such a risk, both of them being together in Pete's room in the hostel. It was Roger's idea – he's a born risk-taker. I think secretly he wants to put pressure on Pete to come out. Except I can quite understand why Peter's worried about the effect it would have in college. And despite all his physical bravery, it turns out Roger is scared of flying too. So we've booked him a place on my Fear of Flying course on Saturday!'

'So it's this weekend,' Lesley said.

'Yes.' Joy had to admit to herself that her attitude to-wards the course had changed. It was no longer such an insurmountable hurdle. Having Roger's company would be fun, and learning how not to be frightened might prove very instructive, especially as she was beginning to develop a new idea, one she wished to talk about now with her best friend. First there was the Fear of Flying course. The word 'flying' sent little eddies of fear through her. The course part was OK – it was the plane ride that scared her. What if it crashed? There was no guarantee it wouldn't. Imagine the headlines in the *Manchester Evening News* – FEAR OF FLYING PROVES ALL TOO REAL!

'It's one ordeal after another with you, Joy.' Lesley commented. 'First your abseil, now your flight and then your interview.'

Joy swallowed hard. 'You've forgotten one.'

Lesley raised her eyebrows in enquiry.

'My seduction of Lawrence.'

'Lawrence!' exclaimed Lesley in delight. She enjoyed talking about Joy's love life. Even here in her office. This was possibly because Joy's love life only ever seemed to exist in the potential, rather than in the actual. But this seduction was a new development. 'So you've slept with him?'

'Ah, no. But I'm coming round to your point of view that perhaps I should. Otherwise, how will I ever know whether we're right for each other?'

'My point precisely,' said Lesley, glad.

'So I'm going to try,' said Joy, rather lamely.

Lesley sensed her diffidence. This seduction of Lawrence was a project that interested her. Sex interested her. Lesley decided that she would do all she could to help.

'Tell me your plan.'

'I haven't got a plan,' Joy said reproachfully. 'I'm sort of hoping it will just kind of happen.'

'Sounds too vague to me,' Les said. 'Now let's get thinking. When are you planning your first advance?'

She reminded Joy momentarily of an army general putting the final touches to a campaign.

'I don't know. I'll have to invite him to my house, but it's still so full of Michael, if you know what I mean. It's bound to be a disaster.'

'Then come to my house.' Lesley thought rapidly and with growing pleasure. 'This Saturday night I'm scheduled to pick Rennie up from the station around ten – he had some sort of exhibition in London. So this is what we'll do. I'll invite you and Lawrence over for dinner, but we won't tell him about Rennie. I'll get Rennie to ring me from the station and ask me to spend the night with him. Then at ten I'll ask you to mind my house for the night. The scene is set.'

'But that's directly after the Fear of Flying course,' Joy objected.

'Good. It'll give you something else to think about.' Lesley thought it would give her something else to think about too. Spending all Saturday alone hoping that Rennie would choose to see her that night was not a prospect she relished.

'That's very good of you, Les.'

'Not at all. It's what you need.'

That was an ambiguous comment, Joy thought. Did Les think she needed sex? Joy had temporarily forgotten her fear that she might be frigid. Frigidity wasn't a subject spoken about much these days, when everybody was supposed to be having it with everybody else. Perhaps she didn't enjoy sex because Michael was such an awful lover. But if she didn't enjoy sex with Lawrence either, then something was certainly wrong with her. She bit her lip anxiously. And what if Lawrence didn't want to be seduced? What if he took her hand away as she was trying to unbutton his shirt and said no? A dreadful thought.

Joy rebuked herself. She was the woman who had abseiled down a cliff only two days ago. Compared to that, sex should be a walk-over. Her lips were dry. Joy licked them.

'I'll do it,' Joy said.

'Excellent!'

There was a knock at the door. Another interruption. It was Lucy, with a large black bin-liner full of rubbish.

'I've finished, Miss Wright. Oh, hello, Miss Freeman!'

Lucy looked surprisingly cheerful for someone who was on college service for a week, to atone for her escape to the Hill Beck Arms.

'Shall I just take this to the caretaker?'

'That's right, Lucy,' Lesley said briskly.

Lucy stood there, by the door, giving the strong impression that she wanted to join the conversation. Joy smiled at her encouragingly. She remembered Lucy's lack of a mother. Older woman naturally held an attraction for her. Joy decided to include her in their talk.

'Did your dad give you a hard time when you got back?'

'No. He thought it was a laugh. He said that's what he would've done. What's an adventure holiday for, if it isn't having adventures? That's what he said. That's my dad for you. Anyway, he's off on his own adventure next weekend.'

'Adventure?' asked Joy.

'Well, not really an adventure. He's involved in some sort of course at Ruskin College, but it's his chance to get away from me, I suppose.'

Joy felt herself stiffening with disapproval. A father who condoned drinking and left his sixteen-year-old daughter alone in the house for a whole weekend.

'I don't mind,' Lucy said, looking cheerfully at both Lesley and Joy. 'Liam's got tickets for this birthday bash at the Mission in town on Friday. His dad's a friend of this geezer who knows an A&R bloke for the Fever label. I might meet someone famous.'

And older, thought Joy. Once again she felt an overpowering need to protect this girl. But what could she do?

'So you're all alone this weekend?' Joy enquired.

'Sure am!'

'I think you'd better take my phone number. I know you'll think I'm being fussy, but you never know what might happen. Just in case of an emergency.' Joy had already ripped a piece of paper from Lesley's message pad and was writing down the necessary details.

'Here's my number. I might not be at home all the time. On Saturday I'm at Manchester Airport – I'm taking a Fear of Flying course. On Sunday –' Joy paused. 'On Sunday I'll be at Miss Wright's house. I'm staying with her on Saturday night. Here's her number too.'

Lucy took the piece of paper gratefully.

'That's cool, Miss Freeman. Everything will be all right, though. Dad's left me alone before. I'd better get rid of this rubbish now.' Lucy grinned, and left them.

'You're fond of that girl, aren't you, Joy?' Lesley said, not without approval.

'I can't imagine being that age and not having a mother,' Joy replied, knowing that was not all the answer. As much as she was horrified by Lucy's recklessness, she envied it. She lived vicariously through it. Part of her thought, if Lucy can do it, so can I. Lucy proved something to her. And Lucy needed protecting too. It was a paradox, but there it was.

'So,' said Lesley, 'are you all right for Saturday?'

'As long as it's a big one,' Joy said. 'With little ones, you can feel all the movement.'

'I should think it was the other way around,' Lesley said, somewhat surprised.

'Oh no,' Joy said. 'I've heard that on the jumbo jets you hardly know you're moving. And it's the tiny planes that have all the crashes.'

'Ah, you're talking about planes,' Lesley said, relieved.

'What else did you think I was – oh, I see.' Joy blushed. Lesley laughed.

'Don't worry, Joy. Size doesn't matter.'

Joy pretended to laugh as a mask for her anxiety. What had she let herself in for? An air journey, responsibility for Lucy and a night of passionate love. None of them seemed to her to fit together. If the plane crashed she would be no good for any of them. And how could she have sex with Lawrence while she was being mother? The thought was almost blasphemous. She lifted her eyes to the model of the Madonna and Child above Lesley's desk, which she had never taken down. Help, she said silently.

Joy stood in the check-in hall at Manchester Airport and wondered how she was ever going to find Roger in the constant flow of people. In front of her were ranged the baggage-handlers' booths with illuminated signs above them – Lufthansa, Air France, British Airways. Queues of men, women and children stood with trolleys and suitcases waiting for attention. It seemed odd to Joy that people should voluntarily submit themselves to the risks of air travel, and even more odd that she should be here, doing just that, when she was neither going on holiday nor travelling on business.

But Roger, where was Roger? She glanced at her watch – it was getting late – and scanned the incoming passengers. Perhaps even now Peter was pulling Roger, screaming, from his car. Or maybe he'd refused to come at all. Then she would have to do this thing by herself, just when the idea of having a companion seemed so attractive. Where was Roger?

From the direction of the Gents she finally saw Peter walking sombrely towards her with his lover. Roger had his jacket folded over his arm and was wearing a red and brown sweater and brown cords. Peter was svelte and elegant beside him.

'Well, this is it,' said Peter unnecessarily to both of them. Joy attempted a small smile. Then Peter did an unexpected thing. He put his arms round her and kissed her swiftly. Then, disengaging himself, he did the same to

Roger. Joy realized why he had kissed her and felt a wave of sympathy for him. He had used her as a cover; otherwise he couldn't kiss Roger without feeling he was exciting attention. In her charged emotional state, Joy thought she could almost cry.

Joy and Roger made their way through the departure lounge, past W. H. Smith on one side, the Tie Rack and the Sock Shop on the other, to the suite of rooms where their course was to take place.

'It's just like an ordinary shopping mall,' Joy said comfortingly to Roger.

He nodded. But it was a lie, and she knew it. For there they were, at the very end of the concourse, lurking behind a huge plate-glass window – the planes. Several of them, huge metal tubes with triangular wings like sharks' fins. Joy and Roger hurried to the Pegasus suite.

They entered a big carpeted hall, which Joy could not help think was large enough for a good-size *Bar Mitzvah* party. Except this morning it had been laid out with rows of chairs facing a white screen, and a table had been prepared for the speakers. Away from those were a few low coffee-tables, where other course participants were drinking coffee and talking in hushed voices. There were a lot of them. So all these people, thought Joy, were scared of flying too. She didn't know if that made her feel better or worse. On one hand, she was not alone in her fears; on the other, if so many people were scared of flying, then she might have good reason to be scared. She touched Roger's arm lightly and led him to a table where there were two empty seats. Once they had sat down, a waiter appeared with a jug of hot coffee and served them.

Once he had gone, there was silence. No one seemed prepared to start up a conversation. It was worse, Joy thought, than a doctor's waiting room, or even a male-impotence clinic. Feeling desperately in need of a diversion and abhorring the vacuum, Joy began to talk.

'Why are you here?' she asked the short bearded man on her right.

'I'm a journalist,' he replied laconically.

Fancy picking the one person in the room who wasn't scared of flying! Joy supposed he was with them to report on the course for his paper. There was a notebook on his lap. She turned instead to the elderly lady next to him.

'And why are you here?'

'Well, love, I don't know if I'm a nervous passenger because I haven't actually flown before. George never trusted aeroplanes. He always used to say that if God meant us to fly he would have given us wings. He's got his wings now, has George. Passed away four months ago.' She gave Joy a conspiratorial wink. 'I've had enough coach tours to last me a lifetime. I'm ready to learn how to fly!'

This encouraged the woman next to her to speak. 'What a coincidence! I'm not exactly frightened myself either. It's my husband who's scared of flying.'

Joy looked around for her husband.

'When he sees a plane, he breaks up,' she continued. 'He's in bits.'

Joy was pleased that someone here was as frightened as she and Roger were. She hunted, unsuccessfully, for this fragmented husband. She noticed the Gents at the side of the room and looked pointedly at it, saying to the wife, 'Is he . . .'

'In the lav? You must be joking! He wouldn't go within five miles of the airport. I'm taking the course for him. I'll tell him all about it when I get home.'

'*I*'m scared of flying,' said the young, pretty, blonde woman next to Roger. Joy turned to her with relief. 'I wasn't so scared when I was younger, but after I had the kids, that was when it started. I found I couldn't get on a plane without imagining what could happen. Now I'm scared I'll pass my fear on to the children.'

Joy nodded vigorously in sympathy.

'Roger and I, we're terrified of flying too. I think it's the feeling of being out of control. And just the merest possibility of a crash makes me imagine one happening – and being so high up, and thinking of all that nothingness between you and the ground,' Joy gushed.

The journalist suddenly stood up, put his notebook in his pocket and went to take a chair facing the screen. Joy hardly noticed. Fear made her talkative, and now she was in full flow.

'I also have this belief that if I can imagine the plane crashing, then it won't. So I have to make myself see it crashing. And to be honest, I don't even see how a plane can stay up there. I mean, it's heavier than the air.'

'Excuse me,' said Roger, and headed in the direction of the Gents.

'And you keep reading in the paper about all these near misses and the fact that mobile phones and laptop computers interfere with the plane's electronics and, before the pilot knows it, the plane's drifting dangerously off course.'

The young mother looked slightly green and murmured something about having to ring home.

Joy wished someone would stop her babble and tell her she was being silly. But the two older women failed to react as she wanted. Instead they listened sympathetically to her. As she drew to a close Joy saw, out of the corner of her eye, three men emerge from a door marked 'private', and stroll over to the table. One of these men had little wings stitched on to the sleeves of his jacket. He must be a pilot, Joy deduced. A particularly good-looking pilot, short, but with intelligent, attractive eyes and a firm, no-nonsense chin.

As the men reached the table, laid out their notes and conferred with each other, there was a general movement from the coffee tables to the seating in front of the screen. Joy rose, looking anxiously for Roger. At last he came out of the Gents and joined her. They took seats in the middle and picked up a leaflet that gave a run-down of the events of the day.

'Feeling OK?' Joy asked Roger.

'Just about,' he said.

'The pilot's rather dishy,' she said, in an attempt to cheer him up.

Roger lifted his eyes. Usually a connoisseur of male flesh, all he could register at this time was a blur of uniform and the plate-glass window on one side of the room where planes were visible below on the tarmac. Fear was tangible to him. It was an opaque mist that distorted and clouded his vision.

'Don't worry,' Joy continued. 'All that's going to happen now is that they're going to talk to us. It says here the captain's going to explain to us how the plane works.'

The lights dimmed, and the pilot, with just a trace of an Edinburgh accent, began his account.

It was lunch-time. There were plates of sandwiches on the tables now, and Joy attacked them with gusto.

'I mean, it's just incredible! I never realized that planes

floated on the air, just as ships do on the sea. And that even if the engines fail we just glide down to earth!'

Roger tried to join in. 'It's thirty times more dangerous travelling in a car.'

'That's right. I think I'll fly to work in future,' Joy laughed. 'Seriously, I feel much better. Just knowing that flight is taking advantage of the laws of nature rather than flagrantly disobeying them is reassuring, don't you think?'

'Reassuring,' echoed Roger.

'And I was impressed with the thoroughness of the security checks. I think even my mother would be satisfied. And turbulence is uncomfortable, but not dangerous,' she concluded, mimicking the accent of the pilot.

Roger gave her a strained smile. Joy was concerned. Although she was beginning to feel as if the short flight scheduled for that afternoon might be a challenge she was prepared to take on, Roger looked a lot less confident than her.

'You're doing well,' she told him. 'It's brilliant that you've even come on the course – you heard what the pilot said. The most difficult thing is walking into this room.' Roger was quiet; he was no longer the fearless, persuasive outdoors-pursuits teacher she'd met last week. More than anything Joy wanted to take him out of himself. It was important he shouldn't obsess about the forthcoming flight.

'Are you and Peter going out tonight?' Joy asked. She always told her exam candidates at college never to worry about the exams, but instead to fantasize about how they would enjoy themselves afterwards.

'We'll go out if we feel like it,' Roger said, looking at his sandwiches rather than eating them.

'I'm going to attempt to seduce my new boyfriend tonight,' Joy announced. That worked. Roger looked at her with surprise. She decided to go on.

'I have to find out if he's right for me, you see. Lawrence is a bit shy, and I'm not much better. One of us has to make the first move. I've decided it's got to be me. Maybe you can give me some tips,' she said confidentially. There, that should do it. Sex was the ultimate distraction. She glanced over the tarmac below, where the planes suddenly seemed to her like so many phallic symbols.

Joy had succeeded in pressing the 'sex' button in Roger's brain. He supposed that the method of any seduction was basically the same, gay or straight. He tried to think what his first move would be.

'Go on,' Joy prompted him. 'Imagine you were trying to pick up the pilot. What would you do?' Sorry, Peter, she said to herself.

For the first time Roger began to appreciate the neatly tailored uniform of the pilot, who was standing in discussion with some eager women. Roger had always liked uniforms.

'A pick-up's slightly different,' Roger explained. 'It's a matter first of establishing whether he'd be interested. I'd brush past him, make eye contact, and –'

'You don't mind if I join you?' It was the merry widow from earlier that morning. 'I've just been chatting with the psychologist who's talking to us after lunch. He's an expert on bed-wetting, you know! He has an excellent success rate; kiddies from all over the North-West come to his clinic in Oldham. I think that's wonderful. Have you ever been to Marbella?' she asked them. 'It's my ambition to get there one day.'

★

The psychologist spoke as if he were thinking aloud, and Joy found this immensely soothing. His comments had the force of carefully considered deliberations and therefore seemed all the more true.

'Worriers are hyper-vigilant,' he explained. 'They misinterpret events around them, imagining disasters where there are none. Worrying encourages fear. So we must vigorously challenge our negative, self-defeating thinking.'

Joy imagined her negative thinking as a black knight, a medieval villain skulking on a flea-ridden, mangy mount, whereas her positive thinking was a white knight, on an Arabian steed, with shining lance and shield, vigorously challenging him. Her lunch had left her feeling rather sleepy. She was glad when the psychologist explained that he was going to take them through some relaxation exercises. They would give her a chance to drift off.

According to what she had heard that day, there really was nothing for her to worry about. Flying was natural and safe. Her fears were understandable but unfounded. As instructed, she clenched her muscles and then let go. The instructions of the psychologist washed over her. She thought of all the people she had seen that morning, going to all those destinations on the departures board: Paris, Düsseldorf, Rome, Athens, Montego Bay. All ordinary people, flying to these exotic places as if it was their right. It was her right too.

This realization made her tense her toes instead of relaxing them. Just now Joy didn't feel like relaxing. She began to think of the lives of the people who weren't frightened of flying, and how they brazenly took holidays all over the world. They went to Disneyland and met Mickey Mouse. They sunned themselves on Caribbean beaches. They went on safaris across Africa. They looked out of their windows as their plane crossed over the North Pole and marvelled at the glaciers, almost blinding in the strong sunlight. They walked out of the airport at Rome and tried to decide where to eat that night.

Joy felt like a mole who had just crawled, blinking, into a world which wasn't dark and damp and confined but gloriously bright and dazzling. She could be one of those people who travelled fearlessly around the world, if she would let the course work for her. Was a new Joy Freeman being born, who would one day walk boldly towards the departure gate, her travel bag in her hand, relaxed and assured, on her way to the United States – to New York! – as if she was accustomed to doing so every day?

Then the psychologist told them to open their eyes and to follow the hostesses to the boarding gate for their flight over the Isle of Man. Joy was alert in an instant. Her fantasy of a flight to the USA was shattered. She wasn't on her way to New York. She was here in Manchester Airport, still tense and nervous, about to board a plane with a man who was even more terrified than she was.

Remembering Roger, she took his hand. 'It's over the top with us,' she said.

'I know,' said Roger.

His breath was sour.

'It's only a short flight,' said Joy, as much to convince herself as Roger. 'We won't be going that high. For a rock-climber, the whole thing should be a cinch!'

They queued for their boarding passes, attracting inquisitive looks from other domestic-flight passengers. Joy felt like a freak. She continued to whisper words of encouragement to Roger. 'Listen to what I've learnt.

Things are never as bad as you imagine them, so there really is no point worrying. The future can just as easily be good as bad. And you feel brilliant when you overcome a fear – that's what you taught me. That's when the exhilaration kicks in. I know what I'm talking about – remember my abseil?' Joy squeezed Roger's hand in gratitude and empathy. There was no answering pressure.

As they walked towards the boarding gate, where a plane sat quietly on the tarmac, Joy felt increasingly desperate. Roger was clearly terrified. She sat with him near the gate, opposite the journalist they'd talked to in the morning.

'That must be our plane,' Joy said to Roger. 'It's only small. I think we have to climb up those stairs to get to it.'

'I can't go through with this,' Roger said.

'You can,' Joy urged him. 'It's surprising what you can do when you have to.' Joy thought of Michael's appearance before her abseil. 'Come on, they're calling our flight.'

Taking Roger by the hand, Joy guided him to the boarding gate. A smiling hostess collected their passes. They emerged on to the tarmac, amongst trucks and airport personnel, and next to the metallic solidity of the aeroplane itself, with its steps leading to a slit of a door.

I'm not going to think about this, Joy decided. I'm going to think about Roger.

'We're almost there,' she said to him. 'Once we're on board there's nothing for us to do – we just sit there. The pilot does all the work.'

Roger paused by the plane. Joy prayed he would have the courage to get on. Behind them she could hear the comforting voice of the course psychologist.

'I know how you feel,' he crooned. 'Remember I'll be with you all the time. You've done well to get so far.'

Joy and Roger turned to see who he was talking to. It was the journalist. He was visibly quaking with fear.

'But you're a reporter,' Joy said to him, astonished. 'I thought you were only here to write about the rest of us!'

'They thought that at the office too,' he told her. 'It's all those years of writing up flight horror stories – it's just got to me,' he muttered brokenly.

'Come on,' Joy said, in her best schoolteacher manner, and taking both the journalist and Roger by the arm, she marched them up the steps.

Joy found a seat near the front of the plane, fastened her safety-belt and found herself crushed between the porthole of a window and Roger's bulk. Lucky she wasn't one of the people on the course who suffered from claustrophobia. There was no way of getting out. The engine throbbed impatiently. More passengers filed on, some white and silent, others giggling nervously.

'I was in an aborted take-off once,' Roger said suddenly.

Aha! That explains it, thought Joy.

'It terrified me. I thought I was going to die. That's why I've never flown since.'

The air hostesses began their mime with the life-jackets and oxygen masks. Joy squeezed Roger's hand again. She could think of nothing to say. It was mocking his fear to tell him it wouldn't happen this time. Then a realization came to her.

'My father died suddenly, when I was small. That's why I'm always preparing myself for something bad to happen.'

A flash of recognition illuminated their darkness.

There were two of them, not one. The air crew took their seats for take-off. Joy and Roger's hands were locked together. The voice of the pilot explained what was happening, but it was drowned by the roar of the engine as the plane gathered speed. Roger gripped ever more tightly on to Joy's hand, the wheels lifted and the plane rose sharply into the sky.

Joy felt a lightness in her stomach which was not entirely unpleasant. She looked out of the window. The ground was at a crazy angle and disappearing fast. Her new-found confidence deserted her. She was pointing up, up into the sky. What if they never levelled out, and the plane went on for ever? Hysteria gripped her. She turned to Roger.

'We've done it. We're up,' he told her, almost disbelieving.

Joy could see the lines of his face relaxing. She realized that for him the take-off had been the insuperable obstacle. Already he was feeling a sense of achievement. Her personal hell was being trapped thousands of feet above the earth, and she was beginning to feel bad now. A *ping* announced that the passengers could remove their seatbelts. Joy declined. A quick glance out of the window revealed that they were going through a bank of cloud. How did the pilot know which direction to take?

'Joy, it's OK,' came Roger's voice.

She nodded, unconvinced.

'Tell me about your boyfriend,' Roger insisted, trying to distract her. 'Is he nice? Is he good-looking?'

It seemed bizarre to Joy to talk about Lawrence at a time like this, but it was impolite not to answer questions.

'He's very nice,' she said. 'Probably the nicest man I've ever been out with. He looks like Moses.'

'But you've not slept with him yet?'

'We've only been out a few times, to eat, to the ice-rink, and I suppose we're waiting until we get to know each other better.'

'Do you fancy him?' Roger said.

There was the movement of passengers in the aisle, as the cabin staff were offering visits to the cockpit.

'What do you mean by "fancy"?' Joy asked.

'Does he turn you on?'

'Well, I don't know until I've tried, do I?'

'So tell me, what are your plans tonight?'

'I shall go home and get ready, have a bath, put on some make-up. Then drive over to Heptonstall where Lesley is cooking us dinner. Then she's going to spend the night with her bloke, leaving us her house.'

'Excuse me, sir. Would you like to visit the cockpit?' At the sound of that Roger swivelled round and saw a young air steward. He rose immediately, and Joy was on her own. Another brief glance out of the window revealed that they were above the cloud, and she could almost believe they were floating on air. What were her plans for Lawrence tonight? Ought she to say straight out that she thought they ought to sleep together, citing her own sexual difficulties as reason? Hardly erotic. Or should she just start by kissing him and move on, or down, from there. What if he was too embarrassed to continue? What if he wasn't? Joy tried to imagine Lawrence making love to her. She frowned in concentration. As they descended through clouds again, her mental picture turned fuzzy. Concentrate! She tried to imagine him turning from her, reaching for a condom.

A condom! What if he didn't have one? Why should he have one? Only she knew what was going to happen that night. She bit her lip. She would have to buy some as soon as she reached land again. There was a Boot's in the departure concourse and they would be bound to have some.

Roger took his seat again, looking remarkably cheerful.

'The view's fantastic in there!' he assured her.

The pilot announced the imminent landing. Joy was relieved. The nearer she got to the ground, the better she felt.

'You've done it,' Roger whispered to her.

The plane was flying lower and lower, there was a slight bump, a burst of applause, cheering and whistling. She had done it after all. She couldn't wait to get back into the airport and resume normal life.

As the passengers milled in the arrivals area, there was much mutual congratulation. Joy saw the young mother hug their earlier companion who'd been taking the course by proxy.

'I feel so much better,' said the mother. 'I'm going home and telling the kids all about it.'

'I'll tell Trevor,' said his wife. 'But I'm not sure it'll make much difference. I'll just have to go to Skiathos on my own again this year.' She sounded remarkably cheerful at the prospect.

'I feel great,' Roger said. He hugged Joy, and she was warmed by his pleasure. 'And you? Are you cured?' he asked her.

'Oh, I don't know,' she said, running her hands through her dishevelled hair. 'I know I've done it, but I'm not sure if I enjoyed it, and anyway, I cheated, because I was worrying about Lawrence instead.'

'Don't be such a bloomin' perfectionist!' Roger said to her jocularly. 'It's a start, isn't it?'

He was right. It was a start. Together they made their way through Departures to where Peter had arranged to collect Roger. Approaching Boot's, Joy stopped.

'You go ahead,' she said to Roger. 'I need to get something for the weekend.' Roger stopped and grinned at her.

'It's been a good day,' he said. 'Excellent company, first-class course and as for that captain! Did you fancy the captain too?'

'I should say,' Joy agreed.

'Think about it,' Roger told her, and walked off, waving as he went.

He was being annoyingly obscure. Joy didn't have a clue what he meant and didn't have the inclination to work it out. She had other things on her mind. She had to go into Boot's the Chemist and buy some condoms. At which point it occurred to Joy that she had never bought condoms before in her life. That was something Michael did, or didn't, take care of. Now, as an independent seductress, she had to enter Boot's and buy them. Joy felt deliciously wicked.

She walked into Boot's and made her way past the suntan lotions and shades. Who was that curly-headed, frowning, suspicious-looking woman in front of her? Joy looked into the mirror and recognized herself. She paused. Guilt was written all over her face. She smiled at herself. For a moment even she could see the liveliness and responsiveness that could make her attractive. Would Lawrence find her attractive? That was the question.

There they were, at the back of the shop. A bewildering variety of condoms were laid out in rows. Which ought she to buy? Ribbed? What were they for? She could hardly imagine Lawrence in a coloured condom, and anyway, she was planning on having the lights out. Seeing a familiar brand with the words 'extra safe' she lifted them from the rack.

. This was the decisive moment. Buying the condoms was a pledge that she would make love with Lawrence tonight. She took them to the sales assistant, who wrapped them up without so much as a glance at her, as if he'd sold thousands of these in his lifetime. Which he probably had.

For Joy, however, this was a first. Feeling excitingly wicked, she left the chemist's.

At first she thought it was divine vengeance.

'Joy Freeman!'

She heard her own name resound through the concourse. It echoed through the air, bounced off the walls – it was everywhere. Sorry, God, she thought to herself, I'll put them back immediately.

'Could Joy Freeman, passenger from the Isle of Man, come to the information desk.'

Joy stood paralysed listening to her message. A thousand possibilities careered through her mind, but as she looked wildly around for the information desk, quizzed a porter and fled through several corridors until she reached Arrivals and the desk next to the Thomas Cook window, all the possibilities melted into one dreadful certainty – there was something wrong with her mother. While Joy had been abseiling, flying, planning seductions, her mother had been taken ill, had been run over, had been burgled.

She reached the information desk.

'I'm Joy Freeman,' she blurted out.

The young, lipsticked airline employee seemed not to know what to do with this information.

'I'm Joy Freeman. There's a message for me.'

'Oh yes,' she said. She looked down at a message pad on her desk. 'Could you call round at Lucy Marshall's directly. She says she's in trouble.'

Relief flooded Joy, which turned almost instantly to guilty concern. She had forgotten all about Lucy. And the girl was in trouble, which was not surprising. Lawrence would have to have her just as she was. No time for a bath or make-up. She would go straight from the airport to Lucy. Lucy needed her.

CHAPTER EIGHTEEN

Once in Radcliffe, Joy found she had little trouble remembering the street where Lucy lived. Identifying her house was going to be more of a problem, as all the terraces looked identical. Yet she need not have worried; cruising slowly down the road, she saw Lucy sitting on her doorstep, stroking the cat. Joy drew to a halt outside the house and scrambled out of the car. Lucy got to her feet.

'Lucy! Why are you waiting outside?'

'No keys,' Lucy said.

Lucy was shivering, even though she was wrapped in a large brown coat, one that Joy did not recognize.

'Get in the car,' Joy instructed. 'You'll be warmer there.'

Lucy did as she was told. Joy switched on the engine and there was a blast of warmth. Lucy held her hands to the vents.

'How long have you been sitting on your doorstep?' Joy asked.

'Only a couple of hours. Up to now I've been round the shops.'

Joy looked at the car clock. It was nearly six o'clock.

'I came back to wait for you,' Lucy added.

'Where are your keys?'

'In this bloke's house in Cheetham Hill, along with all my money and ID card and combat jacket.'

'What bloke? What are they doing there?'

'I went on to this party. I'm starving, Miss Freeman. So is Trotsky. I haven't fed him since last night.'

'Get the cat and bring him in the car.'

Lucy came back and sat in the front with the cat squirming on her knee. As the car pulled away, the cat set up an unearthly, excruciating howl.

'He doesn't like cars,' Lucy said unnecessarily. 'Oh, bugger!'

'What now?'

'He's peed all over me. He does that when he's scared.'

The acrid stench of cat urine spread throughout the car. Lucy began to wind down the window, holding on to Trotsky with one hand.

'Does he eat any sort of cat food?' Joy asked.

'No. He's on the Science diet.'

'Tough. He's having whatever I can find at Patel's.'

Joy stopped the car outside a mini-market and ran inside. Lucy waited and watched her teacher re-emerge with a full plastic carrier bag. Throwing the bag in the back, Joy started up the engine again.

'We're all going to my place,' Joy said. 'You can change and borrow some of my clothes, and we'll feed the cat, and you can tell me what you've been up to.'

'Yes, Miss,' Lucy said, teasingly.

Trotsky ate his Felix as if there was no tomorrow. Lucy sat curled on the settee in a pair of Joy's black leggings and one of her old jumpers.

'That's really grungy!' she'd said with delight when Joy had withdrawn it from her wardrobe.

'Now tell me what's been happening,' Joy demanded.

Lucy acquiesced.

'Like I told you, I went to this birthday do at the Mission. Me and Kel and Liam. There were, like, older people there. It was this bloke's birthday. We danced and that, and all these men were watching us. Liam said they were all in the record business and he said I should try and blag my way into getting a contract with someone. He said that's how you do it, right? So after a time this bloke comes along and offers me a drink. So I said, yeah, and we went under the stairs where there was this table and he was coming over dead friendly, and I'm telling him about our band, and he lets on he's really interested.'

'Hmm,' said Joy, unimpressed.

'So he gets hold of my hand, and then he was, like, you're really gorgeous, and I can tell you've got a brain too, all that shite. I'm a bit suspicious, like, but then it turns out he's the bloke whose birthday it is, Tom, and he says to come back to his house where the party's carrying on and he'll introduce me to some people.'

Joy shook her head reproachfully, just like her mother would have done.

'Well, I did ask Kel if she wanted to go, but she'd copped off with this bloke, and I couldn't find Liam, so I thought I'd go cos there'd be other people there and, like, if I could find someone to listen to our band, it'd be, like, wow!

'So we get in a taxi and go to Cheetham Hill, behind the Ukrainian church on the Old Road. There's a kind of terrace opposite a playground, and this house was the last on the row. Well, it was two houses knocked into one and done up really cool. This bloke Tom knocks, and someone lets him in, and there's all these people standing around drinking, and they're like, hello Mitch, so I take off my jacket and hang it up. Then Tom goes, there's some A&R bloke upstairs, so I follow him up the stairs, and on the wall there's all these gold discs in boxes hung up, so I'm thinking, he's not lied about the record company, and he opens this door, and we go inside, and there's no one there, just a brass bed, and he shuts the door and grabs me and starts kissing me and saying stuff about how he can't help it and he's ripping at my dress, and I'm panicking now and fighting back and screaming, but the music's so loud no one's hearing me.

'Well, it was lucky I was wearing my Docs – I gave him this big kick straight in his balls, and he's swearing at me and everything, so I just opened the door and ran, ran out of the house and into the High Street, and I saw this taxi, so I got in and asked to go home. Then as I'm sitting there I realize my wallet and keys and everything are in my combat jacket and it's in that house. Well, I wasn't going back there. So I told the driver to take me to Kelly's house. Kelly's dad paid the taxi bloke, but Kelly wasn't in yet. He was mad at her, and when she got in he was bawling at her and that. I slept there, but in the morning he says they're spending the day in Fleetwood with Kelly's gran, who's in a rest-home, and she's got to go with. He said I could go, but I thought I'd ring you instead.

'So I've been ringing you all day, but you weren't in. I kept leaving messages on your answering machine. Then I remembered about your flying course, so I left a message at the airport, and I went back to my house to wait for you. What was your course like? Have you stopped being scared of flying?'

'Oh, Lucy,' was all Joy could say.

The cat twisted so he could reach to wash his hind parts, one leg sticking straight up in the air. As Joy watched him, she filled with anger. What scum would dare try to force himself on Lucy? It was a dreadful thing to happen, absolutely dreadful. As she swelled with indignation, she imagined what she would like to do this man Tom. Something unspeakably violent and messy.

Life kept presenting her with challenges. She'd abseiled, she'd flown without panicking, and, now, she was going to drive straight round to this bastard's house, get Lucy's coat and keys and tell him exactly what she thought of him. No one, but no one took advantage of her Lucy. If she was learning to be brave, she knew now it was for this moment.

'I think I know the house you mean,' Joy told her with deceptive calm. 'It's only ten minutes in the car from here. I'm going straight round to get your coat now. You and Trotsky make yourself at home. See you later.'

Grabbing her handbag and coat, not stopping to consider the consequences of what she was about to do, Joy went out into the chilly, damp night. He would not get away with it. That toerag would face up to what he had tried to do to Lucy. The accelerator pedal quaked under her foot, and her car shot off into the darkness.

Normally the prospect of walking alone in the backstreets of Cheetham Hill would have made Joy nervous. Before tonight she would have recounted to herself the stories of gangland warfare and drug dealing and mugging and car thefts which the papers were so keen to dredge up. Not so any more. She ignored the two lads on mountain bikes, who watched with curiosity as she got out of the car, and she didn't see the man on the other side of the road, who was rooting about in a waste-paper bin.

She saw the terrace behind the Ukrainian church and made straight for it. She walked briskly to the end of the terrace, holding on to her anger like a hand-grenade. There was a light in the window of the last house in the row. She banged hard on the door. A tall blond man in his forties opened the door to her, with a faint look of surprise.

'You,' Joy said accusingly, 'must be Tom. I am Lucy's English teacher.' Joy drew herself up to her full height, but was still dwarfed by the man in front of her. 'Last night you brought a sixteen-year-old girl – yes! she was only sixteen – back to a party at this house with the express intention of seducing her. You lied to her about your influence with a record company, just to get her into your bed. She was so frightened she attacked you in self-defence, and ran out, leaving her coat behind. I hope she hurt you. I hope she hurt you very much!' Joy paused for breath.

Tom smiled amusedly at her. 'Come in. I was expecting this.'

'Come in! I wouldn't step in there if you paid me!'

'Since you are getting paid, come in. We don't want to entertain the whole street.'

Before she knew it, Joy found herself in an unexpectedly luxurious open-plan room, with a fire burning brightly in one corner. Tom went over to the settee, sat down cross-legged and looked at her.

'You can go on now,' he said.

'Look, I don't know what kind of man you are, but I can hardly believe that you are taking this so lightly. My student was thoroughly frightened.' Joy looked around the room again. There, on a coat-stand, was Lucy's jacket. Made bold by her discovery, she proceeded.

'Men like you disgust me!' she spat with venom. 'Just because you have influence in the music business you think you can treat young girls as playthings – and worse!' she shouted.

'That's good,' Tom said.

'I don't believe you. I'm warning you, Tom whoever you are, that what you did to Lucy constitutes an assault, and as soon as her father gets back, I'm placing the matter in his hands. Please may I have Lucy's jacket.'

'When are you going to start taking your clothes off?' Tom said.

'How dare you! You're a filthy pervert.'

'What is this? An abuse-o-gram?'

'Just Lucy's teacher, demanding her student's coat and an apology.'

Tom began to applaud. 'Look, it's OK. You can stop now. A mate tipped me off that I was being sent a strip-o-gram. Was it Mitch who hired you? You don't have to take your clothes off. In fact I don't much go for this sort of thing. Are you a drama student at the uni?'

'No,' said Joy, faltering for the first time. 'I'm an English teacher. St Ignatius' sixth-form college. Miss Freeman. Joy Freeman.'

'Tom Quinn,' said Tom, putting out his hand. 'I think there may have been some sort of mix-up.'

Joy stood rooted to the spot. Tom Quinn? Not *the* Tom Quinn, *her* Tom Quinn. She looked at the man again. Why on earth didn't she recognize him before? He was in the music business after all. It really was Tom Quinn – Tom Quinn of the Law Enforcers. What was he doing here? Nothing was making any sense.

'If you're not a strip-o-gram, then I've been unforgivably rude. Please sit down, Miss . . . Joy. Yes, I can tell now. You're not a stripper. I'm so sorry. Can I get you a drink?'

'But Lucy, you tried to . . .'

'I never brought any young girl back here. There was a

314

party here last night. It's my birthday today. It wasn't Mitch, was it?'

Joy remembered something in Lucy's account that did not fit.

'She did say someone called him Mitch.'

'John Mitchell used to be my roadie. It's not the first time he's pulled a stunt like this, the bastard! Look, Joy, I'm so sorry. I believe you now. I just don't know what to say. You have every right to be angry, both with him and with me. Look, there's some wine. Have some.'

Joy, stunned, watched him run over to a kitchen extension where a bottle of wine lay on a work surface. As far as she was concerned, the laws of nature had stopped working according to the textbooks. Here she was, alone with Tom Quinn (Tom Quinn!) in his house, and he was bringing her a drink. And she had just been roundly abusing him when he hadn't done anything wrong. Would he ever forgive her?

He came back with two glasses of wine and gave her one.

'You meet some prize creeps in this business, and Mitch is one of them. I apologize for him and for my dreadful mistake. I can see you don't look anything like a stripper.'

'It's all right,' Joy said. 'All those things I called you!'

'They won't be as bad as the things I'm going to say to Mitch,' Tom declared.

'Thank you.' Joy took a sip of wine.

'Are you feeling better?' he asked her with concern.

Joy stopped to think how she was feeling. First, there was her flight, second, the shock of finding Lucy in trouble, and then her wild dash here, only to hurl invective at the one man she had loved, in her own way, all her adult life. How did she feel? Terrible! And realizing this, a tear escaped her.

'Oh no, I've upset you!' Tom looked aghast. He came over to her, knelt by her chair, put a hand on her arm. 'Don't cry. Look, it's my birthday. Stay and eat with me. We've made such a disastrous beginning, things can only get better.'

'Stay here?'

'Look, I was going to stay in tonight. I've had enough of this birthday business. I couldn't face another celebration. I was feeling thoroughly pissed off before you arrived. Some guy rang from *Q* magazine to do a "where are they now?" feature on me. On my forty-second birthday. I put the phone down and thought Kurt Cobain had the right idea. And then you were banging on my door. I'm grateful. Please stay.'

'Tell me I'm not imagining this,' Joy said. 'You're Tom Quinn. I've worshipped you all my life. You're asking me to have dinner with you?'

'I am,' Tom said. 'Would you like it in writing?'

'In triplicate,' Joy said. 'No, it's OK. I'll stay.'

Tom's face lit up. 'Do you like pasta?' he asked her. 'I have some smoked salmon and avocado I can throw in. I'm a whizz with pasta. Take your coat off – only your coat!' he joked.

Joy did. She stood there in her sweatshirt and jeans, bitterly regretting that she hadn't washed or changed. Seeing a mirror, she turned and glanced at herself. She looked flushed and harassed. She began to tidy her hair with her fingers.

'You look great,' Tom called to her from the kitchen.

'I look great,' Joy thought. The events of that evening had an unassailable logic, yet Joy could still not believe that this was happening to her. She surveyed the room she was in. Indian rugs were scattered on the parquet flooring, and in front of the fire was a rich red carpet with a notebook on it. Tom, understandably, was wealthy. An abstract painting, in slabs of red and grey, hung on a wall next to an antique grandfather clock, which chimed half past seven.

'Can I make a phone call?' she shouted to him.

'Feel free,' he said. 'The phone's in the hall.'

Quickly Joy dialled her own number. She crossed her fingers in preparation for a lie.

'Lucy? It's me, Miss Freeman. I've got your coat and keys, but it's late now. I must go straight on to Miss Wright's. Can you spend the night in my house? I don't know what time I'll be back. But everything's safe.'

'No sweat, Miss F. It's brill here. I've started reading this book, *Great Expectations*. And I'm listening to this old album – the Law Enforcers. They're cool.'

'Excellent. Make yourself completely at home.'

To Lesley she would have to tell the truth.

'Lesley? It's me, Joy. Is Lawrence there yet? No? Good. It's probably too late to stop him, though. Something amazing has happened. I've met another man. I can't explain who now. I can't come tonight. Would you do something for me – look after Lawrence? What should you tell him? That I'm ill. That my mother's ill. I don't know. Oh, God, Lesley, I can hardly stand upright. I'll explain everything tomorrow.'

She replaced the receiver. Seize the day, she said to herself, seize the day.

'You must be Lawrence!' Lesley stepped back to get a good look at this poor man whom Joy had decided to stand up. She was pleasantly surprised. Joy was right – his beard and soft brown eyes gave him a biblical air. Yet he was also exotic, foreign-looking, sensuous. A sort of Jewish D. H. Lawrence. Lesley was impressed. He had a startled look in his eyes, and Lesley began to wonder what she could say to him that would hurt least. The last thing she could do, she decided, was send him all the way back to Manchester, especially as there was a vegetable casserole simmering on the stove.

'Joy isn't here yet,' she said cheerfully, intending the lie to give her time to think. 'Come through and I'll get us both a drink. What will you have? Try this single malt – Strathisla. It's rather special. Go on – take the chair by the Dragon, it's warmer over there. Throw the cats off – they're used to it!'

Pleasantly disorientated, Lawrence looked about him. The shady elegance of Lesley's living room appealed to him. It was so unlike his mother's fussy front room where everything had to be placed on mats and even the fruit bowl had cling film on it. He liked, too, being told what to do. He carefully picked up the cats and placed them on the floor and, pulling up his trousers, sat down. Lesley gave him a small tumbler of amber liquid, and he sipped it. It was smooth as he drank, and then a delicious heat radiated from his chest and warmed his body.

'Do you know how Joy got on today?' he asked Lesley.

'Ah,' said Lesley. 'I was coming to that.'

Tom stood at the chopping board, a blue and white apron tied round his waist. Joy sat on a kitchen stool, sipping her second glass of wine. Tom was talkative.

'Why am I back in Manchester? It sounds corny, but my musical roots are here. This is where we started and this is where we got our breaks. The years in London don't seem real now. I thought if I could come back here and make it like it was when I started out, the inspiration would come back. That's why I'm living in Cheetham Hill rather than Worsley.' He laughed. There was something resigned in his laughter.

'Has it worked?' asked Joy. 'Are you writing again?'

Tom sliced the salmon ferociously. 'I'm writing – and tearing it all up. Everything I do sounds so old. Law Enforcers for geriatrics. It's a curse, this fame thing. You're fixed permanently at the moment you find success – other people label you, and you label yourself. All the time you're looking backwards to what you were and you watch kids making it and you're not sure whether they're rubbish or whether to envy them.'

'Like "Andrea Del Sarto"!' Joy announced.

'Andrea who?'

'Oh, it's just a poem. By Browning. About this painter who was never able to achieve what he thought he should. Except in his case, he blamed it on his wife, and Browning hints that he might be right, or it might be his fault. It's a wonderful poem.'

'I have no wife to blame it on,' Tom remarked. Joy was glad.

'Were you ever . . . is there a woman?' She tensed, waiting for the blow.

'Not now. I've had relationships,' he said, 'but they ended. All sorts of reasons. You?' Tom pushed the salmon to one side and picked up the avocado, tossing it in his hand as if it were a ball. He looked across at Joy. He was warmed by her unaffectedness. The other women he knew lived on the surface, existed in their clothes, their carefully honed figures, those modulated laughs and calculating eyes. Here was someone he could have gone to school with. He felt unaccountably comfortable with her and very desirous to talk. But for all he knew, she had popped out before to ring her husband and kids to tell them she'd been invited to dinner with *the* Tom Quinn, and when she got home she would tell them all about it. 'Do you have a man?'

Joy lifted her eyebrows in mock horror. 'Me? Have a man? What an obscene suggestion. A nice Jewish girl working at a Catholic college? No, I live alone,' she said, and she was glad.

Their eyes met. It was an unintentional meeting, but an eloquent one. Joy understood it and could hardly believe what she had read in his eyes, his questioning, soft hazel eyes. He was interested in her, Tom Quinn was interested in her. But this beautiful man, in a striped apron, his hair temporarily tied back, flecks of grey showing just behind the ears, was no longer the Tom Quinn of her bedroom wall, but Tom. Just Tom. The torment was in her effort not to look at him, when all she wanted to do was feast her eyes on him, memorize him, drink him up.

'I live alone, too,' Tom said. 'So that I can get up in the night if I want to and write. When the inspiration comes. Which it doesn't,' he added with just a trace of self-pity. 'Can you throw the pasta in?'

Joy took handfuls of fusilli pasta and placed them in the boiling water. 'Are you trying too hard?' she asked him.

He chuckled, to indicate she might have hit on the truth.

'Have a night off,' Joy said. Tom turned, looked at her and gave a slow, long smile.

'I might just do that,' he said.

The swede was rather tough. Lawrence found he had to

chew very, very hard in order to swallow it. He wondered if Lesley was having the same difficulty and noticed that she didn't seem to be eating at all, but was watching him. He was pleasantly disconcerted. The evening had not turned out at all as he'd expected. He'd imagined himself and Joy at a dinner party with her teacher friends, discussing the National Curriculum, and here he was, alone with a disturbingly attractive woman who was doing her utmost to make him feel at home. Who would have imagined that Sister Maureen, the principal at St Ignatius', would have needed to see Joy that very night in order to discuss some details of the English department's development plan? Lesley was right, of course. Joy had to go, given that she was a front runner for head of department. It was kind of Lesley to let him stay and eat. Lawrence wondered why it was he was experiencing a profound reluctance to go. Was it that whisky? He rather hoped Lesley would offer him another. He put down his knife and fork and gave up on the casserole.

'It must be a responsible job, being vice-principal,' he suggested to Lesley, wanting her to talk again. He found the way she clipped her words, her precise manner of speaking, unusual and attractive.

'These days it's more or less an administrative job. It pays the bills and occupies me during the day,' she said. 'I do other things at night.' At these words, Lawrence felt an unfamiliar stirring in his loins. He was surprised at himself. He swallowed hard. There was nothing in his twelve-step programme to deal with this.

'What other things?'

'I draw and paint,' she told him, smilingly. 'Everyone needs an outlet for their creativity. Repression is bad for the spirit.'

'Is it?' he said.

Lesley was squeezing every ounce of pleasure from this all-too-brief dinner with Lawrence. Soon, she knew, Rennie would call, and, as usual, his voice would have that irresistible demand in it, and she would go and, as the price of his love-making, she would have to listen to tales of his ego and protestations that she was only part of his life, a necessary part, but only a part. And you are a part of my life, she would tell him. And thus it was she tried to hold him at a distance.

She noticed Lawrence had hardly eaten.

'Aren't you hungry?' she asked him. 'Do you like vegetables? I thought you would want to eat *kosher*, and –'

'Thank you,' Lawrence stopped her. 'I appreciate that. But I'm not hungry. The food was delicious. But I couldn't trouble you for more whisky?'

Lesley got up and made for the cabinet where her spirits were stored. Lawrence admired the neat contour of her back and her shapely calves. *Repression is bad for the spirit.* He jumped when the phone rang. Instantly he was flooded with guilt. It was bound to be Joy.

Lesley answered the phone. Lawrence could just about make out what she was saying.

'Now? No, Rennie, sorry, I have a visitor. You can get a taxi . . . I'm sure there's a cash-card machine somewhere . . . No . . . Yes, I know what this means . . . Yes, I know it's my only opportunity to see you this month . . . OK. Good-bye.'

Lawrence saw that Lesley looked flushed and watched her run her hands through her hair in what seemed to him almost to be anguish.

'Is anything wrong?' he asked her, rising from his chair.

Approaching her, to his surprise, Lawrence saw that Lesley's face was tear-stained. Immediately he took her hands.

'Bad news?' he asked her.

'No, no. I'm sorry. There was a difficult decision to be made, and I've made it. It's over now.'

Lawrence did not let go of her hands. To his surprise and delight he felt an answering pressure in her fingers, as they curled around his. They stood by the telephone, holding hands, in a sudden intimacy that neither of them had expected. Lawrence found that by pulling gently, Lesley came closer to him. And closer still.

There was no sound except for the cats purring by the fire and the rustle of Lawrence's shirt as it made contact with Lesley's silk blouse.

Joy and Tom sat opposite each other across the black dining table. After a few mouthfuls of pasta, as appetizing as it was, Joy found that her appetite had deserted her. Food held little attraction. She stroked the stem of her wine glass slowly.

'My English teacher was nothing like you,' Tom remarked, as he drank another sip of wine. 'She was called Mrs Soothill. We called her Sooty. Old woman, hair in a bun, gave us all these impossible comprehensions.'

Joy laughed. 'Give me a few years and that'll be me,' she said.

'Come on,' he wheedled. 'You're not a typical teacher.'

'Ah, but I am! Through and through. You know what they say – those who can, do, and those who can't, teach.'

'What can't you do, Joy?' Tom asked her. He had stopped eating.

'Most things,' Joy said. 'Because I worry too much.

No, don't shake your head! Worrying is my tragic flaw. I see the risk in everything, so I don't do anything.' Joy realized the wine was giving her an unusual eloquence. She would try to explain further to Tom. No one had ever listened to her quite so closely before. 'I don't know where it came from, this sense that life is fundamentally dangerous, but most of the time I'm just plain scared. College to me is like the Lady of Shalott's tower, and literature is my mirror, where I see life reflected, so I don't have to experience it.'

'When you burst in here tonight you didn't seem afraid.'

'Ah, but I was doing that for Lucy! And anyway, I've been especially brave today. I've been on an aeroplane,' she said in mock pride. 'On a Fear of Flying course, actually.' Tom laughed, but his laughter was kind and encouraging. 'And last weekend, I abseiled down a forty-foot cliff. I'm trying, you see.'

'Is there anything I can do?' Tom asked. 'To help?'

Joy experienced a feeling so equally balanced between fear and excitement that she hardly knew what to call it.

'I'll tell you if I think of anything,' she said in a small voice, and took some more wine.

'So why is it you're so fearful?' Tom persisted. He found her frankness engaging and wanted her to go on talking. More than that, he discovered he really wanted to know this woman. It seemed important to him.

'I've worked out that it may have something to do with the early death of my father,' Joy said. 'Not that I had an unhappy childhood. My mother and I are very close, very close. She treated me more as an adult than a child. She's coming to live with me soon,' Joy said, and for the first time she experienced a disloyal sinking feeling. No time to think about that now.

'Why? Is she ill?' Tom asked.

'No. She's lost her job. And having her with me will stop me worrying about her. I'm a sort of James Morrison, you see.'

'Jim Morrison? The Doors?'

'No, James James Morrison Morrison,' she explained. 'Weatherby George Dupree. Took great care of his mother. Though he was only three.'

'I know that!' Tom joined in. 'Something about not going down to the end of town.'

'A. A. Milne,' Joy said. 'He's great. Do you know "Halfway up the Stairs"?' She recited it. She felt Tom's eyes upon her. They made her self-conscious. She was an English teacher through and through, all right. Here she was, having dinner with the most fanciable man she had ever met in her life, and she was reciting children's verse at him.

'Would you like "Christopher Robin went down with Alice"?' she asked.

'Yes,' Tom said, not taking his eyes off her. 'But let's go and sit in front of the fire.'

Obediently she took her wine glass and handbag and followed Tom to the brightly burning fire. She placed her glass on the hearth and her handbag in front of her. Tom sat on the rug in front of it and beckoned to her to join him.

'They're changing guard at Buckingham Palace,' she began.

'Sshh,' Tom said. The firelight flickered in his face. There was a hum from the CD player, which he had forgotten to turn off. The silence made Joy nervous and yet, while she prickled with her characteristic anxiety, she could half-imagine what it would be like to abandon herself to the moment and just let go. No, impossible.

'The king asked the queen, and the queen asked the dairymaid –'

The rest of the words were muffled. Tom had reached across, over her handbag, and kissed her. His tongue met her tongue, and the tension ebbed from it as she opened herself up to him and allowed him to enter. She was both conscious of her body and not conscious of it. Something softened inside her. The sensation was one she did not remember experiencing before, but it seemed familiar, almost as if in a past life . . .

Tom broke away, and smiled at her. 'Do I get a mark, teacher?' he said.

'A double plus,' said Joy.

'Here, let's get rid of this,' Tom said, picking up her handbag. Joy had not fastened it properly. As Tom lifted it, some of the contents spilled on to the floor: a comb, a biro and a packet of extra-safe condoms.

Joy was gripped by an anxiety greater than any she had ever known. Tom would think she had done all this deliberately to get him into bed, or that she was the sort of woman who carried condoms in her handbag just on the off chance, as she had already explained she was single. She had to say something, and it was best if it was the truth.

'Those were meant for someone else,' Joy faltered. 'I was supposed to be seeing someone tonight, a man my cousin introduced me to. I was supposed to try to make something happen between us, as a sort of test for me – another fear to overcome –' Joy laughed hollowly. 'Except I don't think it was a fear. I just didn't fancy him.'

She understood what Roger had been trying to point out earlier.

'Some people are meant to be just platonic friends,' Tom remarked.

There was another agonizing silence. Joy summoned up all her courage.

'Not us, I hope.' Her remark was barely audible, but Tom heard it.

'Not us,' he said, and reached out to stroke her face. 'Definitely not us.'

He withdrew his hand and picked up the condoms. 'Pity to waste these, though, don't you think?'

They were locked together on the settee. Lesley's mouth was sore from Lawrence's repeated kisses. Beards had their disadvantages. Yet still he had done no more than kiss her. Lesley ached with desire and realized, with growing delight, that it was up to her to express her needs. She was no longer Rennie's handmaiden. She was in charge now, and the idea thrilled her. Here was a man whose latent sexuality almost overpowered her, but who knew nothing, not the first thing, about its expression. He could have no better teacher than her, she thought, as she gently disengaged herself from him and began to unbutton her blouse.

Lawrence looked at her with wonder. He could hardly believe this was happening to him. As Lesley's blouse slipped to the floor he was entranced by the lacy cups of her bra, and they sent everything reeling from his mind – Joy, his mother, his insurance exams. He watched the woman in front of him reach behind her, unhook her bra, and he watched her breasts fall free of their restraint. The stirring in his loins was unmistakable now.

In a practised manoeuvre, Lesley reached over to the belt of his trousers and, as her hands met his flesh, he was transformed and, for the first time, he knew precisely what it was he wanted to do.

Tom's hands moved like a magician's over Joy's body, making it beautiful to her and infinitely desirable, whereas before it had been just a body like anyone's else's. As his hand moved between her thighs, she gasped to discover that she was designed to receive so much pleasure. What could she do to him to repay him those liquid, golden moments that exploded so gloriously and shook her in wave after wave? She clung to him, pulling him to her, drowning in satisfaction as she felt him inside her.

Lawrence lay on his back in Lesley's bed, a sense of well-being irradiating his whole body. This was the best moment of his life so far. Lesley lay cradled in his arm, smiling to herself. He had satisfied her, over and over again. He felt newly born; everything was clear to him for the first time. In the lulls in their love-making they had talked and talked. He wondered who Joy had met and was glad for her. As Lesley had suggested, he was going to forget the insurance and work with Howard. He could do anything he wanted now.

He kissed Lesley lightly on her brow. He needed to get up to use the bathroom. Once on his feet, another wave of euphoria enveloped him. He stretched and flung his arms wide.

Suddenly there was the sound of china shattering. Lawrence jumped in alarm.

Lesley sat up on the bed.

'What have I done?' asked Lawrence in dismay.

'Something I was going to do, if you hadn't,' Lesley told him, smiling. 'But I'm rather glad you did it. Come here,' she said, holding out her arms. 'We'll clear up the mess later.'

CHAPTER NINETEEN

What have I done?

This was Joy's immediate thought when she woke beside Tom very early on Sunday morning, and again when she woke an hour later. She thought it yet again when the bedroom began to fill with light, illuminating Tom's peaceful, sleeping face. Tom Quinn's face. Fantasy and reality had collided for her in a way that challenged all her preconceptions about life. Life wasn't a troll that lurked under bridges springing unpleasant surprises. It was a firework display, filling the dark sky with colour and light and wonder.

Life was also rather embarrassing. When Tom woke, and he was stirring now, they would each have to face the fact that they were lying in bed together naked and would have to make conversation. Joy moved herself closer to Tom, luxuriating in the firmness and warmth of his body. Her mind ranged over the scenes in plays and poems she knew when the lovers woke on the morning after. She remembered John Donne – her favourite love poet – and smiled to herself. She'd always suspected he'd got it right and now she knew for sure, although her proof of his rightness was hardly something she could tell her upper sixth about. She thought also of other literary lovers. Troilus and Criseyde. Hero and Leander. Romeo and Juliet. All of them lovers who begged the night would last just a little longer, yet all of them having finally to submit to the laws of nature.

These violent delights have violent ends.

Do they? Joy curled her leg round Tom's as she pondered this. What was going to happen next? How could she be sure he didn't only want her for one night? And what about Lucy? She was alone, unprotected, in Joy's house. And Lawrence? She had stood him up – there was no getting away from it. And her mother. She had not rung her mother for nearly a week. Was she all right? And ought she to tell her mother about Tom?

A familiar tension gripped her, and she would have got out of bed then, washed and dressed, made some coffee and sat by the breakfast bar in the kitchen to do some heavy-duty worrying were it not for Tom, who stirred and pulled her to him. And once again the present demanded her complete attention.

Later, Joy did sit at the breakfast bar, wrapped in Tom's navy bathrobe, sipping coffee, watching Tom make toast. Now she was hungry, very hungry. Yet fingers of anxiety were probing her sense of well-being. Was this all? Would she breakfast with him and then go? She was silent, her dread making it impossible for her to think of any small talk.

Tom was humming a tune.

'Go on,' he said. 'Tell me another one of those rhymes.'

'A. A. Milne's?' Joy said, surprised.

'That's right.'

'"There was once a dormouse,"' she told him, '"who lived in a bed, of delphiniums (blue) and geraniums (red) . . ."'

'That's good,' Tom said when she had finished. 'Have some toast.'

They faced each other over the breakfast bar. Joy

spread a swirl of blackcurrant jam over her slice of toast. She summoned all her courage.

'I shall have to go soon,' she ventured, her heart thumping, waiting to see how he would respond.

'Why?'

'I have Lucy at home, and I must see how she is. And I shall have to apologize to Lesley and Lawrence, as I explained to you. And I must phone my mother.'

'Why?' Tom said, his mouth full of toast. 'What are you going to tell her?'

'Check she's OK,' Joy mumbled.

'Are you going to tell her about us?' Tom asked.

'No!' Joy said, shocked.

'Oh,' Tom said. There was an uneasy silence. Joy glanced quickly at Tom and saw a shadow cross his face, and for a moment she could almost believe it was disappointment.

'Do you want me to tell her about us?' Joy asked.

'Why won't you?' Tom would still not commit himself.

'I don't talk to my mother about sex,' Joy said primly.

Tom smiled. 'Is that all?'

'What do you mean, all? I've spent the best years of my life successfully protecting my mother from the permissive society, and you dismiss my achievement by saying "is that all?"'

'So your mother believes you're a virgin?' Tom asked Joy.

'No – she must have guessed I'm not, although I never actually told her, the first time. I'm sure she prefers to think of me as pure in mind and body.'

Tom stroked his chin.

'Tell her,' he said. 'Tell her about us. I want you to.'

'You do?'

'Yeah. It'll do you good. It'll do her good. Take a risk.'

A risk. Joy's four-letter word. She bit her lip.

'Anyway,' Tom continued. 'I'd like to meet your mother. I shall have to if she comes and lives with you.'

Joy was alert instantly to the implications of those words. She filled with an exultation it was impossible to express except by smiling at Tom, who answered her smile and reached out and gripped her hand hard.

'The truth is,' Joy said, 'I feel as if I want to tell everybody. I'll put a notice in the college bulletin, if you like.'

Tom laughed. 'Stay with me today,' he said.

'Yes,' Joy said. 'I mean, no. There's Lucy. And Lesley and Lawrence. I must go.'

'Go and come back. Have lunch with me. I'll walk over to Brackman's and get some bagels.'

'"A bear,"' said Joy, '"however hard he tries, grows tubby without exercise!"'

'And what do you want with the bagels?' asked Tom. 'Smoked salmon, chopped herring? I'm crazy about chopped herring.'

'That would be lovely,' she said. And stopped and thought. Her mother had always said that chopped herring was an acquired taste. That was her phrase. An acquired taste. Ruth said that only Jews liked chopped herring. It reminded Joy of something else she had noticed when they were making love, which had slipped her mind.

'Tom,' she said. 'Are you Jewish?'

'My mother is,' he said. 'And I was packed off to *cheder* when I was small. I was even *Bar Mitzvahed*. Then I went through this thing of rejecting it all. I hung around with lads at school who weren't Jewish. You know Chris Chapman, bass guitar in the Law Enforcers? He was one.

His dad had a garage we used to practise in. I didn't look Jewish, so I decided to hide it. I didn't think it was important to me.'

'I just drifted,' Joy said. 'I never had the courage to rebel.'

'So you're Jewish too. I thought you were. Practising?'

'I practise, but I'm still not very good at it.'

'I'm getting better,' Tom said. 'It's kind of interesting when you find out more about it.'

'You said your parents emigrated,' Joy reminded him, keen to find out about this other side of Tom.

'To Israel. It was my mother's ambition. My father thought it would be like a permanent holiday, and so I paid for an apartment for them in Eilat.'

'Don't you miss them?' Joy asked.

'Not particularly. I fly over to see them. Perhaps I'll take you.'

Joy thought of her flight yesterday and was about to suggest that a cruise might be nice.

'You don't have a copy of those A. A. Milne poems, do you?' Tom asked suddenly.

'Yes. At home. Next to Milton on my shelf.'

'Bring it,' Tom instructed her. 'When you come back for lunch.'

As Joy unlocked her front door she heard the sound of voices.

Her first thought was that Lucy was listening to the radio. Yet as she paused to try to make out what station Lucy had tuned in to, she realized one of the voices was Lucy's and the other was one she knew equally well. She was not surprised. Lesley had every right to demand an explanation.

Then a thought occurred to her. She had told Lucy that she was spending the night with Miss Wright. Her alibi was blown. What on earth would Lucy think of her? All her moral authority – vanished in a puff of smoke. Just as Lucy had found an older woman to trust in, she turns out to be the epitome of lust and deception. And Lesley! Joy remembered with horror that she had planned to spend the night with Rennie. Had Joy in her selfishness put paid to that too? She must apologize immediately.

'It's me,' she cried out. 'I'm ever so sorry!'

With that, she entered the lounge. Lucy turned to her with interest.

'Where were you last night? We're dying to know!'

'I met an old friend,' Joy said. It was imperative she conceal the truth from Lucy.

'Male or female?' Lucy asked.

'Female – no, male,' said Joy desperately.

'Aren't you sure?' Lucy asked.

'Male,' said Joy finally.

'Hey, that's great!' Lucy said. 'Tell us all about it. I love hearing about other people's boyfriends.'

Joy shot a glance at Lesley, who didn't seem at all at ease. She was biting her nails. Joy had not seen her do that before. Something was up. She decided to take action.

'I promised my old friend that I'd return for lunch, so I don't have a lot of time. Tell you what, Lucy, I'll take you and the cat home now – here are your keys – and I'll talk to you in the car. Miss Wright will look after the house till I get back.'

Once again Joy entered her house. She'd deflected Lucy's interest in her private life by explaining exactly who Tom was. Lucy had been impressed and had begged to be able to meet him. Perhaps, Joy had said.

And now for Lesley. Lesley would be able to tell her how Lawrence had taken her defection. Yet the strange thing was that she almost felt that if, instead of Lesley, Lawrence had been in her front room, she would have found it just as easy to tell him about Tom, knowing he would be glad for her.

When Joy entered her lounge, Lesley looked far from glad. An uncharacteristic anxiety played across her features. Immediately Joy feared that Lawrence had not believed whatever story Les had cooked up and had given her a hard time. She joined Les on the settee and apologized again.

'I'm sorry.'

'I'm sorry, too,' said Lesley.

'What did you say to him?' Joy asked.

'Oh, something about Sister wanting to see you.'

'On Saturday night?' Joy said incredulously. 'He believed that?'

'I – I prevented him from thinking about it too closely.'

'Was he upset? What did he say?'

'He . . . he got over it.'

'Well done!' said Joy. 'Lesley pulls it off again!'

'Pulls it off,' echoed Lesley. 'That was more or less what happened.'

'What did you pull off?'

'I began with his outer garments, naturally. And things progressed from there.'

A wholly incredible, incongruous, stupendous and thoroughly desirable idea entered Joy's mind. She looked at Lesley. She had never seen Lesley blush before, and it made her look uncharacteristically vulnerable.

'You mean, you seduced Lawrence?'

'Well, somebody had to!'

Joy hugged her friend tightly. This was the best possible thing that could have happened. Astonishment and pleasure competed for expression. Except Lesley got in first.

'I'm so sorry. I wouldn't have done it, except you said you'd met someone else, and being together like that –'

'Listen, Lesley – I'm thrilled!'

'– and I've been so worried about telling you. I've never done anything like this before. He was your man, and –'

'But I don't want him – not like that. He's free. I wish you both *mazeltov*!'

'And then I was worried he would think I made love to any unsuspecting man who walked into my cottage. He reassured me he didn't, and I think I believed him. He's at home now – we've arranged to see each other later. But I'm worried that his mother will disapprove of me, not being Jewish. But that's not all. I'm worried that when Lawrence thinks of what he's done, he'll hate both me and himself.' Lesley's eyes filled with tears. 'I've not met a man like him ever before. I don't know what's come over me. I'm just so frightened of losing him.' And she burst into tears.

Joy handed her some tissues.

'Poor Lesley! But believe me, there's no point in worrying. It's because you've fallen for him. Love and worry are inseparable.' Do I sound smug? I don't mean to, thought Joy. 'Les – you need distracting. Let me tell you what happened to me last night.'

'All right,' sniffed Lesley.

★

Joy looked at her watch. Midday, and Lesley had only just gone. She really ought to be getting back to Tom, but there was just one more thing she had to do.

With anticipation and dread equally mixed, Joy dialled her mother's number.

'Hello, Mum,' she said.

'Oh, Joy. It's you.' Ruth sounded flustered, possibly even distressed.

'Is there anything wrong?' asked Joy.

'No, no. Nothing's wrong.'

'Are you sure nothing's wrong?'

'I'm sure nothing's wrong.' Ruth sounded irritated. Time to change the subject.

'Mum, I have some good news.'

'Really? Are you head of department?'

'No, no, the interview's not for a fortnight. This is something completely different. Do you remember that when I was younger I used to like a singer called Tom Quinn?'

'You liked so many singers. And you stuck all those posters up on your wall with Sellotape, so that when you removed them, the wallpaper was ruined, and I had to get your bedroom redecorated.'

'Yes, I know, but I liked Tom Quinn best. Don't you remember me watching him on *Top of the Pops*? With the Law Enforcers? And you said they sounded as if they were all on drugs?'

'I remember vaguely.'

'Well, the band broke up after two albums, and Tom never recorded anything after that. It was lucky he invested his money wisely. He wanted to write again, and so he came back to Manchester, thinking it would help him rediscover his roots. He's Jewish, you see.' Joy could

338

feel her mother's attention wandering. Yet she was finding it hard to come to the point. 'I only found all this out last night, because I met him!'

'Very nice,' Ruth said. 'Did Lawrence take you to a concert?'

'No, it wasn't like that. It was through one of the students at college. I had to pick something up from his house for her.' Joy paused and took a deep breath. 'I stayed and Tom Quinn cooked dinner for me.' For the moment she could go no further. She could not talk about her own sex life to her mother. To Ruth and Joy, female reproductive equipment was something you couldn't see that occasionally alarmed you by going wrong. Easier to talk about a smear test than sex. Joy played for time.

'It's funny meeting someone famous.'

'I met Frankie Vaughan once at Henry's *Bar Mitzvah* party. He's even better-looking in real life.'

Joy knew she had reached a crossroads. Either they could talk about Frankie Vaughan and Uncle Henry, or she could press on with her revelations about Tom.

'Did I tell you what happened the last time I saw Henry?' Ruth remarked.

'Mum,' said Joy, gripping the telephone as if it were a club with which she was going to hit her. 'There was more to it than just meeting him.'

'There wasn't. He was invited as a celebrity guest. I shook his hand –'

'No, Mum, listen. I'm talking about Tom Quinn. Like I said, I had dinner at his house, and we got talking. We got on very well. I liked him even more than I do Lawrence. And then, I don't know what happened, but one thing led to another, and –' Joy realized she was talking to her

339

mother in clichés, Ruth's own clichés. She knew she had to find her own voice.

'And so later on we made love,' she said. 'It was absolutely wonderful. I never knew how good sex could be. Mum? Mum? Are you still there?'

'I'm still here.'

'Don't sound like that. I wanted to do it. It was me – I wanted it. I don't regret a thing. I want you to imagine how it was – I used to have fantasies about Tom Quinn making love to me, and they've come true. And the truth was even better than the fantasy!'

Joy could hardly believe she'd said all that. At first she experienced a moment of pure, unadulterated liberation. She was free. And then the guilt set in. She had upset her mother. She never should have said those things. She was unutterably selfish.

'Mum?'

'Very nice,' Ruth said. 'And are you going to see this man again?'

'I'm going back there now. He said he'd like to meet you!'

'Me? So what happened to Lawrence?'

'Don't worry about him – he met someone else too.' Just like in *A Midsummer Night's Dream*. Joy cast herself and Lesley as Hermia and Helena – and Michael as Bottom, perhaps?

'So you have a new boyfriend,' Ruth said. Joy thought her voice sounded flat. Why couldn't her mother be glad for her? A mother should be someone who sat in the front row of the audience of your life and clapped wildly and stamped her feet.

'Aren't you glad for me?' Joy asked.

'Yes, I'm glad.'

'You're not angry?'

'Why should I be angry?'

'I still want you to come and live here,' Joy hastened to reassure her mother, in case she thought Joy was trying to wriggle out of their arrangement.

'Are you sure?' Ruth said.

Joy knew she had successfully identified the reason for her mother's lack of excitement. Ruth was worried her daughter would no longer want her. It was up to Joy to show her how wrong she was.

'Mum, Tom changes nothing between us, absolutely nothing. I always want you with me, you know that. I can't wait for you to start living here. I told you about Tom so we shouldn't have any secrets between us.'

'Look, Joy, you've picked a bad time to talk. Barney is picking me up shortly. There's a quiz at his *shul*. I'll speak to you later. And don't worry – I'm very happy for you.'

'I've got to rush too,' Joy said. 'Tom's getting us both some bagels. Enjoy yourself, Mum!'

'I'll try to,' said Ruth.

'Love you.'

'Go on,' Ruth said in affectionate exasperation. 'Go back to your boyfriend.'

Joy was glad. She had been given the permission she craved.

'Bye!'

Ruth replaced the receiver and shook her head. She walked into her kitchen and sat down on an old wooden chair by the small table. She sat very still, and thought. A few moments later she rose and began to prepare a cup of tea. She boiled the kettle and warmed the pot. She stopped, gazed at the shed at the bottom of the garden and watched a starling who had been perching there fly

341

off to a neighbouring tree. Ruth continued to think, and the teapot lay forgotten by the kettle.

There was a lot to think about.

CHAPTER TWENTY

Lesley appeared at the door of the English office.

'I've come to wish you good luck!'

Joy was alone, looking out of the window, over the garage. She had not heard Lesley come in. She was contemplating the impossibility of calling Tom's face to mind, as much as she loved him. It was as if he was so near her, he was out of focus, but at the same time, everywhere. It was easier to recall his caresses that morning, the way he had of rubbing his cheek against hers, as a cat might do.

'Joy!' Lesley said again, more urgently.

Jolted from her reverie, Joy turned swiftly round, saw Lesley, smiled dazedly at her and yawned.

'Good luck,' Les said again.

'Thank you,' said Joy.

'When are you going down to Sister's? Did you know that two of the governors have asked to sit in on the interview?'

Joy looked at her watch. 'Oh look! The interview's in five minutes. Lucky you came along. What did you say about the governors?'

'That two of them will be present at the interview.'

'That's nice,' Joy said.

'I thought I'd come to check you weren't worrying.'

'No, I've stopped worrying,' Joy said dreamily. 'I'm pleased you've come in, because I've something to tell you. Tom's written a song. It's called "Delphiniums Blue". It's sort of urban romantic, he says. He's gone to London today to see his management company.'

'That's great, Joy. Listen carefully. I saw the governors go into Sister's office. I know one of them – Neville Ross of Wilcox Engineering. What he's doing here sitting in on an English post I don't know. He's the one who's pushing Sister into trying to get us an Investors in People award and told her that financial health is the only certain indicator of the success of a higher education institution. One of those men who can only see education as a business. The other governor is a woman, the magistrate type, tall, dog-tooth suit, knowing eyes – almost certainly a practising Catholic.'

Joy struggled to see the relevance of this to her forthcoming interview. They were bound to be nice people anyway. Really, Joy thought, it was amazing how she had come on since the beginning of term. She used to be such a worrier, and now here she was, utterly relaxed, feeling equal to any question they might throw at her. Joy tried to decide what the chief factors that had caused this stupendous change were. Pre-eminent among them must be Tom. She allowed a little sigh of pleasure to escape her. She brought her thoughts back to the present. Here was Lesley in front of her. That brought something to mind.

'How's Lawrence?' Joy asked. Her own happiness still allowed her time to think of other people. 'Did you enjoy meeting Deborah and Howard?'

'Your interview's in a few minutes,' Lesley reminded Joy. 'Why don't you look over your development-plan notes?'

Joy smiled fondly at Lesley, who had become such a worrier.

'Have you seen Peter this morning?' Joy asked her.

'Yes. He's in the staff room. He's being interviewed

directly after you. I'm just off to wish him good luck as well.'

'Give him my love,' Joy said. 'Did I tell you Roger used to like the Law Enforcers?'

'We'll talk about that another time,' said Lesley. 'Now you're going to your interview for head of department.'

'Sister said I shouldn't worry, and here I am, not in the least bit worried,' Joy declared. 'Time to be off!' she said contentedly to Lesley. 'Let's walk down together.'

Sister and the two governors rose, and Joy smiled dazzlingly at them. She shook their proffered hands warmly and then settled herself comfortably in the chair behind Sister's desk. She had a good view of all three of her interviewers.

'Why don't you start by telling Mr Ross and Mrs Webster a little bit about your career here, Joy?' Sister Maureen suggested.

'Certainly. I started at St Ignatius' in 19 – when was it? Was it four or five years ago? Never mind. I came here as an English teacher with no special responsibilities, and then Betty asked me if I'd take over trips and visits –'

A window-cleaner had appeared at the large window behind Sister and the two governors. Joy was surprised. Normally window-cleaners worked after college hours. Perhaps Lesley was trying a new firm. Joy found herself listening to the squeak of the squeezy mop. Now, where was she?

'I've been closely involved with the writing of the department's development plan, and I worked with Betty on something else last year. Isn't that funny? I can't remember what it was!'

The window was completely covered with bubbles

now. Joy waited for the sponge to come and clear the suds.

'Miss Freeman,' interjected Mr Ross. 'What are your plans for ensuring an increase in capitation in the next academic year, and how far do you intend to increase the provision of new courses in order to remain competitive in the market-place?'

Joy tore her eyes from the window. *Concentrate!* She looked Neville Ross straight in the eye. He looked surprisingly familiar. Did she know him from somewhere? Suddenly the suds were cleared from the window. Joy could see the window-cleaner again.

'Capitation,' she repeated, giving herself time to absorb the question and prepare a reply.

She looked at Mr Ross again. His hair was white, with just a tinge of yellow. He was probably a drinker, as the red veins in his cheeks testified. His bulbous nose was reddish too. As the window-cleaner moved off across the playing fields, Joy noticed he was wearing a tartan scarf. A tartan scarf . . . red veins . . . white hair. Surely Neville Ross wasn't the man she'd sent flying twice on the ice-rink a few weeks ago? Could he be? Ought she to say something to him? No – best to proceed with answering the question. What was it about? Capitation!

'I believe the projected capitation for the next academic year has been increased slightly, in line with –' With what? Joy had forgotten. Why was Mr Ross looking at her so oddly? Did he recognize her? '– increased slightly, in line with the FEFC's recommendations.' She took a deep breath. 'Sometimes increased expenditure is necessary to improve facilities in order to attract students. I'd like to invest in computers for the English department, although I know I'm on slippery ground here.' Slippery ground. She'd said 'slippery ground'. He was bound to remember her. She glanced at Neville Ross. He sat there, impassive as a rock.

'So putting aside a figure of eight –' Joy cursed herself. She'd done it again. Figure of eight. She felt herself glowing scarlet. 'A figure of £8,000, and –' Joy tried to recall what she was going to say next. She felt her mind seize up and atrophy. She thought again how tired she was and tried to suppress a yawn.

'I'm so sorry.' Joy paused, trying to collect herself. Each fraction of a second seemed like an eternity. She watched herself saying nothing, doing nothing, and was fascinated by the spectacle. No, not fascinated. That wasn't quite the right word. Horrified. She was horrified. Yet the more she thought about the fact that her mind was a blank, the more it became so.

'I'm sorry,' Joy said again. 'Figures were never my strong point. Which isn't to say I can't handle them – just because I'm an English teacher, it doesn't mean I'm innumerate. Oh no!' Joy felt she was gathering momentum now. 'I do understand figures; it's just that I see them as secondary to other things, like the quality of education. Like human relations. That's my philosophy – that people count. At the end of the day it's not figures we should be worrying about but people. And when I say "worry", I don't mean "worry", but care. The two words are semantically similar, of course. However, worry is fear-driven and incapacitates, whereas caring – respecting the rights and the needs of others – is the basis of all morality – humanist, Catholic, Jewish. I'm Jewish,' Joy reminded Mrs Webster. 'It helps when you're teaching *The Merchant of Venice*.' And she stopped.

There was silence. Sister looked at her quizzically.

Slowly it began to occur to Joy that what had sounded a moment ago like inspired rhetoric was nothing more than drivel. She had astonished the interviewers with her remarkable unsuitability for the job. A tidal wave of embarrassment and humiliation threatened to engulf her. Her only wish now was to get out of Sister's study as quickly as possible. She saw Sister try to communicate her concern with her eyes. Joy smiled bravely back at her to indicate she would be all right to continue with the interview.

Sister Maureen glanced at the papers on her desk and began with the next question.

Joy closed Sister's door softly. It was finally over. She could imagine Sister desperately trying to explain to the two governors how she could ever have encouraged Joy to put in her application. She allowed herself a moment of pure self-hatred. As she walked on in the direction of the staff room, she breathed in the aroma of Calvin Klein's Obsession aftershave, and then saw Peter Worthington coming towards her, smarter than ever in his interview suit. He stopped when he reached Joy and immediately saw the distress writ large on her face.

'Whatever happened in there?' he asked her, concerned.

Joy found that her voice was breaking as she tried to explain. 'I don't know what came over me. I just couldn't concentrate, I couldn't answer the questions and then said all the wrong things in desperation. Sister almost stopped the interview. I've blown it completely.'

'Are you sure you're not imagining this?'

'Not this time,' Joy said, sniffing back her tears. 'All those months learning not to worry, and in the end I wasn't worried enough.' She tried to laugh at the irony. 'But it's all right,' she told him. 'Both the governors seem very human. You'll do well. Good luck!'

'Thanks.' Peter strode off determinedly in the direction of Sister's study.

As she walked on through the corridor, Joy became aware that her legs could hardly carry her. She wanted more than anything to sit down. Lessons were going on in the classrooms she passed. Across the courtyard she could see that the chapel door was slightly ajar. This meant it might be empty. Quickly crossing the courtyard, she made her way there.

It was empty. Joy breathed in the cool, damp air, passing rows of wooden chairs on her way to the front, directly opposite the table overspread with a white cloth that served as an altar. She sunk on to a chair and cupped her head in her hands.

It was hard to accept that all her dreams of having her own department had come to nothing, and harder still to accept that it was all her fault. She was too anguished to cry. Even thoughts of Tom did not cheer her. She felt thoroughly stupid, thoroughly undeserving of him. Here was Joy Freeman, who had prated to her students about the need not to be too laid-back when taking exams and hadn't followed her own advice. She began to realize how much of her time in the past few months had been spent idly imagining what she would do if she had been appointed. Joy felt utterly drained. She looked up forlornly at the crucifix above her and empathized with Christ in his agony.

At first she didn't hear the door open. It was only when footsteps proceeded up the aisle between the chairs that she started and turned round. It was Peter. He stopped in his advance towards her as soon as she noticed him.

'Sister wants to see you,' he informed her.

Joy nodded. 'Thanks, Peter. How was your interview?'

'Fine,' he said. 'I managed to get across what I'd intended.'

'That's good,' she said, smiling at him. She was sure she'd be able to work under Peter, even if he was younger than her. At the door of the chapel he waved briefly to her and walked off in the direction of the English office.

Joy retraced her path to Sister's study and knocked on the door. When Sister called for her to enter, Joy saw that the two governors had gone. That was something to be grateful for.

'Do sit down, Joy.'

Joy sat.

'I've called you back to ask you if you will accept the position of head of the English department at St Ignatius'.'

Since it wasn't what she was expecting to hear, Joy found she couldn't make out what Sister said and asked her to repeat it.

'I'm asking you if you will accept the position of head of English at St Ignatius'.'

'But my interview was dreadful!' Joy exclaimed, still not quite believing what she was hearing.

'Yes, dear. Your interview was dreadful. I had quite a hard time persuading Ellen Webster and Neville Ross that you weren't really like that. But it was Peter who won them over. When he came in here and withdrew his application, and spoke so strongly in support of you, I could see they were both very impressed. As I was. Peter told them that you were a gifted teacher, popular with your colleagues, enviably well-organized, and full of ideas for developing yourself and the department. If I didn't know better, I'd think he had quite a crush on you!'

Once again Joy couldn't quite suppress those tears. Sister reached across with a tissue and handed it to her.

'So do I take it you accept?'

Joy nodded and blew her nose.

'Good. I'm thinking that in view of the inspection you will need a strong second in department and I'm proposing to offer that post to Peter.'

'Oh, yes,' Joy agreed.

'Well, that's all settled.' Joy looked up and saw Sister Maureen beaming. 'I can see the day has been quite an ordeal for you, and I'm perfectly happy for you to go home now. Both of you deserve a day off. Perhaps you'll want to go and tell the good news to that nice new boyfriend of yours. A pop star, is he?'

'Yes, Sister.'

'Congratulations, Joy.'

Peter had proved impossible to thank. He had taken advantage of Sister's offer of time off and was not at home when Joy tried to ring. She knew not to be too effusive, as Peter disliked shows of emotion. This was a problem, insofar as Joy was awash with emotion and needed to express it. Tom was uncontactable for two days, she knew, but in a way, it didn't matter. It didn't matter because the one person who would fully understand everything she had been through, who would relish her blow-by-blow account of the interview and its aftermath was not Tom, but her mother. Arriving home, pouring a coffee, and settling by the telephone, her first instinct and desire was to ring her mother. Her fingers automatically pressed the digits that would connect her to Ruth. Joy waited.

There was no reply.

It was frustrating that her mother should have chosen to go shopping now, when there was so much to say to her. However, Joy partly blamed herself. She had not rung Ruth for the best part of a week, and had she done so she would have known that her mother had planned to be out today. She sipped her coffee resignedly. She would have to wait.

She waited a couple of hours and rang again. Come on, Mum, she said to herself, you must be in by now.

There was no reply.

Joy checked her watch again. It was five o'clock. It was possible that if Ruth had gone into Romford, or was with Uncle Barney and Aunty Miriam, she might not be home yet. The reasoning part of her mind told her that. Yet the facts – her mother not at home all afternoon – were enough to strike the tinder of her anxiety. What if something was wrong?

No, it couldn't be. Her mother had a perfect right to spend the afternoon out. Joy decided to ring again after six.

At one minute past six she rang again. The space between the conclusion of her dialling and the commencement of the ring of her mother's telephone seemed an age.

There was no reply.

Joy resolved to be logical. It was unlikely her mother was out shopping then. She was almost certainly with Uncle Barney and, if she wasn't, at least Uncle Barney would know where she was. Joy dialled Uncle Barney's number.

There was no reply.

Joy rang Deborah. This time the phone was picked up immediately by Hayleigh, who breathlessly rushed through her telephone number and screeched to a halt.

'It's me, Aunty Joy. Is Mummy there?'

'Mummy! Aunty Joy on the phone!'

A pause, then Deborah began to talk. 'Joy. Hi! What's new?'

'Look, I can't get an answer on my mother's phone, and I thought your parents might know where she is, but they're out too.'

'I know. There's a *shul* trip to the Golders Green Hippodrome.'

'Do you think my mother's with them?' asked Joy, relief sweeping through her.

'No, she's not,' Deborah said with emphasis. 'I know Dad tried to persuade her, but she refused absolutely. Said she wasn't in the mood for that sort of thing. I think he was a little hurt.'

'Could she have changed her mind?'

'I don't think so. She hadn't last night when I spoke to them. Don't worry, Joy. I'm sure there's a logical explanation.'

After she had replaced the receiver Joy tried to think of a logical explanation. Perhaps her mother had fallen down the stairs and couldn't move to answer the phone. Perhaps she had been knocked over while crossing the road, and the hospital even now were trying to find details of a next of kin. Perhaps she was very ill and had collapsed in the bathroom, knocking her head against the bath, and was now lying there unconscious. Perhaps she had come in and surprised some burglars, who had tied her up, and were tormenting her, or worse.

Joy dialled her mother's number again.

There was no reply.

At quarter to seven in the morning, when Joy finally emerged from the short spells of semi-consciousness and lurid half-dreams which had constituted her night's sleep, she reached over to the bedside telephone and dialled her mother's number again. There was still no reply.

Now Joy knew that something had to be done. There wasn't a fault on her mother's line; that she had checked last night. Perhaps now she should ring the police, or Whipps Cross Hospital. Did they have a casualty department? The horror of having to do all this made her shudder. She decided then to go into college and ring from there. At college she would have people around her. Lesley would be there, and Peter, Betty and, best of all, Sister. If anyone knew what to do, it would be Sister.

White, and shaking, Joy washed and dressed and forced herself to eat some cereal. The milk seemed bitter to her. She threw on her jacket and went to check that the back door was locked. She put on her answering machine and shut the door, double-locking it with the Yale. She made her way to her car.

As she was waiting on the corner of her street to turn into the traffic, it occurred to her that she had missed something out of her morning routine. What could it be? Her briefcase – it was still lying by the side of the settee in the lounge. She couldn't go to college without her briefcase.

So once she was on the main road, she took the next right and returned to her house. She had plenty of time for the detour. It was still only half past seven.

When she entered her house again, the red light on her answering machine was flashing. Joy was surprised. No one ever rang in the morning, unless it was her mother. It was her mother, she was sure of it! Eagerly she pressed the message button, and waited. Thank God, she was right. It was Ruth. Joy stood rigid with attention by the telephone.

Joy? It's Mum. Now I don't want you to worry. I had a lovely flight and I'm ringing from Aunty Faye's apartment. I didn't tell you I was going to New York because I knew you would worry. But I thought I needed a holiday. It was my last chance –

Joy? Is that Joy? This is your Aunty Faye. Now you mustn't worry. I can look after Ruth. I'm just so thrilled to see her. So you mustn't worry! –

Joy? It's Mum again. I'm afraid this is costing your aunt a lot of money. I'll ring another time. Have a nice day!

Two beeps. Then silence. Stunned, Joy could hardly think what to do next. Was this a practical joke? She rewound the message and played it again.

Her mother had gone to New York without telling her because she didn't want her to worry. Why did she think she would worry? Was there something to worry about? What did Ruth mean by saying it was her last chance? Why did Aunty Faye keep repeating that she wasn't to worry? The lady doth protest too much. The conviction they they were hiding something from her grew rapidly.

She played her mother's message again. And again, until she had memorized it completely.

Forgetting her briefcase once more, she set off for college.

Luckily the door to Sister Maureen's study was open, and Sister herself was sitting at her desk, looking at some papers in front of her.

Joy knocked, entered and closed the door behind her.

'Joy? Are you all right?' Sister said, alarmed.

For the second time in less than twenty-four hours, Joy burst into tears in Sister Maureen's study.

'My mother's gone,' Joy said.

'I didn't know she was ill,' Sister said softly.

'No, no – God forbid. She's not ill, or at least I don't think she is. She's gone to New York, without telling me. She left a message on my answering machine.' Joy repeated the substance of it. 'She said it was her last chance. I'm so scared, Sister. What if she really is ill and doesn't want me to see her suffer? It's the only explanation that fits the facts! Otherwise, why wouldn't she tell me why she was going? She was supposed to be coming to live with me. I don't know what to think.'

'Does your mother often go on holiday on her own?' Sister asked.

'Never. And whenever she does go, she tells me. And whatever I do, I tell her. Ever since my father died, we've been as close as sisters. That's why this is so odd.'

'You think she might be ill.'

'She said it was her last chance. I've been thinking about this. If she was dying, she would want to see Aunty Faye once more! And I can't ring her back because I don't have Aunty Faye's number. No one in England has it, I don't think, except for my mother. And even when I do speak to her, it's so easy to lie on the phone. I want to see her. I need to see her!'

'St Patrick's is a fine cathedral,' mused Sister. 'Just along Fifth Avenue, it is. You must call in there and light a candle.'

Joy despaired. Sister had not been listening to her.

'What shall I do about my mother?'

'Take her with you. And your aunt as well. A walk down Fifth Avenue is a must for all of you. And I'm sure I could arrange for you all to visit our sister college in Connecticut while you're there.'

'What do you mean?'

'You must go and find your mother, Joy. It's a wonderful thing, this close relationship between you. Only when you see her will your mind be at rest.'

'But it's the middle of term!'

Sister raised her eyebrows as if to express her contempt for college routine. Joy was not surprised. Sister was a maverick, and everyone knew it. She made up her own rules as she went along.

'I'm happy for you to have a week off. I'm sure your department can cover for you. You need a break.' Sister sighed pleasurably. 'Do you know the Book of Ruth? Wherever you go, I shall go. Your people shall be my people, and your God, my God. Ruth was a convert, you know, a Moabitess.'

'My mother's name is Ruth,' Joy said wonderingly.

'There. It's all meant. You must follow your mother.'

Joy began to contemplate a lone voyage to New York.

'I'm very interested in the Jewish attitude to conversion,' Sister continued, in reflective vein. 'I believe the conversion process was made so difficult in order to dissuade false converts. The traditions of Judaism and

357

Catholicism are rooted deep in history. I think Lesley found her first interview with the rabbi quite challenging. But she speaks warmly of the synagogue. I must say I had hopes of her embracing Catholicism, but converting to Judaism is almost as good.'

CHAPTER TWENTY-ONE

The plane taxied past other planes, stationary at their departure gates, and moved circuitously in the direction of the main runway. It stood expectantly as another plane rose into the sky. Then, after a pause in which one could almost imagine it gathering breath, it began its powerful acceleration, tilted ever so slightly upward and left the ground.

Joy stared straight in front of her at the panel which divided the rear of the plane from its middle section. She would not look out of the window. That way madness lay. It was a matter of enduring the period when the plane breasted the sky and levelled out for its journey across the Atlantic. She wished again that Tom had been able to come with her. She knew it was impossible. Tom's management company was delighted with his idea for the concept album *Lines and Squares* and, enthused by their interest, Tom was at his piano night and day. He'd promised to try to join her, and she knew that was the best she could hope for.

So here she was alone – a sign said she could remove her seat-belt – flying to New York. She knew that as soon as she allowed herself to think how high she was, she would panic. The art of flying, Joy had discovered, was to let the pilot get on with it, and to distract herself by thinking of other things.

First among these was that her mother had sat here, perhaps in this very same seat, flying at the same altitude and in the same direction. What were the thoughts in her head? Ruth had always been philosophical about flying, so it was doubtful the flight itself would have bothered her. Was she nursing her knowledge of the doctor's pessimistic prognosis of the pains she had been suffering? Was she feeling guilty that she'd left for this holiday so suddenly, without telling Joy, or David, or even Barney and Miriam?

For that was the part neither Joy nor Deborah could understand. Ruth Freeman had gone to America telling no one of her plans. It was almost possible to imagine she'd been involved in some tax fraud or drug-smuggling ring.

Joy started guiltily as a cheerful air steward clad in red came up behind her and offered her a drink. She asked for some wine, which was presented to her in a tiny plastic bottle, along with a plastic tumbler and a miniature packet of nuts in silver foil. Joy paused in her reverie long enough to open the bottle and take a sip, noticing how the pressure in the cabin gave the wine the strange sensation of weightlessness in her mouth, as if it were rising up in her palate.

It had turned out that Uncle Barney had Aunty Faye's address and telephone number, although it had taken him the best part of an evening to find it, hunting in an old John Collier carrier bag where he kept his important family documents. He had driven her to Heathrow early this morning, and she had made him promise faithfully not to ring Faye to say that Joy was on her way. Joy wanted her visit to be every bit as much a secret as her mother's. This was partly out of revenge, she knew, but partly because she believed that only by surprising her mother would she be able to arrive at the truth, whatever that was. She was dimly conscious of another reason too; if her mother could fly the Atlantic alone, so could she.

Joy still kept her vision confined to the interior of the aircraft, despite having been given a window seat. She looked at the other passengers, each cocooned in their own little world, watching films, reading papers, preparing for the tedium of the seven or so hours aloft. When the plane began to shake slightly, Joy remembered that this was caused by turbulence and was not dangerous. It was comforting to know this, and she recalled the pilot at Manchester Airport with a feeling of gratitude. It was also comforting to know that she was floating on air – she tried not to think about how much air – and that she was a graduate of the Fear of Flying course.

If she had done well, Roger had graduated *summa cum laude*. On the Monday after the course, Peter had informed her, he had booked a Christmas holiday for the two of them in the Seychelles. Although the news had delighted Joy, it did not surprise her. What still had the capacity to surprise her every time she thought about it was Lesley's unexpected interest in Judaism. Joy wondered whether Lesley's overwhelming attraction to Lawrence was largely because he was Jewish. Floating over Ireland, Joy began to see how the three of them might have been looking for something central and firm to believe in.

I'm flying. Joy checked to see if she was afraid. She was, of course she was, but now she was aware that she was controlling her fear, self-consciously, like a toddler who, surprised that what he or she is doing is possible, takes his or her first walk across a room. Was that what her mother had been doing? Testing herself in some way? The sky was gloriously, unnaturally blue outside the window and tempted Joy to peek, just a little. She could see the wing of the plane and the red V painted on it. A sense of exhilaration swept through her. She was swooping through the air, on a chariot of fire, crossing the Atlantic just as her mother had, as Aunty Faye once had, as many, many other people had done. She was an adventurer too.

A few hours later it occurred to Joy that it was pretty boring, being an adventurer. It was a matter of sitting there and waiting. The films, the novel she had brought with her, nothing could hold her attention. All she could think of, as the plane edged slowly forward over the water, was that she was getting nearer and nearer to finding out why her mother had left so suddenly. Was it Joy she was leaving? Could Ruth not bear the thought of living with her? Had she been too protective of her own mother? She thought of James James Morrison Morrison, whose mother was also prohibited from going down to the end of town, had decamped one day and was never found again, despite the best efforts of the king, the queen and the prince.

Joy felt an exquisite yearning for her mother, which intertwined itself among the airline's modern red-and-grey-and-white seats, through the bright blue of the sky around them, and the yearning seemed to fuel the plane as it fought the winds to America.

Joy allowed herself a brief glance out of the window. There was land below her. So that was America. Just now it looked like any other land, but the sense of it actually being the country she had only seen depicted in films and in books excited her imagination. It was beautiful. At last she was going there too. She could make out tiny cars below and houses, and hoped that she would be able to get her first sight of Manhattan from the plane.

She craned her neck eagerly. Then, with a shock, she realized she had being looking out of the window for some time, entirely unafraid, enjoying the experience and loving the land beneath her, blessing it unawares – just like Coleridge had those water-snakes in *The Ancient Mariner*. She had looked out of the window like the Lady of Shalott, but the mirror had not smashed from side to side. There was no curse. It was perfectly safe out there.

More than ever, Joy had to find her mother. She had to tell her what she had discovered. She glanced at her watch. Only an hour to go.

Joy sat in the back of a yellow cab holding on tightly to the seat as the cab swung round corners as if auditioning for a part in a cop thriller. Joy looked at the mugshot of the driver in front of her – a startled-looking Puerto Rican. The driver, silent, kept his eyes on the road. Joy looked about her. Having come off Triboro Bridge, she was now entering Manhattan itself. Apartment blocks reared up on either side of her, grey and forbidding. 'Walk' 'Don't walk,' flashed the pedestrian signals. Cars hooted. A man walked by as her taxi stopped at a junction, surrounded by a dozen dogs on leads marching obediently through the busy street.

She had given the cab driver the address of Aunty Faye's apartment – East 79th Street. She had no idea where it was. She waited expectantly as they crossed junction after junction. The cab crossed from a wide avenue into a smaller street and pulled to a halt outside a green awning which bisected the pavement, near a newsstand with piles of papers stacked at its side. To Joy the building looked like a hotel. Disorientated, jet lagged and desperate for a drink of water, she stood looking at it, praying that this was the right place.

She entered the lobby. A uniformed doorman stood behind a desk and nodded politely at her. Joy saw she was expected to use an intercom system. Finding the correct apartment number, she pressed the buzzer and waited.

In the event, it was a man's voice that replied.

'It's Joy. Ruth's Joy. I've come to see if she's all right.' As Joy said this, the absurdity of what she had just done struck her forcibly, and for the first time. She had crossed the Atlantic just to see if her mother was all right. Surely no one in the world had ever worried as much as her? Was there some kind of award you could win for worrying?

'Joy!' exclaimed the man's voice. 'You'd better come right up!'

Joy wheeled her case over to the elevator, pressed a button and walked in to the carpeted interior. A few moments later she emerged on the eighth floor and found the apartment whose address she had so carefully memorized.

Behind that door was her mother.

She took a deep breath and rapped on the wood. The door opened to reveal a good-looking man of medium height who, although no longer young, was too sprightly and alert to deserve the label of elderly.

He beamed at her.

'Joy! Of course it is! I can see your mother in you, and Faye as well. Sammy, this is Joy.'

Joy found herself ushered into the apartment. It was a spacious open-plan apartment, with white walls, a beech-wood unit, a black-and-white cat washing itself on a rug and numerous paintings displayed on the walls, giving it the air of an upscale art gallery. Joy looked around her in wonder. But where was her mother?

'Joy – now you sit yourself down and I'll fix you a

drink. Sammy will make you a Bloody Mary – he makes the best Bloody Marys on the East Side.'

'You're Uncle Benjy, aren't you?' Joy said, her voice sounding curiously flat against her uncle's colourful Manhattan accent. 'Where's Mum?'

Benjy punched the flat of his hand with the ball of the other in a near-miss gesture. 'They're out. Faye's taken her to the World Trade Center this afternoon. If they'd have known you were coming . . . What brought you? Business?'

The other man in the apartment, a chubby, greying man, left the room to get the drinks, Joy guessed. But she didn't want anything to drink. She wanted her mother.

'Is it far, the World Trade Center?'

'Downtown,' said Uncle Benjy unhelpfully.

'Look – is it all right if I just have a glass of water and go and join them?'

'You're welcome to wait here. They'll only be a few hours, unless they decide to eat out someplace.'

That sounded too long to Joy. 'I'd like to join them,' she said, thinking that the World Trade Center sounded a pretty safe sort of place.

'I tell you what,' Benjy announced. 'I'll get Faye on the mobile. I bought her a mobile for her sixtieth birthday. She won't go anywhere without it. So she doesn't have to worry about me. Just some water for Joy, Sammy!'

Benjy moved over to the telephone.

'Faye, honey, it's me. Listen – I have Joy here. No, not on the phone. She's here, in the apartment.' There was a long pause. 'No – she wants to join you there. Yes, she's fine. Nothing's wrong.' A pause. 'No problem! Sure, I'll tell her where to find you. Love you!'

Benjy's friend Sammy brought her an ice-cold glass of water, which she drank gratefully.

Benjy returned to her. 'They'll meet you there,' he said, seeming pleased at the plan. So you can either take a cab – what will that cost her, Sammy?'

'Twenty dollars, thirty dollars?'

Joy thought that seemed a lot. She remembered New York had a subway system like London's Tube. Surely that would be quicker, and cheaper than a cab?

'Can I take the subway?' she asked.

'The subway?' Benjy said questioningly and looked at Sammy. Joy noticed their hesitation. She was getting impatient now. She wanted to be on her way.

'Look, it's OK. I was born and brought up a Londoner. I'm used to the Underground. I won't get lost.'

'I wouldn't recommend the subway,' Benjy said. 'We don't want you ending up in the Bronx, and there are rats. Sammy – I shouldn't be telling her this. But there are rats.'

At that moment Joy realized that she was going to fit into New York like a hand in a glove. Here, everyone was as neurotic as she was. Or as neurotic as she used to be. For she discovered that, in her haste to see her mother, she didn't care about the rats, or the Bronx, or drug-crazed youths on the subway.

'I'll take the subway,' she insisted. 'Just tell me which line I need and where to get off.'

Benjy, amazed at his niece's temerity, consulted a subway map by the telephone, brought it over to Joy and traced with her the green line that snaked down to the tip of Manhattan.

'So you change at Union Square and get off at Fulton Square and then just look up and there are twin towers.

Or just ask. You'll need a token,' he added. Sammy rose and held out to Joy two small metal discs with holes in the centres.

'Take these,' he said to her.

She accepted them.

'Now, Faye said they'll be at the top – not the outdoor viewing platform, but indoors on the floor below, looking over Manhattan. And what a view!' Benjy concluded.

'Oh? Is it high?' Joy asked.

'Don't worry,' said Benjy. 'It only sways a few inches in the wind.'

The New York subway was not quite as cosy as London Underground. The aggressively metallic trains clattered downtown, while Joy read the ads recommending the Mount Sinai Hospital, or offering competitively cheap dental treatment. She glanced at the other passengers, who looked just as locked-in and remote as Londoners do when travelling on the Tube. Yet all of this passed as in a dream. Joy was getting nearer and nearer her mother. Childe Roland to the dark tower came. Except in this case, she reminded herself, she was looking for twin towers.

Joy left the subway station and could not help but lift her eyes to trace the upward-reaching lines of the skyscrapers. There were the twin white towers her uncle had spoken of and, to her mounting horror, Joy saw that they were much, much higher than any of the surrounding buildings. Her heart beat rapidly. Her mother was up there, and she was bound there too. I can't go up there, Joy decided. But she had no choice: the umbilical cord was pulling her. She would have to go. And the sooner she did it, the better.

From outside the building it was impossible to crane her neck far enough back to see the top. She entered the lobby and found the queue which snaked to the ticket booth. She joined it. It occurred to her as she moved slowly forward that if her mother had come all the way here with Aunty Faye, it was unlikely she was seriously ill, and Uncle Benjy's unaffected delight at seeing her suggested there was no dark secret lurking in that airy modern apartment. Which made the mystery all the more maddening. Why, why had her mother vanished without telling anyone?

Joy joined a group which was ushered into an elevator. Still exhausted from her flight, Joy felt almost as if she were acting in one of her own dreams and that in a moment she would wake up in bed in Manchester and everything would be back to normal. But what was normal? Would she wake up and find herself still with Michael? Would her mother still be in Manhattan? The elevator bumped to a halt, and the group got out. It was shepherded to yet another elevator, smaller, less plush. Nearer and nearer all the time.

The elevator stopped, and they were there. Three eager Chinese women pushed out ahead of Joy. Light poured in from the huge windows that encircled the viewing area. Joy's eyes were drawn to the windows. She gasped in horror. The skyscrapers of Manhattan were minute now, like a child's Lego bricks, and Joy was towering sickeningly high above them all.

But where was her mother?

Staying close to the rail at the back of the viewing area, Joy edged her way around the platform. Huddles of people stood at the windows gazing down at the city displayed beneath, so remote and unconnected to them.

There were tourists of all nationalities, as if representatives from all countries had gathered together to look at the world, and to see that it was good.

At present Joy was blinded to its beauty. She wanted her mother. She edged round further. She saw a woman with her back to her, dressed in an off-white fur coat and trainers. And next to her was a familiar navy coat, her mother's, and there, indubitably and unmistakably, was the back of her mother's head. The woman turned round and, most assuredly, most definitely, it was Ruth.

'Mum!' cried Joy, and fell into her arms.

'I'm going to the souvenir shop,' said Faye, unnecessarily loudly. 'I'm going to find something for you to take back for Debbie's children. I'll just leave you two to talk!'

So Joy and Ruth were left alone together, their coffees untouched. From the side of the café area where they were seated Joy could not see Manhattan. She could almost pretend she was on ground level. Except her fear of heights didn't matter any more. What mattered was listening to her mother and watching her mother who, far from looking haggard and ill, looked bright-eyed and alive, more alive than Joy had seen her for some time.

'Please tell me what's going on,' Joy asked.

Ruth laughed. It was partly her usual ironic laugh, but there was a new tone too. Excitement?

'Where shall I begin? Maybe it was when I was fired and everyone seemed to think my life was over and you and your brother were making plans for my old age. That night I looked in the mirror and, sure enough, there was an old woman, but inside, I still felt young. When I was younger I thought I would grow old gracefully like my mother did, or like I thought she did. But here I am, still young, and everybody thinking I'm old!'

'You're not old!' interrupted Joy.

Ruth didn't seem to hear her. 'And so I got rather low. I thought of Faye and, to tell the truth, I was jealous. But I would never have come here if it weren't for you.'

'Me? What did I do?' Joy was mystified.

'You and your pop star,' Ruth said. 'You ring me up and give me this *megillah* about this night you spent with him. You sound like you want to shock me. I put the phone down and I'm not shocked. Why should I be shocked? I'm jealous. I'm jealous of my own daughter. Your father died young, and to you, he was a saint. But maybe he wasn't such a saint. One day, who knows, I'll tell you more. Like mother, like daughter. We make the same mistakes. At least you didn't *marry* Michael.

'So here I am, about to be sixty years old, and what have I done with my life? They tell me I've been a good mother. But have I been such a wonderful mother? David I never see hide nor hair of, and you, you worry about me all the time. And I worry about you. So we never do anything. But you go and do something.

'Then it happens very quickly. Faye actually rings me – she says it's wrong we haven't spoken for so long. And she says, come over, why don't you? So I said yes and bought the ticket. And I didn't tell you because I knew you would worry, and I didn't tell Barney because I felt guilty. I felt guilty because I know I'm coming here for another reason. Because Faye has been telling me about Sammy Liebermann. He was there at the airport to meet me.' Ruth blushed. 'So I like him. So what?'

'Sammy, who was with Uncle Benjy?'

'Sammy,' Ruth continued. 'And at our age, why wait around?'

'Mum!' Joy exclaimed.

'I admit you're right about this sex thing. It's not over-rated after all.'

Joy gaped at her mother.

'And I thought it would do you good to be without me for a bit. I was thinking maybe I needed to let go of you for a while.'

'Oh no,' said Joy. 'You're wrong about that. It's me who needed to learn to let go of you. I'm as bad as you. Worse!'

'We're terrible,' Ruth said complacently. 'Absolutely terrible.'

'Wicked!' said Joy.

Later they stood with Faye, arms linked together, gazing over the vista of New York. Joy knew her legs were weak, but was uncertain now from what cause. She recognized the figure in the distance with her outstretched arm as the Statue of Liberty, from this height looking as if she were life-size, and was waving at them, friend to friends.

As they walked from Grand Central in the direction of the Royalton, the glimpses Joy received of the arrow-straight streets with slabs of blue sky at the ends energized and excited her. It would be impossible to be depressed in a city like this, she thought, pausing at the crossing and watching as a yellow cab swung round the corner. Then she allowed her eyes to travel skywards, soaring up with the giant office buildings, tiered like square wedding-cakes. She realized without any shame that she preferred looking up at the skyscrapers, rather than looking down from them. From the top, one was removed from it all; down here, in the middle of things, surrounded by buildings that jubilantly punctured the sky, there was the sense of what could be achieved, of infinite potential, of aspiration, of a future.

Or perhaps all these thoughts were just a reflection of her mood. Certainly, she was feeling the lack of sleep. On her first night she had lain under a duvet on her aunt's spare mattress, looking at her mother dreaming peacefully on the sofa bed. She was thrilled for her mother; she was astonished by her mother. A lethal cocktail of feelings – a sure recipe for insomnia. Joy decided they would have to get to know each other all over again. Every time she drifted off towards sleep she would wake with a jolt as she remembered her mother's words. Ruth has a lover. And she, Joy, had met him and had paid no attention!

No matter, for they were going to meet him this afternoon, after their lunch at the Royalton. Lunch was Tom's idea. He had rung last night from Heathrow. He was able to come at last and had arranged to stay at the Royalton. Which was why Joy, her mother, Aunty Faye and Uncle Benjy were walking through mid-town Manhattan to 44th Street.

It was Uncle Benjy who spotted it first. It was an unimposing building, its wooden doors shut tight, with a long-haired doorman outside hailing a taxi. Inside was Tom Quinn.

To Joy this reunion with Tom seemed as unreal as everything else that had happened, and it was with some dread that she waited to see him again. Would she feel the same way? Would he feel the same way? Now that his career was about to take off again, what interest could he possibly have in her, the English teacher, even if she was a head of department elect? And how would he get on with her mother?

Ruth pushed open the door of the hotel.

'It's the wrong place,' she said in a stage whisper.

Faye and Joy joined her.

'Or they have the decorators in,' Ruth continued. 'They have dust sheets on all the chairs.'

Joy peered in, saw the plush blue carpet that led into the interior of the hotel and looked again at the elegant white upholstery.

'No,' she said, whispering too. 'I think it's meant to be like this. It's Philippe Starck.'

'You'd think he could afford proper furniture,' Ruth remarked to Faye as they entered, Joy walking ahead now, passing the reception desk and anxiously scanning the tables they passed, looking for Tom. Ahead of her was a restaurant.

She saw him immediately. He was waiting for her. Tom Quinn. More beautiful, more desirable than ever, and so intimately familiar, yet strange in this ultra-sophisticated setting. In a moment they were in each other's arms.

'Not bad-looking,' said Ruth to Faye.

Tom helped them all to seats, called over a waiter and ordered drinks. Joy looked around her and knew from the quiet, understated behaviour of the clients of the hotel and their sleek, affluent appearance that she was in the presence of the cream of New York. Tom seemed at home. He indicated a man seated at a table at the back.

'That's Calvin Klein,' he said. Joy was thrilled. She would tell Peter when she got home.

'Calvin Klein!' said Ruth, impressed. 'You mean the underwear? He's the underwear, Faye!'

'Mum!' said Joy, warningly.

'You see his Y-fronts everywhere,' Ruth continued, loudly.

It was lucky that the complicated procedure of ordering a meal occupied their first few minutes. It gave Ruth sufficient time to observe Tom. Tom would not let go of Joy's hand.

'My management company have paid for this,' he gestured expansively. 'An American label is seriously interested in *Lines and Squares*. My agent flew over with me. There's a copyright deal to be struck with the A. A. Milne estate, but that shouldn't be a problem. So you've found Mrs Weatherby George Dupree!' Tom smiled at Ruth.

'Mrs Freeman,' Ruth corrected him, somewhat bemused. 'Pleased to meet you. Now I remember him, Joy. On the right of your bookshelves, by the window. You were younger then,' she said to Tom, 'but you look better now.'

'I'm sure the same is true of you,' Tom said gallantly.

'A *schmoozer*,' said Ruth to Joy. 'But I like *schmoozers*.'

It was going well. Joy began to relax. She was happy to let things take their course. Her only slight regret was that she did not have time to be alone with Tom for a little while before this meeting. Although she had been able to briefly reassure him that her quest had ended successfully, she badly wanted to tell him about Sammy. Not only that, for all her new-found confidence, Joy still needed the reassurance that he loved her.

She prayed that today he would have the chance to say something to her, something firm for her to grasp. Why, thought Joy, am I even using euphemisms to myself? Who am I trying to kid here? When all's said and done,

I'm just a nice Jewish girl. She looked at Tom and imagined herself married to him. No – that would never happen. She forced her attention back to the conversation. Ruth was on top form.

'So after she told me all about you, it made me think of Sammy Liebermann. He was always the one for me, you know what I mean? He came to meet me at the airport, and I knew then that nothing had changed. Some things had changed. There wasn't so much hair and a tooth or two missing. But once again he's swept me off my feet. He's not with us yet as he's helping his nephew this morning – his nephew has a concession with Crabtree and Evelyn. We're meeting my Sammy later, outside the Rockefeller Center. Come with and meet him.'

'I'd love that,' said Tom.

The Rockefeller Center rose palatially in front of them. Flags of all colours rippled in the wind above a large golden statue. What Joy did not expect was the ice-skating rink. For there, in front of them, New Yorkers glided gracefully on the ice, and Joy could not help but think of Lawrence, and Lesley, and just for a moment envied Lesley Lawrence's steadiness.

Deborah and Howard too – their marriage was better than ever now Debbie was fully stretched. And Kosher Comforts was going from strength to strength. Lucy was helping Debbie two evenings a week and saving up to get her first single pressed. Tom promised he would take it in to his management company. He agreed with Joy that they owed her something.

Joy watched the skaters weave in and out of each others' paths, making circles and patterns, creating harmony from a riot of colour and music. Over the loudspeakers came the suggestive notes of 'Hernando's Hideaway'.

'There he is!' announced Ruth.

Tom's hand on her shoulder, Joy followed her mother's gaze on to the ice. Now she looked more closely she could see that there was one man who was not skating like the rest. Oblivious of the music, of the amused glances of the other skaters, he twirled and pirouetted in a world of his own, a single arm outstretched in a bravura performance. Joy recognized him. It was Sammy. He looked up and saw them, and waved.

Ruth waved back, as did Joy, who was standing by her side. He was splendid, she thought.

'When we get married,' Ruth said very, very casually, 'I'll be able to live over here. I'm thinking I might like to do that.'

Joy felt an increased pressure from Tom's hand on her shoulder. She needed it to steady her. Her mother was remarrying.

'When Joy and I marry,' Tom said, 'if she wants to – I dare say we'll commute regularly over the Atlantic, now that Joy's lost her fear of flying. Make sure you get an apartment big enough for us to stay in.'

'But not a penthouse,' Joy added, turning to face Tom.

Joy could speak no more. Her happiness choked her. In a moment she would embrace Tom, and that would be the answer to his question. And she would not care what the mass of people around her thought.

But for now she turned again to watch Sammy. He too did not care what others thought. He cut his own path, an ageing romantic, enjoying every moment, neither dwarfed by the immense thrust of the Rockefeller Center behind him nor concerned by the sniggers of the youths who passed him. They were just the crowd. He was the individual, exquisitely himself. It was the only way to be.

He skated free from self-consciousness, free from all fear.

Joy thought she might go down there and join him.